The Truth Will Out

Anna McPartlin

POOLBEG

This novel is entirely a work of fiction. The names, characters and incidents portrayed in it are the work of the author's imagination. Any resemblance to actual persons, living or dead, events or localities is entirely coincidental.

Published 2008
by Poolbeg Press Ltd
123 Grange Hill, Baldoyle
Dublin 13, Ireland
E-mail: poolbeg@poolbeg.com
www.poolbeg.com

1 3 5 7 9 10 8 6 4 2

A catalogue record for this book is available from the British Library.

ISBN 978 1 84223 295 8

Typeset by Type Design in Bembo 11.75/15

Printed by Litografia Rosés, S.A, Barcelona, Spain

www.poolbeg.com

About the Author

Anna McPartlin was born in 1972. Her early years were spent in Dublin but, due to illness in her immediate family, she later moved to Kenmare, County Kerry, when fostered by her aunt and uncle. Anna studied marketing in college and dabbled as an actor and stand-up comedian before discovering her true love, writing. While working in the arts, she met her husband Donal. They now live in Dublin.

Apart From The Crowd and *Pack Up The Moon* have become bestsellers. This is her third novel.

Also published by Poolbeg

Apart from the Crowd
Pack Up The Moon

Acknowledgements

Firstly I'd like to thank John Goodman for the excellent tour of Wicklow and his wife Joanne Costello for taking my husband horse-riding so that I could actually get some work done. Cheers, amigos! Always top of my list, thanks to my family: Mary and Tony O'Shea, Denis and Lisa, Siobhan and Paul, Brenda and Mark, Caroline and Ger and Aisling; it was great to spend time with you all in Auckland despite the circumstances of my travel – our time together reminded me how much I miss you all. To the kids beginning with the eldest: Daniel, Nicole, Conor, David, Tara, Katie and of course little Ashling; you are all incredible little people and I love you all. To all the Floods: Mary and Kevin, Eoin and Marcella, Dara, Conall and Ruairi; my love and thanks. To Paudie McSwiney: you are refusing to come for Christmas this year because I'm a rubbish cook – I forgive you for you are correct. To the McPartlin family: Don and Terry, Ruth and Mick Lambert, Felicity and Mick Creedon, Rebecca and Aidan Cornally; rather like lambs to the slaughter, you are coming to me for Christmas. My tip would be to fill up on booze. To their kids, henceforth to be known as victims of their parents' bad decision-making: Daniel, Jessica, Hannah, Con, Abby, Harry and Bill. I would like to apologise in advance and advise you to fill up on sweets. To all the McSwineys: Bertie Snr, Colette, Bertie Jnr and his wife Noreen, Conor, Aileen, Eoin and Mary; my love and thanks. To Claire and Michael Collins and Claire's mother Mary; thank you for your support and kindness. To my husband: you still haven't a clue what I do but I wouldn't have it any other way. Thank you and I love you. To my friends: Valerie and Dermot Kerins, Martin and Trish

Clancy, Leonie Kerins and Steph Duclot, John Goodman and Joanne Costello, Tracy Kennedy, Enda Barron, Fergus Egan, Lucy and Darren Walsh, Edel and Noel Simpson, Graham and Bernice Darcy, Angela Delaney, David Constantine, Garrett and Emma Tierney, Clifton Moore, John and Aoife Hicky; friends make life that much sweeter so thank you. To the band: Seminey, Lisa, Barry, Alan and again my husband Donal; it was a pleasure working with you. To Lyndsey for helping Lisa to mind the dogs; you two are life savers. Again to the buyers and sellers in Easons, Hughes and Hughes, Dubray and Tesco, for your continued support. To Paula Campbell who despite overwhelming odds manages to always get it right. To all at Poolbeg as always, my sincerest thanks. To my agent Faith O'Grady for your patience and Jennifer Griffin for being the first to support my ambition to write for TV. To my editor, Gaye Shortland: Thank you, Thank you, Thank you. And finally I promised a little lady that I'd be sure to compliment her beautiful eyes on paper so, Milly Kerins, you have the most beautiful eyes.

In Memory of Ciara Collins

Dedicated to Caroline, Ger and Ashling Collins

Chapter one

The wedding: take two

The date was May 1st 2006, it was the morning of Harri's 30th birthday and the day she was set to marry.

She'd woken up only once the night before, humming the tune to 'Get Me to the Church on Time'. *I'm getting married in a few hours. Holy crap, I think I'm going to cry. La la, lala la. I wish I wasn't losing my mind.* She wasn't awake for long, just time enough for a mini freak-out, to indulge in a tear or two, blow her nose and hit her head on the Edwardian mahogany headboard with its checkered stringing. *Bastard* – the bed not the fiancé, she loved her fiancé. Harri was just nervous. When she got nervous she got confused or maybe it was the other way around. Either way, nervousness and confusion usually ended up in minor injury. *Don't be all my left foot about it, Harri. It will all go beautifully. Everything will be fine. You will not mess this day up. Go back to sleep.* She obeyed herself and despite a slight sore head managed to return to the Land of Nod within minutes with no real harm done.

"Big day," her dad greeted her with a wink on the landing.

"Big day, Dad," she agreed sheepishly, rubbing a particularly stubborn piece of crap from the darkest and deepest corner of her right eye.

"Don't pull your eye out, love," he warned.

"I'll try not to," she said, kissing him on his hairy cheek as he passed with his paper heading toward his en-suite bathroom where he would spend what he often described as a well-earned hour on the loo.

Soon after, when she'd emerged from a pounding shower, her mother was waiting in her bedroom with a full Irish breakfast including toast, tea, coffee and a range of croissants and cheese.

"Morning, my darling," she said with a smiling sigh while placing the breakfast tray on the table by the window that looked down on a pretty stone patio and across to an ancient oak tree.

"Morning, Mum," she grinned while holding a cloth up against the eye she'd all but pulled out despite the earlier promise made. She took the cloth away from her face.

"Holy hell, darling, how'd you manage that?"

"Sleep crap."

"Ah," her mother said with a smile, "so you slept." She was nodding her head approvingly. "Good girl. Don't worry, darling. Mona will sort it out. Mona could conceal a baboon's arse stuck out of a white Fiat Uno."

"Oh, Mum!"

Her mum was laughing. Harri's mum, Gloria, didn't curse or engage in conversation deemed to be lewd a lot but when she did she made sure her verbal misdemeanour was for comic effect. Harri joined in, always pleased when her mother allowed herself to participate in what she deemed to be misbehaviour. She made her way over to and sat on the chair that accompanied the table that looked down on the pretty stone patio and across to the ancient oak tree. The sun shone a bright yellow against a light blue cloudless sky. "It's a nice day," she commented, hugging herself in the comfortable towelling dressing gown her mother had given her six years before when she'd first left home to move twenty minutes down the road to the UCD college campus. "Always buy quality, darling," Gloria had said, "anything else is simply false economy."

Gloria was all about quality. She had expensive taste and found it difficult to tolerate anything but the finer things in life. She had grown up as the only child to a wealthy landowner. There was a time when her parents owned a quarter of South Dublin. Harri's granddad died in his late forties, leaving the house to her nana and mum. Nana suffered from epilepsy and because of this Gloria would never leave her. She met Harri's dad when the house was broken into in the early seventies and he came to investigate the crime. They fell in love quickly and were married within a year. Harri's dad, Duncan, originated from North Dublin and initially he was uncomfortable with his new-found wealthy lifestyle. Gloria said he was like a duck in a desert but his work kept him satisfied and rooted in the familiar gritty reality that his new-found home life shielded him from and so he retained a balance. Also he was fond of Nana. She was a lady but she was also tough as old boots and a whiz at chess and together they played games that would last up to a month.

Duncan had joined the guards straight out of school. He was third generation and moved up the ranks quickly, making detective in his early twenties. He had worked on some of the most tragic cases Ireland had seen. Harri would often wonder how he managed to leave all that terror at the door. Her mum said he wiped his feet on the mat and there he'd leave his day.

Harri only ever witnessed her dad cry once. She could have been nine maybe ten. He was sitting at his desk in his attic office. Harri was holding a tray with his lunch and so she didn't knock. He was looking at a photograph with his hand held up to his face and tears flowing. He shoved the photo into the file that had been opened out on his desk, closing it quickly, hugging it to his chest, and then he spun toward the window, wiping his eyes obviously in the hope that she hadn't seen. In Harri's house they never really made a habit of talking about anything anyone felt uncomfortable about. Duncan's job ensured that he was obligated to be silent on many matters and so it became his habit. Gloria was far too ladylike and unlike Nana too fragile for any kind of confrontation and Nana when she was still in the land of the living didn't believe in discussing anything that verged on boring. Feelings, she had once decreed, were boring. George and Harri grew up in a house that was all about being lovely. Crying had no place in this home and so Harri pretended she hadn't witnessed her father weep on that day, but years later if she closed her eyes she could still see those fat tears splash on white paper.

"It's a fabulous morning." Gloria smiled and kissed the top of her daughter's head.

"I'm never going to be able to eat this," Harri said, surveying the ridiculous amount of food placed before her.

"I know," Gloria nodded before moving toward the end of the bed and bending over to pull out a blue box from under it. "For you," she said, smiling. "Happy birthday, darling!"

"Thanks, Mum," Harri grinned. She was thirty but still got giddy around presents. She opened the box to reveal a beautiful art deco pendant. Gloria loved art deco and Harri did too. Duncan used to say they were two peas in a pod. She held it up against the window. It was beautiful, gleaming in daylight with stones that glistened. "I love it!" she said with a kiss.

George was in and lying on the bed before Harri's lips had left her mother's head. "So, Mum, where's my present?"

"Under your bed."

"Aah!" he said with a disappointed sigh.

"What's wrong?"

"That's two floors down."

"Don't be so lazy, darling, it's a staircase not blooming Everest."

"So what is it?"

"I'm not telling you," Gloria said smiling.

"And how come I didn't get breakfast in bed?" he queried while examining a strand of his hair.

"Because you're not getting married. So happy birthday, Nuisance. Now please be an adult." She often called George "Nuisance" and was smiling as she said it because if the truth be told she liked it when he acted like a child. It made her feel needed. "My twins," she smiled. "Both so grown up but deep down and where it counts you will always be my babies." The end of her little speech had a touch of mad old dear menace about it but the sweet sentiment was there.

George jumped up and kissed Harri on the head. "Happy birthday, Harri!"

She hugged him tight "Happy birthday, George!"

Harri idolised her twin brother. He was everything she wasn't. George could stand centre stage and hold any room while Harri could only ever be found in its corner. He was adventurous, having travelled around the world, spending summers in the snow and winters in the sun. He surfed, skied and dived and did so well. He loved to paraglide and was considering helicopter lessons. Harri was not much of an explorer. She hadn't managed to move farther than twenty minutes down the road from her parents. Hot sun brought her out in heat rash and the one time she skied she broke her wrist. He was athletic, she was bookish. He was loud, she was quiet. He was a playboy, she was a worker. He was gay, she was straight. They didn't even really look alike aside from both having thick wavy brunette hair. He was tall, she was average. He was broad, she was petite. He had a square-shaped face while hers was oval. They were so different in so many ways and yet they didn't need to use words the way others did. They understood each other. They knew one another. George would have jumped any bridge for his sister. The Ryan twins had always been extremely close.

"Time to let go, little sister," George said, pulling away from her grip.

"I'm older," she smiled.

"You're smaller!" he grinned.

And really between the sunny morning, the new shiny jewellery, the big breakfast, Gloria's tasteful décor, her warmth and kindness, Harri's anxious bride and George's playful neediness, that moment if captured would have been considered Rockwellesque, in that it depicted a picture-perfect family life. The only thing spoiling it in Harri's mind was the impending nuptials.

Stay calm, Harri. Don't mess this up.

But unbeknownst to her there was a far greater menace underlying this ideal family on this ideal day.

* * *

The dress was slightly too tight and Mona's perfectly coiffed up-style was bringing on a headache but even Harri was forced to admit that she had done a fantastic job despite a broken finger.

"What happened?"

"Desmond happened."

"I need more."

"I had a child who turned into a teenager who turned into an asshole who thinks nothing of leaving a skateboard at the top of a staircase."

"You're lucky you didn't break your neck."

"He's lucky I didn't break *his* neck! Seriously, Harri, think before you copulate."

Harri enjoyed Mona. She was named well for she loved to moan but did so with likable verve. George called her Moaning and she never seemed to mind.

"Wow, Moaning, you make breeding sound so romantic!" he chimed in from the doorway.

"Tell me you're going to let me do something with that hair?" Mona asked him, well versed in ignoring his attempted witticisms.

"What's wrong with it?"

"Nothing if you're emulating a fop."

"Well, I was going for Hugh Grant circa *Four Weddings.*" He stood behind her, examining himself in the mirror.

"Well then, dear, the look has been achieved beautifully."

"Moaning, you're such a bitch but I love it."

He sighed and sat in the corner of the sitting room, the room where Harri was standing in her slightly too tight wedding dress, and with pretty but headache-inducing hair.

Duncan coughed outside, knocked and crept into the room with a camera. "Oh now. What?" Duncan often said 'what' out of context as though someone unseen had whispered a remark or query into his ear. He mostly did it when he was happy. "Fantastic. Fantastic!" He also repeated himself a lot and in a tone that suggested childish delight. "Jaysus, you're smashing. Isn't she smashing?" He was looking around at George and Mona who both smiled and nodded to assure him. It would seem that the dress clearly made up for in wow-factor what it sorely lacked in comfort, its sheer splendour managing to bring a tear to Duncan's usually stubbornly dry eyes. To avoid uncomfortable emotion George made a joke suggesting that his father's tears had more to do with cost than visual appeal. Awkward moment averted, Duncan grinned, and despite his jibe Harri's twin brother's good-natured shove suggested her appearance had met with his high if not foppish standards.

Melissa rang. Mona handed Harri the phone with a warning. "Two minutes."

"Hi, Melissa."

"Still with us?"

"I am."

"Excellent."

"Where are you?" she asked, confused by the sound of passing traffic.

"I'm in the church car park changing a nappy."

"You're at the church already?"

She could hear the panic in Harri's voice. "Stop. Breathe. I'm just checking the flowers. You still have an hour."

"Okay," she exhaled as much as the dress would allow.

"Jacob, get in the car. Jacob, get in the car. Jacob . . ."

"Melissa?"

"Sorry. Get in the bloody car!"

Shuffling ensued and she could hear Jacob moan something about wanting a sandwich from the car boot.

"You keep sandwiches in the boot?"

"Sandwiches, yogurts, nappies, towels, Cheese Strings, formula, a six-pack of Caprisun, play dough, knickers. You name it, I have it."

"Get off the phone!" Mona said.

"I have to get off the phone."

"Okay. Everything's going to be fine."

"I know."

"Oh, James is here."

Harri's stomach turned. James was at the church. She hung up.

Mona dragged her to the dining table near the big window that overlooked Nana's bench and let in lots of required light. She'd pulled an eye pencil out of her bulging bag of tricks.

"Are you okay?" she asked.

"I'm fine," Harri agreed.

Mona pushed her into the chair. "Look up!" she ordered. Harri looked up. "Are you sure you're okay? Suddenly you seem pale."

Harri gave her the thumbs up, afraid that if she spoke she'd throw up.

Duncan had gone to pick Gloria up from Shoe World in Sandycove where she'd insisted on going half an hour earlier when the strap of her brand-new sandals snapped.

"Holy hell, I can't believe it!" she'd cried. "These shoes cost five hundred euro!"

"What?" Duncan had roared. "Five hundred euro? Have you lost your mind, woman?"

Gloria hadn't realised he was in earshot and she was in no mood for a price war. "Darling, we both know you weren't meant to hear that so let's just pretend that you didn't."

Duncan grumbled something about five hundred Jaysusing euro but he could see sense in her argument and so he let it go. Sandycove is a small village and they lived a stone's throw away from it so he dropped her off, returning home with just enough time to take photos before the retrieval call came. He had made his way to the car mumbling about the cost of everything and wondering how much these new bloody toe-curlers were going to set them back.

Harri didn't feel like moving or sitting or drinking or even the Valium that Mona offered with the advice that it had worked wonders on her neighbour's daughter Cliona. Apparently Cliona often suffered with her nerves but according to Mona this was due to her being a self-centred ungrateful brat who didn't give half enough of a stuff about her hardworking mother or indeed her father who often smelt of chip fat, a man who apparently had built an empire out of chip fat and was a gentleman to go along with it. George laughed, enjoying Mona's chat. Harri feigned engagement but inside felt numb.

"Do you feel sick?" George asked from the corner of the room where he had made himself comfortable in his mother's favourite antique rocking chair.

"A little," she admitted as there was little point in lying to him.

"You'll be okay," Mona said, applying a second coat of ruby-red lipstick. "Now smack your lips."

"And breathe!" George instructed before returning to read an article on a new species of Sri Lankan tree frog. "Take a look at those weird staring red eyes. If frogs could kill . . ."

⋆ ⋆ ⋆

Harri's fiancé James liked frogs, believing them necessary to a well-balanced ecosystem. He had a strange fixation with all amphibians and reptiles; where most saw ick, he saw wonder.

"Did you know that when snakes strike they have a near 100 per cent success rate?" he'd casually mentioned on their first date.

"I did not know that," she'd responded while thinking he was a mental case and deciding against ordering dessert.

He believed that reptiles were most especially marginalised. "I mean, what have lizards ever done to anyone?"

She didn't respond, hoping he'd change the subject. He didn't. Instead he told her about his pet snake, Ronnie, who he had for about three years until it died of organ failure. He had blamed himself for not having read the signs. "He definitely didn't look sick," he said, shaking his head, leaving Harri a moment to ponder as to what a sick snake would actually look like. "I loved that snake."

He had a cute wrinkle that appeared just over his eye which she later associated with him suffering an upset. James worked as an architect. His great love was all things building-related. James wasn't just a contractor – he was an artist in that he was passionate and strove for perfection. He controlled every aspect of the job from the foundations to the roof, and seeing and walking around his finished building was a high akin to that of a rock star walking onto a Wembley stage and playing to a full house. James was a builder from a different age and yet he could only be described as being fierce about the environment, insisting that he only worked on eco-friendly structures.

They had met six years earlier through work. He was building a house and Harri and Susan Shannon, her business partner, were decorating it. On that very day Susan had said she hoped he wasn't stupid because if he had any kind of decent IQ Harri should marry him. Harri had laughed her off, thinking nothing more of it. Susan always did have a keen interest in matchmaking and did so with anyone who would let her. She said it was a replacement for having sex. From the offset she was sure Harri and James had chemistry and was decidedly happy when, within weeks of their meeting, they proved her correct.

Susan had recently turned forty-six and for her birthday her husband had bought her a garden hose. It was an expensive garden hose with lots of handy attachments and powerful enough to clean a stone patio as well as sprinkle the plants but still she wanted to shove it down his throat.

"James would never buy you a garden hose," Harri said and she was right, he wouldn't. However she did mention that he'd bought her a shredder after watching a news report on identity fraud.

Susan shook her head and sighed. "Whatever happened to romance?"

"I think it's a casualty of feminism."

"The question was rhetorical and you think too much."

She was right, Harri did think too much. Over-thinking was probably her biggest problem.

Anyway two days after Susan had made her little remark about

James being marriage material, he asked Harri out.

Even though their first date had begun a little strangely, by the end of the evening and whilst sitting outside the Dun Laoghaire apartment that she shared with a blue-eye-shadow-leotard-and-puffball-skirt-wearing contemporary dancer called Tina Tingle, the evening improved considerably.

The car stopped. She immediately put her hand on the door handle to suggest she was getting out without delay.

"Sorry," he said, "I'm a little out of practice."

"It's okay," she blushed, embarrassed by his frankness.

"Where did I lose you?" he asked with a slight grin.

"Your in-depth description of the texture of Ronnie's scales."

He laughed and nodded. 'I was nervous. I talk utter shit when I'm nervous."

She smiled. "My brother does that. After my nana's funeral he talked about belly-button fluff for a whole hour."

There was silence for a moment or two and James noticed that Harri's hand was no longer holding the door handle.

"So you're out of practice?" Harri said, scratching the back of her neck and facing the front window but out of the corner of her eye she could see him rub his forehead and the crinkles around his eyes suggested a smile.

"It's been a while."

"Oh," she said nodding, "and a while would be what?" She attempted to inject nonchalance into her voice.

He laughed. "You're not behind the door, are you?"

"Usually I am," she admitted. "Usually I'm behind the door, down the hall and into the boxroom on the left."

He was laughing. He had a full dirty laugh.

"So?" she probed. *I can't believe I'm being so pushy.*

"Two years."

"Can I ask?"

"We were together for four years and she got sick."

"Oh my God! I'm so sorry. I was being way too nosey."

"No, it's okay. It took some time but she got better." He laughed a short laugh tinged with bitterness. "She got better and decided she wanted a different kind of life so she broke my heart and moved to Australia where I believe she married a surfer six months later."

"Right." Harri was bloody sorry she'd started her interrogation. Normally she was disinterested in the lives of strangers. "I feel terrible."

"Why?" His smile had returned.

"Just do," she sighed, shrugging her shoulders.

Harri didn't engage in the lives of those not close because sad stories affected her way too much. She took them on board and lived them when she was alone. Sadness haunted her and it didn't have to be her own.

"What about you?" he asked, lightening the tone and noticing that not only had Harri removed her hand from the door but her knees had turned to face his.

"I was going out with a carpenter called Simon for nearly a year. We split up six months ago. It wasn't anything in particular, we just didn't fit."

"And before Simon?"

"College thing. Ian Grace. He was engineer student. We were together for just over three years."

"Trinity?"

"UCD."

"What happened with you two?"

"He took a job in Saudi. I don't really like the sun."

"Harri?"

"Yes."

"If I promise not to talk shit would you agree to see me again?"

"Yes."

"Good," he said, nodding to himself. "Harri?"

"Yes?"

"Would you mind terribly if I leaned in for a kiss? I don't mind if you say no."

"No."

"Oh bollocks!"

"Only joking!" she laughed and that was it after that.

They just fit.

They were both hard workers, both liked to read, neither of them were particularly into music or TV, preferring a silent room as a background to conversation. They both liked to talk and to cook and to laugh. James was funny, not in a conventional ha-ha-what-a-comedian sense but he could always make Harri laugh nonetheless.

"Knock, knock?"

"No."

"Ah, come on! Knock, knock!"

"James."

"Knock, knock?"

"God almighty, who's there?"

"Gorilla."

"Gorilla who?"

"Gorilla me a cheese sandwich."

You know, when someone tells you such an utterly stupid unfunny joke and all you can do is laugh at the ridiculousness of it? Well, Harri would laugh and he'd clap his hands together delighting in his hilarity.

"There is something wrong with you."

"Yeah, there is! I'm hungry so gorilla me a cheese sandwich."

"Oh sweet God, don't drag the thing on!"

"You love my jokes."

She really didn't but she did love him.

* * *

She was lost and gazing past Nana's bench and out onto a clean street lined with white blossom trees heralding spring and a time for change. It was while adrift in a place beyond white blossoms that the awful feeling came in the form of a large and sweeping wave. Terror rose from within and threatened to engulf not only her but the entire room. Her head got busy buzzing. Everything felt suddenly wrong. She was drowning in the room, now blurry. Everything inside shouted that something was off. *Oh no, not again!* An overpowering and insane notion crossed her now-manic mind, telling her she didn't belong. She had been here before. She could feel her hands becoming clammy and within seconds her heart rate increased, another second or two passed before it began pounding deep within her chest. *Just breathe, Harri. Just like George said.* Clammy hands threatened to shake despite her core temperature increasing at an alarming rate. *Just calm down, Harri. Don't be a dick, please.* She knew that at any moment she would begin to feel dizzy and then she would completely disconnect. *Mom is going to kill me.* Just as she attempted to call out, her breath shortened, clammy hands rose to her throat signalling that she was choking.

Mona was the first to notice. "Oh Christ, she's at it again! George, call an ambulance before she goes bloody blue on us!"

May 1st 1975 - Thursday

Mam was crying again last night. I heard *him* come in. He was shouting at her calling her, "Deirdre, Deirdre, Deirdre!" Someday he'll wear her name out. I heard him bang at her door. She must have locked it. "Deirdre, open the door, you miserable bitch!" "I won't!" she said. Can you believe she answered to him calling her a miserable bitch? What's wrong with her? At least she locked her door. I locked mine too. He's a freak. I hate him. He stormed out screaming that he'd be back and made his way down the road cursing loud enough for Nosey Crowley in number seven to hear. I saw her curtain twitching as he passed her house swearing at nothing and everything. You could see she was delighted, that will keep her talking, the nosy old biddy.

Sometimes I lie awake and I wonder why did she have to marry him? Did she really love him or was she just lonely after Dad? I thought we were happy. In fact I know we were happy, that is until he came along. She rushed into it, at least that's what I heard Nosey Crowley say in the chemist when I was hiding behind shelving and she was talking with Mrs Stephens about the last time he left our house cursing. Nosey called her stupid and to be fair to Nosey she's not wrong. My mother is a stupid woman. I'd never be stupid enough to fall for a horrible man like him and I'll never marry.

School's a nightmare, can't wait for the holidays. Don't know what I'm going to do, he says I'll have to get a job. Maybe I will but not because of him. In two weeks I'll be fifteen. Mam said I could get a bottle of Charlie and a Bay City Rollers tape. I hope it happens. I hope he doesn't drink all the money. I adore the smell of Charlie.

In one year I'll be gone from here. I can't wait. Every day feels like a year and some days feel like ten years. Sheila says she's going to join the bank. Last week she wanted to do hairdressing and a month ago she was thinking of teaching. I don't know what I want to be. I just know that I want to be anywhere but Wicklow.

I saw that doctor again - he was fishing off the rocks. He looks my age, maybe a year or two older. I'd put him at nineteen at a push. Sheila says he's at least mid-twenties. He doesn't look it. He always looks sad even when he smiles. He's shy too. It must be hard for him in a new town. I'd hate to be a doctor, people are disgusting. I wonder where he's from.

I had a dream last night. I dreamt that I was on a boat that kept returning to shore. Every time the boat inched out to sea it was pulled back. It scared me. I'm obsessing. Sheila says I obsess. She thinks I should relax and enjoy life. Easy for her to say - she doesn't live with a drunk - in fact her father is getting rich serving all the drunks in town. She's never had to hide in her room. She gets to sit with her dad watching Morecambe & Wise on a colour TV so it's easy for her to relax and enjoy life. I miss Sheila. I wish she wasn't with that Dave. So what's so great about Dave? He has a rubbish Kevin Keegan perm. Sheila thinks it's cool and it's really, really not. He stinks of his dad's Brut and he's always pawing her. Yesterday he kept putting her down trying to be funny which he wasn't. I wanted to punch him hard. Mam says that sometimes I get a look and it frightens her.

It's after ten and I'm tired. *He's* still in the pub. If I go to sleep now maybe I won't hear him. First I'll lock the door. Sheila's dad says that you should never lock a bedroom door in case of fire. It's not fire I'm scared of. I'd rather burn.

I just decided tomorrow I'm going to look for a summer job, anything to get me out of this house. It makes me laugh. He says I have to get a job, while he sits in a pub or leans on the bank wall with his mate all day every day. Mam always makes excuses, she says dockers can only work when the coasters come in but Anita Shea's dad is a docker and he paints and wallpapers houses and Tim Healy's dad takes shifts behind the bar in The Pole instead of sitting in front of it drinking all the money he's earned for two days' work in two hours. Anyway I don't care about that. He can do what he wants. I'm gone from here. One year can feel like forever or a day. My dad used to say that. I think I'll sit with him for a while tomorrow. Maybe I'll clean his headstone. Birds seem to think it's a toilet and it's funny because Rita Heneghan is right beside him and her headstone is always clean as a whistle and I've never seen anyone visit her. Once a bird actually did a shit on his one while I was sitting there! I think my dad would think that was funny. He used to laugh a lot. I miss his laugh. I miss him. I wish he was here but he's not so what's the point in wishing? He's gone. Feck him for that.

Oh and just so I never forget, today in the woods I heard spring. I actually heard it, in the trees and the breeze and the dogs barking along the trails and the sky was so, so blue and the grass was the brightest green. I leaned on brown bark and inhaled fresh air. When all is said and done I'll miss those woods.

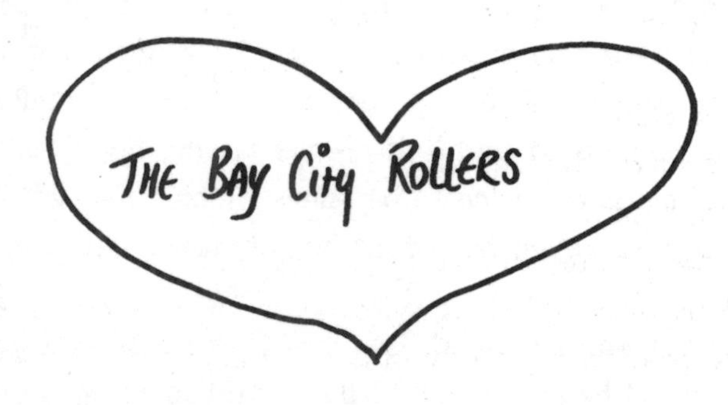

Chapter two

A & E

Harri woke up lying on a gurney in the hospital Accident & Emergency. Her mother and father were sitting at either side. There was no sign of her fiancé. George was standing by the window looking out and commenting on a woman who was clearly making an arse of an attempt to parallel park.

"Good God, woman, you could fit a small island in there!"

Harri was awake long before she could bring herself to open her eyes. *I can't believe I've done it again.* Her parents were silent. Eventually she could feign slumber no more.

"There she is," her father said with a warm smile, "there's our girl."

"I'm sorry, Dad."

"Don't be sorry," he smiled.

"I'm sorry, Mum."

"Shussh, my darling, everything is fine now."

George was over and lying with her on her bed with her head resting in the crook of his arm within seconds. "If it's any consolation you are the most glamorous patient in this place."

Harri realised she was still in her wedding dress. She fought tears. "Where's James?"

Duncan's brother, Father Ryan, came into the room with four coffees. Harri's parents relieved him of theirs and his mother passed George his.

"Do you want a coffee, my darling?"

"No thanks, Mum."

"She's back," Gloria said to her brother-in-law.

Father Ryan leaned over the bed. "Well, hello there," he said. "You'll be the death of one of us, Harriet Ryan."

"Sorry, Uncle Thomas."

Father Ryan only allowed the twins to call him Uncle Thomas. To everyone else, including his brother and sister-in-law, he was Father Ryan.

"Well, they say three times is a charm." He was referring to the fact that this latest panic attack was Harri's second, the first having occurred on the eve of her first aborted wedding six months previously.

"Where's James?" she asked again.

Gloria's hands began to flutter toward her neck the way they always did when she was anxious. Duncan remained silent and Father Ryan was busy drinking from his coffee cup. George spoke up. "He was here, Harri. He made sure you were okay and then he left."

"He hates me." she said before burying her head in the pillow.

"He doesn't hate you," said George. "He's just upset."

"I've left him at the altar twice, George."

"You didn't do it on purpose."

"There's something wrong. I'm obviously mental."

"No, of course there isn't!" Gloria said, attempting a smile. "Every bride gets nervous."

"But they don't end up in A&E!" Harri replied in a voice suggesting anger.

"Harri, mind your tone!" her dad warned.

"Sorry, Dad."

"That's all right, love, we're all a little tense," he said lightly.

"Where's Melissa?"

"She's settling the kids. She's going to leave them with Gerry and then she'll meet us at my place," George replied before spluttering some coffee. "Awful, just bloody awful!" He was referring to the coffee but it summed the day up beautifully.

Harri lay on the gurney on the day that was her second attempt at marrying the man she loved, surrounded by her family, and yet she was completely and utterly alone. The terror had subsided and resting in its place was horror and a sinking depression that was turning her brain into glue. *He'll never forgive me. I can't believe I've done it again. What's wrong with me?*

* * *

George's apartment was a penthouse in Temple Bar. He loved the bustle of living in the city centre. He'd bought it four years before after Nana died leaving the twins what she described as healthy nest eggs. It was spacious with three large bedrooms; it had two floors and high ceilings. It was painted white throughout and the walls were covered in African and European art collected on many different trips. At night the city lights made for a spectacular view but tonight the blinds were drawn with a low lamp providing the only break in the darkness.

"Can the patient drink wine?" Melissa asked George as she poured him a glass while he tucked a blanket around his sister's legs, having insisted she lay on the sofa.

"Her doctor would say no but I, like the man from Del Monte, say yes," he grinned and patted his sister's flat hair. "You really need to wash that before something decides to land on it."

Melissa handed Harri a drink before curling up and making herself comfortable in George's favourite oversized armchair.

"Do I really need this blanket?" Harri asked while pulling at it.

"Yes," her brother argued.

"I'm so tired," she admitted.

Melissa sighed long and loudly and after a time said, "I just don't get it. I mean we all know how you hate to be the centre of attention but this is ridiculous. I don't get it."

"Me neither," Harri repeated while suppressing tears.

After George had demanded her parents take their leave of the hospital and while she was awaiting discharge she'd broken down, wailing and bawling, and only stopping when her doctor pondered aloud as to whether or not she required sectioning. Then and there she had pledged no more tears and she was determined to uphold her promise.

"I do," George said before swishing his wine vigorously around his glass, checking its colour and clarity.

"And?" Melissa said, almost annoyed to be made witness to what she would often describe as the bullshit tasting techniques he'd learned in his bullshit wine-tasting course.

"She's not ready for marriage, that's all."

"What do you mean she's not ready? She's thirty. They've been going out for six years. They've got an apartment together, a rundown cottage in Wexford and a tank full of exotic fish."

"So what's your point?" George asked, once again swishing vigorously enough to cause a minor spillage.

"My point is that she committed three years ago on the day she signed for the apartment, she again committed two years ago when against my advice they bought that shithole in Wexford and once again when they inherited his Great-auntie Edna's freaky-looking fish and will you please stop swishing and just drink the stuffing wine!"

"That's just ownership. Ownership and commitment are two totally different things and it's my apartment so I'll swish if I want to swish."

"Homo!"

"Witch!"

"Could you both shut up?" Harri said before ill-advisedly draining her glass.

"Sorry," George said.

"Me too," Melissa echoed.

Melissa had been Harri's best friend since they were both aged five. She had been George's first and only girlfriend aged sixteen. He broke up with her exactly two weeks and one kiss into their short-lived affair. Six months later he came out to his mother while she was putting out the washing. She pretended to have gone momentarily deaf and it would be another four years before George's sexuality was mentioned in the house again.

An hour had passed and Harri felt the need to throw up. Melissa held her flattened hair away from her face while she vomited red wine and the half a croissant she'd eaten earlier that day. Afterwards Melissa took her to George's spare room and tucked her into bed.

"Melissa, do you ever wonder why things happen?" Harri asked.

"All the time," Melissa said.

"Do you think George is right?"

"Well, he never has been before." Melissa laughed a little.

"I don't know what's going on."

"I know but give it time."

"James won't talk to me." She was crying again.

"Give him a little space."

"How much space? A day, a week, a year?"

"Harri, in the church . . . well, he was devastated too."

"I didn't mean to hurt him."

"I know. We'll get to the bottom of it, Harri. I promise."

Harri nodded and Melissa turned out the light and closed the door.

"Too late," Harri whispered, "I've lost him." She lay in darkness, allowing it creep up and envelop her.

Melissa sat outside the door and listened to her best friend sob. Melissa cried herself. She couldn't help it. She had seen it in James's face. She saw something break. There was no going back. Harri was right, she had lost him, and it felt like a death and a time to grieve.

George had another glass of wine waiting for Melissa when at last she returned. They sat opposite one another, comfortable in each other's company like family.

"Is she okay?" he asked.

Melissa shook her head to suggest that no, maybe she was not. George became unusually quiet.

"What?" Melissa asked after a while.

"James believes it's all about him."

"Well, he wouldn't be far off. Two attempted weddings, two pretty serious panic attacks."

"It's not the only time," George said with his hand rubbing his chin in what appeared to be a demonstration of careful consideration.

"I don't understand."

"When we were kids it happened a lot, maybe until Harri hit five or six. I can't remember exactly."

"But she said . . ."

"She doesn't remember."

"But your parents, they told the doctor . . ."

"They lied."

"Why? Why would they do that?" she asked, leaning forward and whispering despite her friend being a floor away.

"I don't know."

"And why didn't you say anything?"

"I don't know."

"All that stuff earlier about Harri not being ready for commitment . . ."

"That could still be the case. I just don't understand why my parents are lying."

"She needs to know."

"I agree."

"So?" she pushed.

"So I'll talk to them, I'll see what they say. Harri's upset enough – I need to understand before I bother her with this."

"And James?"

"James needs space. I mean, wouldn't you?"

Melissa nodded. "I just don't get it."

"Me neither," George shrugged, "but something's off."

* * *

Gloria picked at her evening meal. She'd put together a pasta dish with leftovers from the night before. Father Ryan was starving, having travelled from Galway earlier that morning and skipping lunch, barely making it to the church in time to hear that his niece would not be joining the congregation. It was James who had driven him from the church to the hospital. *Poor boy*. He had tried to speak words of comfort but James had been silent and far away, too far to be reached. The journey to St Vincent's had seemed to last an eternity, especially as James had a tendency toward aggressive manoeuvring. Father Ryan favoured travelling by bike. His parish was a small one just outside Galway city. He only used the car when he had to travel between parishes to say Mass, other than that he favoured his bike. "Nothing like a bit of fresh air," he'd say. Father Ryan wasn't afraid of the cold, in fact he welcomed it. He couldn't stand his brother's central heating, it brought him out in a rash but of course he'd never say it, even going as far as to thank Gloria for remembering to put on the electric blanket. *It's May! What on earth is the woman thinking?* He was looking forward to going home on the train the next day. He'd sit and eat some lunch and watch the countryside pass him by and attempt to quell his fears and any associated guilt. *I did it for you, Harri. Mostly I did it for you.*

Duncan looked over at his wife picking at her food. He watched her carefully, afraid that she might break. Duncan was ever mindful that at any moment he could lose her to a deep depression that had once all but stolen her away. Days like this day were testing. He was determined to protect her, he just wasn't sure how.

"Are you still with me, Glory?" He always called his wife Glory.

She looked up absentmindedly.

"I'm cold," she said.

Bloody hell Father Ryan thought to himself.

"Maybe you'd like to go to bed?" Duncan offered. "It's been a long day."

"No," she said, "I wouldn't sleep."

"I'll turn up the heat." Duncan got up and went out, leaving his wife and brother alone.

"Is this our fault?" Gloria whispered to Father Ryan.

"Don't think that," he said, shrugging. "How could it be?"

"I'm scared," she said, "I can't lose her again." Tears welled in her dark eyes.

"You've never lost her," he reminded his sister-in-law, squeezing her hand.

"You know what I mean," she said, allowing a tear escape. "I can't lose my child again."

Duncan came back in time to see his wife wipe away a second tear. "Glory?"

"I'm fine," she lied. She stood up as he sat down and she kissed the top of his head. "Maybe I will have an early night."

Duncan again rose to his feet.

"No," she was adamant, "I'm fine. Stay here with Father Ryan. Finish your dinner."

"Goodnight, my love," he said from his chair.

"Goodnight, my darling," she responded from the door.

Father Ryan sat quietly by the thankfully empty fireplace staring into his glass. Duncan sat in the chair opposite. Both spirits were somewhere else. After a time Father Ryan broached Gloria's fears with his younger brother.

"Harri's scared of something unseen, something unknown," he said.

"She shouldn't be."

"You're still so sure she doesn't deserve the truth? You're still so sure that there's a part of her that doesn't already know?" he asked, unafraid of his brother's wrath.

"There is nothing to know!" Duncan said, slamming his glass down on the table holding the lamp beside him.

"Today –"

"Today has nothing to do with anything!"

"Duncan –"

"Thomas."

Father Ryan knew that when his brother called him by his given name he meant business.

"Maybe her panic attacks have nothing to do with anything and maybe they do – all I know is that in the end the truth will out," he warned. "No matter what, the truth will out."

He headed up the stairs toward his uncomfortably warm bed, leaving his brother alone to contemplate.

Duncan drank two more glasses of whiskey before heading up to his attic office, to the drawer that held the copy of the file he hadn't had reason to look at for many years.

He opened it and a picture spilled out. He picked it up and turned on his desk light. The girl's hair was long and dark, her staring eyes deep green, her skin the palest white and her lips were in part purple in part blue. She was seventeen and she was dead.

May 10th 1975 - Saturday

It's the tenth of May already. Today I am sixteen! Sixteen! Can you believe it? I can't. Sixteen years ago my mother gave birth to me. It was a warm spring afternoon in 1959. Mam said that my dad nearly crashed the car trying to get her to the hospital. She said it was a miracle that we all survived the drive. He nearly drove into a tree, a wall and an old man in a cart. He had borrowed his boss's Ford Fairlane and Mam said that he wasn't a practised driver at the time and all she could think about was how would they pay for a replacement fancy car if they survived the crash. Thinking of him driving like a madman with Mam roaring at him makes me laugh. I can hear him. "Hang on, Deirdre. We're nearly there, girly girl!" He always called her "girly girl". I can hear her too. "Hang on? I'm hanging on for dear life! Slow down, you maniac!" She used to be so strong. She never let my dad get away with anything. What happened to her?

I'm sixteen. It's so weird. I used to think I'd never make it to sixteen. When I was tenth, sixteen seemed so far away and after Dad died I was convinced I'd die too. I don't know why but for the longest time I had a sense I'd die young. I still do but only sometimes and anyway now I'm sixteen and that's not so young. This time next year I'll be seventeen and let's face it seventeen is practically ancient.

Mam actually lived up to her promise. She said she'd get me a bottle of Charlie and a Bay City Rollers tape and she did. Wonders will never cease. Now that I think of it, she used to always keep her promises before *he* came along and now, well, I know it's not really her fault. She's doing her best. I had a good day. We had cake for tea. Sheila came and it was nice even if she brought stupid Dave. Still he gave me a bunch of flowers. He'd picked them himself and they were mucky but still they're nice. He didn't have to do that. Even Sheila seemed surprised. It made me feel mean for thinking he's a thick even though I still do.

He was nowhere to be seen, TG. Mam says he hasn't been drinking for over a week now. He's been quiet, no banging doors, no shouting, no nothing. He still can't look me in the eye but I'm glad. Let him keep his eyes on the floor. Let him rot.

Today after school I went to sit by the painting of The Eliana on the pier. I love looking out across the water and far away. On a clear day you can see Wales. Well, not really, but kind of. The doctor was fishing again. He hasn't been there for a few days. I tripped and hurt my ankle. He came over to help so I pretended it was worse than it was. I don't know why, I just wanted to talk to him. Sheila thinks I like him. She's wrong. It's nothing like that. I mean I do like him but not the way she likes Dave. He helped me up and he sat me on one of the flatter rocks. I said I was okay and I asked him his name. He told me, Brendan. He's from Cork. I like his accent - it's sing-songy. He's only in town until Dr Anderson gets better. Dr Anderson is about 107 and has had four heart attacks. I told him the old man should stay at home and let him keep the job. He laughed but he says he belongs somewhere else. I know the feeling.

Henry from Delameres' riding school phoned and told Mam that there was a summer job there if I wanted it. I'm not sure. Cleaning stables is pretty low - horse manure morning noon and night.

PUKE!!!!!!! Still, there's nothing else out there. I've tried every coffee shop in town and the restaurants and the shops. Henry is the manager, he seems nice, and the owner is never really there. He's a horse trainer and spends a lot of time away. Good, I've heard he's a bit of a bastard from Jessica Harney whose brother is a jockey. He's twenty-five and half my size so I suppose it's a good thing he can ride. It's a nice place. I'd never been there before the interview. The house is huge!!!!! I wasn't inside it though. Henry walked me around the stables and the paddocks while we talked. The horses were lovely. A brown one called Betsy really took to me - well, she made lots of noise, tried to head-butt me and dribbled on my shoulder but Henry said that's a good sign. WEIRD. Maybe I'll take it and then if something else comes up I can always leave. HE'S working since yesterday and the job will run on till tomorrow. The load is spirits so he'll sneak some to sell or to drink and either way he'll be delighted with himself, that is until he gets so drunk that he wants to do nothing but hurt someone. First he'll come home with flowers and a box of Milk Tray and Mam will wear her best dress and she could really do with a new best dress and they'll dance in the sitting room and he'll whisper to her and kiss her neck even if I'm in the room. And when I leave I'll hear her laugh and although she's laughing I know that she knows that in another few hours it's likely she will be crying and I just don't understand.

I might be knee deep in horseshit but I'll do my best to make the most out of working at Delameres'. The summer holiday is just around the corner and I'm going to do my best to make it a good one. I'm sitting in my room listening to the Bay City Rollers and I smell great. My flowers are in one of Mam's vases. Happy Birthday to me!

PUKE!!! Still, there's nothing else out there. I've tried every [illegible] shop in town and [illegible] and the [illegible]. Henry is the manager, he seems nice, and the owner is never really around. He's a horse trainer and spends a lot of time away. Good. I've found out a bit of gossip from Jessica Harvey whose brother is a jockey. He's twenty-five and pretty [illegible] so [illegible] there's [illegible] on that. It's a nice place. I [illegible] there before the interview, the house is lovely. I wasn't inside it though. Henry walked me around the stables and the paddocks while we talked. The horses were lovely. A large one called Betsy really took to me. Henry said most [illegible] and dribbled on my shoulder but Henry [illegible] said, 'WELL DONE. [illegible]' [illegible] I can always tell [illegible] working since [illegible] and the job [illegible] tomorrow. [illegible] so he'll [illegible] either way he'll be [illegible] with [illegible] until he gets [illegible] that he wants to do nothing but [illegible]. [illegible] come home with flowers and a [illegible] Mum [illegible] her best dress and she could [illegible] with [illegible] best dress [illegible] in the [illegible] and [illegible] and [illegible] and [illegible] [illegible] and [illegible] anything I [illegible] she [illegible] [illegible] she will be crying and [illegible]

[illegible] I'll do my best to make the [illegible] [illegible] to do [illegible] make [illegible] and [illegible] [illegible] Happy Birthday to [illegible]

Chapter three

Broken

It was after two when Harri unlocked the door to the apartment she shared with James. When they had first decided to buy she had insisted that any property purchased would be south-side and by the sea. She didn't want to move far from her parents and although James was initially reluctant, when they eventually found a two-bed apartment in Monkstown he was first to fall in love. The apartment was empty as she had suspected it would be. The hall remained unchanged, unopened post lay on the floor. The plant on the table across from the door was as usual in desperate need of hydration. The full-length gilt-edged mirror revealed Harri to be a shadow of the girl who had left the apartment three days earlier. She hadn't slept one wink in two nights. James was still not speaking to her. His phone was permanently off. George had insisted that if she was intent upon going to the apartment that she at least permit him to accompany her.

"No," she had said firmly.

"But . . ."

"But no." Harri needed to go home. She needed to go home and she needed to wait there until James returned. She had to see him, to explain, possibly to beg. "I need to see him . . . to explain . . ."

"Explain what?"

"I don't know," she admitted.

"Stay one more day."

She shook her head. "Thanks for minding me, George, but it's time to leave."

He stepped aside to allow her to exit. "I'm always going to be here."

"I know," she smiled at her brother. *I know.*

She hung her coat on the rack and opened the door to the kitchen. Healthy plants rested on the windowsill over the sink. She opened the window behind them allowing sea air to circulate. She put the kettle on and ventured from kitchen to sitting room. It was the sitting room that hit. Boxes sat in the middle of the floor. The boxes contained belongings, specifically James's belongings. The realisation smacked her with the force of a bus. Her legs felt weak and so she sat quickly and with a thud onto the sofa behind her. She sat looking at the boxes for the longest time, digesting their meaning. *He's leaving me.* In the large tank, James's Auntie Edna's exotic fish swam unperturbed by the boxes or indeed the woman crying and in a ball on the sofa that lay a distance away behind thick glass.

It was after six when she heard the key in the door. She hadn't stirred for a few hours and was afraid to risk movement for fear of her body's retribution in the form of stabbing pins and needles. It was a few minutes before he appeared. She was staring at the door waiting for it to open. His face betrayed slight shock, making it clear that he hadn't noticed her coat hanging in the hall.

"Harri," he said quietly.

"James," she replied.

"How are you feeling?" he asked politely.

"Fine. Better. No, actually I'm worse. With every passing moment I feel a little worse."

"I'm sorry," he said, still standing by the door with both arms hanging limply by his sides.

"Why are you sorry? I'm the one who did this," she said, looking from him to the boxes.

"It's not your fault," he said, looking toward his exotic fish swimming and carefree.

"So forgive me."

He shook his head. "It's not about forgiveness."

"Don't leave."

"I have to."

"Why?"

"I can't do this again."

"Well, let's just not get married – let's just stay as we are. I love the way we are."

"I can't," he whispered and his big grey eyes filled. He shook his head. "I just can't."

"It's not you!" Harri cried.

"How can it not be?" he asked.

Harri's head hung low. She was dissolving and James fought the urge to hold her. He moved to leave.

"James."

"Yes."

"I should go. You should stay."

"No. I won't have that. I'll be staying with Malcolm until I find a place."

"What about the apartment?" she asked dully.

"In a few months when we're settled we can think about selling this place and the place in Wexford."

"Okay." She shook her head. "And the fish?"

"I'll come and get them when I find a place."

"Okay." She shook her head, her eyes leaking fiercely. "I really hate those fish – they freak me out."

"I know. I'll pick them up as soon as –"

"I'm sorry – I'm just not a fish person," she interrupted.

"I know. It's okay."

"I'll take care of them. I won't let you down. I mean, not again."

"Thanks. I should go," he said, backing away.

"Please don't," she begged with her hands clasped.

"I have to."

Afraid of breaking, he almost ran from the place, forgetting his boxes. The door slammed and she was alone once more, her heart's blood and the last grains of dignity pooling on the floor. All the while the voyeuristic freaky fishes' indifference taunted her. *Bastards.* Soon she would be hollow so soon she wouldn't care. *Is this what it's like to want to die?*

* * *

A day later and George had spent a good portion of his morning on the phone to a number of Italian winemakers. His latest venture was a wine shop in Clontarf and he was determined to supply only the finest vino sans the middle man, and so he was working on the basis of a charm offensive. During his flitting from here to there he'd become fluent in a number of languages, French and Italian included. He had always found languages came easily. He'd laugh and tell Harri that talk was cheap in any dialect. He was also good at accents. He had an ear. He could be funny as a Texan or an Italian, a Mexican, an Englishman, a German or a Frenchman. He could do each and every Dublin accent, Cork, Galway, Kerry, Belfast and so on. He understood nuance. He heard it and remembered it. His mum said he could have been an actor to which he had once retorted that he was gay but not that gay. He was due in France the following week and he figured he would just cross the border to Italy and kill two birds with one stone. He thought about taking Harri. He figured she could do with getting away but first he had a dinner to attend.

* * *

Gloria had spent most of the day with her daughter. She had arrived at Harri's early and with a basket full of food. Harri had granted her entrance after a few minutes of furious knocking. Her daughter looked terrible. It was clear that she hadn't eaten; she was drawn and seemed almost vacant.

"He'll be back," Gloria had said.

"No, he won't," Harri had replied, blinking in an attempt to relieve tired eyes that burned.

"He will," Gloria repeated, "he'll be back."

Harri ignored her mother.

"George is coming for dinner, won't you come?" Gloria asked.

"No."

"Please."

"I'm drained."

"Okay," her mother said.

Harri was silent. Her heard hurt, she still hadn't slept. She felt so lost and alone and yet craved her mother's departure. *You can't help me, Mum. I wish I knew what was going on.*

"Last night I dreamt that your father was Mel Gibson – 'Mad Max' Mel." Gloria laughed a little. "He was driving a Ford Capri and complaining about the Jaysusing brakes."

"Last night I slept for maybe an hour," said Harri, "and during that hour I dreamt I was lying on cold ground, dying."

"Oh, I'm sure it's just exhaustion, my darling," her mother soothed her, somewhat paler than she had been mere seconds before.

Soon after Gloria left and drove into the Superquinn supermarket car park. There she parked and cried. Five minutes later she emerged, make-up flawless and in time to catch up with Mona heading towards the butcher.

"Have you time for a coffee?" Gloria asked.

"Of course," Mona smiled.

Sitting in the coffee shop Gloria told her friend about her damaged daughter.

"Of course she's upset. She should be on honeymoon; instead she's alone in a flat with those bearded fish."

"Mona!"

"Well, they may be exotic but they are bloody ugly along with it."

"There's one in particular that makes my stomach turn," Gloria admitted.

"She'll get over it," Mona said after a minute or two's contemplation.

"I don't know," Gloria sighed. "She loves him. If I had lost Duncan I would have died."

"She's not you," Mona said kindly and with a smile.

"No," Gloria admitted. *She's definitely not me.*

"Gloria, worse things happen. I don't want to sound cold but it's true. God knows your Duncan knows all about it."

"I've never seen her so down."

"She's bound to be."

"I think it's more."

"More than the second wedding that never was?" Mona's voice suggested a hint of sarcasm.

Gloria clammed up. "You're probably right."

"Of course I'm right. I'm always right when it comes to other people."

Gloria managed a smile.

They split up.

Gloria procured the required shopping to entertain her son. He was home before her and Duncan arrived soon after. George helped his mother prepare dinner while Duncan read the newspaper. He had called in to see his daughter an hour after her mother left. He found her listless. She had taken something to sleep. He carried her to bed and tucked her in, the way he had when she was a child.

"Dad."

"Yes, dear."

"Have you ever felt that you were a piece from another jigsaw?"

"Everything will be fine," he said but inside his heart was beating as wildly as it ever before had.

"I have this creepy feeling."

"Go to sleep," he said, fearing to hear any more, "go to sleep now."

He closed the door and leaned heavily against it. His brother's words ringing in his ears. *The truth will out. No matter what, the truth will out.*

Duncan was quiet at dinner. Gloria talked about her 'Mad Max' Mel dream, making her son laugh.

"I find it hard to see Mel Gibson using the term 'Jaysusing'."

"As I find it hard to see your dad in a wife-beater and driving a Ford Capri. That, my son, is the beauty of REM." Gloria smiled at her son. She was desperate to leave the image of her tattered daughter behind her in the Superquinn car park.

It was only during dessert that George found the necessary courage to tackle his parents on a subject he knew they both would do their utmost to avoid.

"Do you remember when Harri and I were kids?"

"Of course," his mother said. "It seems like only yesterday."

"Do you remember Harri's panic attacks?" He felt it was best not to dick around.

"Excuse me?" Duncan said sternly.

"You had her checked for epilepsy. I remember it. I remember she always put her hands to her throat as though she was choking the way Mum does when she's nervous."

By coincidence, as he spoke Gloria's hands were indeed fluttering toward her neck.

"You don't know what you're talking about," Duncan said firmly.

"So explain it," George challenged.

"I don't have to explain anything to you," Duncan said, standing.

"Sit down, Duncan." Gloria was alarmed by his tone and towering stature.

He sat as instructed while eyeing his son dangerously.

George would not be undermined. "Why did you lie to the doctor?"

"We did not lie," Duncan said, his voice hoarse.

"Why are you lying to me?"

Gloria was suddenly crying. "We didn't want to."

George looked at his mother. Duncan rested his head in his hands.

"What the hell?" said George.

"We just didn't want to open a can of worms," said Gloria. "They ask so many questions – question after question – it gets so hard to keep everything straight."

Duncan's eyes darted from his crying wife to his disenchanted son, remembering his daughter's earlier disturbing query and deep down he knew that the time for avoidance had past. *The truth will out.*

"Dad?"

"We love you both so much," Duncan said with all traces of previous anger now gone.

"I know," George said and suddenly his insides squirmed.

"You are my twins," Gloria said, pale and shaking, "you're my babies."

Duncan's attention was drawn to his shaking wife. "Glory?"

"I won't lose her again," she said, breathing deeply.

"I know. I know, my love. You have to calm down now. Okay?"

"I can't lose her, Duncan. Oh, God help us!"

George was alarmed at the state his mother was getting herself into. He had grown up being careful around her, warned of her delicacy, but because her equilibrium had always been well checked he had never experienced her breaking down, not in thirty years.

The conversation was abandoned. Duncan took his wife upstairs to bed and spent an hour settling her. By the time he returned George was on his third glass of wine.

"She hasn't been like that since . . ."

"Since when, Dad?"

"Well, it's been a long time."

George had never seen his dad so rattled. It was deeply disquieting. Duncan poured himself a whiskey and sat in his favourite chair by the empty fireplace.

"Does Mum have some sort of mental condition? Has it been passed on to Harri?"

"No." Duncan shook his head. "Well, yes. Your mother has suffered with her nerves in the past but it was as a result of something terrible. She's been fine all these years. And Harri, well, no, your mother hasn't passed anything down to Harri."

"Something terrible?" George pushed.

"I can't say."

"You can't *not* say."

"You're right but not tonight. Your sister has a right to know what you know so I'm asking you to wait. Give me one week. Give your mother and your sister one week."

"I'm going to France on Monday."

"Cancel it."

George didn't argue. "Okay," he said, shaking his head, "one week."

"Thank you, son." Duncan drained his glass and made his way upstairs past his wife's bedroom and into his attic office.

George finished his glass of wine and left his childhood home. He stood on the street lined with white blossom trees waiting for a taxi to pass. He looked back at the house and felt like a stranger to the people inside. *What the hell is going on?*

* * *

Susan left her fourth message that day.

"Harri, it's me again. I'm desperate to talk to you. I just want to hear that you're okay. Please call me. I swear I won't talk. I won't say a word. Just phone me, just talk to me. I love you. It's Susan by the way."

Susan always identified herself. It was like there was a part of her that felt she was invisible to those around her, making it necessary to remind the people she cared for who she was. She hung up the phone and sipped on a coffee, sitting at her kitchen counter. She was playing Moby's album *Play*.

Beth, her sixteen-year-old daughter, smiled to herself. *Bloody Play! There are other albums in the world, Mother.* Suddenly she was sitting in front of Susan, clicking her fingers. "Where were you?"

Susan sighed and smiled. "Far from here."

"You heard from Harri?"

"No."

"You okay?"

"I wish she'd call."

"She will, Mum."

"Are you hungry?"

"No."

"Are you sure?"

"I'm sure."

"I feel like crying," Susan admitted.

"So cry."

"I can't. I'm too old to cry."

"No, you're not."

"How did you get to be so sensible?"

"Good parenting."

"Smooth. You're going to ask me for money in the next five minutes, aren't you?"

"No, but I might do in the morning."

"Beth?"

"What?"

"Are we close?"

Beth's face reddened slightly. "Of course."

Susan pretended not to notice her child blush. "Good."

"Mum, sometimes I worry about you."

"Don't be silly."

"I'm not being silly. Sometimes I wish you were happier."

"I am happy."

"Now you're being silly. If you think I don't notice. I notice."

Susan smiled, with eyes filling and head nodding. "Okay, I stand corrected. I did not raise a fool."

"So leave him."

Susan laughed. "It's not that easy."

"It is."

"No, Beth, it's really not."

"I love my dad but he's an arsehole to you and it makes me not like him."

"He does his best."

"No, Mum, *you* do your best – he does everyone else."

"Beth!" Shock brought stinging tears to her eyes.

"I'm sorry, Mum, I shouldn't have said that." She kissed her mother on her forehead. "I love you, Mum. Goodnight." And then she was gone.

"Goodnight, sweetheart."

Susan was alone and wide awake in her large and empty marital bed.

It was after midnight when Harri rang.

"I'm so sorry. I was asleep most of the evening. I just picked up your messages."

"I don't mind. I'm just glad to hear your voice."

"Is everything okay with work?"

"Don't ask about that. Everything is fine."

"Me too. I'm fine."

"Liar."

Harri laughed a little. "You're right. I'm lying."

"Tell me what you're thinking."

"Can't, too fuzzy."

"Try."

"I'm sure you said that you weren't going to talk and talking includes asking questions."

"So we're both liars." Susan laughed before falling silent, waiting for Harri to speak. After a moment or two Harri obliged. "I think I'm losing my mind. I think that I've been fighting this meltdown for a really, really long time. I think there's something eating me from inside out. My head hurts, my body aches, I'm perpetually scared. I'm teetering on the edge, Susan, and any minute now if I let go or if I just give in and allow gravity to take over I think I could disappear."

Susan sighed and closed her eyes for a second before reopening and focusing. "Well, the good news is that you are not depressive."

"Excuse me."

"Depression runs in my family. You, my friend, are far too self-aware to be clinically depressed. That's good news, trust me it's really good news."

"And so?" Harri asked from her bed, tears welling once more.

"And so whatever is going on you have control. You can control it."

"I don't know."

"You do."

"Susan."

"Yes."

"I'm still really tired."

"So sleep."

"Okay."

"I'll call you tomorrow and you will pick up the phone!" Susan ordered.

"Okay."

"Okay." Susan hung up the phone.

It was close to twenty past twelve and still her husband had not returned from work – no phone call, no explanation, and no nothing. Beth was right, it was simple, but she was also wrong. After all what does a sixteen-year-old know about the world?

May 27th 1975 - Friday

Today was the last day of school for eight whole weeks. Whahay! I don't know how to write whahay properly but it's how I feel. Mr Murphy let us out early. Sheila, Dave and I headed for the woods. He's not so bad, Dave. I mean he's still a complete thick but I like him a little more every time I see him. He's kind, annoying but kind. He's tries to be a man and when it doesn't work he reverts to being a little boy - mostly he's a little boy. Sheila doesn't see that. She sees something else. People are funny. Life is funny. Dave smokes so now Sheila smokes. Sad! She smells nasty and coughs a lot but she says it's cool and she likes it. Dave said when he smokes he feels like Steve McQueen. Maybe he does but he sure as hell doesn't look like him. Sheila asked me to try a smoke but life is hard enough without coughing and smelling nasty and my Charlie is reaching its end. I need to earn money to smell good.

I'm starting my new job on Monday. It's okay, I'm looking forward to it. Henry said that I was a natural with horses last Saturday when I went for orientation. I'm not really sure what that means but I do like them. I like their eyes, especially Betsy - it's as though she sees my soul. It sounds weird and maybe it is but she does. I really like her. She's old. Learners ride on Betsy, she's slow and careful and wise enough to know that really she's the one in control. Betsy's kind. She makes me unafraid. She makes me want to ride. Henry said I can if I want to. It's a perk of the job. A few weeks ago I would have thought bollocks to that but now I'd like to. I'd like to canter with Betsy.

I saw the doctor today. He was walking through town with Father Ryan. They were deep in conversation. I didn't like to intrude. Father Ryan's fairly strict and he wouldn't have appreciated teenage interruption. I wonder what they were talking about. What do they have to say to one another? Maybe someone had died or was dying or something else, something terrible. Dr Brendan smiled at me, that sad smile of his. I wish I knew what's wrong. I feel like I know him but I don't. Sheila is still teasing me about liking him but she hasn't a clue. The doctor is broken. I know broken. My dad was broken before he died. My mam is broken now and me, well, I'm on the way. I'm not there yet though.

Mam was crying again last night but not because *he* was here but because he wasn't. I don't understand her. He was quiet for a while and now he's gone. I think that's good. I love that he's gone but all she can do is cry. He was working and coming home and being normal, well, as normal as he can be. He wasn't drinking. He wasn't being loud and Mr Funny or mean and moody. He wasn't doing much of anything. Mostly he just sat around looking sad. The other night when he tried to apologise to me when Mam was asleep I told him it was fine. He knew I was lying. He put his hand on my shoulder and I flinched. I wanted to punch him in his face. He knew it. He kept saying sorry. Sorry doesn't mean anything. It doesn't take away the fear. He can be sorry but I can be vigilant. My mam is sad. She doesn't see or maybe she doesn't want to see. She married a loser. She married a weirdo. He can be sorry. We can all be sorry. He asked me if I hated him. I said nothing but I suppose I gave him one of those 'I could kill you' looks that my mam talks about. He was gone the next day. He hasn't been home in ten days. I hope he never comes back.

Chapter four

Crabs

It had been one full week since Harri had failed to turn up to her wedding. It had been four full days since she'd ventured further than her own bedroom and two days since she'd bothered to shower. Gloria arrived early. She looked as bad as Harri felt.

"Mum, you look terrible."

Gloria surveyed her daughter whose pyjama bottoms and string-vest top belonged to different sets; her hair was standing on end and dark circles once confined to her eye area were spreading fast and threatening to take over her entire face. "That makes two of us, my darling."

Harri caught a glimpse of herself in the long gilt-edged mirror in the hallway. *I really need to bin that mirror.* She followed her mother into the kitchen.

"I'm cooking," her mother warned, "and you are eating."

"I feel hungry."

"You do?" Her voice was injected with hope.

"Yeah."

"You're feeling better?"

"Well, I'm not feeling worse."

"Good," Gloria was encouraged, "that's good."

Harri sat at the counter nursing a mug of tea while her mother made her favourite risotto. Gloria was quieter than usual. They chatted a little and then lapsed into silence.

Harri, while glad of the silence, was also perturbed by it. "What's going on with you, Mum?" she said at last.

"Oh, nothing, nothing at all!" Her mother was shaking her head too rapidly and was clearly flustered with hands fluttering toward her neckline. Gloria of course was lying. When Duncan had made it clear that they had no option but to tell Harri the truth she had fought him.

"Tell George but we can't tell Harri."

"Oh, Glory," he said, shaking his head, "we can't do that, love."

"But George will torture us but eventually he will forgive us."

"And Harri won't?"

"She might not."

"I don't believe that." He was resolute.

She had cried more in the preceding few days then she had in many a long year, only endeavouring to pull herself together when it became evident that her delicate state was tearing a hole in both her husband and son. *Buck up, Gloria. She'll understand. She's your daughter. She loves you.*

"Well, I think I might be coming down with something," Gloria said after a moment or two. "I doubt it's catching though."

"Right." Harri nodded, unsure.

"You could do with a wash but you do seem a little better," Gloria observed with a smile.

"I promised Susan I'd go to her house for dinner tomorrow," said Harri.

"Good for you."

"Melissa's going."

"A girl's night?"

"No, Aidan will be there but George can't make it. Have you

spoken to him lately?"

"No, darling." *He's calling every five minutes*

"Huh, he's being weird."

"Really?"

"No, maybe it's just me."

"You're still coming to dinner on Monday?"

"Yes."

"George will be there."

Harri spun in her stool. "He left a message, he was pretty adamant that I go."

"Don't spin, Harri."

"Sorry."

Gloria placed a plate of risotto in front of her daughter. "Darling, you know that I would die for you, don't you?"

The fork stopped short of Harri's mouth. "Excuse me?"

"I would, you know. I would gladly die for you both. You, George and of course your dad are my world. You know that, don't you?"

Are mental breakdowns contagious? Have I infected my entire family? "I hadn't really ever thought about you dying for anyone and I seriously hope that it never becomes an issue – but thank you. I love you too."

Her mother smiled. "Good girl." She seemed relieved. "I should go."

Harri walked her mother to her front door. They embraced and her mother held on for the longest time.

"I'll see you on Monday?" Gloria said.

"I promise."

"Good girl."

Gloria was gone leaving her daughter in a state of suspicion. *This is not just me losing it – there is something going on.* And as her brother was intent on avoiding her she knew just who to pressure for information.

* * *

Susan checked on the lamb – it was cooking nicely. Beth had abandoned ship, creeping upstairs as soon as her mother's back was turned despite promising to prepare the starter. *Beth's so jumpy this evening.*

Melissa was the first to arrive, thrilled to bits for an excuse to leave her home, her husband and their two children.

"I can't believe you managed to talk her into this," she said, referring to Harri, while pouring two large glasses of wine.

"I was pretty surprised myself."

"Is George coming?"

"Apparently he's busy. He sounded odd."

"He and Aidan haven't split up again?"

"No," she said, handing Melissa a knife. "Start chopping."

"Will do, boss."

Aidan was next to arrive. He was in and pouring wine before the door was closed. "Kisses," he said before taking a long sip from the glass. The term 'kisses' was never intended as a request – in fact it was instead a replacement for an actual physical kiss.

"What's up with George?" Susan asked.

"Can't say."

"So there *is* something up with George." said Melissa.

"I can't say."

"So what is it?"

"Allow me to refer you to my previous statement."

"Don't be ridiculous, Aidan, you've never kept a secret in your life," said Susan while covering a bowl of salad in way too much cling film.

"It's not my secret."

"So there *is* a secret!" Melissa said, nodding to herself in a manner not too distant from Sherlock Holmes' good friend Watson.

"I can't say."

"Of course you can," said Susan. "That is, of course you can if you ever want a referral again."

"Below the belt, Susan, and no I can't. George doesn't know what's going on. A dinner will be held in the Ryan household on Monday night and all will be revealed."

"Does this have to do with Harri's panic attacks?" Melissa said, remembering her conversation with George.

"Maybe, then again maybe not."

The two women looked at one another and then back to Aidan. It was all terribly dramatic. Aidan loved drama so he hammed it up as much as possible. The doorbell rang.

"That's Harri," Susan said in a whisper.

"Say nothing," Aidan warned.

"There's nothing to say. We don't actually know anything," Melissa reminded him.

"A good reason to say nothing," Aidan said, nodding.

The doorbell rang again. "Oh, for God's sake answer the door, Susan!"

Harri had washed and put on something respectable.

Susan welcomed her warmly. "It's so good to see you. You've lost weight. Bitch!" She laughed nervously.

"Thanks." Harri felt awkward. She had thought about backing out but had second thoughts, fearing the wrath of her well-meaning friends.

Melissa greeted her with a freshly poured drink.

"I'm driving."

"Oh well, the more for me!" Melissa seemed a little too jovial but then Melissa didn't get out much.

Aidan hadn't seen Harri since she didn't turn up to her own wedding. "I'm really sorry, Hars."

"Thanks. So what's going on with George?"

Aidan paled a little. Melissa and Susan were left a little dumbfounded, allowing Harri time to assess the situation. *They all know. Bastards.* "Well?"

"No idea," Aidan said unconvincingly.

"Susan?"

"How would I know?"

Susan lied almost as badly as Aidan.

"Melissa?"

"I can't say," she said in faltering manner.

Harri nodded. "Okay. I was beginning to think I was going mad, I mean really mad, but I'm not, am I? Something's going on? What is it, Aidan?"

"Okay, you're right." He seemed relieved to be forced to capitulate. "Your parents are going to make some sort of announcement on Monday."

"What kind of announcement?"

"I swear I don't know. They wouldn't say."

"Try again."

"It's about you."

Harri felt the breath leave her. Her knees shook a little.

Susan gently assisted her toward a chair. "I'm sure it's nothing."

"George doesn't know what it is?"

"They want to tell you together. If he knew I'd said anything he'd kill me. He didn't want to upset you. "

"I won't say a word," Harri promised.

During dinner she was quiet and her friends allowed her silence. *What could it be? What could it be?*

Aidan, Melissa and Susan managed to get through three bottles of wine and were on another planet. Harri figured she'd stayed long enough to be polite. She made her way to the bathroom before saying her goodbyes.

But on exiting the bathroom she bumped into Beth.

"Beth, you scared me!"

"Sorry, Harri."

"It's okay, I was dreaming." She moved to pass her friend's daughter.

"Harri?"

"Yes."

"I'm sorry about the whole wedding fiasco."

Harri laughed a little. Beth was the first one with balls enough to call a spade a spade. "Thanks."

"Harri?"

"Yes?"

"Can I talk to you in my bedroom?"

"Oh. Okay," she said, looking around, feeling suddenly awkward.

They were sitting on Beth's bed. The room was cosy and clean with a study desk, a computer, TV, DVD and a sound system with speakers mounted on the wall.

"God, we could be in Dixons!" said Harri.

"Yeah. Listen, I'm in a little bit of trouble." Beth was sitting awkwardly and she seemed a little jumpy.

"Shouldn't you be talking to your mother?" Harri was beginning to panic.

"No. I really don't want to."

"So why me?"

"Well, you're mum's business partner and friend, I've known you most of my life and I've kind of fucked up and, well, you tend to fuck up so I thought you might understand."

Good argument.

"No offence."

"None taken."

They sat in silence for a moment or two. "So what's the problem?" *Please don't be pregnant.*

Beth laughed. "I'm not pregnant."

Thank you, God. "I never said you were."

"You were thinking it."

"Yes, I was."

Beth laughed again. She liked Harri. "I've got crabs."

"Oh." Harri stood up.

"Will you take me to a clinic in town? I couldn't bear to tell my GP."

"You're sure?"

"Positive. I've been tearing the fanny off myself all day and you can actually see them."

"Oh God."

"I know. Have you ever had them?"

"No."

"You're lucky."

Harri sat on the hard chair by the computer. She contemplated wiping it but feared it would be impolite. “Can I ask how you caught crabs?”

“I’m not a slut.”

“I didn’t say you were.”

“But you were thinking it.”

“I certainly was not.”

“Okay.” Beth smiled. She believed Harri.

“So?”

“So I was going out a guy for six months. We were doing it and being careful. His parents took him skiing last month. He met a slut, slutted with the slut and long story short I’ve got an ice pack shoved down my knickers.”

“I’m sorry.”

“I don’t care, he’s a slut.”

“You care.”

“Yeah, I do, but I’m all cried out.”

“I know the feeling.” Harri stood up. “I’ll make an appointment tomorrow.”

Beth handed Harri her card. “Call me directly, okay?”

“You have a card? Sixteen-year-olds have cards?”

Beth shrugged. “It’s easy. Anyone can do it with a computer and colour printer.”

“When I was your age we really didn’t have a clue.”

“Yeah, well, think about my poor mother – she has sixteen years on you. Can you image how green she was?”

“Green but very likely crab-free.” Harri smiled and Beth laughed a little.

“You won’t say anything?” she asked and Harri promised to remain silent for the second time that night.

* * *

Later while alone in bed Harri remained wide awake. Her head was full and yet empty, so many questions and bloody no answers.

What’s going on? I don’t know. What could it be? I have no idea. Is it about me alone or George and me? I should have pushed Aidan more. Is it my health? I'm thirty years old – surely I'd know more about the state of my health than my parents. Wouldn't I? Why did Mum say she'd die for me? Why does George feel like he has to avoid me? What could be so bad? How upset does he think I'm going to get? Surely this week couldn't get any bloody worse. I should be on honeymoon for God's sake. God, I ache for James. Please come home! Please forgive me. I'm lost without you. And what about Beth having crabs? Jesus, I didn't see that coming. Should I tell Susan? No, I shouldn't break Beth's trust. It's good that she came to me. I'm an adult. It was responsible of her. Why didn't she tell Susan? They're so close – maybe that's why. Oh God, maybe should I tell Susan? Definitely not. I'd love to hunt that dirty little bastard down. I wish I could talk to James. He'd think this was funny – the crabs not the secret. The secret would freak him out. I feel like tea but I better not – I'll end up pouring it all over myself. Why do I always become awkward and accident-prone when I'm upset? Holy hell, Susan's baby has crabs! Well, now, what do I really think about that . . .

It was after three when Harri finally dozed off. Beth may have been a teenager with a VD but she had managed to help take Harri's mind off her parents' secret, allowing her to face away into a dream state and for that she was grateful.

June 2nd 1975 - Monday

HE came home last night. I knew it couldn't last. He was out of his mind. He hit Mam over and over. I ran to Nosey Crowley's but she was on the phone to the police before I knocked on the door. Good for her. She was on her own and was too afraid of him to help. I was too scared to go back. I feel terrible but the police and Nosey Crowley said I was right to stay out of harm's way. Easy for them to say, they weren't getting their faces punched in. They locked him up and I went with Mam in the ambulance. She kept saying she was fine and she didn't look as bad as I thought she would. She's been worse. Her lip is in bits though. Mam's staying in again tonight. Of course he was let out this morning. Typical. She said that it was the end of it.

He wasn't welcome at home again. I'll believe it when I see it. Why is she so weak?

Dr B. That's what I'm calling Brendan now, Dr B. It has a nice ring to it. Anyway Dr B was in the hospital last night. He was visiting one of his patients. She's eighty-eight and dying. He's so nice. I saw her, she's bonkers and he could have easily got away without visiting but he did anyway. He asked after Mam. I told him straight out, he seemed shocked. He tried to talk to her but she wasn't having any of it. He bought me a coffee later after she'd kicked us out of her room. He said I was strong. I'm not strong. If I was strong HE would be pushing up daisies. It was nice to hear though in that sing-songy voice. He said he wasn't used to people being so open. He said it was a nice change. I don't know what he means. I'm hardly in a position to pretend. The whole town knows what he's like. Well, most of it. What am I supposed to do - bury my head in the sand along with my mam? No thanks.

I started work today. Mam insisted. I'm glad. I hate sitting around hospitals. Besides I was actually starting to look forward to cleaning up horseshit. So how great is my life? Henry was nice. He showed me around again and introduced me to the people I'll be working with. Delamere's son Matthew will be home all summer. He's working in the stables too. He's my age but I don't really know him, only to see. He goes to a boarding school in Dublin. He's really tall and cute, really cute, but I think he's a bit stuck up or maybe he's shy. I haven't made my mind up yet. He was mucking out in the stable next to me and didn't say a word - well, not to me - he talked to the horse a lot though. WEIRDO. It wasn't a bad day actually. I even got to ride Betsy. I was ready to wee my pants but I thought why not? It was scary. I felt so high up but it was fun. Matthew was flying around the place on his horse Nero - he was jumping over fences and everything. I was being led around by Henry. I felt a bit of a twit but Henry says I'll be galloping in no time. I don't know whether I like that idea. I'll see. It's weird being home alone. Father Ryan called earlier to check on me. He told me Dr B had filled him in and asked if I was all right. What is it with Dr B and the priest? I said I was fine but I offered him tea. We hadn't much to talk about but it felt better having him in the house. He said I could stop by the parish house any time. Why would I do that??? He said he'd called in to Mam but she was sedated. Sedated my eye, she was pretending. Oh and just to note - Matthew Delamere looks really REALLY like Starsky from Starsky & Hutch or maybe it's Hutch I always get them confused. He looks like the blonde one except he has brown hair. He has a black cord jacket with patches on the sleeves and I know it sounds nerdy but it looks really good. I think I'll talk to him tomorrow.

Chapter five

Ms Know-it-all

The following morning a horribly hung-over Melissa woke up to the sound of crying. Gerry turned over and snored a little for effect. *I know you're awake, wanker.* It was just after 5 a.m. and the fifth morning in a row that Carrie, the baby, had woken for no apparent rhyme or reason. Melissa dragged her body into sitting position and pulled herself into standing. *I'm coming, I'm coming.* Carrie stopped crying as soon as she was picked up. In the week just past Carrie had decided that it suited her to be walked between the hours of 5 a.m. and 7 a.m. As soon as Jacob, Melissa's four-year-old, and her husband awoke to prepare for school and work Carrie was ready for a snooze.

The night before Gerry had promised he'd get up when Melissa was so tired that she'd threatened to pull out of dinner in Susan's despite being desperate for a night out, not to mention being the designated and obligatory shoulder for her newly separated best friend to cry upon. He had looked her in the eye and told her emphatically that he would take his turn without word or grumble. He had lied. Carrie had started crying and he ignored her. Melissa had nudged her husband gently and he turned stiffly. She had poked him again and his movement became more aggressive and accompanied by a huffing soundtrack. The child was near hysterical by the time she'd at last risen. She could have shouted but what would be the point? Gerry was a nightmare in the mornings.

With the baby secure in the crook of her arm she went about securing headache tablets and a badly needed pint of any available liquid. With medication ingested and venturing through her system she sat on the loo with the babe in arms gurgling and staring at the ceiling with the kind of intensity that made Melissa wonder if the child could see something that she could not. Carrie didn't like it if her mother sat for long between the hours of 5 a.m. and 7 a.m. and so the business in the loo was concluded quickly and before Carrie realised the woman who gave birth to her roaring was standing, walking or swaying in a manner that some might deem slightly manic. Melissa felt sick and hoped to God her system wouldn't require purging. *How can I walk, hold the baby and vomit? Can't hold baby and basin at the same time but maybe I could manage a pot. God Almighty, please just let me get through the morning.* Of course there was no rest for Melissa once the men of the house rose from their uninterrupted slumber. There was breakfast and lunches to be made, necessary items to be found.

"Mom, where's my Bart T-shirt?"

"Melissa, have you seen my phone?"

"Mom, where's my runners?"

"I could have sworn that I put my briefcase by the sofa in the sitting room. Have you seen it?"

"Mom, where's my lunch box?"

"My keys. My keys. Have you seen my poxy keys?"

"Mom, where's my pencil with the picture of Captain Jack Sparrow with the rubber on top?"

She'd have to shower, iron clothes, make her child's lunch, steam bottles, drink a coffee, fix her hair and apply enough make-up to hide the fact that she was haggard and ready to give up. *I might just need a roller.*

Gerry was bright as a button and pretending he hadn't let her down. "Good morning, good wench."

"Don't good wench me!"

After acquiring his briefcase and keys he kissed her on her forehead and she momentarily contemplated head-butting him. She didn't for fear of mentally scarring her eldest child so instead she stormed out of the room, banging the door for effect.

"Jacob, is Mommy in bad humour?" Gerry asked while ruffling his son's hair.

"She told me to shove my Captain Jack Sparrow pencil with the rubber on top where the sun don't shine," he said between mouthfuls of cereal.

"Well, I'm sure Captain Jack has no business going there," he said before drinking out of the orange carton.

"Dad?"

"Ah ha?"

"Where doesn't the sun shine?"

"In the shade, son."

"Oh. I don't think he'd really mind so."

Melissa packed her son's lunch into his schoolbag before pulling the Captain Jack pencil from her pocket and handing it to him.

"Where'd you find it?"

"In the treasure trove that resides underneath your bed."

"Thanks, Mom," he said, making his way outside to the car.

Gerry pretended he hadn't noticed she was annoyed. "Where's my kiss?"

"Go fuck yourself, Gerry."

"That's nice."

"Not as nice as being a lone parent."

"Oh for God's sake!" he said, sighing dramatically.

"Get out! Get out before I knife you."

It struck him that she meant it. "Melissa, you seriously need help," he said, shaking his head as though her outburst had been somehow irrational.

"Yes, Gerry, I do. I need your help but it looks I'm not going to get it so fuck off out before I do you in, okay?"

Gerry left quickly. The babyminder arrived just in time to give Melissa half an hour to get to a budget meeting that would start in ten minutes and last the next four hours. She would eat a sandwich at her desk before enduring a further sales meeting which would no doubt last another four hours, forcing her to take her paperwork home. She'd feed her baby, work on her sales figures, burp her baby, work on graphs, and rock her baby to sleep while printing off her sales proposals. The baby would sleep, Jacob would need dinner, help with homework, then they would fight over the TV and what he wanted to watch as opposed to what he was allowed to watch, she'd shout, he'd sulk. She'd all but force-feed him his dinner, negotiations breaking down early in the proceedings. "Just eat the food, Jacob, eat the bloody food!" Gerry would get home just a little after seven thirty. He'd dish his dinner from the oven, take it into the sitting room and there he would sit with a tray and his four-year-old, now jaded from his campaign to break his overworked mother and together they would vegetate in front of the sports channel. *I hate my life. I can't do this any more.* Melissa had been unable to take any longer than six weeks' maternity leave because of her position as team leader on a massive account that required her constant supervision.

"If it was last year or next year, Melissa, we could have accommodated you but this year you're killing us."

Of course she had made the sacrifice for the sake of the team because Melissa was a team player. She was suffering from a mild case of post-natal depression when she did go back and although that passed it felt like a lifetime had passed since she could breathe. She had broached the subject of leaving work with Gerry on a number of occasions but he was adamant they couldn't afford it. She had broached the subject of working part-time with her boss but he was adamant that they needed her full time and working longer hours rather than shorter. She spent her time juggling her work and home life and all she seemed to be doing was apologising to all and sundry for her inability to split herself in two while battling exhaustion. It felt like she was on a never-ending treadmill going nowhere fast. *I'm so, so tired.*

It was just before nine and both kids were in bed when she eventually had time to stop, to sit down and to phone Harri.

"Hi," she opened the conversation wearily.

"Hi, yourself."

"Are you okay?" Melissa asked in a tone that suggested that she wasn't.

"Can't wait for Monday!" Harri said airily as though it was a joke. She wasn't fooling anyone.

"I don't know what to say to you except that I'm sorry for getting so drunk last night."

"You needed blow off some steam," Harri said knowingly.

"I did."

"How are you feeling?"

"Like crying." Melissa laughed a little but she too wasn't capable of fooling anyone.

"We're a fine pair."

"Undeniably."

"Melissa?"

"Yes."

"We'll just get over it, okay?"

"Yeah, we will."

"Promise."

"I promise."

After that they talked about a book that Harri had been trying to read followed by a show that Melissa had been watching and a song that a girl in Melissa's office had been humming that went la la la la la la la la. Harri said it definitely sounded familiar but couldn't pinpoint it and Melissa maintained it was at the tip of her tongue and driving her insane and she couldn't stop humming it all the time.

"Just ask her," Harri said.

"She'll think I'm nuts."

"She's the hummer."

"She is the hummer."

"Hummers are notoriously unstable," Harri said without actual facts to back up her point but she was confident that her friend was too tired to delve into her reasoning.

"You're right. I'll just ask her."

"You'll have to wait until Monday."

"Oh Mother of God!" Melissa said, realising that she had a full weekend of head-wrecking humming before her.

* * *

It was a little before eleven. The clinic was busy enough. Harri took a number and pointed Beth to a chair in the corner and away from the man who looked like a stalker. Beth was quiet and determined to keep her head down. She didn't talk for a little while – instead she buried her head in *In Style* magazine. Harri picked up *Time*. A woman in a nice suit sat next to Beth. Beth made a face to Harri. Harri pretended not to notice. They returned to their magazines. The woman got up and walked down the hall, possibly toward a coffee shop or somewhere else unseen and unknown to those sitting in chairs.

"I wonder what's wrong with her?" Beth whispered from behind her magazine.

"I have no idea," Harri replied in a similar whisper.

"I hope it's not catching." Beth said making the face again.

"You mean like crabs?"

"Ouch!"

"Just reminding you that you are in no position to judge."

"Fair enough. I do like her suit."

Minutes passed. Harri was reading about the environment and how we are all pretty much dead in the toxic water. Beth was looking at nice shoes. Beth raised her magazine to just below her eyes.

"Harri?"

"Hmmm."

"Do you think I'll be with a woman doctor?"

"I don't know."

"I don't want a man."

"You'll be fine."

"Do you think I'll have to take anything off?"

"I'm not sure but probably."

Tears welled in Beth's eyes. "I don't want to take anything off."

Harri smiled at her. It was easy to forget she was only sixteen. She looked and acted so grown up but when she cried, she was, as Bob Dylan had once so beautifully put it, just like a little girl.

"They see this every day," she said, nudging Beth the way George often nudged her.

"They don't see me every day," Beth said with tears suddenly dripping from her chin.

"I know it's embarrassing," Harri said. "Wait until you're my age and have to go for a smear test every year!" She raised her eyes to heaven.

Beth's eyes dried slightly.

"Is that sore?"

"Just embarrassing."

"You get embarrassed?"

"I lose the power of speech."

Beth laughed a little.

"I used to live with a girl once called Tina Tingle," said Harri.

"Tina Tingle?" Beth asked in a voice that suggested she didn't believe.

"Tina Tingle," Harri confirmed. "During Tina's first smear test she farted." She smiled at Beth. "Loudly. It was no real surprise as the woman lived on Indian takeaways."

Beth dropped her magazine to just under her nose and laughed.

"You'll be fine," Harri said.

Beth grinned. "I suppose if I'm old enough to have sex I should be old enough to handle the consequences."

Harri leaned back in her chair, sighing. "How did you get to be so emotionally intelligent at sixteen? Compared to you I was a dribbling dope."

"All of life's bigger questions are asked and answered in teen dramas," Beth smiled, "especially *Dawson's Creek*. It's a cliché-ridden classic. I have seasons 1 to 3 on DVD if you're interested."

Harri laughed at her young friend and shook her head. "I think I'm past teen dramas but thanks for the offer."

Beth was called in soon after. Harri gave her the thumbs up, she grew pale once more but she went in regardless. *Good for you. I would have been scratching for years.*

Later, after Harri had paid the bill and purchased the required medicine, and Beth had spent an inordinate time in the ladies' toilet of The Elephant & Castle restaurant in Temple Bar and close to George's apartment, they ate lunch in a seat by the large window.

"You're staring out the window," Beth pointed out.

"So I am."

"So you're looking for George."

"He comes here a lot," Harri said as though to herself.

"I heard the drunkards talk last night after you left. They're worried about you and about the secret."

"Do you know about the secret?" Harri asked, betraying a little alarm.

"I know there is a secret."

Harri looked back toward the window. "He's avoiding me."

"He thinks he's shielding you."

Harri laughed. "Is that what you think?"

"No, that's what Aidan said after you left."

"Oh. So what do you think about all of this? Any *Daniel's Peak* related light to shed on the matter?" She was amused by her new sixteen-year-old friend's supposed clarity.

"It's *Dawson's Creek* and this secret, well, it's probably nothing." Beth nodded to agree with herself. "Adults tend to overcomplicate things."

Harri smiled. "I'll bear that in mind."

They had finished their buffalo wings and Beth was waiting on an ice-cream-based dessert.

"Harri?"

"Yes."

"What do you think about my dad?"

Harri didn't know what to say. She shook her head. "I don't know what to say about that." Harri had a habit of saying exactly what was on her mind which is probably why the sixteen-year-old warmed to her.

"He's a dick," Beth said categorically.

"Beth!"

"Don't defend him. He's been missing in action for over six months. He's treating my mum like crap. I see how she suffers."

"Life is not that simple."

"That's what she says but that's bull because I'm the one listening to her cry."

"It's a bad time but they might recover," Harri said cautiously, knowing she was treading on dangerous ground.

"He's obviously having an affair. God, for all we know he could have a whole other family."

"I think you watch too much TV."

"Yeah, well, I don't think you watch enough."

Harri took her statement on board with a smile. *Maybe she's right.*

"Beth, sometimes what we see isn't all it seems. I know you love your mum and you're fiercely protective and that's great – but you know she's capable right?"

"I used to think so."

"She is, so I'm asking you to just back off and give them a chance. They need to work it out themselves, either way."

Beth considered for a moment. Her ice-cream appeared, she tucked in and silence resumed for three or four minutes.

"Harri?"

"Yes."

"Do you miss James?"

"Yes."

"Do you want him back?"

Tears stung Harri's eyes. "Yes."

"Does he want you?"

"I don't know. Probably not."

"I'm really sorry. I really am."

"Thanks."

Harri pressed on her eyes before gathered tears gained enough weight to fall. "What about you?"

"What about me?" Beth asked, shrugging between ice-cream scoops.

"Do you miss your boyfriend? What was his name?"

"Mark."

"Do you miss Mark?"

"Mark is a slutty slut-riding slut machine."

"That's not what I asked."

Beth stopped, she sighed and then she allowed a moment to pass. "I do."

"You really liked him."

"I thought I loved him." Beth's eyes were now focussed on her feet. "I might still."

"I understand."

"I don't. I've cried more than I've ever cried before and that includes when Mr Bo Jangles died when I was nine," Beth admitted with a sad sigh. "That dog was my life and I've shed more tears for a boy who gave me crabs. I feel sick about that."

"Hang in there, kiddo!"

"You too."

Harri dropped Beth to the dart station. Beth had hugged and thanked her and Harri told her friend's daughter that their day spent in a VD clinic was a pleasure.

June 9th 1975 - Monday

Okay so it's been a full week but at last today I talked to Matthew. I was cleaning a stable door which was covered in God knows what but whatever it was it was hard to get off. He was passing, taking Lovely Lucinda for a trot and as he was passing his dad the Dreaded Delamere shouted to him. He had come down from the posh part of the grounds where they train the posh horses and where the rich people helicopter in. I'm not allowed over there - it's a whole courtyard and field over. It even has its own entrance. He was wearing wellies. I don't know him but he looked weird in wellies as though it was a wrong fit. Matthew froze. I could see his back straighten the way mine does when I hear HIM come in. Anyway Dreaded Delamere started shouting about Nero, the horse Matthew exercises. He said he was lame and it was Matthew's fault. Matthew didn't talk, he didn't defend himself. I wanted to say it's not his fault and how dare you but I don't know if it is and I don't want to get fired. I really like this job. Dreaded Delamere stormed off leaving Matthew standing in front of me upset and embarrassed. I said dads were dicks. He agreed. I said mine was dead and he apologised which I thought was nice. I told him I had a stepdad and he made his dad look like a saint. He disagreed. He said my stepdad would have to go a long way to beat his dad. I know the man only shouted at him and I know I don't know him or his dad but I think deep down he has a case. I don't trust the Dreaded Delamere. He makes me feel weird. I don't care how rich he is.

Sheila had a fight with Dave. She said he doesn't understand her, whatever that means. Sheila's losing it. I think it's because Dave keeps dropping the hand and she said the other night that last week he shoved his fingers up her privates. Apparently that's not comfortable.

Mam's bruises are going down, her lip is still cut but it's not as fat. HE's moved out. She left his stuff in the garden and he picked it up with a friend from the docks. Maybe this time it's for good. I really hope so. Father Ryan was back around. He and Mam sat in the sitting room alone for over an hour. I tried to listen at the door but Father Ryan is an awful man for whispering. Dr B called too. He was checking in on Mam. I didn't know her rib was broken. He was making sure it was healing well. He said it was. I made him tea and put out a plate of custard creams which I didn't realise had gone soft. NIGHTMARE. Mam was way nicer to him than she had been in the hospital - she even apologised. He said there was no need. That's just like him. We walked out together. He asked me about my new job and I told him about Matthew. He teased me about liking him and I blushed!!! What a SPAZ. I told him later that he had sad eyes and I swear I saw a tear although it disappeared quickly but I know what I saw.

The other evening when I left Delameres' and walked home though Devil's Glen, I was surrounded by tall leafy trees, the waterfall, the bending trickling river, the well-worn closeted trails and I felt full. As though my heart was bursting and I don't know why but it felt warm. In Devil's Glen I can breathe, slow and hard, my head and heart full of the whole world and for that short time I'm in love with this life no matter how horrible it can be.

I had a dream last night. I dreamt that I was riding Betsy and she was galloping faster and faster into and through the woods and every now and then I'd have to duck to miss a branch in the head and my heart was beating wildly and I could feel the saddle under me and the reins pulled tight. We emerged from the wood and suddenly we were on The Head and speeding toward the two lighthouses and then beyond them down the steep pathway that zigged-zagged toward the cliffs and to the third white lighthouse that seems like it belongs in another country somewhere that is never without sun. Just as we passed it and before we reached the cliff's edge I saw Matthew and he waved and I let go of the reins so that I could wave back and then we were falling through the air, Betsy and I, and I didn't care. I was happy to fall. There was silence, no screaming or neighing. I woke up before we hit the water and although I was sweating I wasn't scared. It sounds strange but it was a good dream.

Chapter six

I'm not scared

James arrived a little after ten on Monday morning. He brought Malcolm. His former best man was now reduced to labourer and possible buffer.

"Coffee?" Harri asked as nonchalantly as possible under the circumstances. James was noncommittal but Malcolm was gasping.

"I thought you were going to wait until you found a place before you picked up the fish?" she asked although in truth the sooner they were gone the better.

"I know you hate them." He tried to smile.

You're a gentlemen and too good for me. "I wouldn't have minded, besides it's really only three of them. The others are fine."

Malcolm took one look at the tank "It's him, him and him, isn't it?" he said pointing.

She nodded.

"If they were people they'd be warlords," he concluded.

Harri didn't quite understand where this notion came from but it instantly made sense to her. She nodded thoughtfully. "I think you're right."

James shook his head and sighed to himself. Obviously he didn't see it. He got busy with the tank. Malcolm followed Harri into the kitchen. She was making coffee.

"So?" he said aggressively.

"So?"

"How many times do you plan on breaking my best friend's heart?"

"I think I'm done," she said, pouring coffee.

"I hope so," he replied, accepting coffee in his cup. "And so what now?"

"I haven't a clue."

"He will always love you."

"You sound like Whitney Houston."

"Don't joke, he's devastated."

"Sorry." Suddenly Harri was crying. *Stop crying, you fool!*

Malcolm's momentary bout of anger disappeared and they found themselves hugging.

"I'll miss you, Harri Ryan."

Harry couldn't respond, so busy was she sobbing on her ex-fiancé's best friend's shoulder. When eventually she managed to bring to a halt her torrent of tears, they pulled apart, and Malcolm gratefully took his leave of the kitchen, taking his coffee together with a coffee for his best and equally devastated friend who was deliberating on the most feasible way to dismantle an extremely large fish tank without risking the life of its inhabitants.

This is going to be a long day.

They were gone before three whole hours had passed.

Harri searched the apartment but all trace of James was gone so she sat on the sofa, curled up and didn't move for hours.

George buzzed Harri's apartment a little after six. She made her way to the front where he was parked. She settled in the passenger seat.

"Aidan admitted he blurted," he said with a sigh.

"Aidan's as spreadable as butter." She attempted a laugh. Harri hated tension.

"In so many ways," he joked before returning to serious. "I'm sorry for the silence."

"Don't be."

"I saw Mum freak out and I couldn't handle it." George was not used to witnessing his mother's outbursts. She had seemed so unstable it had terrified him.

"Mum freaked out?" Harri asked a little breathlessly.

"Don't you freak out Harri, Okay?"

"Okay," she said, slowing her breathing.

"I don't know what's going on," he said.

"Okay," she said, practising her slow breaths without knowing why.

"But I know one thing – whatever it is we'll get through it."

"We will."

"Agreed," he confirmed. "And it could be nothing."

"Agreed," she repeated. "But, George?"

"Yeah?"

"Everything in me is screaming life is never going to be the same again."

"Drama queen!" he teased and laughed at his twin but deep inside he knew she was right. They drove the rest of the way in silence.

* * *

Father Ryan had just come out of Mass two days earlier when the call came.

"We need you to come to Dublin."

"Tell me why?"

"We're telling them."

"You're doing the right thing."

"We have no choice."

"You're doing the right thing."

"I wish I had your confidence."

"She has to know."

"There could be repercussions for both of us."

"Duncan, it was a different time. The church and state had a lot more power then. Besides, Harri is your daughter."

"She'll hate us."

"Maybe for a time but in the end she's a Ryan."

"We can't lose her."

"You won't."

"So you'll definitely be there."

"Of course."

"Thank you, Father Ryan."

"You're welcome, brother."

* * *

George used his key. Harri followed her brother, holding on to his coat-tails like a peasant from another time and place. *Can I have more cheese, sir?*

They sat at the dining table. Duncan was busy opening wine. Gloria was nowhere to be seen. Father Ryan's presence was a surprise. He was smoking in the back garden.

George looked longingly through patio glass. "Do you mind if I join him?" he asked Harri.

"Okay," she smiled.

"I'll be back in a minute."

"Okay," she agreed. *Stop saying okay, Harri.*

Outside Father Ryan greeted his nephew. "George."

"Uncle Thomas."

"You look well."

"I feel well."

"Good for you."

"So you're in on it too." George was never one to dilly-dally.

"It's not for me to talk on this occasion," Father Ryan said before taking a large drag. George followed suit. "And yet you're here."

They were silent for a few moments.

"George?"

"Uncle Thomas."

"No matter what happens here tonight, your parents – my brother and his wife – and I – well, we did what we all believed to be best. I want you to know that."

Before George could respond Father Ryan had stubbed out his cigarette and was gone indoors.

The meal passed in silence. Gloria had been last to join the table. She was pale and, although smiling and pleasant, her hands were rarely away from her neck. They all picked at their meals. No one pretended to be in the humour for small talk. Harri and George remained silent despite minds swimming with questions. They waited. Everyone seemed to be waiting.

Eventually it was Duncan who spoke. He stood as though he was giving a speech.

"I'm not sure what to say," he opened. "Harri, I'm not sure what to say," he repeated, looking directly at his daughter.

Her eyes filled. George held her hand while wondering what the hell was going on. Gloria was crying while still feigning a smile and it was frightening.

"You need to understand that you are," he faltered, "you are our miracle."

Suddenly Harri was back in time to when she was barely ten and sharing a seat with Nana on Nana's bench.

"Harri," Nana said, "did I ever tell you that you are a little miracle?"

"Why, Nana?"

"Because you were sent from the heavens when we needed you most."

Harri controlled her breathing. *I'm not going to panic. I'm fine. I'm perfectly fine.* Duncan continued. "Thirty years ago Glory and I were pregnant with twins." He smiled at Gloria and she bowed her head to signal that he could continue. "It was one of those times," he smiled at the memory, "a great time."

Father Ryan scratched his hand loudly, momentarily distracting everyone. "Sorry," he said, slightly embarrassed. *Bloody central heating will be the death of me.*

Duncan continued, following a small silence. "The pregnancy went perfectly. No problems." He was nodding to himself. "It was just perfect."

Harri's stomach was turning, George's too. *Just say it.*

"Glory went into labour around three o'clock on the thirtieth of April. It was a Friday. I was working on a murder case. They were rare then. Your mother was seven weeks early and I was in Kildare. Nana got her to the hospital." He smiled at his wife while momentarily remembering Nana with warmth. "Don't forget this was before the mobile phone. I didn't even know Glory was in hospital until nine that night when I called home and Nana was waiting. It was another hour before I made it to the hospital. Harri had been born and George was coming. Glory was near dead." His eyes filled and Gloria closed hers and bowed her head. "She was bleeding badly and screaming." He stopped. "She was screaming that she was gone. I thought she was telling me that she was tired and giving up. The doctors and nurses didn't speak – they were too busy trying to save George. And then you came," he turned to George, "and I held you and I don't know if it was moments or minutes before I asked about Harri." He looked at his daughter with eyes brimming. "Your mum's womb was so damaged it was a miracle that George survived. They had to operate. They had to take it." Again he looked at his wife and again she sighed and bowed her head. He stopped talking. He just stopped. Moments passed, it seemed like hours.

Father Ryan stared him down. "Duncan."

"Yes," he said, nodding. He looked weak for the first time in his life. His stature was diminishing before them. His mighty hands that his wife had once described as shovels betrayed fear in the form of the slightest tremble. He clasped them together tightly, so tight that the fingers on his left hand went white.

"Tell them."

"I will," he said, teetering on the edge of a new reality. *No turning back now.*

Harri's heart was beating so hard her chest wall threatened to crumble.

"Dad?" George encouraged, feeling the same pain.

"Harri was dead." Duncan said. "She had died a few minutes after delivery."

Harri instantly disappeared into numbness as though she had been switched to off.

George looked from his sister staring blankly toward the wall opposite her to his mother staring at the floor to his father staring at his daughter and on to his Uncle Thomas who was staring at him and appeared to be silently praying.

"Harri's here, Dad," George heard himself say.

"Harri died soon after birth. We buried her, son, and your mother, well ..."

"They let me hold her," Gloria said out of nowhere. "I got to hold her just that once."

"She's right here," George pleaded.

But already Harri knew because suddenly every misplaced feeling she ever had made sense. *I don't belong here.*

"Harri?" her father pleaded. "Harri?"

"Just talk," she heard herself order.

"I couldn't live with it," Gloria said.

"Mum!" George cried.

"I wanted to disappear. I so desperately wanted to die. I can't describe it. I was lost, George. I loved you but I was so lost without her."

She stopped talking and everyone at the table stared at Harri but Harri was gone, she was in another place, untouchable.

George was still clawing through this new reality. "Mum?"

"I had to stay in a hospital for a while, some weeks, and then I came home to you, George, but I still wasn't right."

"Six weeks after you were born and your sister died I investigated a death in Wicklow," Duncan said taking over from his wife. He looked towards Father Ryan who nodded to him. "Your Uncle Thomas called, he was the one who requested me. It was a young girl. She was seventeen. She'd given birth in a wood. She'd died but against all odds her baby girl survived. The baby is you, Harri."

Harri shot to her feet and, without thought and almost as suddenly as thought, she passed out.

George remained static. His twin sister was on the floor and yet he couldn't move. *My twin sister is on the floor. Get up, George. Move.* But he couldn't because suddenly she wasn't his twin and it was all too incredible for feet or legs to function as normal. Gloria broke down. Duncan moved quickly towards Harri but he was further away than Father Ryan who got down on the floor and held Harri in his arms and whispered in her ear words inaudible to those around. *Damn him and his whisperings.*

She woke after a few seconds or maybe it was a minute; for those observing her collapse, time had stood still.

"Uncle Thomas?"

"Yes, Harri."

"I knew. It sounds insane but deep down I've always known!" She was crying.

"Shush now, angel," he said. "You are loved. You were always loved." He held her tight and in the background Duncan and Gloria and George disappeared if only for a moment.

June 13th 1975 - Friday

They say Friday the 13th is unlucky and maybe it is but not for me. Today has been amazing. First of all HE has moved into a place outside of town with his bank-wall-leaning friend, the one who helped him take his stuff from the garden before. Mam is still determined not to let him in the house no matter what Father Ryan says about the sanctity of marriage. She's got a cleaning job at The Crow's Nest and I told her I could help out with the bills now that I'm working. She's sad but I've seen her a lot sadder. Mostly I think she misses my dad. I know I do. He was sick for so long that sometimes I forget what he was like as a normal dad but then every now and then out of nowhere I see him and he's healthy and virile and smiling and vast and hugging me and protective. I think he really loved me and I think he loved my mam. It's nice to have that. It's nice to hold on to. Matthew took me riding today. It was weird without Henry leading me around but he promised I'd be okay. Betsy knew I was a spaz and so she took care of me. We rode far away from the arena and the trails. I had no idea how big the Delamere property was. It's huge like their big stone house that looks like a castle without the turrets. I'd say it gets really cold in winter. We rode for ages and then we stopped and settled the horses and sat together under a tree. Matthew told me about boarding school. He doesn't really like it much but it's not so bad, it's better than being ignored at home. His mam is dead. She died when he was two. She fell from a horse and broke her neck, not exactly encouraging when I had to ride Betsy back to the yard. He's lovely and he's not stuck up at all. He's just not used to attention. He goes to an all boys boarding school. He says it's okay and he has a few friends but he's not a rugby player and unless you are a rugby player you're no one. I couldn't imagine him being no one. It's impossible.

Sheila and Dave are back together after being off for nearly a whole week. He promised not to shove his fingers up her privates and she promised to allow him to lie under her duvet with her. They haven't met up yet but as soon as they do she's going to call or come over with an update.

I met Dr B down by the pier this evening. I was sitting by The Eliana and he sat beside me. He was quiet, much quieter than usual. I asked what was wrong and he told me it was nothing. He was lying so I asked him again. He shouted at me to go away which was funny because I was there first. I pointed this fact out and asked him what was wrong again. He said I was a kid and wouldn't understand and he got up to walk away. I told him I would. He stopped dead and looked at me like I was some kind of alien. I reminded him that honesty was refreshing. He sat down again and he cried. I sat with him in silence for the longest time looking out over the sea towards where Wales should be. When he stopped crying I asked him what was wrong again. He told me I was too young. I told him that maybe I was young enough. He said that he had left Cork because he had fallen in love. So? I said. He said it was with a man!!!!!!! I didn't see that coming. I nearly fell off the bench. I don't know about much but

I know he's a really good person and I don't warm to many but I warmed to him. I told him that. He thanked me but I know my words mean little. Dr B hates himself. He thinks there is something wrong with him. I don't. I think he's lovely. I wish he could see that. I don't care who he loves and I promised I'd never tell. I'll keep his secret. Oh, I've just thought of something - is Father Ryan telling him he's wrong to love a man the way he's telling my mam she's wrong to leave my stepfather? FATHER RYAN, PLEASE SHUT UP!

Chapter seven

Gone

Harri was lying face down on the pillow, her mobile phone resting beside her. *Go away. Go away. Go away*. She picked it up with the intention of throwing it against her hotel bedroom wall, risking damage to the expensive wallpaper. She needed to aim correctly so as to risk minimum damage because even in the most terrible turmoil Harri appreciated good décor. She used to think she was like her mother that way. Before she took aim she realised it was a call from George.

"Harri?"

"George."

"I'm sorry for running."

"It's okay."

"You were on the floor. First I couldn't move and than I all could do was run."

"You left your car in the driveway," she said as though it was important.

"I don't know what to say," he admitted quietly.

"Me neither."

"I don't know how to be."

"Me neither. We need some time away, George," she said, knowing his feelings mirrored her own.

"I'm going to Italy." He had re-booked his flight one hour earlier.

"Good idea."

"You sound far away."

It was odd that he should say that as Harri was staying in The Clarence Hotel which was only around the corner from her brother's apartment. She was closer than ever, at least geographically, but then being close has nothing to do with geography, being close is a state of mind and so yes Harri was far away and moving further with each passing moment.

"George?" She sounded fuzzy like she was drugged but she wasn't – she was just numbed to her very core.

"Yes?"

"You're the eldest now."

"I suppose so," he said, bringing the phone back to his ear.

"By six weeks," she whispered, "you're older by six weeks and a lifetime."

George allowed the tears to fall. He was alone and it was okay to cry because their world as it was had ended and his twin sister had died.

"Let's not talk for a while," she said.

"No, Harri."

"Don't call me that."

"It's your name."

"It's someone else's name."

"Please."

"George, I can't breathe. Let me be, I'm begging you."

"Whatever you want."

She hung up. She turned off her phone, lay face down and then she disappeared.

* * *

George woke up to a blinding light. He batted the sun-bleached white shutter back in place while shielding his tired eyes. The required level of dullness restored, he slumped back down on his bed. On the pillow next to him lay his phone. Seven missed calls. *Go away, Dad.* The unreliable shutter attempted to once more creep away from the window. He slapped it back into place. *Don't make me break you.* He checked his watch on the pretty white faux-antique locker. It was after two. He had missed a meeting in a local vineyard, a meeting he had been attempting to secure for weeks and yet he couldn't bring himself to care. The previous night he had sat in the local village bar alone while locals spoke about him, muttering aloud about the drunken Irishman and debating as to why he looked so shattered. They assumed he didn't speak the language and so he listened to them comment upon his sadness, his floppy hair and his expensive-looking suit and even managed to enjoy two women argue over who had the best chance with him. He gave them both a smile of encouragement, allowing them to believe that maybe they both had a chance with him. He liked it when women were attracted to him – it appealed to his masculinity and vanity. Having said that, he remained where he was at the bar and all the while he continued to drink. He drank until he could no longer feel his legs. A stranger who disliked his hair but coveted his suit was forced to carry him to the entrance of his hotel. He had attempted to tip the guy but he was polite and refused despite earlier asserting that the Irishman was the Italian for a waster.

Now in the cold light of day his head hurt and he was in no mood to talk business. He stood up and into vomit. *Oh nice, George, very nice.* He cleaned the floor after which, exhausted, he returned to his bed. He must have drifted off into the deepest sleep. He didn't even hear Aidan arrive; he didn't even hear him when he banged his suitcase against the doorframe, knocking the corner of it back against his bad knee. "Oh bollocks, that hurt!" He didn't hear the kettle being boiled for a badly needed coffee. "Bloody Ryanair! How do you manage to run out of coffee?" Nor did he hear the shower run or Aidan dancing under it. "Hot, hot, hot!" When George eventually woke up, he woke up to the back of a head. *What the hell?* He was about to panic when he noticed a familiar tattoo.

"Aidan?"

"Five more minutes," he mumbled sleepily.

"Aidan," he nudged him.

"Three more minutes."

"Aidan!" he roared into his ear.

Aidan shot up in the bed. He took a second or two to orientate. "What?"

"What are you doing here?"

"I'm your boyfriend. You've had some bad news. I'm here for you."

"Your calling what happened 'bad news'?" George asked a little incredulously.

"Well, dear, it's not good news."

"You shouldn't have come."

"Of course I should."

"I don't want you here."

"Of course you don't."

George sat at the side of the bed with his head in his hands. "Aidan, I can't do homotastic witty repartee today."

"I'm not asking you to, mostly because you're not very good at it." He smiled at George who betrayed a slight grin. "Good. Let's take a walk."

"I don't feel like walking."

"Fine. I'll hire you a wheelchair."

It was early evening and the sun was still warm. The little cobbled streets were busy with people walking dogs, couples strolling and some with kids in buggies. The old were holding hands and taking it slow, breathing in fresh air.

George and Aidan sat just inside an empty café watching the world go by. George had been quiet and Aidan had allowed him to be.

"Have you seen Harri?" George asked after careful consideration.

"No," Aidan said, shaking his head. "She checked into The

Clarence for two days, checked out and she hasn't gone home."

"What about Melissa or Susan?"

"Nothing. She can't talk. She can't think. She needs to be gone for a while."

"Like you?"

"But she's not like me. is she?"

"George . . ."

"I always knew we were different but still we were the same." He paused to collect himself. "I think I've just have lost the part of myself that I liked the most."

"You haven't lost her."

George shook his head. "Did I tell you that she said she knew? She told Uncle Thomas that deep down she'd always known." He bit his lower lip remembering that it was that very second in which he regained the use of his legs and had run. "You know what I knew? I knew I had a twin sister." He shrugged. "What I didn't know was that she was dead."

"Harri is not –"

"Harri is dead, Aidan. They didn't even give her replacement a different name. How fucked up is that?"

"It's pretty fucked up," Aidan was forced to agree.

"I keep trying to get my head around it but I can't. My whole life had been a gigantic and pretty fucking mesmerising lie."

"Okay I'm the drama queen in the relationship and it just won't work with two."

"You think I'm being dramatic?"

"I think that you and Harri may not have shared a womb but you have shared a life, every memory and every milestone. You grew up in one another's pockets, finished one another's sentences; you speak in code for God's sake. No one gets you the way she does, not even me and no one gets her like you. So history has been re-written but history is just a list of facts. You and Harri are real and who and what you are together has not changed."

"Nice speech," George said.

"Thanks, I practised on the flight."

"It's not that simple."

"I know. It will take time to get your head around it but after that it really is up to you, both of you," Aidan said, taking his lover's hand and kissing it.

He didn't mind that George pulled away quickly. George hated public displays of affection. It made him uncomfortable. Aidan was tactile and although mostly he kept his affection in check sometimes he slipped. Mostly this would end in a fight but on this night George was too tired to fight so instead he pulled his hand away slowly and stared at the passers-by without another word. Later they walked back through the old stone village to the hotel where they ordered room service and ate dinner in bed before making love and afterwards they turned away happily, moving to the edge of each side of the bed. Aidan was out cold in no time. George lay awake having slept most of the day away.

I can't talk to her. She doesn't want me to. What can either of us say? If nothing really has changed why does nothing feel the same?

⋆ ⋆ ⋆

Gloria was a surprise. She had managed to hold it together exceedingly well and beyond her husband's wildest expectations. She cried of course but that deep dark depression that had once all but consumed her appeared to have no hold. She was upset but she wasn't clinically so. Duncan was grateful for that. His kids were in chaos and so they should be. He understood. He knew it was something they had to be allowed to go through. He just wished he could fast-forward time so that they would understand and see that all was well and they were loved and then the Ryans could be a happy family again.

To Duncan it seemed odd that Harri hadn't asked any questions once revived. She had sat silently in the aftermath of her brother's flat-footed flight.

⋆ ⋆ ⋆

Harri had all but disappeared inside herself. After an hour of silence she'd asked for a taxi, further silence ensued, the taxi arrived, her mother kissed her tearfully, Duncan hugged her so tight she thought her arms would snap, Father Ryan said he was sorry for all the pain she was about to feel. He reminded her that she was viewed as a miracle and that she was forever held dear. Harri didn't stop to ask any questions. Her mind was too full to accept answers. She just wanted out. The taxi man had talked about the cost of concert tickets. "€100-odd euro for George Michael me hole, do you know what I mean, love? Don't get me wrong, he's good, but he's not that bleedin' good. I could get me knob sucked for half that, no offence, love. I mean to say, tickets to a gig or a blow job? A bleedin' blow job wins every time. No offence, love, after all a reality is a reality. Of course George Michael knows all about that. Are you with me?" He laughed away to himself and didn't even notice that the girl in his back seat was crying.

Harri fell into bed and slept soundly that night. Her life was a sham with unfathomable connotations and yet she lay down numb and exhausted. She closed her eyes, happily sleep came quickly and she was gone.

⋆ ⋆ ⋆

On the night of revelation George had run all the way home and screamed the truth to Aidan. Aidan had waited until his boyfriend was calm enough before calling Susan, who after an hour of ohhing and ahhing and Oh-my-Goding, phoned Melissa who sat silent.

"I know them since they were kids," she said at last.

"I know you do."

"No," Melissa had said. "No way. This is Dublin not Hollywood."

"It's true."

"Harri's not Harri?"

"Harri is Harri, she's just Harri 2 The Return." In other circumstances Susan's comment would be funny but neither woman laughed.

"It's just not possible." Melissa sighed.

"It is."

"It's impossible."

"Maybe today but back then in 1970s Ireland . . ." Susan said remembering the time well.

"It's just so macabre."

"You know what's really weird?" Susan said.

"What?"

"I could be my business partner's mother."

"Excuse me?"

"I've just turned forty-six, Harri's thirty, the dead girl in the woods was seventeen."

"Oh, that's so . . . that poor girl."

The phone call ended soon after that. Neither party slept well that night, disturbed by their friend's tragedy.

* * *

Harri didn't answer her phone except that one time to George. She left The Clarence when Aidan managed to track her down and when the coast was clear she returned to her apartment, packed, locked up and drove to the cottage in Wexford she had bought with James, the one that Melissa deemed to be a moth-eaten money pit. Melissa was right but that was okay because for the first time in seventy-two hours Harri could breathe. She was cold and uncomfortable but she could inhale and exhale easily and right about then that was good enough.

June 21st 1975 - Saturday

Dr B is avoiding me. I can't believe it. He hasn't been fishing at the pier and yesterday in town he crossed the road when he saw me. I don't understand. If he keeps it up I'm not sure what I'll do but I'll do something because he needs to cop on – having said that I haven't a clue what to do though. I'll think about it.

HE's still living somewhere else. I don't know exactly where and I don't care. Mam seems to be doing okay. Her face has healed nicely and she's enjoying working in The Crow's Nest. She says the staff are good fun. I'm glad, cleaning is a spaz of a job and I swear I'd hate it but if she's happy I'm happy. Just please, God, make sure she doesn't break and bring him back home.

Sheila is fighting with me. I can't believe it. She says that I've been flirting with Dave. She's obviously gone a bit bell-jar, in other words she's a mental case. I don't flirt with Dave - I interact with him more kindly now than before because I feel sorry for him. I pity him. Poor Dave is not my idea of the ideal man. But Sheila is going nuts. I really don't get it. She says I lean a lot when I'm around him. What does that mean? Maybe I lean because I'm taller than him? Sheila is getting weirder and more annoying by the day.

I've been spending more time with Matthew. We talk all the time and he keeps finding reasons to touch me - my hand, my elbow, my shoulder, my face. Every time he does I feel like throwing up but in a good way. Stupid I know but true. Yesterday after we'd finished work he walked me home through Devil's Glen. We talked about the things we loved. I told him about my inexplicable desire to leave this place even though when I think about it I love it. He talked about wanting to be heard. I asked him what he meant but he said he didn't know but he was sick of living in the shadows. Children are seen and not heard!! That's what his dad always says. Poor Matthew, he's been silent for so long. In school he says a lot of it is silence. He makes me weak. When we talk I feel weak. What's that about? When I'm with him the most mundane incident seems almost magical and when he's not there what I would have previously deemed interesting is now dull. I crave him. And so what's that about? Maybe I'm going mental. He talks and I listen like I've never listened before. He smiles and I light up. PUKE. I know and I sound like a dick but it's true, I can't help it. Sometimes I disgust myself and I want to run away but then I wouldn't see him and that would be bad, really bad. I look at him and my stomach flip-flops. Sometimes that's uncomfortable depending on what I've eaten.

Matthew asked me to meet him in Devil's Glen after nine tonight. I'm scared. I want to go but I'm really stomach-flipping scared. I feel stupid like a kid. I want to go but what's going to happen? Is he going to kiss me? What else? Will it be weird? I really REALLY like him. I can't stop thinking about him. What he likes, what he says, what he eats, even what he drinks and of course what he listens to. Just to note he hates the Bay City Rollers. He's into David Bowie. I still like the Bay City Rollers but not as much as I did and that bothers me. Am I one of those girls???? I want to go but I don't want to go. When I'm with him I don't feel myself and it's nice but it's not nice. I like alone-me and I'm not sure I like the me that's me when I'm with him. Mam said once, you can't choose love, love chooses you. I thought she was full of it. I might have been wrong.

Dave found me sitting by The Eliana today. He said he'd come to apologise about Sheila fighting with me. That was nice of him. I told him it didn't matter and she'd get over it. Sheila's always been moody. I was reading and he asked if it was all right if he sat for a while. The pier is a public place and it's a free world so I said fine. I just continued reading and he stayed sitting beside me for the longest time. Just before he left he told me that he really did like Sheila but sometimes the things she said and did made him feel horrible. I told him that I think that's what happens when you love someone - after all look what happened to my mam when she met HIM. It made me kind of sad and now I'm not sure if I'll meet Matthew. I really want to but what if it turns out badly? Then again I'm no coward. But then I'm not a fool for anyone either. Oh, I don't know.

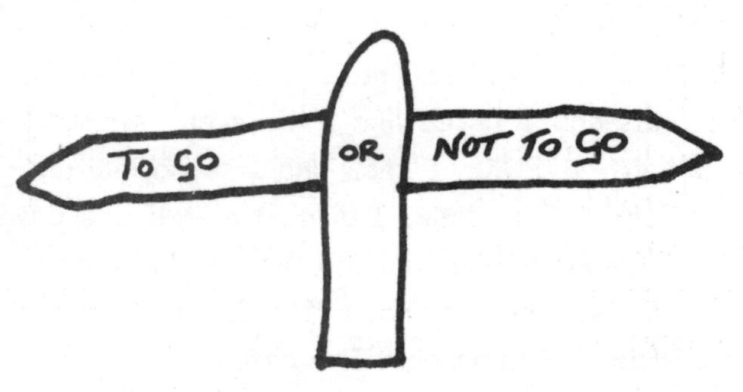

Chapter eight

All to forget

Susan usually liked to spend Saturday lunchtime in the Avoca shop in Ashford. It was only a spin away in the car, the food was great and so was the shopping. She could stock up in the speciality supermarket, she could browse the cookbooks, the clothes, the novelties but mostly she could salivate over the utensils. Susan loved utensils – can-and-jar openers, colanders, strainers, graters, thermometers, whisks and spatulas. All of which she had multiples of but what was most interesting about her psychology was her slavish propensity to buy pastry tools and cake-decorating cutlery despite having an aversion to baking. Susan had more utensils than she had counter space, and so many duplicates lay in draws unseen and forgotten that space was becoming limited.

Today's the day, she had thought upon silencing her alarm clock. *Time for a clear out.* Susan got busy emptying overstuffed drawers. Susan liked to clear cupboards, clean toilets, hand-wash clothes, grout tiles or prune hedges when burdened by unwanted thought. She hadn't engaged in one proper conversation with her husband

Andrew in over a week. Mostly he was gone before she rose and he didn't come home until he was sure that she was asleep. Susan needed her eight hours, she couldn't function without them. She'd usually be comatose by eleven thirty with the TV blaring or glasses halfway down her nose and a book on her chest.

Thank Heavens for small mercies, he'd think passing their room in favour of the guest room. He was tired and the game of avoidance was becoming more trying. Maybe that's why he overslept. *Bollocks.* He could hear the kitchen drawers rattling from the top of the landing despite a staircase and wide hall separating him from his wife. She was being loud on purpose, she was making a point or maybe she was just attempting to remind him that she was still alive. Dying of thirst he entered the kitchen quietly. Susan was sitting in the middle of the floor surrounded by utensils. Neither spoke. Andrew poured himself a coffee. Susan continued to sort whisks from spatulas and colanders from strainers. Sunlight was streaming through the kitchen windows and it was warm enough to open the french doors leading to a carefully kept garden. Andrew took his coffee, newspaper and himself out to the patio area. The radio housed on the shelf next to various hanging plants over the window above the sink was on low, the disc jockeys debating on their favourite version of Leonard Cohen's 'Hallelujah'. Jeff Buckley won. They spoke of the young man himself in rapturous terms, declaring him to be remarkable, and then of his voice which all agreed was best described as poignant. One girl used the word evocative, the other DJs said nothing but Susan could imagine them nodding in the studio. After that they spoke of his untimely death and of the music world's great loss and suddenly Susan found herself crossed-legged and crying for a dead rock star she'd never before heard of. *I must google him.*

* * *

It had been one full week since the revelation and although Harri had escaped to her modest Wexford crumbling cottage it was impossible to flee this new reality no matter how hard she tried.

Anxiety had returned and become a staple part of her existence. It didn't come on her fast and from nowhere, rendering her incapable of breath and tormented by the very real fear of imminent death. Instead she suffered a deep dread that crept into her bones insidiously so that although she wasn't blindsided or dizzy, it was palpable and constant. Concentration was fast becoming Harri's enemy. *Where are my keys? In my handbag so where's my handbag? I'm sure I left my handbag by the door. Christ, where is it? On my shoulder. Right. Now where was I going?* She had gone out and filled a shopping-basket full of books so that she could dodge irrational thought and her distastefully decorated hideaway. *I don't exist. Not only do I not exist but I don't exist in a horrible kip in Wexford.* Reading had often been Harri's escape. The plan was simple. She would read and read and read until numb and apart from herself. *Genius.* Unfortunately reading requires concentration. *Ah crap.* And a lack of concentration compounded by a terrible restlessness made escaping into a book impossible. Harri's new-found jumpy disposition manifested itself both emotionally and physically in the form of minor tremors and jitters. Once while attempting to apply lipstick she noticed her lip twitch. *One twitch, two twitches and here comes three. Oh my God, I'm a bottle of vodka away from morphing into Sue-Ellen Ewing.* The physicality of her new-found fear was not content to remain within the muscular domain. Harri felt exhausted, completely and utterly shattered, her stomach felt constantly sick and when she did manage to eat on the odd occasion her oesophagus opened enough to allow food past her larynx, she suffered stomach-crunching cramps before speeding to the loo to embark on a very necessary and aggressively swift evacuation. The odour of her innards was not of this earth and suggested the possibility that she was rotting from the inside out. *Jesus, the smell! It's bringing tears to my eyes.* If Harri could have run away from Harri she would have done so. Despite the bad state she was in, despite mounting confusion and anger and being incapable of any sort of verbal communication she didn't want the people she loved to worry. Each day she would text the man and woman who had pretended to be her parents and her overwhelmed friends the same message.

<< I'm fine. I need more time. >>

Each day the man and woman who had pretended to be her parents and her overwhelmed friends texted back various messages.

Mum << We're so sorry, darling. We love you.>>

Dad << It's your dad. We need to talk. Please call soon.>>

Melissa << Jesus, Harri, where are you? I wish I knew what to say.>>

Susan << Please come home. I miss you.>>

Aidan << In Italy with George. What doesn't kill us makes us stronger. >>

Aidan << Me again. Ignore last text. Talking through my arse. Sorry.>>

Harri tried to clean the place to keep her mind off things but she was too tired. She tried to sleep but her mind was too restless. She tried to eat but not too much as she was afraid of shitting her pants. *That really would be the icing on the cake.* Her insides were raw and torn. Her eyes burned holes in her head, her skin dehydrated, dried and itching, and each moment that passed she felt a little closer to the edge of reason. *Harri is dead and I'm a Jerry Springer guest. Go, Jerry! Go, Jerry!* She was so tired and so incapable of rational thinking that familiar clumsiness ensued. When attempting to make a cup of tea, one twitch, jitter or possibly a tremor later and the boiling water missed the cup and instead flowed from her hand down her arm before being soaked up by a gathered sleeve. *You are fine. Do not let this get to you. You are better than this.* She turned on the tap and placed her hand under it. Unfortunately it was the hot water tap as opposed to the cold. *You bast– Breathe. It's fine, just turn off the hot tap and turn on the cold. Breathe again.* She pulled at a tea cloth so as to douse it in cold water and the cup that lay on its edge fell hard onto her foot before bouncing and smashing on the tiled floor. *Okay, just limp up stairs, open the bedroom window and fuck yourself out of it.* She could have screamed loudly but she didn't. She could have roared obscenities but roaring obscenities required cognitive thought and strength and in both she was lacking, so she sat quietly on the hard cold tiles and nursed her burned hand and bruised foot and she didn't cry. She hadn't cried once in the entire week.

James pulled into the driveway just after seven. Harri had been sitting on the hard cold tiles since four. She didn't hear him approach. The back door was open and he was standing in front of her.

She blinked. "James?" she asked as though she was unsure as to whether he was a vision or living flesh.

"It's me," he said and he sat down on the cold tiles opposite her. He took her hand in his and unwrapped the wet towel. "What happened?"

"I burnt it."

"Doesn't look too bad," he smiled.

"No, I suppose it isn't," she agreed.

"How about standing up?" he suggested kindly. He could sense she'd been on the floor a while. She looked terrible – thin, pallid, drawn – and it was clear she was so tired that her eyes found focussing a challenge.

"My legs are numb," she said.

"That's okay. I'll lift you."

"I might fall," she said factually and without any associated worry. *If I do I hope I land on my head.*

"I promise I won't let you."

"It doesn't matter," she mumbled. Having stubbed her big toe, smacked her face against a press door, jammed a tweezers into her eye and now this latest burnt-hand-bruised-foot combo, short sharp bouts of physical pain was something she was beginning to become accustomed to.

He lifted her up in his arms and took her from the kitchen into the small sitting room that looked onto the overgrown back garden. He placed her on the sofa and closed the tatty curtains so as to shield himself from the bad state of the garden.

"I'm making you dinner," he said and entered the kitchen, leaving the sitting-room door open so that they could converse.

"I can't really eat," she said.

"I'll make something light."

It would want to be bloody light. Two people, one bathroom, this could be a long night. "Please don't fuss," she begged.

He came back into the room. "Neither of us will. Okay?"

She smiled and nodded. "Susan called you?"

"Susan, George, Aidan, Melissa and your dad. Actually your dad called about nine times."

"How did you know I was here?"

"I went to the apartment. Your passport was in the kitchen drawer so I took a chance."

"Melissa is right – this place is a shithole," she said looking around at the crumbling plaster.

"Yes, but it had potential."

Harri was tired but not tired enough not to note that he was using past tense. "I suppose it had." *Just like we once had.*

Later he insisted that she ate propped up on the sofa. She managed a good few spoonfuls, seemed grateful and then went to the bathroom where she refused to exit long after her colon was well and truly evacuated.

"Harri, let me in."

"No."

"Please."

You really don't want to be in here. "No."

"You're scaring me."

Oh my God, he thinks I'm trying to kill myself. "Do you think I'm trying to kill myself?"

"No."

Silence.

"Yes."

Silence.

"No. Well maybe. Jesus, Harri, I don't know. Are you?"

She sighed while sitting, pants down, with her head in her hands. "I have the runs."

"Oh."

"So do you still want to come in?"

"No. No, no. I'm fine. I'll be in the sitting room." James suffered from a weak stomach and strong smells of any kind were no friend to him.

Twenty minutes later Harri returned and slumped on the sofa.

"Sorry," James said.

"Do you really think I'd hurt myself?"

"I don't know," he answered honestly. "Would you?"

"I don't know," she answered honestly. "Earlier I momentarily considered throwing myself out a window." She shrugged.

James smiled at her. "So why didn't you?"

"I was too tired," she sighed.

"I'm so sorry about the whole bloody lot of it," he said.

Harri nodded. "Me too."

Just after the word "me" and exactly on the word "too" Harri's carefully constructed dam burst and she was crying loud and hard with streaming eyes, nose and mouth which unattractively appeared to be gushing wave after wave of built-up pain, confusion and anger. But mostly she leaked grief. She grieved for the dead girl who gave birth to her. She grieved for the mother she'd always known and for that woman's dead baby girl. She grieved for her father, the stranger, the one she thought she knew and the architect of this most terrible deceit who felt somehow lost to her. She grieved for her twin who was now no relation. She grieved for the man she'd loved and lost despite him being beside her and rocking her. She grieved for all that she used to be and for all that she never was. Harri Ryan cried in her ex-fiancé's arms for hours that night and when she was spent, completely and utterly drained, she fell asleep so soundly that she didn't wake when he lifted her awkwardly, nearly dropping her such was her dead weight nor did she wake when he banged her burnt arm off the narrow doorway or when he placed her on the bed, moving her roughly so that he could wrangle the duvet from under her. She didn't wake for another fourteen hours but when she did the man she'd lost was waiting for her.

* * *

Melissa hadn't really had time to talk to Gerry until he had surprised her with a babysitter and a meal out. The babysitter was a fifteen-year-old neighbour who four weeks previously had been caught sleeping with her boyfriend by her mother who Melissa had befriended while on maternity leave. Melissa didn't worry about what would happen when she left the house. *Hey kid, use our bed. I don't give a stuff. I'm going out.* She dressed quickly, left her randy babysitter alone with a stash of biscuits and a stack of DVDs and hightailed it out the door to the restaurant where her husband was waiting. Once they were sitting and he was pouring wine she couldn't help but query his intention.

"Gerry?"

"What?"

"What's going on?"

He grinned. "Nothing."

"I don't believe you."

"I'm just sorry about the other night," he admitted.

"You say it like it was a one-off," she reminded him.

"I don't want to fight."

"Me neither."

"So let's not."

"Okay, let's not."

"But?"

"But I really need help with the kids."

"Fine. Now are you done?"

She grinned. "I am."

They clinked glasses and drank. They had ordered and were awaiting starters before she got around to telling him about Harri and her implausible predicament.

"Whoah!" he said, hands up. Gerry was all hands. "I know you said they adopted her but . . ."

"I didn't say they adopted her – I said they replaced her."

"Excuse me?"

"Put down your hands, Gerry, you look like you're attempting the Mexican wave."

"What are you saying?"

"I'm saying. They had a daughter who was born alive."

"Okay."

"Therefore there was a birth cert."

"Okay."

"She died a few minutes after birth."

"So there was a death cert?"

"Never completed."

"Excuse me?"

"Gerry, don't be dense. Six weeks after the child was born and died, Harri, our Harri, was born in some field or barn or ditch or something in Wicklow. Duncan somehow got his hands on her and then he collected his twins' birth certs."

"What about the death cert?"

"I don't know."

"So the birth cert became Harri's – our Harri's? Is that really possible?"

"Well, it happened so it must be," she said, nodding knowingly.

"It's true, stranger things have happened. After all, who ever thought the Terminator would become a governor or the Crocodile Man would get killed by a fish? The world is mad!" Gerry laughed before shoving a large piece of bread into his mouth.

The waiter placed a plate in front of Gerry who smiled at him despite his full mouth and nodded to himself. When the waiter had finished serving, Gerry looked at his wife.

"Duncan and Gloria Ryan are dark horses all the same," he said.

Melissa thought about it for a moment or two. "Yes, I suppose they are."

"So what are the chances of us having a little rough and tumble later?"

"Very little."

"Fair enough, I'll have dessert."

"Well, maybe," she said thinking aloud.

"Look, we either are or we aren't. You know I hate having sex on a full stomach."

"I'm tired."

"Fine, I'll have the banoffi."

"But then again it's been a while."

"The waiter is on his way over," he pressed.

"Fine, have the banoffi!" She hated being pressed.

"Fine," he said, smiling at the waiter.

"You don't have to look so bloody pleased," she huffed.

He ignored her. Gerry loved a good banoffi.

June 22nd 1975 - Sunday

All through Mass all I could think was Matthew, Matthew, Matthew! Father Ryan seemed to go on forever. I've no clue what he said but no doubt he was sitting atop an invisible high horse. I saw Dr B standing at the back. He looked uncomfortable as though he was loitering and didn't belong. Maybe he feels he doesn't but he has a right to bore himself to death as much as anyone else. When I leave home I'm never going to Mass again. I'm never going to Mass and I'm eating cake for breakfast. I can't wait.

I saw HIM standing left of Dr B. I can't believe he has the neck to come to church. He had his hat in his hands and they were clasped. What a creep. I hate him. I hate him. I hate him. He took Communion. He took Communion but Dr B didn't. That says it all. This world is a sad, sad place. How can obviously good people be made to feel abnormal and those full of badness allowed to feel as though they fit in? Is it normal to be twisted? Is it normal to cause torment? Maybe but I can't decide where God is supposed to fit in.

Father Ryan has almost taken up residence in the house. He was back again this afternoon. Mam has agreed to go to prayer meetings. She feels bad about her marriage falling apart. She feels bad that she's let God down by protecting herself and me from a bastard from hell. That's what Matthew called him when I told him what he did to my mam. I never said what he tried to do to me. It doesn't matter. I stopped him. It really doesn't matter. Father Ryan has spoken to HIM and he told Father Ryan he wouldn't hurt her again.

Father Ryan believes him. Father Ryan is a fool. So far she's praying for forgiveness but she hasn't allowed him back. All I can do is wait. I hate it. I hate it. I hate it.

Last night, in Devil's Glen with Matthew it had all seemed so far away. He'd brought a blanket from the stables which smelled weird and he'd stolen three cans of beer from his dad's fridge. I had one, he had two. I hate the taste of beer but it felt nice afterwards when I couldn't taste it any more. We sat by the waterfall but not close enough to fall in like that stupid couple six months back. She nearly died – they're both fine now but they broke up soon after it. The sky was black, not a star to be seen, and the moon was big and bright. Matthew looked toward the sky and put on a deep voice and said "Man's colony on the Moon – a whole new generation has been born and is living there a quarter-million miles from Earth." He said that loads of times. It sounds rubbish now but it was funny when he said it. He's a massive *2001: A Space Odyssey* fan. He said people either love or hate that film. He's right. I think it's a pile of shit. He brought a flash light so that we wouldn't trip on roots while trailing home. We sat and we talked and I told him about Mam and about school and about my teacher saying I had a great command of the English language but no discipline, I didn't apply myself and she wished I could learn to shut up in class. He told me about his mam and her death and his dad and his dad's girlfriends and boarding school and his wooden cubicle and a beating he'd once got with a cane. He showed me the scar on his hand. It was small but that's probably because it happened a long time ago. Mostly he keeps his head down. He just tries to get by until he leaves school and home. He's going to America. Why does everyone go to America? He says his dad will never let him ride the way he wants to. He's too tall to be a jockey, he's at least six foot maybe six-one or two. He says he doesn't want to be a jockey but his dad won't even let him near the bred horses. He wants to break them the way his dad does and like his mam did. He says he'll find a way to do it in America. I don't know why his dad won't let him – he's brilliant with the horses. Even Henry says so. Matthew's a natural, not like me. I'm still a bit scared but every day

I like them more. He kissed me with tongue and he tasted of beer but it was way nicer than drinking the stuff. It was brilliant. We kissed and we kissed and we kissed until we were tired and sore. And still I would have kissed him some more. I'm running out of diary space again.

Just to note horses have their own personalities. It's weird. Betsy is old and wise, calm and strong. Nero is young and foolhardy and excitable. Lovely Lucinda is a lady, she likes to be petted and she bows her head a lot. Paddyman joke-looks at you out of the corner of his eye and he likes his ears scratched but only for a minute or two. He's randy too. He likes the ladies!!! At least that's what Matthew says. I really love my job. I can't wait for tomorrow.

Chapter nine

Every time we say goodbye

James rose at seven. He could never sleep after that and the idea of lying in bed staring at a ceiling never appealed, especially when it was apparent that this particular ceiling was all but coming down. He showered in the bathroom using the old shower with very little power, so little in fact that he found it necessary to shake water violently out of the shower-head. He finished up using a facecloth in the sink. He sighed as he looked around the old place, with plaster crumbling and damp stains the size of a fat man's jocks. He traced the black crack-lines in the Shires porcelain sink. The arched sash window would have once been beautiful but now the wood was rotten and the thin single sheet of glass was on the verge of falling out. Within a minute the broken-down images faded and instead when he looked around he saw a lost future and all that the bathroom could have been. He glimpsed the arched sash window restored to its former glory, the sink a treated laminated warm wood and instead of black cracks in his mind's eye he was tracing wood grain. He saw a large matching wooden bath in the centre of the room, big enough for two. A Raindance Rainmaker shower-head was perched above with its mood lights, gentle rain flow with optional jets for an intense massage experience. It would have worked so beautifully in the room. *Christ, I wanted that Raindance Rainmaker.* Very few cottage bathrooms were big enough to carry it off but this one was. *One in a million.* When he had finished shaving and returned to the present he would mourn the Raindance Rainmaker for some minutes more. *two feet in diameter, pressure assisted, it literally creates rain. Ah well.* Mourning a shower was better than mourning his soul mate. At least he had believed Harri to be his soul mate. After the two aborted weddings he was sure that Harri's mind and body had sabotaged them for a reason and, aside from the recent revelation, it was still possible that reason was that she didn't love him enough. Once again a woman he had loved had abandoned him and this time not to travel far away to marry a surfer but instead despite herself and twice in front of all his family and friends. He couldn't go through it all again, that was for sure. He couldn't let her steal away his last shred of dignity and all that was left was the merest shred – in fact it would be fairer to say it was a shred of a shred. Malcolm had been kind in letting him camp with him. Thankfully his friend was resolutely single which meant he wasn't playing gooseberry. Yet still sitting alone in his friend's apartment he had mourned her every minute since he'd picked up his aunt's rotten fish that mostly he pretended to like and because the woman, having observed his love for all things aquatic, amphibian and reptilian, had bequeathed them to him in her will. Therefore being the type he was he couldn't find it in his heart to dispose of them. He hadn't returned to work, having booked holidays to accommodate his honeymoon. Instead he slept and walked aimlessly and visited showrooms test-driving cars he would never in a million years have dreamt of buying.

"She's lovely," he'd point to a Mini Cooper, "I'll try her."

The sales man would look at him oddly, up and down, judging him to be at least six foot three maybe even six foot four. Then he'd look at the tiny car before them. "Are you sure Sir wouldn't like to try something a little larger?"

"No, Sir's happy in the mini," James would say firmly before getting in, pulling the seat back as far as it would go and driving off with his knees in his mouth and a circus clown overenthusiastic wave.

That kept him humoured for a few days but it didn't dull the pain. He didn't dare drink because he knew if he did he'd cry just like his dad did every Christmas when he'd talk about how he was a laggard when he met James's mother, before lamenting over how she'd helped to save him and made something out him. He had a pride in himself that he accredited to her. James felt that way about Harri, not that she had changed him but that she had accepted him wholly for the man he was and that made him feel the same immense and combustible pride his dad cried over each year. But that was gone. He was raw and sore and desperately empty, so empty he thought it possible that he'd never again know what it was to be full.

But then from nowhere the phone started to ring.

First it was Susan. "I had to tell you . . ."

Then Aidan. "You need to know . . ."

After that it was Duncan. ' Please, James. She loves you. She needs you . . ."

Melissa was last. "I know the others have called and I know it's a lot to ask . . ."

And then Duncan again. "James, even if you phoned her . . ." And again Duncan over and over until he was forced to switch off his phone. He was numb at first. How was he supposed to respond? What were these people trying to tell him? That his weddings were aborted for a reason other than a lack of love? Were they trying to link his fiancé's panic at marrying him to a dead girl in the Wicklow woods and a life born from a lie? Did their argument hold water? And poor, poor Harri, how she must be suffering and what a nightmare she had found herself embroiled in! Incidents came back to him in flashes. Her nightmares that had once made no sense still made little sense and yet somehow they resonated more. That awkwardness, that jagged misplacement, the same one that forced her into every corner but nevertheless ensured she stood out, now made sense. Her charming inability to lie despite having come from a house built on obfuscation. In James's mind she had always stood apart from her family. From her brother who, though he had the fortitude to be who he was despite encircling homophobia, was also a man desperate to hide the tiniest part of himself that agreed with his detractors, and to suffocate the mushrooming self-hatred it had created within him. From a mother who allowed herself to be treated as a fragile maiden from another era despite clearly having an unyielding strength, ruling those around her in an almost passive-aggressive manner. From a father who had long ago halved himself into the detective who dealt with hate, intolerance, anger, violence, victims, death and dismemberment on almost a daily basis and the husband who wiped his day on the mat to play the affable king of his wife's castle. To James, Harri had stood out from her family because Harri had always been straightforward Harri. He discussed it with a fascinated Malcolm. Was this because she wasn't really a true-blue Ryan? Were her strands of DNA so powerful that nature beat nurture hands down? Was there a part of her that always knew? Was getting married and the father of the bride's symbolic handing over of his daughter to the groom her trigger? Was he talking bollocks? Was it all just a coincidence? Did it really have anything to do with him?

The final question was the only one that he and the ever-patient Malcolm agreed on over a super-sized pizza. It did have something to do with him because he loved her and so he would search until he found her and he would ensure she was upright on her own two feet before he would leave. Maybe her fear of marriage was connected to a large lie lived and maybe it wasn't, but either way this was no time for her to deal with their relationship. She had to find herself again before she could find him or even them if there was a them, and he hoped and prayed there was. James would wait for her, at least that's what he told himself, being that it would be the only way he could say goodbye to the devastated, vulnerable, tormented, innocent, beautiful Harri.

James never ate fried food in Dublin. His father had been a bacon, egg and chips junkie and endured high cholesterol, two heart attacks and a bypass because of it. But when in Wexford James did like to cook a fried breakfast from scratch. The local butcher had good quality herb sausages, delicious black pudding and lean bacon that emitted a hickory-based aroma that made him dribble. He had foregone his luxury breakfast for the three mornings since his arrival. Harri had been too ill to have endured the smell of fried pig's blood, but yesterday he felt had been a breakthrough, having managed to get her out of bed, out of the house and into the fresh warm air. They had walked over the grassy hill that led to sand dunes and a waiting beach. The tide was far out, so that they walked toward the water rather than by it. Fresh air blasted their faces, turning them pink, and entered their lungs encouraging deep breathing. When the tide turned they quickened their step back toward the grassy hill where they sat and looked far out across the Irish Sea toward Wales.

"I'm sorry," Harri said. "I've been sleeping since you came."

"That's a good thing. You needed it. You resembled the walking dead."

"I felt like it."

"And now?"

"Now it's better, I think I've regained the power of cognitive thought."

"Good," he laughed. "Cognitive thought is pretty important."

"Yeah," she smiled and even laughed a little.

"You will be fine," he said, "better than fine."

"The second I saw you I felt better. I know it didn't look like it but I did."

He detected wistfulness which unnerved him slightly. He didn't want his determination to help the woman he loved to be confused with an attempt at reconciliation. He was also desperate not to disappoint her. He knew only too well what that felt like and she was in enough pain. He needed to clarify his intentions.

"You know, you are probably the kindest and best woman I've known. It's your habit to put others before yourself sometimes to your own detriment. You really listen and so few people really listen. You speak your mind and you care about the people around you even when they disappoint. You have strength. You don't know that about yourself. You see George as the strong one but he's not – he leans on you."

Harri's smile faded and the fresh light in her eye dimmed a little. All these compliments could only mean one thing – goodbye. *Bollocks.* She huddled into herself, waiting for him to finish.

"And ever since I first knew you I knew that a part of you was a little lost."

She raised her head and looked quizzically at him, directly into his eyes.

"And you know what I mean. Don't get me wrong. I liked it that you stood out. I liked your clumsy presence as though you were making a guest appearance in your own life but now I understand. I understand why you never seemed comfortable enough in your skin to fit right in. I understand why you couldn't marry me. You need to find out who you are, Harriet Ryan. You need to do it alone and it will be fine."

Harri didn't speak, instead she smiled and kissed James on his forehead before getting up and leading the way home.

She wouldn't cry all that day or that night, when after eating most of her meal they played dirty-word scrabble into the small hours of the morning.

"'Gap' is not a dirty word!" James argued.

"Not at first glance but it certainly has potential!" Harri retorted.

"Potential?" James wasn't convinced.

"Okay," she sighed and then she grinned, making him grin too. She shook her hair out and winked while valiantly holding back her smile. "Why don't you come on over here and play 'find the gap' . . ."

James turned his head away laughing. He was also blushing. This blush was born from heat as opposed to any embarrassment and if she'd had the guts or gumption to look she would have noticed his trousers had become a little tighter. But she didn't. Instead she bit her lip and nodded knowingly. *Score.*

"You win! 'Gap' is a filthy, filthy word!" he laughed, turning to face her, and for a moment they shared a look and then it was gone.

And although Harri felt like crying she didn't because it wasn't fair on James who had come to save her after everything.

I love you. I love you. I love you. Don't leave.

They wouldn't speak about it again. Instead she would agree that it was time to return to their individual lives. After all it was appropriate, being that the very next day would signal the end of the honeymoon that never was.

* * *

James called up the stairs to Harri, signalling that her fried breakfast was on the table. She arrived moments later and joined him. Her hair was wet from plunging it into the stupid sink when the stupid shower wasn't powerful enough to wash out the shampoo.

"I've only given you a small plate but there's plenty more in the oven."

"Thanks."

"It's probably better to get an early start," he said.

"You should do that. I'm going to leave later."

"Are you sure?"

"Yes."

"Okay," he smiled and proceeded to enjoy masticating sinfully delicious black pudding. Harri drank from her coffee cup while checking her texts.

Dad << When can we see you? Have you heard from George? >>

<< Soon. He's fine, Dad, just give us time. >>

James moaned a little upon introducing crispy bacon into his mouth. He shook his head from side to side. "You have *got* to try the bacon."

She smiled at him as the pure joy he extracted from a simple breakfast had always entertained her.

She was still so angry at her parents but she couldn't hurt them. George was ignoring them so she couldn't ignore them too. They were as lost as she was. She felt she could manage her relationship with her father better by text as she feared that in close proximity to the man she might succumb to the urge to punch him. Either that or she'd fall at his feet and cry until she was nothing more than a puddle. Neither was a preferred option. She needed more time.

The phone beeped.

Dad << Thanks for talking to me. We miss you. >>

Now she wanted to hug him tight and tell him everything would be okay but she wasn't sure that was true and every moment her feelings toward him changed so she didn't write back. She didn't know what to say. George was easier. Initially there had been no contact but for the past four days each morning she woke up she sent a text.

<< I love you.>>

It was simple and to the point and each morning seconds later her phone would beep. George << I love you too.>>

That was it, nothing more and nothing less but it was enough for now.

"Are you going to eat that?" James said pointing to her pudding.

"No," she said, dishing it onto his plate.

"I'll really miss this," he said to her and she noticed his lip quiver ever so slightly. She wanted to beg him to stay with her and to put his lovely little speech aside. She did need him. She couldn't do this alone. She was only functioning because he was beside her. If he left her she would be desperate once more.

"Please don't leave me," she said.

James lowered his fork. "Harri," he said, shaking his head sadly.

"Please don't leave me," she repeated, tears gathering and waiting to fall.

"Don't," he warned.

"I love you. You love me," she begged.

"I can't," he said.

"Why not?" she said loudly and her tone suggested a simmering rage that she could hold back no more.

"You know why not." He tried to stay calm.

"Bullshit!" she heard herself scream. *Oops! Rational has left the building. Fuck it, I'm on a roll* "If you really loved me you'd stay with me!"

"I've done this before," he said before clearing his throat. "You forget I've done this before."

"I don't understand."

"I can't be your nursemaid. I can't be the one you lean on while you find what you're looking for. I've been there, I've done that, and some surfer in Australia benefited."

"I'm not her," she said.

"I know. You mean more to me than she ever did so another disappointment at your hands would kill me." He laughed a little but his eyes were leaking. "Maybe some day when you're whole again we might bump into each other and then who knows?"

"I can't call you after today, can I?" she asked, finally resigned to heartbreak.

"No," he said. "Not for a while."

"Okay," she agreed with tears burning holes into her cheeks. *How long is a while? A week? A week? A month? A year? Should I seek a specific timeframe? No. Damn it. Say something. Stop him.*

"I should go," he said, getting up and leaving the rest of his breakfast.

"Okay," she replied. *Oh God.*

His bag was in the hall. She shadowed him to the door. She could see he wanted to break but he wouldn't, not in front of her. She grabbed him and hugged him tight and her tears wet his shoulder. *Break. Please break. Break and stay. Break and stay.* He squeezed her tight and her head disappeared into his chest, wetting the front of his shirt. *He's not breaking.* They stood in silence until he let go. *He's not staying.*

He opened the door and walked out in his wet suit, leaving his much-longed-for fry, determinedly making his way through the overgrown front garden to his car. He got in and drove.

Harri sat on the step of their holiday home in Wexford shedding tears until there were no more left to shed. Hours later while the night sky descended outside, inside Harri Ryan was doing something that was quite contrary to anything anyone would expect from her. She was wrecking the place, breaking every single thing possible using her ex-fiancé's five-iron. *Fuck strong. Fuck kind. Fuck listening. Fuck lost. Fuck alone. Fuck James. Fuck my father. Fuck my mother. Fuck Father Ryan. Fuck everything and fuck everyone!* She stopped at pulling the sink off the wall. *Fuck me, I've lost it again.*

She vacated the once-tattered, now completely vandalised cottage a little after one, suitcase in hand, and it didn't even occur to her to look back. *No more tears.*

* * *

George was asleep in the passenger seat of the open-top rental and under a bright rich velvet blue sky. Aidan had graciously agreed to drive most of the way through Northwest Italy as his partner was spent from negotiating, finagling and swaggering. George always injected just a hint of swagger into his demeanour in business situations. He felt it was an important function in the sales game. Maybe he was right maybe he was wrong but whether he was or wasn't no one could carry off swagger quite like George Ryan. Aidan had often said it was one of the things that had first attracted him because when George swaggered he carried it off with James Dean cool. Unfortunately for Aidan when he attempted to emulate his lover he only succeeded in appearing as though he was in desperate need of a hip replacement.

"Too light on my feet," he complained. "No weight in my gait."

George had smiled and agreed but he was quick to point out that it made him a better dancer. Aidan agreed he was most definitely a better dancer and so he should be after clocking up many thousand teenage hours in front of '*Footloose*' practising the moves. To this day his 'Footloose and 'Let's Hear It For The Boy' were step perfect. George didn't dance. George didn't do anything he wasn't good at.

They would soon be taking their leave of the Piedmont area, having secured a deal to ship and sell Barolo which according to George was the greatest of all Italian red wines. Aidan didn't know nor did he care much either way, he was just glad to see a smile on his partner's face. The map on George's lap revealed that their destination was not so far which was a good thing because the Barolo meeting had run on and they had less than an hour to make the second and according to George all-important Barbaresco rendezvous so as to secure the high quality yet more affordable wine of choice. Aidan was glad George had this new venture to take his mind from his family troubles. However with each passing day he was becoming more concerned about George's determination to ignore his parents and the problems confronting them all. George could be cold. His parents' pleas went unanswered. "They deserve it," he had declared the evening before at dinner. Aidan disagreed. George clammed up. Aidan changed the subject so as not to endure George's insufferable huffy silence. He was relieved that George was not taking his anger out on Harri. At least he was texting her. *Poor Harri.* Aidan was very fond of his partner's sister and in times of relationship crisis he would often turn to her to help find a road back to the difficult man he loved. They might not be related but Harri knew her brother better than anyone else on this planet. That wouldn't change, of that Aidan was sure, but everything else hung in the balance. He wanted to see Harri to find out where her head was at. He wanted to hear her voice to know she was okay but he wouldn't call until he was home which would be the following day. George couldn't bear to speak to his sister until he had worked out what he would say so it wouldn't be fair for him to overhear a call between Harri and Aidan. At least that's what Aidan told himself. Maybe deep down as much as he missed his pal he was as unsure of what to say as her brother. After all, although George had been deceived he was still a Ryan. Who the hell was Harri?

Aidan drank a glass of wine in the sun looking out from the villa's stone patio onto the tree-lined path that led to the vineyard. Colourful foliage danced in the faint breeze, catching his eye, and time passed quickly. It was so warm Aidan worried for his nose while enjoying the warmth creeping though his sandals from the hot stone beneath his feet. George emerged from the cellar triumphant. He made his way toward Aidan, loosening his tie and swinging his briefcase in a way reminiscent of a schoolboy on the last day of term.

Later, sitting on the train that would take them from Northwest Italy towards the Northeast and on to Verona, the men sat opposite one another, both heads facing the glass, soaking up the view and relaxing a while. They would spend the night in a quaint little hotel before George would talk to a man about sparkling wine and then after a leisurely lunch they would head to the airport and home. At least that was the plan.

It was at dinner later that evening, outdoors under a roaring orange sky, that George admitted his intention to remain in Italy.

"I don't understand," Aidan said in some alarm, "the plan is –"

"The plan was. I've decided to head to Tuscany and pick up some decent Chiantis, then on to Southern Italy."

"Hold on! You said that Southern Italy has nothing to offer but offensive glugging wines."

"No, I said it had little more than offensive glugging wines. It's that 'little' that I'm looking for."

"You're just avoiding."

"Don't start."

"So come home. It's time."

"I'm trying to get a business running here in case you haven't noticed."

"You can pick up a few decent Chiantis over the phone."

"Aidan, I really appreciate you coming on this trip but I'd also appreciate it if you'd allow me to live my own life."

"You are so selfish. Your parents are going through hell and your sister needs you."

"My parents deserve to go through hell and Harri, well, she understands me and she wouldn't change me."

"Not like me," Aidan said nodding. "It always comes back to that, doesn't it?"

"Yes, I suppose it does," George said before sipping from his glass.

"Sometimes I really hate you."

"So go home!" George spat at him and with that disappeared

down the road. He didn't come back to the room that night, choosing instead to book into a single.

Aidan spent a restless night alone before he made his way to the airport and home. *You really are an asshole, George, and I don't know how much more I can take.*

* * *

Harri woke up to her doorbell. She steadied herself knowing instinctively it was her mother or at least the woman who had pretended to be her mother. She opened the door to reveal Gloria, pale, thin and frail.

"Hello, my darling," she said.

"Hello, mo – m." Harri stumbled on the word 'mom'.

Her mother flinched. "Any chance of a coffee?" she asked feigning a smile while consciously trying to keep her hands away from her neck.

Gloria followed her daughter into the kitchen and sat at the counter while Harri put on a pot of coffee.

"How was Wexford?" she asked then.

"Hell."

"Right. I suppose it would be."

Harri couldn't seem to sit still. Instead she was watering the plants on the window, cleaning the counter or fixing her stool.

After a long silence Gloria said, "You must have questions."

"Millions," Harri admitted, "but I'm not sure I'm ready for the answers."

She handed her mother a mug and poured coffee that really wasn't ready to be poured. Gloria didn't complain.

"Will you allow me to explain my part in this?" she said.

Harri nodded. Her mother seemed so vulnerable and scared and she knew the woman's heart was drenched in her own pain.

Gloria took a breath. She closed her eyes for a moment or two and when she opened them she spoke. "I was mad with grief. Not only grief. I plunged headlong into sudden menopause. In the 1970s there wasn't the same understanding that there is now, there weren't the same therapies and God forbid that you'd talk about your feelings or indeed answer that you were anything other than fine." She took another breath and a slug of horrible coffee. "Those first few weeks when I was sectioned they felt that I was a risk to myself and maybe George. Maybe I was, I don't remember much about that. I remember the wards though. They were filled with women. Some were older, some were like me in their thirties and then there was a teenager – her name was Sheena. I remember thinking it was a terribly exotic name." She took another breath before she fixed her skirt and wiped her mouth.

Harri stood by the counter silently.

"Poor Sheena had attempted suicide nine times. She was only eighteen. She was a sweet thing but consumed by a terrible darkness that you have to experience to explain so I won't even try. Sheena and I took walks together around the corridor and around in circles. Sometimes we'd chat and sometimes we'd walk in silence. I'd known her three weeks when her mother brought her some items from the local shop: chocolate, toothpaste, a magazine. An hour after her mother had left Sheena was found dead in the bathroom having suffocated herself using the plastic bag."

"My God!" Harri said having lost herself in the poor young girl's terrible tragedy.

"I left the next day," Gloria continued. "I couldn't stay there, not after that. Duncan took me home to George and Nana but I wasn't right. I lived on prescription pills while Nana was mother to George and Duncan stayed out working late. Then one day that call came and soon after Duncan brought you home and laid you on my knee. I don't remember what he said. I do remember I didn't want to look at you or touch you. I was horrified that he would try to replace my baby girl but then you smiled at me and your hand rose toward mine and you'd grabbed my finger and you had such strength for a little one. I fell in love. There and then I knew that you were sent to me. It took a while to really get back on my feet but that was the first day that I knew I could." Gloria smiled at her daughter sadly. "We should have told you and we were going to when you got older but time passed and it just got harder and harder until we convinced ourselves that it really wasn't important. We were wrong. We know we were wrong and we are so, so sorry, my darling."

"Mom," Harri said and her mother sighed and smiled.

"Yes, my darling."

"I'm glad you think I saved you. I just wish you'd thought to do the same for me."

Gloria's smile faded. "I don't understand."

Harri shook her head sadly. "You knew I felt like I didn't fit all these years. You knew that and yet you let me think that there was something wrong with me."

"No, darling, I swear I didn't."

"Yeah, Mom, you did. I deserved the truth, you should have been honest. Maybe if you had I'd be married today and maybe not but at least I'd know who I was and why I was such a mental case."

"You are Harriet Ryan. You are not a mental case and you are my daughter."

"And yet you seem like a stranger."

"Oh Harri!" her mother called to her crying.

"I'm sorry, Mom, I need to be alone now."

Her mother rose from her chair. "I understand," she said and without another word she left.

After that Harri put on the electric fire because despite the fine night she was cold in her bones. She opened a bottle of red wine, one that George would disgustedly describe as cheap glugging crap, and she turned on the TV and there she sat staring at TV show after TV show many of which were completely alien to her. *Goodbye old life, hello, couch potato existence.*

June 26th 1975 - Thursday

It's been a long week. Betsy got sick with colic and I swear I thought she was going to die. Matthew and me stayed with her (The correct term is 'Matthew and I' but I think 'Matthew and me' sounds better).

But hold on, I should start with Monday. Matthew was wearing a new leather jacket his dad had brought him from Monte Carlo. It's really cool – he looks like The Fonze but way better looking. Anyway along with the jacket came a blonde woman Giselle something (I think she's French or maybe German or Dutch). She looks our age but Matthew says she's twenty-six. His dad has moved her into the house. They look weird together. Matthew's not really interested in talking about it, he says she is one in a long line and soon she'll be gone. She's really beautiful though. I wish I looked like her. So along came Tuesday and after work I called in to see Sheila who wasn't at home and her mam was really awkward about telling me where she was and she even went red in the face and her dad told me to go home which was weird because usually he's as sweet as pie. I was on my way home when I met Dave who said that she was in the hospital being pumped out. I didn't know what that meant so he told me she'd stolen vodka from the bar and she and Dave went to the castle drinking. Obviously Sheila did more drinking than Dave and so she got really sick and he ended up carrying her to the hospital!!!!! He says he's in big trouble at home and Sheila's parents have refused to let him see Sheila again. I felt sorry for him. I mean she robbed the booze, she drank most of it and he got her to the hospital – they should be thanking him. Adults are spazes. Matthew called down to me later (always get embarrassed when he sees my house – I'm such a peasant compared to him) and we went to see her when the coast was clear. It was fun sneaking around and let's face it I know the place well enough to be able to. Once Sheila's mother had left the building Matthew and me went in and Sheila started crying. I felt really sorry for her. There was black stuff all over her face and she said her mother wouldn't let her wash it off and had told the nurses to leave it. She was stuck in bed with a needle in her hand. I told her I'd walk her to the bathroom and I'd help her wash her face. I don't care what her mam says. She didn't want to – she said she felt too sick. She had the shakes like old man Jeffers except Mam says he has Parkinson's and he's expected to die soon. Sad. I like him. Sheila was let out of the hospital on Wednesday but she hasn't been seen since. I've gone up to the telephone box in town a few times to call her but her mam says she's not allowed talk on the phone. It must feel like jail to be grounded in the summer. I wish we had a phone because going up town every time I want to call someone is a nightmare.

Anyway back to Betsy. Last night Matthew came by to tell me that she had colic and she was bad with it. I went back to the stables with him straight away. Poor Betsy was really sick. Henry said she had an increased heart rate, which is bad. She was obviously in a lot of pain, sweating and rolling around. I wanted to cry but I didn't because I didn't want to be a spaz about it. Henry gave her paraffin oil which he said would act as a laxative which basically means that she would shit all over the place. He gave her a sedative too but it didn't seem to help the pain. Matthew and I stayed with her even though it was after eleven and Mam had warned me to be home by then. I didn't care. I wasn't going to leave Betsy. Just after midnight shit came pouring out of her like nothing I'd ever seen. Matthew and I got out of the stable just in time. She shat straight for an hour and then she seemed to improve. I got home after one and I thought Mam would kill me but she didn't notice!!!!! She must have gone to bed early. Thank you, God. Matthew and I didn't kiss while Betsy was sick but we kissed all the way home. I think I could fall in love with him. I think maybe I already have. Tomorrow night we're going to the carnival. God, I love the carnival especially the bumpers. Sometimes when I'm behind the wheel of a bumper car I feel like I'm driving a real car and I'm an adult and I'm heading off into the sunset and free to find my own way in the world. I can't wait to really be able to drive. I can't wait to really live. We're going to try to help Dave sneak Sheila out. Matthew is bringing the ladder! I can't wait.

Chapter ten

Tension Towers

The waiting area was empty save for Susan and her decidedly distant husband Andrew. He chose to sit on the other side of the room camped beside a table piled high with magazines that he pretended to flick through. *Christ, Andrew, I'm not contagious.* It had taken weeks of persuasion and every ounce of guile she could muster to talk him into accompanying her. Although he had remained stubbornly and steadfastly silent in her presence for six months, bar the odd monosyllabic and necessary reply, and it was obvious that he had only nodded his agreement to counselling as an empty gesture or maybe to get her to shut up rather than having any real interest in salvaging the last remnants of their relationship, she was deeply relieved when he had finally acquiesced. Having said that she didn't hold on to much hope. Susan was just tired of talking to a wall and desperate for a conclusion to their misery one way or another. She wished he would sit next to her but didn't dwell on it. Instead she focused on the painting, large and looming on the wall above her defiant husband's head. In it a man and woman sat on the remote ends of a bench both facing forward, both forlorn. At first they seemed completely apart, strangers even, but when studied it became apparent that while the man's hand was tight by his side his index finger was lifted and poised as though it was about to creep toward the woman whose hand lay open and waiting. Susan looked from the painting to her husband's face of thunder. *If I left my hand open he'd slap it.* He hated being in her presence so much he appeared distracted, irritated, itchy even. She wondered why he hadn't left her. *Why don't you just go?* Why had he sworn her to secrecy? He didn't want Beth to know what was going on. That was only one of the things she hoped a visit to therapy could help answer. *She'll hate me not you.* He was adamant. It was all he had said that night six months and four days before.

"Don't you dare involve our daughter in this!"

"But can you forgive me?" she'd begged.

That was the moment when he had stopped speaking and the moment that their relationship had truly ended. What was left was an illusion. They were stuck in some sort of torment-ridden limbo. *Can't you just forgive me?*

The door opened after mere minutes and another couple exited, the man leading the woman, both staring blankly ahead, neither their faces nor posture revealing what might lie waiting inside. The door closed. More minutes passed. The door opened. A man in his early fifties with a full head of wavy salt-and-pepper coloured hair smiled at Susan and Andrew.

They stood.

"Mr and Mrs Shannon?" he clarified pleasantly.

"Yes," Susan replied.

"Good. Come in."

They followed him inside. The room was larger than expected but then again Susan would often comment that the rooms in Georgian houses were often larger than expected. It momentarily occurred to her that the Georgians might not be known for their propensity towards personal hygiene but they did have the luxury of space. She smiled to herself. Andrew gave her a filthy look that suggested he would not tolerate anything that approached optimism. She stopped smiling. There wasn't any sign of a couch. Instead two comfortable chairs were perfectly positioned in front of an antique mahogany desk accompanied by an oxblood leather mahogany captain's desk chair. *At least he has good taste.*

Andrew noted that the chairs were far enough apart so as to negate the necessity for physical contact. *Good.*

The man sat and smiled.

Susan attempted the same but for some reason her lip stuck to her upper front teeth giving her, she was sure, a pretty frightening appearance.

"So firstly let me introduce myself. I'm Vincent Mayers."

"Hello, Vincent," Susan said while mentally trying to inject saliva into a desert-dry mouth.

Andrew said nothing, instead he focused on the framed document indicating the man before him was the beneficiary of a PHD. *It will take more than that.*

"So let's cut to the chase – why are you here, folks?" Vincent asked pleasantly.

Silence.

Vincent nodded. "How about we start with you, Susan. Why are you here?"

Susan's eyes widened in shock as she hadn't expected to be immediately put on the spot. She thought he would start off slowly, maybe get to know them though a little chit chat. He would ask how they met. That was a great story. Or enquire as to whether or not they had kids and they could talk about Beth and how well she was doing in school and what a lovely voice she had or how long they'd been together. A lot happens in twenty-six years – they could have talked for a while about the passage of time. Or even a more basic introductory subject such as the weather especially as it was unseasonably hot for mid-May or the fact that the Kirov Ballet would be performing at The Point the very next night but certainly not anything as pointed as why she was here.

Why am I here? Oh God I feel sick. Her insides were drying, possibly terminally, and the PHD's question had the effect of wiping her once busy mind clean. Another silence.

"Andrew?"

Andrew didn't even pretend to engage, instead he stared blankly ahead.

Vincent nodded to himself and sat back. The silence extended and rested in the room. Andrew stared out the window, acting as though he was calm, but his hands clasped in his lap suggested he was not as comfortable as he pretended. His wife was clearly agitated; her hands moving excessively as though she was seeking out a suitable place to rest them. She was sweating and judging by her involuntary lip-curl her mouth was dry. Vincent offered her water and then he sat back and resumed watching them.

Susan desperately wanted to cry.

After the thirty-third minute had passed Andrew looked her way but a little to the left and beyond her.

"Are you ready to go home now?" he asked.

She nodded sadly that she was and they left without another word. *I don't suppose there's any chance of a refund.* They travelled in separate cars. Susan wasn't ready to return to the house of silence, instead she drove around the city directionless, only guided by the one-way systems those around her found infuriating. The radio played but she didn't hear it. Instead she was remembering the recent past and in her mind she returned to the Shelbourne Hotel and the double bedroom on the second floor.

It was mid-afternoon in deep winter and she was trembling, charged with an erotic excitement she'd forgotten she was capable of. The builder called Keith approached her, handing her a glass of vodka he'd procured from a well-stocked mini bar. She drank it down in one and he had laughed at her and she had laughed along with him, embarrassed that she was shaking visibly.

"I'm sick with nerves and don't tell me I've nothing to be nervous of," she admitted while laughing off her own embarrassment. *I'm worse than a stupid schoolgirl.*

"I promise." He made a Scout's Honour sign with his hand.

"Peanut?" he ventured, holding out a can of dry roasted nuts, making her laugh again.

Hardly champagne and strawberries but my God I'm desperate for you. "Thanks, I'll pass."

He drained his glass so that it was empty, matching hers. He placed it down on the dresser and then took her glass from her hand. Her heart was beating wildly enough to cause her insides to reverberate.

"Did I tell you how stunning you are?" he said.

You lying bastard. I love it. "I remember you mentioning it once or twice."

"Did I tell you how you make me feel?"

Please stop talking. "You don't have to."

"You are the best part of my day."

Okay, seriously, stop talking. "Thanks."

He touched her hand and pulled her close, and every hair stood on end. He leaned in for an electric kiss and she momentarily thanked God that in her handbag in the secret pouch she kept an extra pair of knickers.

And ironically someone beeped their horn, bringing her back to the present and a far from erotic reality.

"Mind where you're going, ya thick!" a faceless man roared as he passed her.

"I'm sorry," she mumbled to herself.

She was on Baggot St, so she parked the car and headed to Searson's Bar which was the venue of the last dangerous liaison with her burly devotee. It wasn't supposed to be. She didn't want it to be and neither did he. They just got lazy or maybe miscalculated or maybe fate intervened or it could have been a simple case of bad luck – either way it was a devastatingly violent and abrupt end. They were kissing across the table in a seductively dimly corner when she first heard Andrew's voice. She leaked a little wee and turned away from the kiss and toward the voice which she silently prayed was a manifestation of guilt and possible indication of a chemical imbalance rather than her real life husband. *Please God, make me be hearing things.*

He was standing in front of her in his business suit holding his briefcase and there was a man standing beside him, a colleague or business associate or someone she didn't know.

"Susan?"

Every inch of her froze. Andrew looked from his wife to his colleague; Tony was the name she remembered him using.

"Tony, this is my wife Susan."

Tony didn't speak, instead his look of shock said it all.

"And I'm not sure who this is," Andrew said while staring pointedly at Keith.

Keith stood. At six foot five and broad he had an overpowering presence but Andrew who was shorter and slighter than his love rival, punched him hard in the face anyway. Keith didn't react. He'd taken the punch with the good grace of a guilty man. Andrew didn't wait for an argument, tears or even apologies. He turned and walked away with his miffed colleague following two steps behind. Keith sat and drained his drink while delicately pushing on his swelling eye.

Susan was in shock. Her mouth was open and she was very still.

"Susan?"

She nodded.

"Susan?"

"Swords," she mumbled after a moment or two.

"Excuse me?"

"Swords, he said he would be in Swords."

He sighed before signalling to the barman that he wanted another drink. The man complied and Susan thought that it was nice of him not to kick them out based on the fact that they were mucky adulterers, stupid enough to be caught and punched on the premises. Of course in Keith's case it was physical, but mentally Susan felt like she'd received a whack from which there might be no recovery.

The barman brought over Keith's drink.

"Thanks," said Keith.

"Sorry," Susan said to the stranger. He smiled at her and walked away. *At least he's got a good story for the regulars.*

Keith drank deeply, almost inhaling the glass. "What now?"

"Now I go home and face my husband," she said.

"And me?"

"You go home, glad it was my husband who caught us and not your wife."

"It's over, isn't it?"

"Oh yeah," she almost laughed, "it's definitely over."

"I'm sorry."

"That makes two of us." She got up.

"I'll walk you to your car," he offered.

"No." She shook her head.

The excitement was gone, everything that she had felt for him minutes before disappeared in an instant to be quickly and nauseatingly replaced with a mixture of dread, self-loathing and terror. *What have I done?* She picked up her handbag and walked away. At the door of the bar she turned to take one last look at the builder named Keith who was not looking back. Instead he was lost staring into the bottom of his empty glass and more than likely contemplating his lucky escape.

That had been six months and four days before. She had gone home to an empty house, her husband having packed a bag of essentials and left without a word or note, only to return one week later and one day before their daughter was due home from a school skiing trip. He told her he had returned for their daughter's sake and despite her begging and pleading he remained cold, uninterested, stoic. He didn't want reasons, explanations or excuses; he didn't want times, dates or details. In fact he didn't want anything but silence, a torturing silence that had run on for days, weeks and now months.

Searson's was quiet and she was grateful that the barman and witness to her scandal didn't appear to be working. Instead a woman served her a badly needed vodka and tonic. She retreated to a booth, deliberately passing the one which was the scene of the beginning of the end of her marriage. She sat and put her bag under her feet. She stroked her glass before tipping its contents down her throat. She was on her second drink before she called Melissa, asking her to meet her. She could hear her friend hesitate but she sounded so desperate and tear-soaked Melissa told her she'd be there in an hour. So as not to make a fool of herself by getting drunk she ordered food. By the time she was finished her meal Melissa was sitting opposite her.

"I'm sorry about the short notice."

"What's wrong?"

"I think my marriage is well and truly over," Susan admitted for the first time.

Melissa nodded. "I take it counselling didn't go as expected."

"It didn't go at all," Susan said sighing. "I couldn't talk. I couldn't admit what I'd done."

"And Andrew?"

"He didn't want to be there anyway. He's never going to forgive me."

"And now you're sure?" Melissa said wearily. She couldn't understand how her friend had allowed her husband to punish her for so long. *Either get over it or get out of it.*

"I know him. We've been married twenty-six years." She shook her head and sighed. "Twenty-six years and now when I look at him all I see is anger and hate. He'll never give me the chance to explain. Sometimes I don't think he'll be happy until it tears me inside out. He doesn't want it to get better. I just want it to end."

Melissa put her hand through her hair. "I don't know what to say." She was glad her friend was hinting toward saving herself but careful not to push too hard. After all, Susan had often talked about having had enough. *I wish I could believe you.*

"Nothing to say." Susan laughed bitterly. "I wanted excitement and drama in my life and, well, I certainly got that." She downed another vodka before shaking the glass at the bar woman who nodded. "My husband is determined that I suffer. I do suffer but apparently it isn't enough." After that final drink she agreed to allow Melissa to drive her home. When they reached the house Melissa went inside with her. *Poor Susan, she's aged six years in six months. She's suffered more than enough. Andrew, you wanker!*

Beth was at the cinema with a friend. Andrew was sitting at the kitchen table reading the paper.

Melissa was first to enter the room. Andrew stood.

"Melissa."

"Andrew."

"I didn't expect to see you."

"Sue needed me to bring her home. She's in the loo."

"Oh," he nodded.

They were both silent, each embarrassed by Melissa's presence during such a delicate time.

"Coffee?" he said after a moment or two.

"No, thanks."

"Tea?"

"No, thanks."

"Water?" He smiled at her.

"Nothing," she said, annoyed that he could find a smile for her while being so cold to the woman who had given him twenty-six years of her life. *We all make mistakes, Andrew. I'm sure you're no angel either.*

"Sit," he ordered.

She did out of habit rather than any desire to please. "Andrew," she said after a minute.

"Yes." Again he smiled.

Stop smiling or I'll murder you. "I don't believe in meddling in other people's marriages. God knows I've enough dealing with my own but what you're doing to Susan is deliberate and cruel."

"What do you suggest?" he asked calmly.

"I suggest you either attempt to work it out or leave."

He laughed a little. "It's all so easy!" He was being dismissive but she let it go.

"Just talk to her."

"And what would you like me to say?" He was laughing again which was really starting to annoy her.

"Okay, fine. Be a baby but how about doing it somewhere else?"

"This is my house," he reasoned calmly and with a grin that suggested that he thought of her argument as nothing more than the mutterings of a mindless woman.

Don't you dare grin. "So let her go. Do something, Andrew, because your silence is destroying her!" Her voice was elevated, hinting at her infuriation.

"Thanks for your input, Melissa, I'll definitely consider it," he replied again calmly with a stupid grin firmly fixed to his face.

He might as well have found and flicked the switch marked 'lunatic' on the back of Melissa's neck because she flipped. "You know, Andrew, it's no frigging wonder Sue had an affair because you are one of the most selfish, self-centred and annoying fuckers I know. You're a cold-hearted, money-orientated, bullshit artist who has never had any time for his wife. So you keep on punishing her until you decide to call time but when you do I honestly hope she hates you enough by then to really stick it to you. And if you think all of this is her fault you're more stupid than I ever gave you credit for!"

Andrew had stopped grinning.

Melissa's heart was racing. *Oh shit, I just may have said too much.*

The downstairs loo flushed and Susan made her way into the kitchen.

"Tea?" she asked Melissa, ignoring her husband and the dense atmosphere in the room. "No, thanks, Sue. I'm leaving."

"Oh. Okay." Susan nodded sadly, upset she would spend another night alone.

"Thanks for calling," Andrew said in a light sing-song manner, attempting to recover from Melissa's tirade.

You smug bastard. "Go fuck yourself, Andrew!" she retorted much to Susan's shock and happily to her amusement.

Susan laughed all the way to the hall door.

"Sorry," Melissa said sheepishly.

"I don't know what happened in there but I'm glad you said what you did. I'll live on that for weeks."

"It's like he knows exactly what button to push."

"It's his gift," Susan smiled.

"I really hope you've had enough."

"Me too."

Melissa and Susan hugged before she closed the door.

Susan didn't attempt to engage her husband and she was still laughing at Melissa as she filled her bath. *Okay, Andrew, have it your way. I give up.*

June 29th 1975 - Sunday

HE's back in the house. He was there on Friday morning when I woke. I heard him downstairs making breakfast. They were laughing together. I felt sick. I didn't want to leave my room. Mam kept calling to me but all I wanted to do was cry. I didn't go to work. I locked my door and hid under my blankets. He's back. I can't believe she's let him back. I hate her for it. I wish Dad was here. I wish she had died and left me my dad. HE hasn't come near me. He knows. Mam told him to give me time. I heard her talk to him about me like I'm the troublemaker. She said something I couldn't hear and he laughed. I hate them.

I didn't want to go to the carnival but Matthew had brought his ladder for Sheila so he used it to climb to my bedroom. I let him in but only because I can't say no to him. I really just wanted to be left alone, besides I hadn't even had a wash so I'm sure I smelled. He knew there was something wrong. I don't like lying to him so I just said 'HE'S back'. That was enough. I didn't have to say any more. He hugged me for the longest time. I wish we could run away. I told him that too. He said maybe one day we would. I hope so. I hope it's soon.

He talked me into going to the carnival. I'm glad he did. It was brilliant. We met Dave at the top of the town and when Sheila climbed down the ladder we all caught a glimpse of her knickers. Dave and Matthew laughed at her because there was a bunny on them. I said nothing 'cause there was a frog on mine. She was like a bird released from a cage. She was dancing her way down the town. Dave kept running after her trying to hold her hand but after being confined to her room for nearly a week she needed to be free. It was after nine when we eventually got to Harrington's field. It's usually so bare and muddy, empty and depressing, but when we turned the corner there it was full of people and lights, red, green, yellow and blues all flashing in time to loud pounding music. Everywhere you looked were bumper cars, boat swings, carousels, aeroplanes, shooting galleries, ring-throwing tents, chip vans, ice-cream vans - there was even a Wurlitzer! The smell of candyfloss was all over the place making Sheila feel a little sick. I think she's still suffering from all the drink. Dave won a Scooby Doo cuddly toy for Sheila. Matthew won me a fish but it died in the passenger seat of a bumper car ten minutes later. RIP. Still Matthew was a brilliant bumper car driver - we hardly got bumped at all even though Dave nearly killed himself and Sheila trying to get at us. Matthew drove with one hand and had his other arm around me the whole time. The queue for the chip van was massive so we had ice-cream, then we went on the Wurlitzer. I nearly died it was so fast. I thought we were going to spin right out of the field. Sheila puked. She missed Matthew and me but she managed to get most of it on Dave's crotch. He seemed really pissed off and he cleaned it off with the Scobby Doo cuddly toy so Sheila wasn't too pleased either. Dave took her home before eleven because she was scared if she left it any later she'd be caught. I didn't want to go home so Matthew and I went and sat by the castle overlooking dark water. There was a car parked far behind us with its headlights on, lighting the water up in just one spot. We sat there for ages talking about where we wanted to go and what we wanted to be. I asked him, if we were still together in a year's time, could I go to America with him? He seemed really pleased and started making plans. He's even going to ring the American embassy!!! Then he told me stories about the places he'd been there, describing New York as bustling, crowded, heaving and electric, remembering in Boston the Harvard grounds, red-brick terraces and orange sunsets and smiling about San Francisco, hills, cable cars, the famous Wharf and in the distance the almighty Alcatraz. It sounds so amazing. Matthew's been to America lots of times and he says it's way better than here. He said I could be anything I wanted over there which is great as I'm not really sure what I want but he says I'll know it when I see it. It was after twelve and I still didn't want to go home. Matthew was worried that my mam would kill me but I didn't care so I went home with him. His dad is away with 'his bit' - that's what Matthew calls her - 'his bit'! We walked through Devil's Glen and it was pitch dark under the trees and only lit by a perfect half moon in the rare moments of open ground. It's weird but I didn't notice the moon over the water earlier by the castle! Anyway it was not a bit scary even though we could hear little animals rustle in the undergrowth. I don't even want to think about what they were. Actually aside from tripping on a root and nearly breaking my knee it was romantic.

Matthew's house is unbelievable. You could fit my entire house in his living room. His room is painted a dark blue with a white ceiling and white wooden door and window frames. He's got four massive stacks of albums piled so high the top one is hard to reach and a really cool record player on his floor. The lamp by his bed shines a red light!!! Like the carnival. His bed is huge, it's even bigger than my mam's and mine is definitely less than half the size. It was good though - we both had loads of room to spread out. We talked for ages under the red light and he played a band I didn't recognise on his record player. The record was scratched so he kept getting up to sort it out but other than that they were really good. We kissed for a while and we hugged and then we went to sleep. It was really nice. I feel safe with him. I hope we make it to America. God bless America!!!!

Okay now I'm running on to Wednesday of next week on my diary. I have to get a bigger one but this is important. I forgot to say Friday night Sheila and Dave had sex behind the bush where we'd hidden the ladder!!! She said that it wasn't planned which was pretty obvious seeing as it was in a bush. She said she doesn't know what came over them. One minute they were fighting over her puking on Dave and Dave cleaning up the puke with her Scooby Doo. Then they were kissing which was the usual and then she doesn't know, she felt something, something new. I asked her to explain but she went red and said she couldn't and that some day I'd understand which was pretty condescending for someone where wears bunny knickers. Anyway she said that after that she couldn't help herself and this is coming from a girl who swore she'd never do it until she left home because if she got pregnant her mother warned her she'd be out on her ear. And she means it. Sheila's mam is very religious and she has always maintained that she will not live under the same roof as a sinner which is funny because she's quite happy to serve them booze. Now Sheila is terrified she's pregnant even though she did a lot of jumping afterwards and thinks she got most of his stuff out. Not a pleasant thought and something I could have done without hearing. I don't know if I'll be able to look at Dave in the same way. I'll see. Anyway she also managed to cut her knee on a sharp rock and she tore her bunny knickers. She still made it home by eleven because it only took five minutes. She doesn't think she'll do it again unless she is pregnant – then she can do it all day long every day at the side of the road where she'll be living! Even if she does do it again I doubt it will be outdoors. She's been stuck in bed for the past two days with a really bad cold.

Chapter eleven

I am I And You Are You

Harri's headache began with a taxi ride to Dublin Airport. This hastily arranged jaunt was followed by a mad dash through customs and through fourteen miles of airport lounges.

In Harri's case any exercise, most especially running, never failed to cause a serious case of profuse sweating combined with a disturbing inability to control rapid breathing. Her gasping and anxious entrance onto the plane was met with several dirty looks from agitated passengers who by all accounts had the decency to embark on time. The familiar pain in her frontal lobe arising from the lack of fluid and oxygen was exacerbated by a nasty bump on the head due to an ill-timed overhead locker mysteriously shooting open just as she passed it. Making her way to her seat she knew that she was about to endure the headache from hell. *Arse.* A man with a beer belly the size of a large hillock stood between her and her seat. His loud and growling tut-tuts suggested he was displeased at the notion of momentarily stirring to stand, never mind moving to the side to allow the visibly shaken and terribly apologetic Harri gain access to her cramped mid-aisle seat. Sometimes Harri's headaches induced vomiting and while squeezing by him she decided that if she was to vomit she would vomit on him. Once seated, with her head buried in the dark sanctuary of her lap, she congratulated herself. *Bloody hell, I made it. I can't believe I made it.* It had only been three hours since she'd received George's SOS call and the Ryanair flight to Bergamo was the only one that could get her to Sirmione that day.

The flight was uncomfortable, mostly because of the mind-numbing headache but also due to the fact that she had only enough time to throw a few items into a case, grab her passport and leave in the clothes she was wearing. Unfortunately, as she had earlier attended a new business meeting with Susan, she was wearing stilettos and having run enough in mileage to qualify for the Olympic Games, they were now embedded so far into her feet that it was possible that they would have to be surgically removed. The sandwich and coffee which had left little change out of twenty euro repeated, so much so that she was forced to discommode beer-belly man further by necessitating his standing so that she could spend some time in the bathroom swirling with a travel-pack-sized mouthwash. She fixed herself as best she could before making her way back to her seat and her new portly nemesis. His face turned a little red when he saw her and when getting up he huffed and puffed in a manner reminiscent of the wolf in a well-known fairytale. *Up yours, fatso!* she thought as she passed him and it really wasn't like her to be surreptitiously obnoxious but it had been a difficult few weeks and the man in seat 13D was clearly an arsehole.

Three hours later, armed with a map of the airport and shuttle bay, she navigated her way to the nearest exit, face toward the floor and blinkered-like, avoiding all staff present that might be on the lookout for someone to help, *go away, go away*, until she reached her desired locale. The bus read Sirmione in bold on the front. She handed the bus driver the exact cost of the bus as directed by the web. *Thank you, God, for the euro.* She was on the shuttle and heading towards Lake Garda and the tiny island of Sirmione without having to engage with one Italian. She sighed. *Okay. I'm fine. Everything's fine.* A woman beside her smiled and made a slight mouth movement that indicated she was about to engage Harri in conversation. *Oh sweet God, a chatty foreigner. Go away. I don't understand.* The woman was either suffering from a mild twitch or had decided against speaking with the lunatic now staring at the floor and with her head moving towards her lap. The bus was small and air-conditioned and although it cost more than the flight she was happy to pay any price so as to avoid a planes, trains and automobiles scenario. Harri was not a happy traveller. In fact the few times she'd bothered to leave her own country, to travel into the abyss she considered abroad to be, had mostly been to either join or rescue the man she had until recently believed to be her twin brother.

George had insisted that they share their twenty-first birthday together although he refused to leave Cape Cod, so ever obliging Harri and their parents had travelled to him. Before that, aged eighteen, she had caught a flight to Biarritz where he was participating in a surfing contest even though he had been banned attending by his parents due to upcoming exams. He'd broken his ankle and needed his sister's savings to pay the hospital bill and her shoulder to lean on when hopping on and off the planes. Their parents had been away for a second and long-overdue honeymoon, spending six weeks in Australia, and by the time they returned to Ireland the cast was off albeit prematurely and they never did hear or know of their son's disobedience or injury. She'd once gone to Venice upon his request. He had broken up with his first love, a man called Jeffrey Moon. He was desperate over the whole thing. Mr Moon really couldn't have given a fig for George but before he realised that sad fact George had lost himself to him. Jeffrey was ten years older than George at the time and saw him as a fling. He broke up with George slowly and painfully by slowing things down and only sleeping with him when he was horny or bored. George tore himself inside out trying to please and appease the man, believing that if he behaved in a certain way, wore a certain fragrance or dressed in a particular manner he'd win him back. Eventually when Jeffrey found someone else around his own age and more to his taste he severed ties completely and in doing so broke a little something in George's heart that was yet to heal. Harri accompanied her brother to Venice and held him like a baby for four days while he cried and cried and cried. He cried in the Ca Rezzonico Museum. He cried in St Mark's Square and on the Bridge Of Sighs. Harri just held his hand. He was crying outside The Basilica Of Santa Maria when an elderly and distinguished Italian gentleman had approached them and was seemingly captivated by the young man unafraid to reveal a broken heart to strangers. He stopped and rested his brown eyes on George and took his free hand in his.

"Perché piangi in una giornata cosí bella?" the old man asked.

"Il mio cuore è spezzato," George answered.

"Guarda verso il cielo," the old man ordered. George looked up and toward the sky.

Harri followed suit. *What the hell is he looking at?*

"Ora chiudi gli occhi e senti il suo calore," the Italian said and curiously George closed his eyes and appeared to bask in the daylight while his hand remained in the Italian's and the Italian spoke huskily.

Harri was left looking around wondering what was going on. *This is just bloody rudeness.*

"Oggi puoi pure piangere, ma domani starai meglio," the old Italian smiled.

"Sei sicuro?" George asked.

"Cosí sicuro come che io sia il cielo ed il sole." The man patted Harri's brother's shoulder and he was gone.

After that George did stop crying, even managing to negotiate The Golden Staircase and wander the halls of The Doge's Apartment without a hint of a tear. His resolve failed him once more that evening over a particularly tasty pizza that reminded him of the time he had broken out in allergy-related hives and Jeffrey Moon had tended to his lotion and potion needs over the period of one long weekend.

Harri decided against asking what the elderly gent had said to her brother and years later she would often reflect and wonder if his words were as spiritual as his tone suggested or if she'd be disappointed by the possibility of a mundane answer, especially as it was clear from his gait and demeanour that it was likely that the old gent had imbibed one glass of vino too many at lunch – well, either that or he had some sort of degenerative disease. There were a few trips after that but thankfully they were to English-speaking countries and so not as stressful for the girl who was pathologically afraid of anything or anyone she didn't understand.

And now once more Harri was travelling to George. He had called, slightly panicked having woken up with what he believed to be a broken nose. Clearly he was still drunk as he started the conversation off in harassed Italian. She had to remind him that she didn't speak Italian and asked if he could manage English. This gave him cause for thought before he conceded that English was possible. He was slurring and it became slowly apparent that he had gone on a three-day drinking binge culminating in a punch in the face.

It was after ten when she made it to his hotel. He was sleeping soundly when she knocked.

"Chi c'è?" came his groggy response.

"George?"

"Chi c'è?" he reiterated.

"George, it's me, Harri." *I really hate this.*

"Harri? Sei tu?" George clearly was still not properly awake.

"It's Harri. Your –" The word sister caught in her throat. "Let me in for the love of God."

The prayer seemed to work. George opened the door, sweeping back a fringe that needed cutting, revealing two black eyes and a swollen nose.

"What are you doing here?" he asked in a tone that suggested he didn't remember their earlier conversation but he was glad to see her. He was smiling.

"Good God, George. Look at the state of you!" She followed him inside.

He took a look in the mirror. "Oh that's why my face is hurting," he said nodding. "I called you, didn't I?" he asked sheepishly.

She nodded.

"Old habits die hard," he said, sitting at the side of his bed. He looked at his watch. "Still, you must have made serious time."

"You've no idea," she smiled at him. The familiarity of their situation was comforting. She sat on the single bed opposite his. "You'll need to see a doctor."

"No, it's fine," he protested.

"No, it's not," she argued.

"I'm sorry I called. I was drunk."

"Don't be and I know."

"I've really missed you, sister."

"I've really missed you too."

"You're still the one I call," he said, smiling to himself. "When I'm down and out you're still the one I call." The realisation felt like an enormous weight lifting.

She grinned. "Lucky me." But she too realised something and for the first time. *I haven't lost him. He hasn't lost me. He's a pain in the arse but he's still my pain in the arse.*

"What are you thinking?" he asked suspiciously.

"That you're a pain in the arse and I'm really glad that you called me."

"Aside from the bender, street fighting, broken nose and black eyes I'm glad too," he laughed but that hurt so he stopped.

"I'm calling the hotel doctor," she said lifting the phone.

Then a woman on reception answered speaking Italian and she froze, a terrible case of xenophobia kicking in. *I have no idea what she's saying. What the hell is she saying?* George grabbed the phone and one medical examination, word of the all-clear, two showers and a number of painkillers later, George and Harri were sitting in a nice restaurant close enough to the imposing Rocca Scalgera and far enough away from the scene of the unfortunate fracas which occurred the night before. The castle was lit up in all its gothic glory.

Harri stared at her menu.

"Do you want me to choose for you?" he said.

"Great." She closed the menu.

The waiter approached. Harri dropped her gaze to the floor. George ordered a number of items she was completely unfamiliar with. He smiled warmly at the waiter and the waiter returned the smile despite George's fearsome appearance. George turned his swollen self on Harri. His eyes rested on her but he said nothing.

"What?"

"You really need to get over your fear of foreigners," he said with authority.

"Why?" she asked like a child chastised.

"Because it's weird, not to mention rude," he said, wagging his finger.

"I'll tell you what weird is. Weird is when you wrap a T-shirt around your feet and hop across a room rather than stand barefoot on a tiled floor." She laughed at his audacity.

"Tiles are cold and hard," he protested. "I have very sensitive feet."

"And as for rude. If rude was an Olympic event you'd take the gold," she laughed.

"Bullshit!"

"What about the time that Tina made a pass at you and you informed her that even if you weren't gay you wouldn't stick someone else's dick in her?"

George sat back in his chair to contemplate. "Tina Tingle, your old flatmate?"

"How many Tinas have you said that to?" Harri grinned.

Laughing, George put up his hands to concede. "That was years ago and I sincerely hope my behaviour has altered for the better in the intervening years."

"Well, my guess is that last night you weren't punched hard in the face for nothing."

"There is that," he said grinning. "I just wish I knew what I'd said so I could avoid any future battering."

The food came and, both ravenous, the Ryans tucked in.

They were finished and strolling arm and arm by the lakeshore. George liked to have his arms around a woman in public. It made him feel masculine and virile and especially so with his diminutive sister who when abroad clung to him like a child afraid of getting lost. They sat on a bench watching the sun go down, both quiet and tired from the incidents of the past few weeks.

"How's Susan?"

"Aidan's fine."

"I didn't ask about Aidan."

She looked away from the pretty view and towards her brother.

"Okay," he agreed, returning his gaze toward the disappearing sun. "How's Aidan?"

"He's annoyed and frustrated and fine."

"He won't take my calls."

"He's punishing you."

"Any idea on for how long?"

"Until you come home."

"Oh."

"You'll come home with me?" Harri asked the question rather than making a statement. She knew George too well to think he would do anything in any time bar his own.

He sulked. "It's only been a few days."

"It's been more than a few days. You have a new business to run, a boyfriend who is waiting for you and a life back home."

"You didn't mention Mom and Dad."

She shrugged.

"Have you seen them?" he asked.

"Mom," she said quietly.

"How is she?" He asked.

"Contrite." She sniffed a little.

"And Dad?"

"We've texted but I can't face him yet."

"Why?"

"You've a neck to ask," she laughed.

"Oh, I know why I can't face him but tell me why can't you?" The answer might seem obvious but George needed to know exactly what Harri was thinking. He needed to feel he knew her as well now on the Sirmione shoreline as he did nearly a month previously lying on her bed on the morning he thought they shared a birthday.

"Because he'll take me into his office and he'll sit me down and he'll take out a file and he'll open it and he'll tell me and show things that I'm not ready for. Don't forget I was once one of his cases."

George was silent for a few minutes, absorbing his sister's words. In his outrage and contempt for his parents' lie and in wallowing in how he had been affected by it, he had forgotten something important. He had forgotten that Harri once lost could soon be found and all the frightening connotations that entailed. *She has another family somewhere. That really should have occurred to me before now. God, I'm such a selfish sod.*

"What are you thinking?" she asked after a minute or two.

"That I'm a dick."

"Oh," she said, nodding agreement and laughing.

"Harri?" he said after another moment or two.

"Yeah."

"Are you scared?"

"Not any more," she smiled at her brother. "Maybe a little nervous but definitely not scared."

"Are you curious?"

"Yeah," she admitted. "I am."

"Are you still my twin sister?"

She nodded. "I am," she admitted.

"But?"

"But," she sighed, "I'm also someone else."

He smiled at her. "I can forgive them but only if you can."

"The parents?"

"Yeah."

"So we'll forgive them."

He stood up and took her hand and together they walked away from the shore and toward their hotel room where twenty minutes later George would make an ill-conceived joke inferring that as they were not now technically related she should probably turn her back so as not to get too aroused in the presence of his muscle-bound body. He didn't duck in time. The pillow hit his face and because of the previous night's injury felt like a brick. *I really need to learn to shut up.*

July 5th 1975 - Saturday

I can't believe it. Dr B has moved into Matthew's gate lodge! Henry asked us to help him unload boxes from his car. I carried the light stuff and he was really strict about us bending our knees before picking anything up. When Matthew went out to get stuff for sandwiches Dr B mentioned he'd seen us at the carnival. I asked him why he hadn't said hello but he mentioned that we seemed to be in a mammoth bumper-car battle at the time of the sighting. He made me laugh. He was right, it was a mammoth battle, Matthew against Dave who took it a little too seriously for my liking. Anyway he said that out of my school uniform and with make-up I looked a lot older than my years. Sheila's Dave said I'd definitely pass for twenty-three! I suppose looking in the mirror at my old face all the time makes me think that others like Dr B are really young when they're not. He's probably twenty-six but he only looks about twenty. It's weird. I hope I don't always look older. That would be terrible - I'll look like my granny at twenty-five. Dr B said with make-up on he almost didn't recognise me. I told him I'd been able to buy beer since I was thirteen. He frowned at that, crinkling his face, but if he can tell me he likes men I can tell him I buy beer. I didn't tell him that I don't like the taste. He conceded that I had made a good argument after going very red and shuffling a bit. He's very sorry he let his secret slip and I don't think he's really sure how or why it happened. I think he was just like a bubble on the verge of bursting and I just happened to be there at the point of disintegration.

Anyway I had Tuesday off so I thumbed to Bray and headed to the bookshop and spent half the day looking for the perfect moving-in present. In the end I came across it by accident. I was looking through some second-hand books in the corner and came across *A Passage To India* which had been a present I'd received from my granny the year before last. I nearly had a fit. I thought it was a travel book and I really don't think I'd like to go there. I mean I wouldn't even know what they were saying and that's just weird.

Anyway I was wrong, it was a brilliant story about a poor Indian doctor who lives under British rule which means they probably do speak English or at least they did. I don't know. God, I'm sooooo ignorant. Anyway he's falsely accused of touching up some stupidly named English woman during a day out at the caves and all hell breaks loose. It's really good. I was glued. Anyway I was looking through the writer's other stuff - Howards' End (looked kind of boring) and A Room With A View which looked like it could be a bit sexy. Then I came across a book called Maurice and it's only a story about homosexuality which is a man loving a man! Unbelievable! So I bought A Room With A View and Maurice and the man behind the counter gave me a dirty look when he saw what I was buying but he didn't ask my age because I wasn't in my uniform and I was wearing make-up. So last night I started reading Maurice (Dr B will never know it's a second-hand book anyway). Holy Mother of God, I think that there will be parts that I'll have to read with one hand over my eyes!!!!! Anyway I'm only at the start of it but already I really feel sorry for Maurice and Clive. I'll give Dr B the book when I'm finished. I hope he likes it. I hope it has a happy ending. If it doesn't have a happy ending maybe I won't give it to him. I don't know. I'll have to think about that.

HE's keeping his head down. He hasn't said a word to me and I haven't said a word to him. Mam is pretending not to notice. Father Ryan has visited twice and the other day the three of them knelt in the sitting room and said the rosary before they had tea and biscuits in the kitchen. It makes me sick to my stomach. Father Ryan asked if I would pray with them but I said no way and Mam said later that I gave him that look, the one that would frighten the Devil himself. Tough! If Father Ryan thinks a rosary or two, a few cups of tea and some biscuits will make any difference he's a fool. If he thinks by talking my mam into letting HIM back into our house that he's done a good thing he's wrong.

I haven't seen Matthew in three days. His dad came home without his bit and took Matthew to somewhere in Spain with him. He didn't say why he wanted Matthew to go with him but then he doesn't really talk to him, instead he just kind of orders him around. Anyway they won't be back until mid next week. I really miss him. I wish he was home. I haven't seen Sheila either, she's still locked in her room. Dave has been up and down Matthew's dad's ladder like nobody's business. Her parents are too busy in the bar to check on her so she and Dave have her room all to themselves. Little do her parents know she's been having the time of her life just above them!!! Having said that, once she found out she wasn't pregnant she told Dave that they couldn't have full sex for a good while as she didn't want to risk it so they are doing other things that she says are private. Suddenly Sheila is private. I've heard it all now.

Henry said I'm getting to be a much better rider. I'm not a natural though not like Matthew. Betsy is good to me. She'd want to be after she almost shat all over me. That will be hard to forget. Anyway although the days are a little longer without Matthew, I still love working with the horses. Maybe I'll go into horse training. Maybe I should be nicer to Matthew's dad. I'll think about that. The door is locked. I'm tired. Going to sleep now.

Chapter twelve

Limbo's just a stopgap

In the weeks preceding Harri's trip to her father's attic and aside from her Wexford and Italian jaunts she had allowed disillusionment to consume and taint her. As Aidan had put it one afternoon, if she was a taste she'd be described as tart with a hint of bitter. He had appeared in her doorway the day after his own return from Italy. She'd opened the door to his annoying rapping. He bustled past her, tanned, wearing white and smelling of a combination of Paco Rabanne and Lynx which he insisted on spraying down his pants in what her brother had once described as an OCD-type manner.

"Is that the TV I hear?" he asked, trailing into the sitting room just to be sure. "Wow, I didn't think that thing actually worked!"

Since returning from her holiday home in Wexford and as the final nail had been well and truly battered into the coffin that was once her relationship with James, mam had done little bar working and watching TV. Television was the greatest thought-antidote imaginable. She could remain awake and free from contemplation, consideration, or deliberation for hours upon hours on end. Instead she was free to live someone else's joy or misery, fear or fortitude. She could stare blankly at the screen and become embroiled in another's nightmare without having to consider or ponder upon her own. She found that she liked crime shows best. *CSI* was particularly fascinating and conveniently seemed to be on every time she turned the TV on. In fact it had such an impact that when her dad did tell her about her origins in the attic two weeks later, one of the few thoughts that passed through her paralysed mind was *There's no way they'd get away with that in Nevada*, not to mention *Jesus Christ, Jesus Christ, Jesus Christ, this would make for a bloody good CSI!*

Aidan made himself tea while cursing her brother. "He's a pig." "I'm sick to death of him." "Selfish selfish selfish!" "Where are the teabags?" "I've reached my limit with him, I really have." "Are you going to say anything?"

"He wants a few days on his own, that's all," she reasoned while squeezing her own teabag as Aidan had a phobia about squeezing other people's tea bags. "It just feels so wrong," he'd once explained. Tea bag squeezed and removed she handed over the cup so that he could pour in the milk before handing it back to her and taking a seat at the counter.

"Excuse me, Harri, but this is your nightmare not his. I mean okay your parents lied to you both and his real twin is dead but boo-hoo-hoo get over it already. You're the one who is the outsider in your own family. You're the one who doesn't know who she is or where she belongs. You, my friend, are the square peg in the round hole."

"Thanks for reminding me and putting it so beautifully," she laughed.

Aidan always could make her laugh, most especially when he was at his inconsiderate best.

"I'm only saying it like it is," he said before drinking from his tea. "Christ, the milk's off!" He made a gagging sound and poured both cups down the sink before opening the fridge and taking out two cans of beer. "How's work?"

"Busy. We've a few projects going. Susan's in Howth working on a penthouse and I'm in Dalkey working on a really nice little café for a couple from Cork. I hope it does well for them."

"Any work going?" he asked after cleaning the taste of rotten milk from his mouth by gargling beer.

"Susan will need you in Howth next week. I think the client wants the place painted top to bottom. They're still at the decision-making stage but give her a call."

"Will do," he said. "And you? Still avoiding your parents?"

"As much as possible. I've seen Mum but I'm keeping clear of Dad for a while."

"Why?"

"I'm not ready."

"Are you angry?"

"Yes."

"You want to punish him?"

"No. Yes. Maybe. I don't know. Mostly I just want to be left alone."

"And why wouldn't you? People are bastards."

They both sat back and contemplated that fact for a minute.

"Still, what a shock. It's all so fucking shocking," he said after a minute.

Harri took a large gulp of beer and nodded her agreement. "If I grew a mini-mickey I'd be less shocked," she said contemplatively, making her pal laugh.

"Interesting," he mused and was relieved that the pre-wedding Harri was making a brief return. Shock and grief had stolen her all but away and one month on he was really beginning to miss his friend. Harri was in freefall and it's hard to do anything bar hold your hands out, yell and hope for the best while freefalling. Hitting the ground would hurt but he counted on her to do so running. *Come back, Miss Harri, we miss you down here.*

"Aidan?"

"What?"

"I think I do want him to suffer."

"Your dad?"

"Yeah and Mum too."

"That's okay."

"I feel sick about it."

"Don't be. You can wallow a while longer but soon, my friend, you will have to change that gloomy tune and return to us the effervescent little do-gooder that you are."

One beer later he was leaving to meet a friend for a pint. "What's the point in getting a tan if you can't go out and sicken a white freckled paddy or two?" he said before kissing her cheek and heading toward the door. "You'll be all right. Everyone thinks George is the strong one but they're wrong."

He had a point because the very next day she was on a plane heading to Italy to bring her battered brother home.

Susan cornered her in the office whenever she could. "Do you want to talk about it?"

"No."

"Are you sure?"

"Yes."

"Sometimes it's best to just let it all out."

"Sometimes it's best not to."

"You're having a really, really terrible time. First ending it with James and now this unbelievable revelation."

"I'm fine."

"Of course you're not fine. Just let me know if there is anything I can do."

"You can shut up."

"Say no more," Susan said while zipping her lip.

Melissa would phone five times a day. "What are you doing?"

"Working."

"I hear noise."

"I'm in an antique shop."

"Anything nice?"

"I'm fine."

"I didn't ask, smartarse!"

"I'm fine."

"Any news?"

"No."

"Are you going to your parents for dinner any time soon?"

"No."

"You have to go sometime."

"So you've said."

"Well, I'm right."

"Is that it? Can I go now?"

"Fine. Go."

Two or three hours would pass.

Melissa again. "Jacob is being kicked out of his nursery for biting some kid with big ears."

"Oh my God, what are you going to do?"

"Sit him on the bold step, threaten his life and then find another nursery."

"Why did he bite the kid?"

"Apparently it was a mission of mercy. He thought if he bit the top bit off each ear the kid would have normal-sized ears."

Harri laughed.

"It's not funny."

"I know, I'm sorry." *It bloody is funny.*

"I was in a meeting with a new client and now I'm on my way to collect him because fucking Gerry is too busy. And didn't you know his job is far more important than mine?"

"I wish I could help but I'm in a traffic jam on the M50."

"It's fine. Don't worry. So have you spoken to your parents?"

"No."

"Are you going to?"

"Not today."

"Right. I'll call you later."

Another few hours would pass.

"Jacob and Gerry had a screaming match. I swear the man is as bad as the child. Jacob threw the tantrum to end all tantrums and eventually cried himself to sleep. Gerry's in the bath in a sulk. They woke Carrie who now thinks it's first thing in the morning and wants to play. Don't eat that, darling. No, darling. Please do not put that in your mouth. Just a second. Carrie, ta ta! Right, where was I?"

"Jacob cried himself to sleep, Gerry's in the bath and Carrie thinks it's morning," Harri summarised.

"I hate my life," Melissa sighed.

Harri laughed. "I'm watching my third *CSI* in a row and I saw this particular episode yesterday and possibly the day before too."

"Oh."

"Yeah."

"Have you talked to your parents?"

"You're relentless."

And so when Harri had eventually returned from Italy with George in tow and had summoned the courage and will to face her parents it was a relief to all.

July 6th 1975 - Sunday

I was sitting by The Eliana and just staring out to sea thinking about nothing. I didn't notice HIM sit beside me. I suppose I was daydreaming and far away. It was early. Nine or maybe nine thirty. I felt his arm on my shoulder. I moved but too slowly. He held me in place. He must have been out drinking all night. I could smell the drink on his breath and when he leaned in for a kiss I stamped on his foot. He cried out and let go a little and I ran. I could hear him shouting that I was waiting for him and I wanted it.

I don't know how I didn't see him, I don't know how I managed to let him get so close, I don't know if he was right. He was so drunk he couldn't have been quiet in his approach, he would have been stumbling and the smell of him alone! Where was I in my head that I didn't see or hear or notice? What's wrong with me? I can't tell Matthew because he'll do something and then we'll end up in trouble and it doesn't make sense that he can get away with it but he can. He can do what he wants because he has a marriage licence and that's a licence to do anything. I didn't want to come home so I walked and walked past the castle and the Strand and on to the head and around by the lighthouses and down to the cliffs. I sat at the edge and I'm not saying I would ever kill myself but for the first time ever I thought how easy it would be. It was only fleeting and I could never leave Matthew but that's it. I realised that he is the only one I have to stay around for. Coming back here was hard. Putting my key in the door and turning it was harder. I used to love this little house on Castle St. I loved that we were in town and beside the pier. I loved my little room that looked onto Mam's well-kept garden and the way the light streamed into the sitting room on a sunny day. I loved the smell of cooking that hit you the second you opened the door. Mam used to cook all the time. She would start the dinner at one to serve it at six. She loved to bake apple tarts, rhubarb tarts, fairy and queen cakes. She doesn't do that any more. The house doesn't smell of cooking any more. The sitting room seems duller, older, and tatty even. The garden is overgrown and my room isn't my room any more. He's taken everything and every day he makes me a little more scared and I'm really scared.

Chapter thirteen

It's been a month but it feels like a year

The trip up the stairs seemed to take longer than ever before. Three floors plus the converted attic made four flights and the combination of expectation, fear, silence and a familiar creeping dread encouraged Harri to believe that the destination might never be reached. *I might have a heart attack. I could easily have one. Beat beat, beat beat beat. It's beating too fast. Don't panic, Harri. Don't be My Left Foot about it and for Christ sake don't die on the stairs.* Once climbed and the door to her father's inner sanctum reached, he turned to her and smiled slightly before turning the key.

* * *

Duncan had aged ten years in one month. When Harri had pulled up in her parents' driveway she had found her father sitting on Nana's bench and when her eyes met his, the anger she had felt all but disappeared. He was old now, his face was lined, his brow furrowed, and when he stood, unsure and eyes watering, inexplicably he seemed smaller. The large hulking gravel-voiced hero of her youth who one month previously had in a moment turned into a stranger who had lied to, stolen from and betrayed her was now lonely, scared and at sea in uncharted waters. *I know how that feels.* Resentment trickled away and instead pity filled her. He seemed unsure for the first and only time in his life. His head was hung low and although he met her stare the man she knew wasn't looking back at her. She couldn't bear his pain, her own was too great and so she smiled at him and walked toward him hugging him tight.

"I just needed time, Dad."

He wrapped his arms around her and right there outside and by Nana's bench her dad the warrior had cried for the love of his daughter Harri.

Gloria was waiting by the stove, having just checked on the shepherd's pie. She was wringing her hands so that they wouldn't flutter.

"There you are, darling," she pointed out, happy that her daughter was arm in arm with her broken husband.

It seemed so odd and so faraway that in the Ryan household it had been Gloria's mental status that had long been cause for concern. Gloria had of course been upset by the events that had led them to this appalling and awkward place. She had worried for her daughter and son and how the terrible truth had affected them and how it would affect them in the future. She worried that she would lose them and specifically Harri. *Will she run off now? Will she find a family somewhere else? Will she no longer need or want us?* But deep down there was a calmness she couldn't quite explain. *We'll be okay. We have each other and we'll be okay.* She had felt sadness and she had cried because memories that were so deeply buried had been exhumed thirty days and nights before. She had once again seen the face of the baby girl she had lost as vividly as though she was pictured on the wall before her. She recalled the contour of her little button nose and her discoloured rosebud lips. She had a head of hair, dark and floppy like her twin brother's. Her nails were so long they needed cutting and her thumb on her left hand curled inwards and toward her palm while her other nine fingers were stretched out as though she was about to yawn. She was long and would have been tall. When Gloria had held her that one and only time thirty years before she had decided that her daughter could have been a concert pianist as her elegant fingers looked like those of a piano player. She knew that night that if given the chance she would have been athletic too just like her twin had turned out to be. Having said that, she had not considered her little girl would jump out of aeroplanes or ski on black ice like her brother who on many occasions had nearly been the death of his mother. Instead she saw her as a tennis player or maybe a golfer or something else that required skill and wasn't life threatening. That night when the doctor and nurses had all but pulled her little girl out of her arms something inside her broke but that had long ago healed and although the scars remained she had always known that deep down she would never break like that again.

And so Gloria had been the strong one and Duncan was the one to fall apart.

His kids hated him. He was full of regret and for the first time a self-doubt seeped inside, threatening to fill the unseen fissure that had begun to creep through him the day his dead daughter was born. Thirty years ago his wife had leaned on him and now thirty years later he would lean on her.

"You see – she's texting," she said when his daughter couldn't bring herself to talk to her father but still couldn't be unkind enough to ignore him. "Don't mind George – we both know he's a selfish sod." She had smiled and squeezed his hand tight before pulling him out of his bed and into a standing position. "We've had thirty years to get used to this – surely you can give them thirty days."

"It'll never be the same," he had mumbled with head in hands.

"No, darling, it won't," she said, putting her hand through his hair. "But that's okay."

She smiled and he kissed her hand. "What would I do without you, Glory?"

"Well, darling, right now you'd probably lose ten pounds and smell."

He laughed.

"Now get in the shower and I'll make you a breakfast fit for a lord!" She had left him to sit on the side of his bed but his mind was elsewhere and back in time in a Wicklow wood where he was pulling his brother's coat away from a dead teenage girl's face.

His brother was standing beside him.

"I knew her," he'd said. "I know her mother."

"Where's the baby?" Duncan had asked.

"She's with the local GP," Father Ryan replied, still staring at the dead teen.

"She has a black eye," Duncan said.

"It's not related."

"Have you contacted her family?"

"No." He shook his head.

"Why not?"

"I want you to come back with me to the GP's house," he said. "Now and before it's too late."

Did we do the right thing? What did we do?

Duncan had relied on his wife more than he ever thought possible and in that month a change of balance had occurred in the Ryan household.

* * *

The key turned in the lock and the door swung open, revealing Harri's dad's office. It always looked the same, dark and dusty even though Mrs Gallo cleaned it along with the rest of the house once a week on a Tuesday. The floor to ceiling shelves filled with endless books and papers gave the place its dusty feel and the dark wooden bookcases, floorboards and office furniture lent themselves toward gloomy despite a large triangular wooden roof window which seemed to be designed to stream light into one place in the corner of the room. That place coincidently held the large locked cabinet which held copies of all her father's case files. It was the untouchable, the Ryan household's Holy Grail, and lit up it appeared portentous and dangerous.

Duncan switched on his desk lamp giving the room an eerie

orange glow. He slumped hard into his chair, causing a slight twinge in or around a weary coccyx.

Harri sat opposite him.

He didn't need to go to his locked cabinet. The file was in his drawer beside him. He opened the drawer and Harri felt her breath slip away. He pulled out a thick cream-coloured file and placed it on the desk before them. The edges were frayed and yellowing. He looked up at her.

"Move around," he said pleasantly as though she was once more a child and he was about to read from a storybook.

She pushed her chair around and sat next to her father. A moment or two passed while they settled themselves.

"Are you ready?" he asked.

She shook her head. "I don't know."

He nodded and put his arm around her shoulder.

"Dad?"

"Yes, love."

"Why don't you just tell me?"

Duncan nodded that he would.

He told her about the morning of July 11th 1976. He had just been escorted from the psychiatric wing of a hospital that was temporarily housing his wife. She had been listless, medicated and a world away from him. He had attempted to discuss her depression with a doctor who didn't seem to be familiar with her case. An argument had broken out and regretfully he had threatened to break the man's nose.

"It was a very stressful time," he remembered ruefully.

Nana had been charged with caring for George who was six weeks old, suffering from colic and no doubt separation anxiety. "Poor Nana! We really landed her in it. George had lost his twin and his mother in a matter of moments." Duncan sighed. "And if I'm honest he had lost me too."

Duncan had returned to work immediately, only taking two days off to attend his brother's Mass for his dead daughter and to cremate her.

One week later he took another day off to section his wife but other than those few days he worked harder and longer hours than he had ever worked.

"It kept me going," he sighed.

Later that day he returned to the office – he was working on an arson case in west Dublin. He spoke of its tragedy. A farmer burnt down a shed he couldn't afford to fix in the hopes of an insurance premium payout. He had no idea that a drunk had taken refuge there and was fast asleep inside. "That fella did five years for that," he said. "We never did identify the corpse and nobody ever came looking."

Harri took a moment to feel sorry for the poor man burnt to death and the arsonist who had become an unwilling murderer.

"That's awful," she said horrified and her dad couldn't help but smile.

"Don't you take that home with you, Harri Ryan," he said, tipping the top of her head. "It was only an aside and not meant to upset you."

"I'm not sure I've room, Dad," she admitted.

"I remember when you were twelve and you found that bird, almost dead, and you took him home," he laughed a little to himself. "You sang to it and it died in your hands."

"George says it was my singing that killed it." She smiled a little.

"You cried for that bird, you mourned it. Such a big heart for such a little girl."

"You're changing the subject."

"I am," he sighed and so he proceeded from where he'd left off.

He was back in July of 1976 late one night, eating at his desk which was something he said he was doing a lot of at the time. The station was quiet and so his feet were on the desk and, exhausted, he fell asleep. The phone woke him up.

"Dad?" said Harri.

"What?"

"When I said tell me I didn't mean every detail."

"Well, I'm telling the story – I should be able to tell it the way I want to tell it."

"Right then. I'm sorry I didn't bring a flask." She sighed and her dad smiled to himself. *She's still my girl.*

He then mentioned that the clock on the wall read that it was after 1 a.m. the man on the phone was his brother and he was verging on hysteria which was disconcerting in that it was highly unusual.

"I need you," Father Ryan had said. "I need you in Wicklow tonight."

Duncan queried him as to why and it was then that he was told that a girl had given birth in the woods and died. "There's more to it," Father Ryan had warned. "Don't tell anyone and come alone."

Duncan didn't waste time arguing. He knew his brother well enough to know that argument wouldn't get either of them anywhere so instead he got into his car and just under an hour later he was in a Wicklow wood by his brother's side and standing over a dead girl covered by a priest's black coat. He stood there silently for what seemed like the longest time while his brother finished a prayer over the girl.

"Dad?" Harri interrupted.

"Yes, love," he said, again returning to the present.

"What was her name?"

"Olivia," he said, "but she was known as Liv."

"Liv?" Harri repeated, contemplating the irony.

Duncan resumed his tale. "We left her there," he said.

Father Ryan had insisted on taking him back to the GP's house where the GP waited with the baby.

"Me," she clarified as though there was some need to do so.

"You," he confirmed.

He remembered how distraught the GP was and that his name was Brendan something but of course all that information was in the file. The three men sat together at the doctor's kitchen table and the doctor outlined the reasons he wanted the child to be kept out of the girl's mother's house and out of the system. Father Ryan had agreed that it was best for the baby that it disappeared; he said he would deal with the girl's mother and stepfather and the boy.

"Her brother?"

"No. The father of . . . the baby."

Harri stayed silent.

"The doctor knew him well," Duncan went on. "In fact he lived on the boy's father's land. She was trying to make her way to the doctor's house, at least that's what we believe."

"And the boy?" Harri's heart began to race again quicker and quicker – any minute a vein would pop in her neck.

"Staying with his grandparents in Meath."

"What was his name?" she asked holding her neck with her hand so as to keep any rogue veins in check.

"Matthew Delamere."

Silence.

"They were both only kids."

Silence.

"But when I met him I could tell he really loved her. He was devastated, broken. And trust me right about then I understood broken."

Silence.

"Harri?"

"He knew?" she asked and for some reason she was filling up as though a kid she didn't know had suddenly betrayed her and her mother who didn't make it past her teens. "He let you take me?"

Duncan nodded. "He did, love."

So, while the girl was cold and the boy was blissfully unaware, asleep in his grandmother's spare room less than two hours away, the priest, the young doctor and the detective had sat up in the doctor's kitchen drinking coffee and smoking cigarettes, and there in the wee hours they had devised a plan. Duncan and Father Ryan would return to the place where the girl was and remove any evidence that she had been found. Duncan would then take the baby girl home. At first light the young doctor would put on his running clothes and he'd take a run before he'd make a call to the local police station about the girl he'd found dead in the woods. Father Ryan would be called and he would insist on his brother, a senior ranking detective, being involved. He'd get his way too because the local sergeant not only owed him a favour, he was afraid of him. Besides, he was well and truly out of his depth. Duncan would return and take over the investigation. The young doctor would sign the death cert and the priest would break the news to the girl's mother.

"But how?" Harri asked in something approaching a strangled whisper. "How did that plan work with no baby?"

"There was a baby," he said.

And if Harri didn't have heart failure right then and there she was never going to. *Holy Fuck!*

"George wasn't the only twin."

"Excuse me?"

"You were barely breathing on your mother's belly. Your sister was dead on the ground."

Harri's hands covered her mouth, she was certain she would throw up. She didn't.

"Take deep breaths," he ordered.

"I'm fine," she replied wearily and with eyes watering.

"You have that look," he said, "the one that frightens people."

"I'm fine, Dad."

"Harri, you've gone very pale."

"Wouldn't you?"

"I suppose so."

Again they sat in silence.

"But why?" she asked after ten long minutes.

"Why what?"

"Why would Uncle Thomas and the doctor be so desperate to make sure that I didn't go to my grandmother?"

"There were problems. Your real grandfather was dead and she'd married again. He was a drunk, violent, and your mother was desperate to get away from him. She had some sort of hold over the young doctor – she wasn't just a patient. I think in some ways he loved her."

"What?" Harri asked in a manner that suggested a little disgust.

"Not like that, Harri, and besides he was little more than a kid himself – twenty-six maybe. Anyway in those days the boy, Matthew, wouldn't have had a look in even if he thought he could manage. His family would never have supported him for fear that the scandal could have destroyed their reputation. His grandfather was a man to be reckoned with, the death was all over the news, and despite the whole town knowing he was going out with the girl his name never made it into the papers. And, well, your grandmother was a weak and unwell woman. And besides, the minute I saw you I fell in love. You were so small, so fragile and still a fighter. You looked at me so fiercely, so fierce it made me laugh. It was the first time I'd laughed in six weeks. I knew in my heart that you were for me and I was for you so I took you home. You were never a replacement, not in our hearts."

Harri was crying, her nose was running like a tap and the tissue she had located up her sleeve was sodden. "What about the boy?" she sobbed.

"Poor kid," her father sighed before he went on to explain that he took Matthew's statement in the young doctor's house. He told them that they were planning to run away and that he had money saved and tickets bought and it was only two weeks away. Duncan remembered that the boy seemed to be fixated on that fact: "Only two weeks away." Matthew had repeated it over and over to himself while gnawing at his knuckles. They had planned to take the boat because of the pregnancy and they would land in Wales and then after that they would take it from there until eventually after the baby was born they'd find their way to the States. At least that was the plan. "Only two weeks away." He was confused because the baby wasn't due for at least another month. And he refused to accept that sometimes babies come early. He had constantly looked at the doctor as though with words he could bring her back. "It was HIM," was the only other thing he repeated. "HE did something." The boy was right. The stepfather had done something two nights before. He had attacked her just as Father Ryan arrived to make a call. He came between them but not before she received a black eye. It was then that the young doctor spoke to the young boy about the baby that lived and he explained to the boy that he and Father Ryan and the kind man in front of them wanted to help. At first Matthew was speechless but the doctor talked and talked and talked and by the end of it the boy had only one request.

"What?" Harri asked as breathless as an asthmatic after a ten-kilometre run.

"He just wanted to meet you once and get a picture. So that's what we did. One week later just after midnight I took you to the pier in Wicklow and we sat on a bench and on the wall behind was a painting of a Greek ship called The Eliana and he held you and kissed you and whispered stories about your mother and you slept the whole time. Two weeks after that he was gone. The death was ruled accidental and thanks to the young man's powerful father his identity was never revealed."

"Case closed," Harri said.

"Case closed," Duncan repeated.

They both sat in silence, Duncan recovering from his emotionally draining recollection and Harri still absorbing a new and disturbing reality.

"You didn't have to tell him," she said after a while.

"I know," he replied.

"That was really brave of you," she said.

"Thanks."

"And really stupid. It all could have blown up in your face."

"I know."

"But right."

"I think so."

"And he's never called or written or anything."

"No."

"Dad."

"Yes, love."

"Have you any pictures in there of Liv when she was alive?"

"I do."

"Maybe you could give me one of those. I don't want to see anything else."

"Good idea," he said. "Tell you what – you go downstairs to your mum and George and I'll fish one out."

"OK," she said, getting up. She kissed her old dad on the

forehead. He said nothing but she could feel his relief because she was relieved too.

George was tipsy on Italian wine and was waltzing his mother around the kitchen as though the past three weeks had been a collective figment of the Ryan family imagination. Gloria was playing along, happy to have her two children under her roof. George was good at pretence. He had decided and agreed upon forgiveness and so there was nothing more to be said. He didn't want details of the twin that died, he didn't want reasons for his parents' actions preceding that death. He had a twin in Harri, he had parents, a boyfriend and a new business and that was enough to be dealing with. His sulk had reached its conclusion and he was ready to move on. Time to go through the motions of forgiving and forgetting.

Gloria, like her son, was happy to side-step anything approaching uncomfortable in favour of equilibrium.

And so Harri's mother and brother dancing around the kitchen told Harri in no uncertain terms that the time for mourning, reflection or introspection had well and truly past.

In the words of a much loved drunken homo: build a bridge and get over it.

July 7th 1975 - Monday

Yesterday on the cliffs I thought about dying but only for a split second. I left and walked home and locked my bedroom door and while I was lying on my bed writing in my diary a boy two years younger from my school fell from the same cliffs. I can't believe it. It's so weird and so awful and he didn't want to die. He was with friends, they were trying to rob the eggs from the gull's nest right on the ledge. They do it all the time and it's madness. I don't think they'll be doing it again. His name was Shane McCafferty and he was fourteen. He was a footballer and he had a girlfriend called Jackie. I don't know her, she's from Rathnew. The boys with him were taken to the local police station to make a statement. Sheila said that her dad said that they were all wailing. Shane's mother was taken to hospital because she went into shock and she suffers with her blood pressure. The coast guard were looking for him and they were trying to be hopeful about finding him but Sheila's dad said that if falling from the cliff didn't kill him, the rocks would, and if the rocks didn't kill him he'd drown. Sheila's dad can be very negative. All the same this time he's probably right. They haven't found the body yet and it's been over twenty-four hours so at this stage they know he's gone. It's so sad I can't stop thinking about it. I didn't really know him and yet he's all I can think about. The poor boy, I wonder where he is now? Is he happy? Is he glad he died or is he sick with himself for being so stupid and risking his life and future for a stupid seagull egg? Matthew and I called to Dr B. He made tea and told us the search was ongoing and mentioned something about the body surfacing in nine days. I didn't know what he was talking about, he mentioned something about the expulsion of body gases and I switched off, it's just so disgusting. Shane's mam is in a terrible way. It made me feel bad about not considering my own mam when I sat up on those cliffs but then she doesn't deserve it. Dr B asked after her. I said she was fine but I was lying. She's acting strange again. She was fine for a while and now she just sits at the table in the kitchen and stares at the wall. She still goes to Mass and she still watches '*Coronation Street*' so that's something. I don't know what's wrong with her. Maybe she's scared too. Maybe that's what being scared does to you. HE hasn't come home. I don't think she even notices. They can't hold a funeral for the boy until they find him. It's so sad. I wish I could do something to help. Maybe when they find him and he's buried maybe I could ask my mam to bake an apple pie and I'll take it to Shane's mam. I don't think apple pie upsets blood pressure. I'll check with Dr B.

Chapter fourteen

I'm Melissa and I google

In the days following Harri's trip to her father's attic she had made a sincere effort to keep to herself. Having the whole sorry situation retold for George's benefit over shepherd's pie had taken its toll and she just needed a few days to quietly reflect. Of course that was never going to happen. She was hounded by all her friends until eventually she agreed to a meal where she would discuss the matter once and once only. The whole nightmare would then be laid to rest and she could get back to normal or at least what normal would become now that she was single, empty and living alone. *Maybe I'll get a rabbit.*

* * *

"You wanker!" Melissa roared at her husband before slamming the front door behind her. Gerry stood mouth agape, holding his infant daughter Carrie with his son Jacob pulling at his trouser leg.

"What's a wanker, Dad?"

Five minutes earlier Gerry had arrived home to find his wife walking around the house in one high heel with a considerable dollop of baby food running down the front of her top and a look on her face that suggested he was a dead man walking. He'd been happy enough up to that point having had a good day at work followed by a pleasant game of squash before partaking in a nice creamy pint or two. Or three. His good humour was destined not to last long.

"What time do you call this?" she greeted him in a manner approaching sinister.

"It's a little after eight," he replied airily after taking a moment to examine his watch.

"I was supposed to meet Susan and Harri at seven thirty!" she screamed with a kind of frustration that was nearing the Land of Hysteria.

"Ah you won't be too late," he said, injecting calmness into his voice in the hope that it would inspire calmness in his wife.

He was wrong. She stopped searching under furniture and behind cushions suddenly and turned on him, walking two steps toward him. One leg shorter than the other seemed to make the situation slightly outlandish. "You promised," she said seething. "You promised to be home by seven so that I could go and have a meal with my friends."

"And you can," he said, hands in the air. "You'll only be an hour late."

If Melissa had a gun she might have used it. "An hour!" she roared. "An hour!" she repeated indignantly and roaring louder while limping toward him as he backed away from her. "My top is ruined, Jacob has forgotten where he's hidden my shoe and it's at least forty minutes from here to the restaurant."

"So sort yourself out, get in the car and go!" He was laughing at her demented demeanour, having morphed from outlandish to comical, especially when she stubbed her toe on the sitting-room door before backing up to kick it only to hurt the toe once more. Maybe it was the fact that he had actually indulged in three pints as opposed to the one he'd admit to or the fact that he was so relaxed after having vented any everyday residual frustration in the squash court or maybe it was because he really didn't have a clue as to how much he was taking for granted, but Gerry's laughter was genuine in the face of her pent-up aggression and overwhelming emotion.

Carrie was on the floor crying and Jacob was jumping up and down in the one spot counting to ten.

Melissa stopped to absorb her husband's ill-considered amusement. *Mental note: buy a gun.* It was ten seconds after that very thought that she'd picked up her crying baby girl, shoved her in her husband's arms and stormed out of the house wearing one shoe, no make-up and with half her baby's dinner down her front.

* * *

Aidan, Susan and Harri were waiting for Melissa patiently while indulging in a bottle of wine accompanied by a basket of breadsticks.

"So, missus, what's going on?" Aidan asked Harri as if he didn't know.

"Apart from the dissolution of my relationship with the love of my life, the discovery that I'm the living twin baby of a dead teenage stranger and swapped for a dead baby, not much, thanks for asking."

Aidan grinned "How about you, Sue, any chance you can beat that?"

"Well, my marriage is in the toilet but then that's not news, Beth is in exam frenzy and in such a bloody mood that it's like living with Barbara Streisand."

"I'd love to live with Barbara Streisand." Aidan said, grinning and winking at a smiling Harri. *Nice to see you smile.*

"Homo," Susan sighed.

"Breeder!" Aidan responded, holding his smile at Harri.

"And two nights ago I bumped into Keith," Susan said pretending to be nonchalant while reading an upside-down menu.

"Keith the builder?" Harri said after removing the glass from her lips.

"Keith the builder," Susan confirmed. "He was in Tesco with his wife."

"Oh," Harri said.

Aidan was too rapt to talk.

"What did you do?" Harri queried.

"I smiled and walked past them."

"Good for you," Harri said helpfully.

Aidan was still rapt, knowing deep down there was more. *Come on, you dirty bitch, tell us something filthy.*

"Then five minutes later he called me, asked if I'd meet him. I did. We had sex in his car. It was great. I've no plans to see him again."

Aidan made a kind of yelping sound. Harri's mouth fell open.

"I thought I'd feel terrible but aside from slight backache I actually feel good," Susan said, nodding to herself. "My husband hates me so why not?"

"Why not indeed?" Aidan agreed raising his glass. "I'm so glad I'm not the only one going to hell! I'll save you a seat." He patted the empty chair beside him. Harri laughed and that reminded him that if she didn't commit some sort of Vatican-certified hell-bound sin soon she might end up in the clouds alone. "We've got two homos, an adulterer and let's face it sooner or later Melissa will be a murderer so what about you, Har? What can you do to hitch a ride on the highway to hell?"

"I'll get back to you," she said smiling while wondering whether or not the serious diseases, pain and torment she had recently wished upon her substitute parents would be enough. She was trying to forgive them, she was pretending as best she could but deep down their deceit was eating away at her slowly and little by little so that one day in the future she wondered if the Harri sitting at that table would be gone and no more. *Good riddance, you didn't exist anyway.* She knew George too was pretending. He had danced with his mother and made nice over dinner. He'd toasted to their family and smiled and was charming and forgiving and deceiving. She could see it in his eyes, the eyes that refused to meet the eyes of either parent. The Ryan family were doing what the Ryan family did best: they were pretending and hiding and lying and sweeping every irritation, uncomfortable emotion and bad feeling under the carpet and how long their charade would last was anybody's guess.

Melissa entered the restaurant barefoot and holding her handbag tight against her chest. She looked the maitre d' straight in the face and with a beaming smile announced that she had seen her party and would not require help being seated. The maitre d' didn't seem to notice the woman had no shoes on but then again how many people look down? Susan was the first to speak.

"Where are your shoes?" she asked, proving that in any situation the saying 'there's always one' has merit.

"Don't ask," Melissa said taking her bag away from her stained top.

Harri poured her a large glass of wine.

"Thanks," said Melissa before taking a long drink.

"Kids are hard work," Susan said sighing.

"Husbands are harder!" Melissa said before taking another gulp.

"I hear that," Susan agreed.

Harri remained silent, avoiding the momentary need to cry as the scene before her only served to remind her that she had neither kids nor a husband. James was gone, she missed him more than she would have thought possible and rabbits were probably banned by the apartment-building committee.

"Are you okay?" Melissa asked her.

"Fine." She grinned for effect.

"You look constipated."

"I'm fine."

"There are prunes on the menu," Aidan interjected.

"I don't need prunes."

"I was only saying. It's not often you see prunes on a menu."

"Where's George? Melissa enquired.

"He's up to his tits in carpenters, electricians and plumbers," Aidan said before clinking his glass with Melissa who then guzzled from hers. "You'd swear he was converting bloody Buckingham Palace. He's had me painting all week and he's a fussy little bastard."

* * *

Aidan was lying a little bit. George was up to his eyes in it but not so much that he couldn't stop for a meal. The real truth was that George didn't enjoy nights on the town with the girls and Aidan was sick of making excuses for him. They'd argued about it earlier that evening when Aidan had begged him to come, especially in light of Harri's latest ordeal. George was adamant he had no intention of wasting time listening to idle bloody gossip, baby talk, marriage talk, bitching on Aidan's part.

"I don't bitch."

"Aidan, have you ever met yourself?"

"Your sister needs you."

"And I'm there for her on our own time."

"You never come out with us."

"Three women and you are not my ideal dinner companions. Melissa and Sue are lovely women, my sister is my world, but just because I'm gay doesn't mean I like girlie nights."

"Isn't it funny how you enjoy their company here in our home but not in a restaurant?"

"Don't start, Aidan."

"Just saying."

"So don't say. I have my friends and you have yours." George was annoyed to be having the same stupid argument for the millionth time.

Aidan gave up because what was the point? George's supposed friends were all adrenaline junkies who when not jumping out of planes or bungee-jumping off buildings were talking about it or planning it or getting pissed on it. They didn't know George, no more than he knew any of them. They had nothing in common bar their hobbies. When George needed help with his business plan it was Melissa who spent three nights drawing up his proposals for the bank, when he needed décor discounts it was Sue who ensured he got what he needed and for everything else he relied on Harri. They were his real friends and his real friends wanted to have a night out with him in lieu of the terrible recent events so that together they could move past them. But why argue reason with a man like George? He'd made his mind up so that was that.

Aidan slammed the door to signal his exit.

George had been tired after a long day spent wrangling with an electrician.

"I'm just not comfortable putting the spots there," the man had said with arms crossed.

"Excuse me?"

"It doesn't feel right to me."

"It doesn't have to feel right. It's what I want," George snapped.

"Yeah, well, that may be the case but I'm the one doing the work and four spots so close together in that particular area does not look right to me."

"I am the fucking customer."

"There is no need to swear."

"I think there is."

"Really there isn't."

"Are you going to put the spots where I've asked or not?"

The man sniffed and rubbed his sleeve under his nose. "It's your funeral."

"Are you trying to say putting them close together is dangerous?"

"No."

"Oh for Christ sake!"

Days before and in a moment of weakness he had agreed to go to the meal but that was only to get Aidan off his back. He'd also forgotten so it was an unpleasant shock when Aidan was waiting for him in his best smart casuals reeking of Paco Rabanne and with a big smile plastered across his face.

"You have half an hour to get ready."

Bollocks. "Aidan, I'm not going."

And the argument took off from there.

After Aidan had slammed the door leaving George alone in his apartment he realised he had no food in the place and was sick at the thought of ordering in once more. He knew Aidan was seething and he knew that the argument could go on for days. There was a part of him that really needed a good night out and of course he loved all the girls – it was just Aidan around the girls that he didn't like. He became giggly, girly, loud and camper than camp and George found it embarrassing. Of course when he brought this fact up Aidan called him a homophobe and screamed and shouted. "You're as bad as them!" "I am what I am." "How dare you judge me?" George had no comeback, at least not one that gained anyone's sympathy. Aidan was effeminate at the best of times and George sometimes found that difficult to handle but he loved him. When Aidan drank he became a little camper and when he drank with the girls he became the king of camp. Suddenly life was a stage and Aidan the main attraction and George couldn't deal with it. Aidan had once argued that he was jealous, being the one used to attention. It wasn't true. George didn't know why he was popular company nor did he spend too much time wondering about it. All he knew was that when he received attention it had nothing to do with him standing on top of a table holding a handbag and singing 'I'm Just a Girl Who Cain't Say No'. Aidan was kind and loving and funny and great in the sack but sometimes he embarrassed him. And it wasn't fair that he couldn't voice it without being called homophobic or self-loathing. So he sat alone waiting for the delivery of his third chicken satay that week, simmering and trying to remember why he and Aidan were together in the first place.

* * *

Harri had talked about her dad, her mum, the two dead twins, the girl in the woods, the dead girl's fragile mother and vicious stepfather, Father Ryan, the young doctor and the boy who'd lost his love.

"I think it's very romantic," Susan declared after one too many.

"If your idea of romance is sharp tacks in your knickers," Aidan said, looking at her oddly. "The girl died alone under a fucking tree with a dead kid between her legs. How is that romantic?"

Harri winced and Melissa kicked him.

"I mean the boy's love for the girl. She was dead and he loved her so much he was willing to let his little girl go just to keep her away and safe from the stepfather the girl loathed. I swear it's like a Mills & Boon."

"You are such a sap, Sue," Aidan said.

"It's a nice thought, Sue, but Aidan's right – you are a sap," Harri concluded.

"Excuse me?" Susan said, opening her mouth so that food was visible.

"Close your mouth!" Melissa ordered as though she was talking to her four-year-old.

"He was just a kid. He didn't want a baby," Harri said while swirling the contents of her glass thoughtfully.

"And now?" Melissa asked.

"Now what?" Harri responded.

"And now he's a grown man."

"My age," Susan reminded them. *I wonder what he looks like.*

"And now nothing," Harri asserted.

"You're not the slightest bit curious?" Aidan asked.

"No," Harri lied.

"Really," Melissa said, "that's a pity because I googled him last night."

Harri went slightly pale. "I can't believe you did that," she said in a whisper.

The other two said nothing.

"Did I step over the line?" Melissa asked, a little alarmed by the silence. Nobody spoke making her panic a little. "Okay, maybe I shouldn't have but I didn't think. My computer was on and open and, you know me, I'm a googler." Melissa was sweating now. *Oh crap.* Aidan and Susan shuffled in their seats uncomfortably.

"So what did it say?" Harri asked after a long and uncomfortable pause.

Melissa cleared her throat, regretting her indiscretion but forced to proceed. "Well, he's a horse breeder. It turns out he's a very well-known trainer and big with the horsy set. He lives in some mansion in Wicklow. He's not married and other than you he doesn't have any kids. Oh and he's minted."

"My parents have money," Harri replied, slightly offended that economics were being mentioned at all.

"Yes, they do, but this guy would make the Ryans look like peasants."

"And he's single?" Susan clarified.

"Well, he's unmarried, he may have a girlfriend."

"So he's rich?" said Aidan.

Melissa ignored him. "I printed off a picture. It's not great, my colour printer is rubbish but if you want to see him . . ."

Susan's mind buzzed. *Please be good looking. Oh Jesus, what am I doing? How desperate am I? Get a grip, Susan.*

Harri looked at Melissa and sighed. "Show me," she said.

"Okay." Melissa nodded and took the picture out from her handbag. She smoothed it out on the table before opening it.

The man before them was dressed in a tuxedo and grinning while holding up a glass of champagne. The caption read: *Matthew Delamere Back on Form.* He had a full head of thick wavy brown hair matching Harri's only shorter. His smile was wide and his eyes had a twinkle in them.

"You have his eyes." Melissa said.

"He's a ride," Aidan said.

"He really is," Susan agreed. *God, I really feel like calling Keith. Don't do it, Sue. You're better than this.*

"He's a rich ride," Aidan said before taking a sip of wine. "Every cloud . . ." he mumbled. Harri gave him a dig.

"Right," he agreed with himself. "Too early to be positive."

Harri felt weird and decided she needed the loo. She excused herself and sat on the toilet for a minute or two trying to regain composure but when it didn't work she cried.

"Are you okay, dear?" a woman asked from behind the next stall.

"Yes, thanks," Harri sobbed.

"Sometimes all you can do is have a good old cry," the woman said.

"True," Harri sobbed.

"Good girl," the woman said before leaving her to it.

August 2nd 1975 - Saturday

It's been a whole month since I wrote in my diary. Damn it, I've missed so much and no matter what I won't remember everything. I broke two fingers on my right hand, that's why I couldn't write. Two really bad breaks. I was in bits and they are still really sore. I was racing with Matthew and I fell off Betsy. Henry said the way I'd fallen I was lucky I didn't break my neck and I seriously don't know how he worked that one out. I landed on my hand not my head. Dr B gave me a letter for the hospital and Matthew came with me. I didn't bother telling my mam, she'd just embarrass me. She's being a psycho at the moment. One minute she's laughing, the next she's crying, then she's laughing again, then she's screaming, then she's apologising before crying, then laughing, and so on. I swear she's got so mad I even felt sorry for HIM one night last week. It was only for a moment, then I wanted him dead again so that's all right. I've been able to continue working in the stables although I've been doing more in the office which I love. The girl on reception got a job in Dublin and left them stuck so my broken fingers couldn't have been better timed. I've been answering phones mostly and taking notes on a chalkboard because chalk is way thicker and easier to hold with the claw I had instead of a hand. It was Matthew's idea and seriously genius. I thought it would be really boring but it wasn't, in fact it was pretty interesting. I was up in the posh trainer's part of the property and holy hell was it posh. At the start Matthew's dad ignored me but then he came into the office one day shouting about a lunch order which had failed to be delivered to him and a Saudi Prince!!! Anyway, the girl who'd gone off to Dublin must have forgotten to order from some posh place, ironically in Dublin, so while he was going mental I rang Sheila's dad and asked him to pack up a traditional pub lunch and deliver it and he was only too happy to oblige and the prince loved it. Afterwards he said I was great at thinking on my feet and said I'd make a great PA. I've no idea what a PA is or exactly what a PA does but it sounds brilliant. He's been all over me since. Well, when I say all over me I mean he thinks I'm brill and I'd say if I didn't want to go back to school to do the Leaving Cert in September he'd keep me on. I don't think Matthew would like that though. Anyway it's only a thought.

Now what else? Sheila and Dave were off for two weeks but they are now back on and she says that they definitely won't break up again. Yeah right and my mam isn't bonkers! Anyway Dave broke it off because he thought she was being too clingy and she wasn't supportive when he said he wanted to be a rock climber for a living. Dave is a total spasm. A rock climber? Who does that? How does that pay? Why would you do it? What is the point? I wouldn't mind only he's the laziest boy I know. He wouldn't scratch himself if he thought someone else would do it and I'm sure behind closed doors his mam does it for him. She's weird-looking and always has a wet hanky at the ready. Dave still wants to be a rock climber and Sheila's pretending she's happy with that because her mother told her it's just a phase. Sheila is now seriously considering becoming a hairdresser and not like before when she was only talking about it. She's even done my hair in an up-style. It wasn't very good, there were loads of lumps and my head hurt but she's only a beginner and hasn't actually had any training yet so you never know.

Dr B! What can I say about Dr B? He's at a crossroads and gone goggle-eyed! We've got closer since I broke my fingers. Oh I forgot to mention that he hated my present of the '*Maurice*' book. He nearly lost the plot when he got around to reading the back of it and we didn't talk for a week and then when I broke my fingers he admitted he did read it and I didn't say that I'd read it because it was really sexy and I didn't want to go red and he said that he loved it and thanked me and told me that it made him feel normal. I understand that. I told him I understood but he laughed and said I couldn't possibly understand what it felt like to be a pariah and I couldn't answer him back at the time because I didn't know what a pariah was, never mind what it was spelt like. Later I looked it up in the dictionary and now that I know what it is, he's wrong. He may like men but nobody knows that only him and me and everyone knows that I'm living in a house of violence, everyone knows my mam is being odd and falling apart and my stepdad is a drunk and everybody thinks they know exactly what goes on and they don't. I hear them talk and whisper and wonder. I watch the world pass me by and just because I'm a teenager it doesn't mean it doesn't affect me. I see the person I want to be and the world I want to live in and it's out of my reach by miles. I'm a stupid kid to be ignored and trodden upon so if anyone knows what it's like to be an outsider I do. Have a wank, Dr B, and get a clue! Well, that's what I thought but I didn't say it. Instead at my next bandage appointment I told him I now understood the term and explained why I was right and he was wrong. He laughed first but then he was sad. He said that my frustration and pain was a rite of passage and his was a burden to bear for eternity. That's Father Ryan talking – I can even hear it come out of his mouth. What a load of old shit! I told him as much. He thinks the Church knows what it's talking about and maybe he's right but maybe he's wrong. I asked if he'd ever considered that and he admitted he hadn't. I told him that my dad's brother (a hippy the family don't talk about) once said to me that there was only one rule that applied: Treat others as you wish them to treat you. It was New Year's Eve and he was drunk but it made loads of sense. He said anything above or below that was utter bollocks. I think he's right. You are who you are and as long as you live a good life and treat people well, aren't you decent and good and worthy of all that heaven has to offer? Dr B didn't talk much after I brought up my drunken uncle on New Year's Eve but he did say he was still glad he met me. That was nice. He seems surprised that I haven't spoken to anyone about him but why would I? He's my friend. Plus he's really sorted out my fingers.

Father Ryan is being weird. He keeps trying to talk to me, asking about how it is at home. I told him it was shit. Well, I didn't say shit but I told him my mam was going mental and HE would explode any day. He asked me what I meant as though I was speaking a different language. What do YOU mean? I said, I swear I did, and it was really cheeky but what does he expect shoving his nose in people's business when he has no idea? Does he live with someone who swears at him and brutalises him every day of the week? Has he ever been in hospital so swollen he couldn't speak? Has he ever locked his door and prayed and prayed he wouldn't be attacked? Father Ryan doesn't have a clue and yet he comes into my home and preaches the Lord's word, the same Lord that hung out with whores and thieves and liked them because at the end of the day he was human and they were probably a better laugh than the pious bullshitters that in the end viciously murdered him. Father Ryan doesn't like it when I say what I think. He twitches and stutters and his neck goes red and then he quotes and reasons and argues and I switch off because I don't care. If he had left well enough alone my mam wouldn't be so mad that she left the house the other day forgetting to put on a skirt but that's another story.

So much more has happened. Matthew and I are brilliant. When I'm with him the world's a better place. We talk and talk and we never seem to run out of things to say and it's never boring or dull. We talk about everything. I even told him about that night a few months back when mam was out walking and HE was drunk and came into my room. I told Matthew everything and I never thought I'd actually say it. He was so angry he wanted to find him and kill him and it was nice that he was so angry, it was nice not to be the only one angry, and now that he wants him dead too it makes me feel a little better about things. I was beginning to think I was a bit sick in the head. Anyway I told him I was fine and I'd be able to fight him off but now he worries. He says he's going to put an extra lock on the door for me, a padlock. I wish he didn't worry. He has enough going on. His dad is being really mean to him. He puts him down all the time and it's getting worse. I don't know why. He'll be back in school in September and I dread it. What will my world be like without him? I can't imagine. I don't want to. He's my world. I won't see him for weeks and weeks because his dad only allows him home for holidays.

What a dick! Matthew is the love of my life. Two weeks ago we lay on the marram grass (which is as soft as any duvet - it's so soft it bounces under your feet - weird) by the castle listening to the sea and watching stars and we put our hands in each other's knickers and it was really really nice and today he whispered that he'd save me and held me so tight it hurt. He'd save me, he said, because he knew I needed saving. I didn't have to ask. I'll love him forever for that. I'll love him forever for everything. I love him so much I miss him when he's with me. Maybe I'm mad like my mother!

Okay, one last thing. I'm listening to Elton John and he is so amazing. 'Rocket Man' has been out forever but for the first time I love it. Matthew has all his 7-inches and I really love 'Candle In The Wind' and 'Don't Let The Sun Go Down On Me'. The Bay City Rollers are over and he's forever, you can just tell.

Anyway I'm going out now. My fingers are liberated and Matthew is taking me for a picnic by the Glen strand. I love the water. Maybe some day I'll work in water. I'm a great swimmer. This morning I opened my window and there was the blackest fattest crow on my ledge and I know everyone hates them but I don't, it was lovely. It sat so still and its neck was arched and proudly facing toward the sea and it turned its head my way slowly and it wasn't scary, it was beautiful. I didn't move once, I just waited and then it looked at straight in the eye. I swear it looked at me for the longest time and I looked at it and then it was gone and I needed to sit down. I don't know why it was weird. Would it be crazy if I thought that the bird knew something I didn't? I suppose so and still . . . Matthew will be here soon. We're going to town to meet Sheila and Dave and his English cousin Simon.

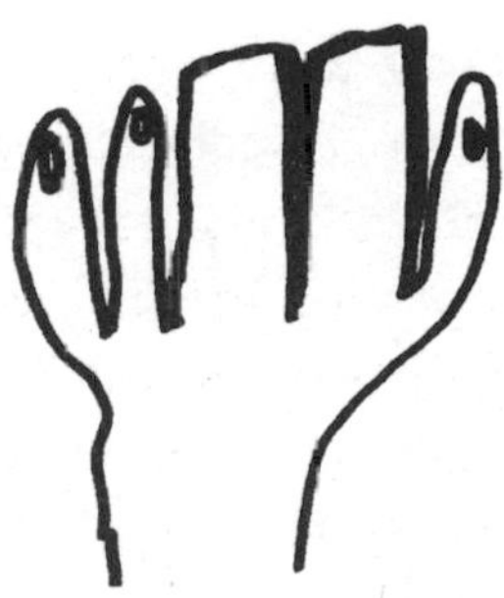

Chapter fifteen

If only

The month of July had been a long one and despite good weather and lots of work Susan was glad to see it end. She had slept with Keith three more times, once in a hotel, once on a king-sized duvet behind some rocks just before dawn on Killiney Beach and once in the middle of the day in Susan's bedroom and on her marital bed. It was after that particular fulfilling but guilt-ridden tryst that she had truly admitted to herself that her marriage was over. Keith had left soon after they'd finished and as the door was closing behind him Susan found herself packing a bag. She didn't cry or even think too much, instead she mechanically packed all that she needed to survive outside of her own home.

She called Harri from the car.

"Can I stay with you?" she asked as soon as Harri picked up the phone.

"Of course," Harri replied without needing to ask any questions. After all, Sue's last desperate act had been a long time coming.

"I'm on my way," she'd said *I'll face Beth when I'm settled. I'll tell her everything. Please God, don't let her hate me.*

Harri was waiting with fresh sheets on the pull-out sofa, tea, biscuits and a bear hug.

"I'm so sorry, Sue," she said. She had expected that Andrew had thrown Sue out, and was shocked to hear that it was Sue who had thrown herself out.

"I couldn't do it any more," she admitted. "I couldn't bear the silence and the lies."

"And what about Beth?" Harri asked, alarmed when she'd realised that Susan's escape had been spur of the moment, unprepared for, unplanned.

"She doesn't know."

Beth was working in a boutique in town and would be home later although Susan wasn't sure when. Harri instructed her to call her. She needed to be told and as a recent victim of lies Harri was adamant. And so Susan left a message on her daughter's mobile phone asking her to come to Harri's after work, noting that it was important.

Beth arrived a little after eight. Harri fussed over her, insisting that she ate some leftover lasagne. Susan remained quiet. Beth was adamant that she didn't want food, instantly sensing that something bad had happened.

Harri left the room for the bathroom where she sat on the loo for a while before deciding to run a bath.

"What has he done?" Beth asked.

"Nothing," Susan said. "He's done nothing."

"I know he has!" Beth said, full of fire.

"It's me," Susan admitted. "I'm the one who had the affair. He caught me seven months ago."

Beth was sitting and yet her legs still managed to go from under her. She visibly sank in the chair. "You?" she questioned in alarm and disbelief.

"I'm sorry," her mother said.

"You?"

Her mother nodded. Beth didn't understand. All the time she had thought her father was the one playing away and that it was her father that was destroying their family and he was the bastard. All that time when she was slagging him off, berating him while standing by and comforting her mother, all that time it was her dad who was the victim. Beth was speechless.

"I'm sorry," Susan said.

Beth regained the power of thought, word and movement and suddenly she was standing, then pacing and thinking aloud and shouting. "He didn't say anything!" "Why didn't he kick you out?" "Why did he let me talk to him like that?" "Why did he cover for you?"

All Susan could do was answer that she didn't know because she didn't know why her husband had been so adamant that their daughter should not be involved in her deception. He had made her promise and she had agreed, willing to do anything to get him to forgive her. It had occurred to her that it had been odd that when Beth was spewing her venom at him he had never once defended himself and never once pointed the finger in the right direction. In the end the lie had imprisoned, demoralised, degraded and trapped her. She had wondered if that had been his intention but it had seemed too Machiavellian and too cruel. She couldn't explain to her daughter why her father had been so desperate to hide her adultery. It made no sense.

"Who was he?" "When and for how long?" "How many times?" "Why?" Beth had shouted over and over again while circling Harri's small sitting room.

"A builder." "Not long." "A few times" "Does it really matter?" "I was lonely." Susan had answered, repeating herself.

Susan didn't want to have to explain her sex life to her daughter. It wasn't right. She wasn't going to tell her daughter that her father had lost interest in sex two whole years before she even dreamed of having an affair. She would never tell her that she had tried everything to entice him, going as far as getting a makeover, losing weight, dressing up, dressing down, boots in the bedroom, she'd even attempted to woo him in peep-hole lingerie. He had laughed at her.

He had laughed at her a lot. She would cry and he'd storm out. Sex was not something he was interested in having with his wife and she missed it. She wanted to feel attractive and alive and loved and not like an old woman, dried up and finished waiting for death. She was forty-six and sexual and horny. She wanted sex from her husband. She bloody deserved it and she was angry because he had made her hate herself and sad because she missed what they once had and guilty because it was wrong to do what she had done with Keith and yet a part of her screamed that she was innocent because Andrew had left her first. He may not have fucked somebody else but he wasn't fucking her either and he should have been because that was his bloody job. She had friends but what she wanted was her husband and he just wasn't there. But she couldn't say that to Beth. All she could say was that she was sorry, but sorry wasn't good enough.

Beth all but spat at her mother. "You disgust me!" she said, grabbing her coat.

"Where are you going?" Susan begged.

"Home to see my dad and to apologise for being such a stupid bitch!"

She slammed Harri's front door.

Harri got out of the bath and into her bathrobe and entered the sitting room to find Susan sitting in the middle of the floor. Susan didn't need to rehash the argument. Harri had heard it all through thin doors and walls. She didn't have to explain her point of view or excuse herself either because Harri knew that Susan's husband had cruelly lost interest in her a long time before.

"I'm sorry," Harri said.

"There's a lot of that going around lately."

"There is."

Later Harri and Sue sat together drinking cocoa and watching an episode of *CSI Miami*, Harri having exhausted *CSI Las Vegas*.

"You really need to get over *CSI*," Susan commented halfway through the show.

"I know. Did I mention there's a *CSI New York*?"

"Oh sweet Jesus!" Sue sighed. "You do know that it's basically the same bloody show over and over and over again, don't you?"

"That's what I like about it," Harri said, nodding. "I find it comforting."

★ ★ ★

Andrew didn't get home until after eleven. Beth was waiting.

She had cried most of the evening. She had phoned four of her friends, her favourite cousin Jessica and the ex-boyfriend that gave her crabs. He was most sympathetic and offered to come over but after serious consideration she decided against allowing him access to her home. Her grief made her weak to his advances and as much as she still missed him she didn't trust him not to give her another dose of something unpleasant. She waited for her dad in the kitchen sitting at the table, back hunched, hands clasped and head held low.

He seemed to receive a slight shock when he opened the kitchen door to reveal her foreign demeanour emphasised by silence. She raised her head slowly.

"Beth?" he said, betraying a slight panic.

"I'm sorry, Dad," she replied.

"Sorry for what, love?" he said with a voice quickly succumbing to a tremor. He sat beside her.

"She told me the truth," Beth said and she was crying.

Andrew blanched.

"She told me what she did."

"Right," seemed to be the only word he could manage.

"She's gone."

"Right," he repeated nodding.

"Why didn't you tell me, Dad?" Beth asked, bewildered. "All those times I attacked you for being a dick to Mum. It was her all along."

"And she's gone?" he said in mumble.

"Dad?"

"Yes."

"Why didn't you tell me?"

"Because I wanted space to forgive her."

"But you couldn't?" she asked in a voice that suggested she knew the answer.

"No, I suppose I couldn't."

"Screw her!" Beth said, hugging her dad. "You have me, Dad, so screw her." And Beth adamantly transposed every single ounce of anger she had held for her father onto her mother in that single moment. *I can't believe she's done this to us.*

Andrew hugged his daughter and although he didn't speak his head was bursting with too many thoughts travelling in too many directions, causing an ache. *She's really gone? She told Beth – the bitch, I begged her not to. Are we over? For how long? For good? What about Beth? Is this what I wanted? I hate her. Where is she? This is my fault. Will I miss her? Twenty-six years. Twenty-six years. Twenty-six years. Why was sex so fucking important to her? Why couldn't she take me as I am? What's wrong with me? Will I be alone now forever? I should have forgiven her or at least pretended to but if I had let her back in she would have worked it out. There's something wrong with me. I'm not a man. Oh God, my wife is gone!*

Andrew returned to the room he had shared with his wife seven months before. The dressing table was void of anything Susan. Her dresser drawers and her side of the wardrobe were empty of clothes. The bedclothes were changed because even as she left him she was kind enough to ensure he returned to a clean bed. He sat down on the left and familiar side of his freshly made marital bed. It was this bed that had broken their marriage. For such a long time Susan and Andrew had worked so beautifully. They laughed together, enjoyed each other's company, shared ideas, opinions and an interest in most things. He never understood her impulse to buy kitchen utensils but aside from that they were usually in unison. In fact up to three years ago they would have been seen as the perfect couple and that's not bad going after twenty-three years of marriage. But then it changed. He changed. Andrew began to experience difficulty in the bedroom. Andrew grew up on a farm and was the son of a wealthy farmer and the middle child of six. He had two sisters, both Irish dancers, and three brothers all strapping big lads and none shorter than six feet-twp. Andrew had been a boxing county champion at sixteen. He was as smart as he was big and the first of his brothers to go to university. He studied law and excelled and when he grew tried of that he bought property and when that no longer satisfied him he lectured part-time before setting up an investment-property consultation business which quickly became a thriving success much like everything else he'd ever done. He liked to drink, play cards, golf and he played football well into his forties. Andrew was a man's man, having come from a long line of men's men and he wasn't used to failure. That is until three years ago when that man, the only one he knew, began to ebb away. At first he thought he was just tired but after a while he wondered if he had actually lost interest in his wife but he hadn't, at least he didn't think so. She was still beautiful to him despite a slight middle-aged spread, a crude C-section scar and stretch marks. In fact he kind of liked those; they were silvery and told the story of their miracle daughter. He used to trace the lines with his finger marvelling at how the little girl fast asleep in the next room had come from such a petite woman. He wondered if he was stressed but he didn't feel stressed except when his wife pressured him for sex. Then he felt nothing but stress, most especially when she went to great lengths to titillate him. And yes he had laughed at her and in truth he didn't know why he'd done so. He could only reason that it was panic-induced. He hadn't meant to laugh and he knew how much he had hurt her and so many times he had thought about talking to her but he couldn't No matter how hard he tried he couldn't bring himself to admit what was really going on. She had got so angry and he was so embarrassed. It sounds stupid for a grown man to be embarrassed in front of his wife but he was and the longer it went on the harder it was to confide in her or anyone. He'd made an appointment with his GP once and he'd even made it to the car park but no further. As he was parking it occurred to him that he was in the same golf club as his GP so obviously that wasn't going to work. He kept hoping the problem would go away but it didn't. Initially three years ago when he began suffering problems he had tried a number of remedies such as vigorous masturbation leading to a strained wrist and a slight penis bleed which almost caused a cardiac arrest. *My dick my dick oh God my dick!* He didn't try that again. Instead he watched porn, all kinds – soft core and sensual, hard core and downright grab-you-by-the-back-of-the-neck filthy but nothing worked. He phoned sex lines and talked with women with names like Busty or Pussy Freak. Busty was nice enough – she had a sexy French accent and was a Neil Simon fan. He didn't stay on the line with Pussy Freak for too long – she came on a little strong and had a voice so deep she could pass for a man. Of course he tried Viagra which did nothing but make him feel dizzy and a little sick. And after he found his wife kissing another man he got into his car and drove until he spotted a whore. She jumped in and ten minutes later he was sitting with his pants around his ankles and she was sucking and sucking but he just couldn't get hard.

"Here, Mister? You'd want to see someone about that."

And now his wife was gone. His marriage as pathetic as it was, was now over and all because of his inability to confess his grotesque disability, his humiliating impotency and if only he'd had the courage. He hated himself, he hated that his stupid stubborn childish ridiculous behaviour had allowed him to stand by while the woman he loved tore herself in two trying to please him; and he hated that he hadn't the courage or strength to ask for help but how could he ask and where would he go and who would he confide in and how would he say it? How does a fifty-year-old man who has never asked for or needed help for anything set about admitting needing help? More importantly how could a man's man and a man like Andrew admit to impotency?

"Dad, you're crying," Beth said and he wiped his tears away. She had knocked on his bedroom door but he hadn't answered.

She put a tray holding a mug of tea and a plate of biscuits on the bed beside him.

"Thanks," he said.

"She doesn't deserve you," Beth said and her father closed his eyes.

"I'm really tired," he admitted.

"Me too," she said.

"I'll see you for breakfast," he promised.

"Okay."

She closed the door behind her and she was gone. He looked around the room and shook his head and resumed crying because his daughter was right. Susan didn't deserve him she deserved better than him and now she'd probably go out into the world and find that better man.

August 3rd 1975 - Sunday

My mam was really weird this morning. I found her sitting in the middle of the front garden. It was raining and she was just sitting there. She was crying and when she saw me for a second it was almost as though she didn't recognise me. Tingles went up and down my back. It was eerie. Then she was fine. I picked her up and we walked inside together and I made her some breakfast and she asked after Matthew and it was like nothing had happened. I really think HE's pushing her over the edge but there's nothing I can do about it. I'm going to stay in tonight just to make sure she's okay. There's a programme on about the ceasefire so I'll watch that with her. She'd like that.

Last night was good. Matthew brought me to a really nice restaurant. The prices were huge but he gets a big allowance so he said I could have whatever I wanted but to be honest it was all a bit too fancy for me. I'd have way preferred a Big Mac Meal and a coke to animal livers and duck. Ducks are cute, I really don't like the idea of eating them but I have to admit it was tasty but only if I closed my eyes because it looked disgusting on the plate. We went back to his place and his dad called us into his drawing room. He was watching 'The Late Late Show' and Gay Byrne was talking to Minnie Brennan from 'The Riordans'. Her hair was lovely. Matthew's dad asked us what we were doing. Matthew told him nothing. His dad told him to tread carefully. Matthew told him to go back to Argentina and his dad threw a glass at him!!!! Matthew ducked but I never saw it coming and it barely missed me. It smashed right over my head. I only got my fingers out of bandages and now my head was nearly split open. Matthew's dad got a shock and started to CRY! Matthew called him a drunk and we went to his bedroom. Matthew put on Elton John and he told me that since his dad split up with his bit he'd been drinking and acting the eejit. That and it will be Matthew's mam's anniversary the day after tomorrow. I told Matthew that we should visit her. He didn't want to but I insisted. I'm going to make a picnic and the weather forecast is good so we can sit and eat with her for a while and it'll be nice. I'm looking forward to it.

I was talking to Christopher Nolan the other day in town. He's a friend of Shane McCafferty's older brother. He said Shane's mam hasn't left the house since he died. I feel bad about not bringing over an apple pie but I asked Mam to make one and she said she was too tired. I should really learn to do it myself. I mean how hard can it be? Although now it's probably a bit too late, she'd probably think I was some sort of weirdo if I arrived up at the door with a pie now. Christopher said Shane's brother Éamonn isn't taking it too great either. He's broken up with his girlfriend Ellen after five years together and he's jacked in the football and he like Shane was a great footballer. I was still talking with Christopher when Father Ryan asked me to help him carry his shopping. It was too heavy for his bike as he'd done a big shop. Get a car, Fr Ryan!!! Anyway he carried two bags on the handlebars, one on the back of the bike with the handles wrapped around the seat and I carried the lightest one which wasn't so light. He asked about my mam and I said I was worried. He said he'd noticed she was a little off, himself. He said he'd found her sleeping in the confession box. I told him she sleeps a lot these days. He asked if HE was hitting her. I wish I could have said yes but he's been too busy staying out drinking to hit her. Suits me, he's at home so rarely it's like he doesn't live there any more. There's a lot of work at the docks and when he's not working he has enough money to keep him in the pub with his stupid toothless friend. Father Ryan thinks that Dr B should take a look at Mam, especially when I told him that sometimes she forgot to put on her skirt. It's weird I didn't think to say anything to Dr B. I knew she was acting weird but everything she does is weird to me. I should have said something. I should have realised something was wrong. My poor mam. What could it be? Father Ryan said it's probably just stress. I hope he's right and if it is I hope he takes one long look at himself because if she's stressed she's stressed because she brought that monster back into our house on Father Ryan's say so. I didn't say that though but he's no fool. He knew what I was thinking because I gave him the look.

Chapter sixteen

Something old something new

By the time Harri arrived George was frantic.

"Where were you?"

"Working."

"Nothing's ready, it's going to be a disaster," he said, shaking his head.

Harri looked around the shop with a smile. "It looks great!" She loved the floor-to-ceiling beechwood shelving running nearly the length of the left wall. The shop was narrow and the arched ceiling gave it a cavernous feel. The artwork that hung behind the till was bright and bold and the refrigerated room on the right was inspired and cold – it was bloody cold.

"George, let me out. Not funny, George."

"I see nipples."

"And I'm looking at a very swollen left testicle."

"Okay, okay!" He let her out as she had that look on her face that meant business – that plus she did three years of kick-boxing in her early twenties.

Upon release she was happy to report that the cold room was

beautifully appointed.

"It's a good finish," she said following him through the shop.

"What do you think of the spot lights? Are they too close together?"

"No. They're perfect."

"The painting?"

"I picked it. I love it."

"What about the flooring?"

"The flooring is exactly like I said it would be. It's fantastic."

It was as though George had forgotten that Harri had quite a large input into the décor but of course that was before her ill-fated wedding and she hadn't been on site since.

"It's all worked out beautifully," she grinned.

"You haven't seen the best bit," he said, grinning back, and she followed him down the spiral staircase into the cellar which had been converted into a tasting area. The room wasn't entirely set up. Aidan was sweeping the old flagstone floor with a sour face on him. The boxes lay open but the wine was yet to be uncorked. The nibbles were stacked and covered in cellophane.

"What do you want me to do?" she asked, taking off her jacket.

"The floor," Aidan said handing her the brush.

"Aidan!" George said in disgust.

"I'm pissed off sweeping, I'll open the wine." He flopped down on the bench and grabbed the opener.

Harri laughed at him and continued with the sweeping. Then George began to lay out the sandwiches and buff the glasses while Harri dusted around the shelving that housed even more wine. Five small round tables with four seats each were scattered around. Ray LeMontagne played on the CD. Once the tablecloths were de-creased and lying flat, the floor clean, the wine open and the food laid out it was time and so they waited, Aidan with a glass of wine, Harri with water because she was driving.

"Still or sparkling?" Aidan had asked.

"Still."

"At least have a sparkling."

"What's the bloody difference?" Harri laughed, shaking her head. She noticed her brother raise his eyebrows.

"Bubbles. Obviously."

"I don't want bubbles."

"You've no sense of adventure, you know that?" Aidan said in a mood approaching a sulk. Aidan was spoiling for a fight. *Uh oh.*

George walked around in circles with a double expresso from the place next door.

"No one's coming," he said.

"It's one minute past eight,' Harri pointed out.

"No one is coming," he repeated.

"And I'm the drama queen!" Aidan pointed out, snickering.

"Calm down," Harri soothed her brother. "They'll be here."

They sat in silence while Ray sang 'Can I stay?'. The door bell rang just as he was asking someone unseen to whisper to him. George was up the stairs in seconds leaving Harri alone with Aidan.

"Everything all right?" she asked.

"Everything's great," he confirmed but his demeanour suggested he was lying.

For a while Harri had sensed all was not well with Aidan and George and wondered how long it would be before they'd split up again. *He's never going to be who you want him to be, Aidan.*

George arrived downstairs followed by four strangers including the very wine critic he had hoped for. After that it was Harri who would trudge up and down the attractive but energy-consuming stairs to answer the door.

The night was in full swing. George was talking business and charming the pants off two middle-aged women one of whom was the critic he was set to impress.

"Oh, here we fucking go! George Clooney has entered the building," Aidan sneered from the corner.

"Aidan!" Harri warned.

"Well, look at him all over them. It makes me sick."

He walked away leaving Harri to worry.

Duncan and Gloria were in the corner talking with Melissa and

Gerry. Duncan was smiling proudly at his son's achievement and when George gave his father a moment of his time he told him so rapturously, slapping him on the back. "I'm proud of you, son!" George was polite and stood with his dad for a minute or two but their encounter was awkward.

George had yet to find it in himself to forgive his parents their terrible lie despite all appearances to the contrary. Gloria didn't notice, she was too busy ignoring her family's new reality and instead devoting herself to catching up with Melissa about the babies and Gerry about work and a shared love of watching golf on TV.

Harri and Aidan were the designated wine-pourers.

Susan arrived with a partner. "This is Keith."

Harri nearly dropped the bottle on the flagstone floor. "Hello, Keith. It's lovely to meet you."

Aidan was a little tipsy. "Not bad, Sue, not bad at all," he said, nodding.

Keith just stood there. Sue went red. Aidan winked at Keith and a clearly perturbed Keith downed his glass of wine.

Harri dragged Aidan into the back storeroom. "What are you doing?"

"Surely you mean what the hell is Sue doing?"

He had a point.

"I don't know – it's a bit weird," she admitted.

"It's fucking insane. Andrew's on the guest list."

Harri nearly fell out of her standing. "He's not coming, is he?"

"Well, he said he might. Actually he said he might bring Beth."

"Sweet Jesus! Red alert! Red alert!" Harri repeated the word red and alert another three times while walking up and down the storeroom.

"Calm down," Aidan said laughing.

Harri was crap in a crisis but always entertaining like the time she was caught up in a bank raid on Henry Street. The raiders told the customers to get on the floor and when they queried as to why she remained standing she admitted it was because she couldn't remember how to bend her knees. The raiders had a sense of humour which her father said was a good thing or else she'd have left the place with a bullet in her.

Aidan promised to deal with Susan if Harri would deal with the tasting table. He was getting tired of using the word 'soupçon'. Initially he had felt the term lent him a certain air of professionalism but four glasses of wine imbibed and twenty-four soupçons later he was reaching his limit.

"Waiter, the Barolo. Mmmm . . . I'm tasting tobacco, vanilla, chocolate and . . ."

"A soupcon of wild strawberry."

The man with the large nose smiled and Aidan smirked. *I'm not a waiter and read the back of the bottle, dicknose!*

Dicknose called Aidan over to him many times that night just so he could talk at him. "Now, young man, the Bardolino – I'd say it's light and fruit-filled with a faint cherry flavour and . . ."

"A soupçon of spiciness." Aidan smiled that really sickly smile that meant bad things could happen, to those who knew him.

"Indeed." The man who didn't know smiled back.

I'm not going to do you, you old queen. Aidan was bored. He wanted to get away from all this stuffy wine crap, he was sick of watching George flirt with the women. *You're gay, okay. You're gay.* He wanted to drink a beer and dance to Kelly Clarkson rather than age to Ray LeMontagne and Peggy bloody Lee.

"Who the hell put on Peggy Lee?" he asked when he approached Sue.

She shrugged her shoulders.

"Right, come on, get your coat, we're leaving."

"I've just got here."

"Andrew and Beth may be coming."

"Keith, drink up."

They were gone before the wine hit the back of the builder's throat.

When George had a minute Harri explained that Aidan had left with Sue.

"Thank God! If he used the term soupçon one more time I was

going to murder him." Andrew and Beth never appeared.

Duncan and Gloria left, having enjoyed a lovely night, with Melissa and Gerry who were running home to have a shag because they had the will and the energy and if they hurried it might just last until they made it into the sack. The tasters and critics left smiling. George closed the shop doors just after eleven.

"Not bad," he said nodding. "Not bad at all."

Harri smiled and agreed. "It went well."

"Have a glass of wine with me," he begged. "I need to come down from all the coffee."

"I'm driving."

"One glass."

"Half a glass."

"Good," he said leading her downstairs.

The candle in the middle of the table was flickering, nearing its end. Harri and George were sitting opposite one another in the dim light clinking glasses.

"I love Paul Weller," George said smiling.

"Who the hell is Paul Weller? Does Aidan know? Is that why he's so angry?" Harri asked, alarmed enough to dribble a little wine.

George laughed at his musically retarded sister. "It's the guy singing on the CD."

"Oh," she said and laughed a little. *It could have been Paul Gascoigne singing for all I know.*

"I asked James," he said.

Harri nearly choked. "You didn't."

"I was hoping he'd come. I know you miss him."

"Understatement," she laughed a little. "What's that saying? You never know what you've got till it's gone."

Her brother squeezed her hand and she smiled at him. "I even miss his stupid knock-knock jokes."

"Don't!" George said laughing at the memory. "Knock-knock!"

"George."

"Knock-knock!"

"Who's there?" Harri said with her head in her hands.

"Wooden."

"Wooden who?"

"Wooden you like to know!"

He was laughing and Harri joined in.

"He'll come back, Harri," he said then, "maybe not tonight but he will be back."

"Nice dream," she smiled. "What about you and Aidan? Why is he so angry?"

"It's hard."

"I know."

"We're so different."

"I know."

"I do care about him."

"I know."

"Stop saying 'I know'."

"Okay," she grinned.

"Who ever said that opposites attract?" George asked, swirling the contents of his glass.

"Paula Abdul."

"Well, then, that says it all, doesn't it?" he grinned.

"You know what he said the other night. He said I hate myself. Can you believe he actually thinks that?"

"I can."

"What?"

The shock registering on George's face was funny, making Harri grin. She wasn't grinning for long.

"Excuse me?" George's tone was elevated, suggesting he was getting snotty.

Oh no and we were having such a nice time.

"Look, George, everyone who loves you knows that there is part of you that would prefer to be straight."

"Bullshit."

"George you're a modern-day Rock Hudson. In public you're every woman's dream only in private you're, you know, yourself."

"Oh, come on! I can't help it if women find me attractive."

"No, you can't, but you don't have to encourage them and you do. You want strangers to think you're straight."

"Because it's easier."

"Easier to pretend to flirt outrageously all night with those two women? That's not easy."

"It's business."

"Okay."

"You don't believe me."

"You forget I'm the one who found you cutting yourself at sixteen. I'm the one who held you when you cried for two days when you couldn't make yourself shag Grace Fanning."

"That was one crisis summer and I came out earlier then most of the gay men I know."

"You came out to Mum, Dad and me. You came out in the Ryan household where nobody talks about anything. You didn't come out to your friends or your classmates or anyone else until you were well into your twenties."

"Just because I'm not Liberace doesn't mean I'm not content with my lot."

"I hope so, George, 'cause you've got a lot."

"And you?" he said, changing the subject as a consensus as to whether or not his sister and boyfriend had a point would not be reached on that night.

"What about me?"

"Aidan told me about Matthew Delamere."

"Oh."

"You're not even curious?"

"I am," she admitted. "I'm very curious."

"So?"

"So tomorrow's my birthday," she said. "My *real* birthday."

"I hadn't registered the date," he admitted.

She shrugged.

"You're going down there, aren't you?" he said.

"Yeah," she nodded.

He sighed. "You're sure?"

"Positive."

"You want me to come with you?"

"No."

"Thank Christ! I've just opened a business."

Harri laughed. George was a selfish old sod but at least he was honest about it.

Later that night when she was tucked up in bed she wondered what she would have done if James had been there. She missed his face, the crinkle under his eyes, the way he grinned, the way he licked his left incisor just before making a point. She missed his hair, his hands and everything else that began with 'h'. *I miss your hamstrings.* She missed all of him and it ached. She wondered about Matthew Delamere and what he must have gone through in the wake of losing his girlfriend. *Did he really love her? Does a seventeen-year-old really understand love? Did he ache? Did he bury a part of himself with her? Does he even remember her?*

Harri stared at the picture her dad had given her of a smiling seventeen-year-old Liv stroking an old horse. She had such light in her eyes and a dirty grin. She was tall, much taller than Harri, and lean. They had the same hair and cheekbones but it was hard to see any other similarities when she looked from the girl in the picture to herself in the mirror before her but then the girl in the photo was just a kid. The very next day, July 11th 2006, was Harri Ryan's actual birthday and Matthew Delamere's girlfriend Liv would be dead thirty years. *I'm so sorry. I wish I could change it for you. I hope you're resting in peace, pretty girl.*

* * *

"Harri?" James repeated. "Harri, I know it's you," he sighed. "Are you going to say something?" A few seconds passed. "Harri, this is ridiculous."

"Sorry."

"At last she speaks."

"How did you know it was me?"

"No one else calls me in the middle of the night with nothing to say."

"Sorry."

"Stop apologising. What time is it?"

"Just after three."

"What's wrong?"

"I have a picture of my mom. My real one, not Gloria."

"Does she look like you?"

"I don't think so. Sue thinks she does and Melissa said so too but I don't see it."

"Does she look happy?" he asked and it made Harri smile.

"Yeah, she does."

"Good," he replied and Harri felt instantly better.

She'd first called him on the night that Melissa had showed her a picture of her father. She had been silent that night too. She had really only wanted to hear James's voice but then she changed her mind and pretended there was something wrong with the line.

"Can you hear me now?" she'd asked.

James's turn to be silent.

"Do you mind that I called?" she'd asked.

"No," he replied. "Nice to hear your voice."

She'd told him about her dad.

"Do you want to meet him?" he'd asked.

"No," she'd said, not really knowing if her answer was true.

"Well, there's plenty of time," he counselled.

"I haven't had a panic attack," she said.

"Of course you haven't. They only tend to happen when you're due to marry me." He said it lightly but she could sense his pain.

"Not true," she said. "My parents admitted it used to happen a lot when I was a kid."

"But they said . . ." He trailed off as it occurred to him that her parents had done a lot of lying and in the general scheme of things that particular lie was inconsequential.

Still it was nice to know and Harri was glad that she had told him. They had talked on and off since that night. It was always on Harri's instigation, when she was at breaking point, and usually the call began with silence. Except for once, two weeks previously when she'd seen him in a coffee shop in Bray with Tina Tingle. Tina was leaning in for a kiss and only for the fact that she was walking with a client discussing fabric samples she would have fallen to her knees right there on the street.

That phone call began with the words. "Tina Fucking Tingle!"

James had laughed but Harri wasn't amused.

"How the hell?" he'd asked.

"I saw you," she said in a tone dripping with disgust.

"Saw us what?" he'd replied with good humour.

"Kissing!" She said the word through gritted teeth.

James laughed. "Since when has a peck on the cheek constituted romance which I presume by your tone is what you believe you witnessed."

"Peck on the cheek?" she said, realising that if anyone had cheek it was her. *Who the hell do I think I am?*

"I'm converting her attic," he said.

Tina Tingle has her own attic. For some reason Harri had seen Tina Tingle as a permanent renter.

"How is she?" she asked, resuming a normal tone as though the call had just begun and therefore was merely continuing on a pleasant note.

"She's fine," he said. "Married."

"Married," Harri repeated slightly winded.

"To a dentist."

"A dentist. Jesus!" Harri had never really seen Tina Tingle married to a dentist. "Did she ask about me?"

"No," he said.

"Oh."

It was weird. Tina and Harri had lived together for some years and yet when Harri moved out their friendship had ended abruptly without malice or an ill word or deed. It just simply ended. It turned out that Tina and Harri had nothing more in common than a shared address. So why would she ask about Harri but then again Harri had asked about her.

"Well, I asked after her."

"No, you didn't," James reminded her. "You saw me with her, presumed an affair and called her names!" He was laughing.

It amazed her how he could be so pleasant to her after she left him at the altar not once but twice. She wondered if he missed her as much or even half as much as she missed him. She knew either way it wouldn't matter because once James had made up his mind to give her space, there was nothing she could say or do that would change his mind. She hoped that he would live up to his promise of waiting for her. She knew if she didn't hurry up and sort herself out he could slip away from her. *What if I never really know who I am? What if the only thing I want is you? What if while I'm flaffing around trying to find myself you find someone else? Bollocks to this finding yourself stuff! Is it really necessary? I mean I am what I am whatever that is and I want my life back with you and me and our little country kip that's falling down around us and maybe a house instead of the apartment and a rabbit. I'm seriously thinking about getting a rabbit. Isn't that enough?*

"I should go," he'd said.

"Right, me too."

"Bye."

"Bye," she repeated.

He used to end every call with 'I love you'. If truth be told it used to get on her wick a bit because it meant she would have to say 'I love you too' and that was okay if she was alone but she felt stupid saying 'I love you too' in front of strangers on public transport or in a shop or in the queue at the bank or God forbid a garage where invariably she'd get some crack from an old fart with too much time on his hands: "Do you love me three, darling? Ha! Do ya see what I did there? Go on, you good thing!" She had often bitched about that very fact to Aidan but she missed it now that it was gone. She had made a real effort to stop calling when she realised that she was averaging a call a week. She was scared she would end up relying on him too much and afraid that if he did find someone new, someone who knew who she was and what she wanted and wasn't verging on being a little bit mental, that she'd be asked by him not to call any more and that would kill her. Still, that night at three o'clock with her mother's photo still in her hand and tears falling from her eyes all she wanted to do was talk to James. And, when after less than three minutes on the phone he had made her feel considerably better and therefore suitably sleepy, she was glad that she'd called even though talking to him was sometimes more painful than not talking to him.

August 9th 1975 - Saturday

I had such a great day with Sheila. It was hot and we spent it on the beach sunning ourselves and catching up. It seems like ages since we'd been alone together. She said that Dave shoves his knickers up his arse and does a funny walk while doing an eerily good impression of her mother giving out about the price of a nice slice of ham. She did an impression of him doing an impression of her mam, shoving her bikini bottoms up her own arse, just as Mrs Brown from Brown's bakery was passing. Mrs Brown didn't seem too impressed but I was rolling around. She said her dad's thinking about selling the bar and retiring. He comes from Kerry and he's always wanted to go back. She says she really doesn't want him to sell and basically threw the hissy fit to beat all hissy fits when he mentioned it. She says if they sell they'll definitely end up in Kerry and where will that leave her? She has one more year left of school and where will she come home to if they bugger off to Kerry? After messing up one too many hair styles she's back to considering nursing now and she's pretty sure that's what she wants to do especially after Dave stood on a piece of glass and she pulled it out and cleaned and bandaged the wound. He was crying like a baby but she said that even though he was wailing and carrying on she did a really brilliant job. I could see her as a nurse. She's definitely bossy enough. If Sheila told you to drop your drawers you would.

Dr B asked me in for a cup of tea on Wednesday. I was passing the gate lodge on my way to the stables. I still can't believe I'm back in the stables. I bet the only reason Matthew's dad kicked me out of the office is because I saw him cry. Anyway it's not so bad. I did miss Betsy and Nero and Henry is a nicer boss by far and it's way nicer to be around Matthew and to watch him ride. He looks amazing on a horse. It's a pity he's way too tall to be a jockey but then again it wouldn't suit him to be short. Anyway Dr B called me in for a cup of tea. We talked about my hand and he made me flex it a few times and we listened to the radio and the DJ played a song called 'Born To Run' by a guy called Bruce Springsteen and Dr B turned it up and we danced in his kitchen. He was twirling me around and we were laughing and that man can really sing and it was weird, I really did feel like I wanted to run somewhere. The DJ said that it wasn't available to buy and that he had got it in America so I've been listening to his show every night since just to hear it. I think Dr B is lonely. He tends to stay away from the crowd keeping himself to himself. It's a pity but I suppose he doesn't like football, drinking and fighting. I told him he should learn to ride. I've got much better and I'd help him out. He could start off on Betsy. Matthew said he'd help him too. So that's what we did. We went riding yesterday. Matthew was on Nero, I took Favourite, she's Henry's best pony, and we put Dr B on Betsy. She was good to him and had him galloping in no time. He really took to it and I'd say he'll keep doing it. He was really happy afterwards.

When he went home Matthew and I went walking in the woods. He looked so handsome in the streaming light and he pulled me in to him and leaned on a tree and kissed me and told me that he loved me and I told him I loved him too and every part of me wanted to burst and it felt so good. Sometimes when I'm alone sitting in this room behind a locked door I wish I didn't love anything or anyone because everybody knows that love hurts, but I do so I'll have to live with it. Since I've met him I've never been happier. He makes me smile and feel warm inside and when he touches me my heart races and my hands sweat and I lose the power of thought and speech and my head buzzes and my heart and stomach dance and spin and I'd die for him. I'd die for him with a smile on my face.

Mam thinks I'm going to Dublin with Sheila and her mother next weekend but I'm not. I'm going camping with Matthew. Mam won't know any different. She has given up her cleaning job and I can't remember the last time she bothered to leave the house. Anyway I don't really think she cares and HE, well he and I don't speak. He stays well clear, knowing I would kill him as soon as look at him.

I can't wait for next weekend for Matthew and me just to be alone together. Matthew will be going back to school in the first week of September and it seems like ages away but it's not. It will fly by and then he'll leave me and I'll be broken-hearted but I can't think about that now, all I can do is live for now and enjoy the time we have together. I'm not going to be miserable, I'm going to be happy and glad and things will work out. I just know they will.

Dr B tried to see Mam but she wouldn't let him in. Father Ryan tried to talk to her too but she shut the door on him too. She's not so bad at the moment though. She's wearing all her clothes and she's started to cook again and the other day she even did a bit of weeding. We watched '*Coronation Street*' together and she laughed at Deirdre and Ray. I can't remember what they were arguing about because I was surprised. I can't remember the last time I heard my mother laugh.

Yesterday morning I woke up crying I have no idea why but I felt a terrible darkness and so alone but that was a dream. I'm not alone at least not anymore. I've got Matthew. Father Ryan told me once that no one was alone as long as they had a relationship with God. Well, that's nice for him but give me Matthew over God any day!!!!!!

Today Matthew kissed me by the old stone wall and under a light blue warm sky with not a cloud in sight and then arm in arm he walked me home and at my door he told me I was the best thing that ever happened to him. I've never been anybody's best thing before. Today was a good day and maybe one of the best.

Chapter seventeen

A secret shared

Matthew Delamere woke a little after six. He lay static for a few minutes listening to the stranger next to him breathe. *What's her name? What's her name? What's her name?* The party the evening before had been impromptu and as a result of the successful purchase of a highly sought-after filly despite strong bidding competition. The hotel had been packed for the auction but there was also a wedding and a ladies' lunch and somehow all three events managed to blend at some point. The excitement had become too great for Henry and after a hearty meal he had been taken home early on in the proceedings by Alfio. Henry was still living in one of the lodges on the Delamere land and, although pushing eighty-two and officially retired, he still tended to the horses and could always be found strolling around the grounds. He loved a good auction especially when Matt flexed his considerable financial muscle.

"Oh, she's worth it, son," he said. "She's worth it all right." "Good man." "Good man yourself!"

Alfio had returned later to find his boss in the bar chatting up two ladies who were finished lunching and looking for something more fulfilling. Matt was only too happy to oblige.

"Ladies, this is Alfio."

Alfio bowed his head and smiled. It became obvious instantly that the blonde with the boob job was the object of Matt's desire. The pretty redhead smiled and patted the seat beside her. Tentatively Alfio sat. *Ambushed! Tomorrow he will suffer.*

"Alfio is a champion polo player," Matt said to the girls before signalling to the barman for more drinks.

"I was," Alfio said in a tone not too distant from huffy.

"Once a champ always a champ," Matt grinned and raised a glass to Alfio. *He's going to kill me. I hope she's worth it.*

"Oh, I loved *The Champ*. I've seen it a hundred times and it still makes me cry," the blonde said, laying her hand across her considerably sized breasts.

"Oh that's the one with the kid from *Silver Spoons* in it." The redhead shook her head. "What a little heartbreaker!"

"Some people shouldn't be allowed grow up," the blonde said with great authority.

Matt nodded his agreement before looking at Alfio who responded with a look that suggested he might be considering shoving a polo stick up his boss's arse.

"Yeah," the redhead said thoughtfully. "The kid from *Silver Spoons*, *The Uncle Buck/Home Alone* kid and that little spiky-haired one from *Jerry McGuire*."

"Ahhhhhhhhhhhhhhhhhhhhh!" the blonde said, slapping her friend's hand. "I love him!"

"Remember the bit about the human head?" the redhead squealed.

"It weighs eight pounds!" the blonde almost shouted. They both laughed.

Matthew put his hand up to his face so Alfio couldn't tell if he was laughing, grinning or reconsidering his need for sex. *Please, please, please reconsider.*

Matt didn't reconsider and so Alfio was forced to listen to

twittering and bullshit talk and bear witness to tentative groping and when it was time to book a room which no doubt Matt would do, he would be obliged to make an excuse to the redhead because he just wasn't interested. Alfio sat quietly while Matt held court, making the two ladies giggle and squeal. He thought about the girl he'd left at home in Argentina, a sweeping brunette beauty with large coffee-brown eyes, mocha skin, full mouth, full bosom, legs long and lithe. She was intelligent, fiery, strong, athletic and funny. She was everything. *Ah Maria, you have ruined me.* He smiled kindly at the tiny redhead who was telling a story that involved traffic.

"Bumper to bumper and no one was going anywhere and I thought 'I'll never hold on'. So two hours later and with tears in my eyes I hitched up my skirt and peed at the side of the car while three builders in a Hiace shouted 'Go on, ya good thing!'"

Cue laughter from the blonde and Matt.

Alfio had had enough.

"Oh no, stay!" the redhead begged.

"I'm really tired," he explained.

"One more drink!"

"No, thank you."

"Ah, come on!"

"No."

"Ah, you will!"

"This is beginning to sound familiar," laughed the blonde. "G'wan, G'wan, G'wan!"

The redhead covered her mouth. "Oh my God, I'm Missus Doyle!"

The two women were laughing raucously again. Alfio hadn't a clue as to the reference nor did he care.

"Oh Alfio, you wouldn't know this but we're quoting from a very funny Irish comedy – it's called *Father Ted*," the redhead said with her hand firmly fixed around his arm. *You're going nowhere, Mister.*

"Really," he sighed.

"Poor Dermot Morgan, he was taken too young." The blonde shook her head.

"RIP," the redhead said solemnly and blessed herself, thereby loosening her grip on Alfio and he was gone.

The disappointed redhead left in a taxi soon after.

Matt and the blonde made their way to his hastily booked suite soon after.

What's her name? What's her name? What's her name?

Now in the cold light of day and with a headache, he was sorry he'd stayed. The blonde was a board in bed. She just lay there with a fixed expression while directing: "No. No. Not down there." "Here touch me here." "I don't like it on top." "I don't want to move." "Have you come yet?" She dropped off after twenty minutes and even as a sleeper she was annoying, being both restless and loud.

He knew by her breathing that she was still sleeping heavily and so he got up and showered leisurely and she only woke when he was shaving.

"Morning, Matt," she said, standing behind him and looking into the bathroom mirror.

"Morning, sexy," he grinned from force of habit rather than anything else.

"Will I order breakfast?" She reciprocated his grin.

"If you're hungry, order what you want, I'll take care of the bill," he winked at her.

"You're not staying?" She sounded disappointed.

"I have an early business meeting. Sorry, sexy."

She smiled and nodded. "OK." *I'm going to order everything on the menu and rob anything that isn't nailed down, you using tosser!* "It was nice while it lasted," she smiled.

"It certainly was," he lied while emptying the sink of water. He put his clothes on in seconds.

Plenty of practice, no doubt, she thought watching him from the bed she had returned to. He was gone in less than five minutes and five minutes after that the blonde began ordering from the extensive menu.

Alfio was waiting in the car with two takeaway coffees, two Danish pastries and an *Irish Times.*

"You're a lifesaver."

"*Beso mi culo, boludo*!"

Matt smiled. "I'll give you that. Last night was not me at my most shining."

"*Come mierda!*"

"You eat shit!" Matt laughed.

"They say that the Argentineans are hot-blooded but I've never known a man to air out his dick as much as you, Matt Delamere," Alfio said in disgust.

"I will take that as a compliment."

"It wasn't meant as one."

"Doesn't matter." Matt grinned at Alfio who was shaking his head and smiling to himself.

It was after eight when Alfio drove into the long winding driveway and past the gatehouse, past the stables, past the training grounds and to the house. Matt got out and Alfio drove on to the car park. He had a full day ahead of him breaking in a Californian thoroughbred stallion.

Matt entered the house by the back door. Patsy Byrne the housekeeper was standing on a chair, cleaning out the presses.

"You'd want to watch yourself, Patsy, that's a broken hip waiting to happen," he said from the doorway.

"Are you trying to say I'm old?"

"No comment," he grinned and she smiled.

"So help me down," she said.

"I'll get you a proper stepladder. Health and safety and all that. Maybe for your birthday," he laughed.

"Charming," she said, pretending to be annoyed.

An hour passed before Matthew left his home again, dressed in riding gear and with a large bunch of flowers he'd grabbed from the vase in the hall. He rode past the training grounds, the stables, the long driveway, the gate lodge, through Devil's Glen and down the narrow road that took him to the graveyard. He tied up the horse at the entrance and walked the rest of the way. It was just after nine thirty and the graveyard was empty save for an old lady hunched over a worn gravestone. The scarf hid her face and he passed her so quickly that she probably hadn't even noticed company.

He made his way down to her grave where he stood resting his free hand on the stone that bore her name while clutching the flowers firmly to his chest.

"Hi there, kiddo," he said. "It's been a while, maybe even the full year. I was away at Christmas, I would have been here otherwise. I see Henry's been though, keeping the place tidy and the roses trimmed. He's good, still going strong. I think he'll outlive us all. Brendan's good too. What's that you used to call him – Dr B?" He laughed and sat on the grass beside her. "He's still living in the gate lodge. Can you believe it? He loves that old house and that old house loves him. He's done a lovely refurbishment job on it. The old fella has taste. Look at me calling Brendan old. He's fifty-five. I remember when Henry was fifty-five we thought he was ancient. I turned forty-seven three months ago, can you believe it? My dad was forty-seven when . . . He was in Monaco, remember? We'd had that massive row before he left. You stopped me from punching him. I was so annoyed with you . . . I'm sorry. Hey, remember the nights we spent by the castle looking up at the stars? I'd go back in a second," he sighed and shook his head. "I swear I'd go back in a second." He stopped talking, instead he just held on tight to her stone. "Hey, Liv, I still love you." He stood up. "But don't tell anyone, okay? It's our secret."

He was gone after ten minutes, leaving her resting place as quiet and serene as he'd found it.

Most of Matthew's day would be spent on the phone. Most of the calls were transatlantic and so he had until after lunch before his workday proper would begin. Brendan was sitting out in his garden when he passed, riding Shadow his favourite horse.

"Brendan."

"Matt. Come in. Have coffee with me."

Matt dismounted and tied and patted Shadow who shook his head vigorously. Matt sat and Brendan poured coffee from the percolator.

"You're expecting company?" Matt asked, referring to the extra cup.

"I was expecting you." Brendan smiled. "How's our girl?"

Matt nodded. "Still gone, Brendan," he sighed.

"Thirty years is a long time."

Matt nodded again. Words always seemed to fail him when Brendan talked of Liv. He never mentioned the baby; neither of them mentioned the baby. Matthew sat back in his chair. *She's thirty today. Happy thirtieth, Harriet Ryan. I wanted to call you Olivia after your mother. Olivia Delamere. Happy thirtieth, Olivia Delamere.* Matthew was miles away even as Brendan talked about his recent trip to Las Vegas.

"Dusty place. I wouldn't go again." He liked San Francisco. "You were right about San Francisco." In fact Brendan had liked San Francisco so much that he wished as a younger man it had occurred to him to get off his arse and move there or anywhere instead of hiding away in a wood in Wicklow. *It could have been so different.*

Later when Matt emerged from his haze he talked about his latest acquisition. They toasted to it with fresh coffee and Brendan's home-made muffins.

"You could have been a baker."

"I could have been a lot of things." Brendan grinned to himself and Matt laughed a little before they fell into a comfortable silence.

"Are you free for dinner tonight?" Brendan asked.

"I'm seeing Clara."

"Ah, the lovely Clara! Are you serious about her yet?"

"Jesus, Brendan, it's only been three months."

"Three months can be a lifetime."

"We'll see. She's a nice woman. Ticks all the boxes."

"Such a romantic," Brendan jested.

"You can talk!" Matt retorted.

"All right, all right," Brendan said with hands in the air. "I give up. I haven't a clue what I'm talking about."

Matt laughed. "We're a right pair!"

"We most certainly are." Brendan grinned. "How about tomorrow? I'll do a rack of lamb, we'll break out the cards and make an evening of it."

"Sounds good," Matt said, getting up. "I'll see you around seven."

Brendan was left alone in his garden after that. He contemplated life and death and the passage of time, he remembered Liv and her grin, her sense, her strength, her stubbornness, her open heart and her inability to lie. He missed his young friend. *What would you be like now?* He wondered. *Would you still be a fighter? Would you have held tight to your beliefs? Would the world have worn you down?*

⋆ ⋆ ⋆

Four miles away in a care home Liv's mother Deirdre sat in her chair by the heater under the large window which looked out onto the grounds. The gardens were separated by the long winding tarmac avenue that led to the electric gate and out of the hospital. The gate was too far to see from her chair but, when she closed her eyes, in her head she could hear the motor whir as it opened and closed. Her hands remained clasped in her lap which is something she did out of habit rather than as a result of any deliberation. She didn't have much use for her hands most of the day. She didn't dress herself, or prepare food or drinks, she didn't salute those who passed her and when she spoke which wasn't often she wasn't animated in any way. She did lift her own skirt when she went to the loo and she pulled down her own pants but after that she couldn't remember if she did much else with the hands she clasped on her lap.

A nurse approached with tea, laying it on the windowsill by the old radio she had constantly playing. She liked talk radio. Gerry Ryan was a great man for chat and in the afternoon she would listen to Joe Duffy. In fact she did use her hands to change the radio dial from Gerry to Joe and Joe to Gerry. And she used them to lift her cup and drink her tea.

It was a Tuesday and Tuesday was hair-wash day. She kept her hair short and even though it was grey and she didn't use much conditioner it was still soft and a little flyaway. She didn't like people touching her head. She didn't like hair-wash day. She didn't struggle or whine or moan, mostly she just cried a little. Tears flowed in silence. She wasn't one for making much noise.

"How you feeling, Deirdre?" Nurse Trisha asked.

"Fine," she said.

"Are you ready for your medication, love?"

Deirdre nodded. Trisha handed her the pills and Deirdre had them swallowed before the nurse had time to hand her a glass of water.

"I see you got some flowers," she said but Deirdre was finished interacting. Instead she was staring out the window at the gardener pruning a hedge.

"By your bed," Trisha said, attempting to reengage her but to no avail.

For Deirdre, Trisha's voice disappeared behind Gerry Ryan talking with some woman about weddings and bad music and drunken fumbling while she watched the sun redden the back of the gardener's neck.

The nurse made her way down the corridor and towards the staff room. Maisie was making coffee.

"Deirdre just got a serious bunch of flowers."

"No card," Maisie said.

"No," Trisha confirmed.

"He never leaves a card," Maisie said ominously, piquing Trisha's interest.

"Who?" Trisha asked, intrigued – after all it had been a slow morning.

"Matt Delamere," Maisie replied, handing Trisha a coffee.

"The trainer?"

"The very one."

"Why?" she asked, being new to both the hospital and the area.

"Did you ever hear about that girl who died giving birth in Devil's Glen in the mid seventies?"

"Yeah, I remember something about that. Very sad."

"Deirdre was the girl's mother. Matt Delamere was the boyfriend."

"Good God!" Trisha sighed.

"I know."

"So where was he when she was bleeding to death in a wood?"

"Who knows? That GP, what's his name, found her."

"Jesus."

"I know."

"And no one knew she was pregnant?"

"Well, if they did they certainly didn't make it known. Anyway back in those days you'd be sent off somewhere so I'd be surprised."

"He must have felt awful," she said, shaking her head.

"Well, he hasn't been paying Deirdre's bills for twenty years for nothing."

"You're joking me!"

Maisie nodded and walked out of the room leaving Trisha to ponder on a nice piece of gossip. *People live mad lives all the same.*

⋆ ⋆ ⋆

Susan was looking through some catalogues in the front passenger seat of the car. "There's some great stuff in here," she said to Harri who was driving. "Do you think we could nip in on our way? After all, Bray is on the way."

Harri sighed. "All right, all right. Don't get your knickers in a knot."

Sue had insisted on coming. As soon as Harri mentioned she was taking the day off, Sue knew something was up and questioned and hounded and annoyed her until eventually she broke. Usually Harri could have escaped Sue but unfortunately, seeing as she was camped out in her sitting room, avoidance was not an option. Already they were on the road four hours later than she'd intended. An order of Valbonne French distressed furniture had gone astray and Sue had spent most of the morning on the phone with the courier company while Harri made excuses to the client. *So much for a day off.*

"It will take less than an hour. We'll be in, we'll be out," Sue said, still flicking.

"Fine," Harri said, slightly aggravated. *I'm only going to visit my dead mother, no need to make it any kind of priority.*

"Great," Sue said happily. "We might stop for a bit of lunch too. I'm starving."

"You're pushing it!" Harri warned and judging by the look on her face she meant it.

Sue remained quiet, then she turned on the radio. Gerry Ryan was talking about wedding bands. Sue laughed. "You know what my wedding band was called?"

"No," Harri sighed.

"Mixed Grill," Sue grinned and Harri couldn't help but smile. "Still they were a ruddy good band." Then her smile faded and she became a little subdued having being reminded that her marriage was over.

The day was bright and warm, a yellow sun hung from a bright blue sky and Harri and Sue drove with the top down. The new motorway stretched before them and with it the promise of the kind of adventure that neither woman felt fully prepared for. For Harri the questions that swam around and around were simple. *What lies ahead? Am I doing the right thing? Do I really want to open this can of worms? Could I even turn around if I wanted to?* For Sue there was only one question. *What do I do if she falls apart?* The car took the women towards Wicklow with the sun on their backs. They smiled at one another intermittently but mostly they kept their eyes forward and their mouths shut.

* * *

Melissa would have loved to have spent the day with her friend on the first time she would celebrate her actual birthday – well, celebrate would be an exaggeration of what she would be doing. Mourning would be more accurate or maybe not mourning. After all, although she was visiting her dead mother, in reality she was merely visiting a dead stranger. Gloria was her mother and still very much alive. It was all a little confusing and hard to grasp, so much so that although she really wanted to be with her friend during her time of great need, she really hadn't a clue what to say to her. 'Chin up' was something she'd often say in the face of gloom and that didn't quite cut it, or her other favourite, 'never mind, it could happen to anyone' wasn't necessarily on the money either. Still she would have liked the opportunity to spend the day with Harri, not necessarily because she felt she could help, but because anything even a trip to the grave of a seventeen-year-old who bled to death in woods would be a break from the increasing demands her boss, her colleagues, her husband and her children were putting upon her. She was halfway through a presentation when the phone call came. She had asked not to be disturbed and poor Ellen was incredibly apologetic when escorting her out of the meeting room and toward the phone at the front desk.

It was Jacob's teacher. "Jacob has a pain in his tummy."

"Is he pale?"

"No."

"Hot?"

"No."

"Has he been sick?"

"No."

"Well, then, I'm sure he's fine."

"He's complaining of pain. I can't just ignore it."

Melissa sighed. "Sometimes he says he has a pain in his tummy if he's doing something he doesn't like doing."

"He's doing what he does every day and likes it just fine plus he didn't eat his lunch and refused a chocolate biscuit."

"I'm on my way." Jacob never refused a chocolate biscuit. *Why the hell didn't she lead with that?*

Jim met her in the cloakroom. "Where the hell are you going?"

"Jacob's sick."

"You're halfway through a presentation."

"I know and I'm sorry but there's nothing I can do."

"Where's your husband, your nanny, your mother?"

"Where indeed? On a day off and retired in Spain."

"Melissa."

"Jim."

"This can't go on. I depend on you. This firm depends on you."

"I'm sorry. I'll sort it."

"What am I supposed to say to the client?"

"Tell them I'm sorry, I'll reschedule for whenever suits them."

"Not good enough," Jim said, shaking his head.

"It's the best I can do," she said before taking her leave.

She tried to call her husband four times from the car but each time his phone went to voicemail. She arrived at Jacob's school a little after eleven. Jacob was waiting for her at the door.

"I have a pain."

"I know, buddy. I'm going to take you home, we'll put on *Thomas* and you can lie with Snuggles on the sofa."

The crèche rang as she was pulling out of Jacob's school. "Carrie vomited."

"Oh God. I'm on the way."

Carrie was asleep when she picked her up. She decided to bring the kids straight to the doctor. Jacob complained that she had promised him the sofa, *Thomas* and Snuggles and the doctor's office could not offer any of the three. She cajoled him with promises of a new *Thomas* toy when he got better. After spending an hour sitting in the doctor's waiting room and receiving his patented dirty look when she couldn't answer what her children had for breakfast as she had left the house early to prepare for the presentation she didn't get to make, and after an examination that lasted mere minutes, he concluded that the ailment was viral in nature and therefore would have to run its course. One prescription for a kiddie pain reliever and €60 later she was back in the car with a now awake and grumpy Carrie and a moaning Jacob. "My stomach still hurts."

The shopping centre car park was jammed but she eventually found parking. Carrie was now crying loudly and Jacob was rubbing his tummy and repeating the word sore over and over again in a particularly annoying sing-song voice. "Sore. Sore. Sore. Sore. Sore." With Carrie in her arms and Jacob by the hand Melissa navigated the busy shopping centre until she reached the chemist. Despite her daughter's wailing and her son's persistent moaning ringing in her ears she acquired the prescribed medicine and, laden with children, near deafened and suffering from an overloaded bladder, she began queuing to pay.

Her phone rang. It was her boss and she thought about ignoring the call but she, unlike her husband who she was contemplating battering to death, had never been able to ignore a phone. She dropped Jacob's hand and held the phone to her ear. Her boss rather snottily reported on their client's not so favourable response to her leaving mid-meeting.

"Mom!"

"Just a second, Jacob." Carrie was still crying. "Can I deal with this tomorrow?"

"Mom!"

"In a minute, Jacob."

"I need your password. I've promised to send on your presentation notes. It's the least we can do."

"Can I not send them on first thing?"

"Mom!"

"I'd rather they had them now."

"I'd prefer to do it myself."

"Well, we'd all prefer that you do it yourself, Melissa, but unfortunately I'm here and you are not."

She argued on that she wasn't comfortable with anyone else going through her computer. Jim argued that he didn't really care what was comfortable bearing in mind that her abrupt exit could lose them a client. She sighed and absentmindedly looked down toward where her son had been standing less then one minute before. He was gone. Initially she was not alarmed but then she looked around and she couldn't see him in the vicinity.

"Jacob!" she shouted into the phone. "Jacob!" she shouted again. She was moving now out of the queue and down the closest aisle.

"Melissa, what's wrong?" Jim asked.

"It's Jacob – he's gone," she said, now running down the next aisle. "Jacob!"

She hung up the phone and was yelling so loudly the manager came to her assistance. He and another girl called Jane also made their way around the shop calling out the name Jacob but he wasn't in the shop. He was gone. Melissa joined Carrie in crying. She sat on the floor and cried and cried and the poor manager did his best to calm her and the girl called Jane ran in and out of the shops next door asking if anyone had seen a little boy called Jacob. Security were then called.

Melissa was now shaking and Carrie was stunned into silence. "He was here and then he was gone," Melissa repeated to herself. "I was holding his hand but then work called." She was crying again. "Oh God, where is he?" She didn't think to try to call her husband. Her mind was a blank and fear had completely engulfed her. She could do nothing but repeat herself and bite her nails. "He's not well," she said a number of times. In her head were images of missing children. Jamie Bulger was abducted in a shopping centre and when he was found he was dead. *Oh my God!* Carrie was now clinging to her mother, wide-eyed and still. Melissa clung to her little girl, praying into her ear. *Please be okay, son. Please come back.*

Twenty long minutes had passed before a security guard called Tim arrived with Jacob by the hand. When she saw him Melissa, who was already crying, burst into larger tears accompanied by louder sobs. Jacob on seeing his mother near hysterical did likewise, jarring Carrie sufficiently for her to resume crying. Melissa hugged her wandering son so tightly the security guard had to separate them for fear the child would lose oxygen. Once calm and approximately another full ten minutes later Tim the security guard explained that he had found Jacob in the toilets.

"I needed to poo," Jacob said. "It was coming."

Melissa didn't scold him for running off. He had tried to get her attention. The child had the runs and she had ignored him in favour of arguing about a stupid bloody presentation. She gathered herself together and thanked the chemist manager, the young girl Jane and Tim the security guard and left the centre with the prescribed medication that the chemist manager had insisted she take for free. At home when her children were bathed and medicated and sleeping she poured herself a large whiskey and cried again. *I just can't do it any more.*

Melissa's problem was greater than exhaustion and a well meaning but ultimately unhelpful husband. Her problem was that she was fast becoming a stranger to herself. Once upon a time she was a dedicated worker and a professional, hailed as a stand-out performer. She had sailed through school, and college was a breeze, and from a very young age she was destined to have the fulfilling career her mother could only have dreamed of. Melissa's professional life was exciting, challenging and rewarding. It afforded her a large bank balance and the comforts associated with that. She was respected and contented. Life was good. Then she had Jacob. Initially on discovering her pregnancy she was delighted. And of course she had a plan. She was only six months gone when she'd found the perfect babyminder. She would take the minimum maternity leave and return to work. She knew that at first there would be teething problems like with any new venture. It was impossible to plan for every eventuality but she felt confident that once a routine was established she could do and have it all. Melissa didn't prepare herself for guilt. She didn't realise that with motherhood came worry like she'd never known, love that was frankly overwhelming and the greatest need to be with her baby. The day she returned to work she cried in the toilets for over an hour. She thought it would get easier to leave him but it didn't. She thought she'd fight the urge to call home twenty-five times a day but she couldn't. She thought that if she could just switch off that little part of her brain that constantly reminded her of what she was missing everything would return to normal and she would be the single-minded dedicated professional she had been before. It didn't return to normal and Melissa found herself to be slightly tortured and very torn. She hadn't spent years in college and working her way to the top of her career for nothing. She couldn't just throw it all away and, looking around her, lots of women were perfectly happy to leave their babies at home while they worked. Mother of four Denise Green had not only said that working was as fulfilling as it had ever been but it was the saviour of her sanity. Melissa was embarrassed by her perceived inadequacy and lived in denial, quashing the urge to renounce her place in the man's world her sisters before her had fought so valiantly to ensure and return to the kitchen where she yearned to be. In her kitchen baking with her son, playing games, watching him grow, being there, and being his mom. Eventually she did fall into a routine and managed her work and home life well and it was only when her perfect babyminder called to tell her that Jacob had clapped or stood or walked or called her mama that her heart threatened to break and those dark thoughts had first emerged. *What if I stayed at home?* Of course that was a ridiculous notion. She would have gone insane just like Denise Green had said. She was a professional not a cookie-cutter. But then Carrie had come along and with her came double the work and double the heartbreak and her job was suffering and her kids were suffering and her marriage was suffering and most of all and in the worst way she was suffering. She was tired all the time. She was haunted by leaving not one but two children and the prospect that yet again she would hear of her own child's development from someone else.

Melissa needed a break. Melissa needed to stop. Melissa needed to come clean. Since Jacob was born she was pretending to be someone that she used to be but wasn't any more and the lie had taken its toll.

August 18th 1975 - Monday

We camped on Brittas Bay and pitched our tent on the grass overlooking miles of white sand dunes. Well, maybe not miles but it seemed like it. The weather was amazing so when we got there (and we biked there by the way which nearly killed me), but when we got there it was heaving with people. Loads of Dubliners down for the day and kids in colourful togs with ice-creams and shovels and old women with big dark-coloured togs and swaddled in towels even though they were complaining about the heat. The sea seemed full as far as the eye could see with people swimming, wading, walking, floating, splashing, jumping and the sounds of seagulls and mothers calling for their kids and kids calling for each other and the men playing football off to the side and the water lapping and swishing and heat on our backs and on the soles of our feet and the way the sun glinted on the water and the way air weighed on me like a cosy old jumper and all the while the DJs played what Matthew called sunny songs. I'll remember my weekend away forever. Matthew did most of the work. He was a Boy Scout and well used to putting up the two-man tent which he managed to carry on the back of his bike along with the sleeping bag. He's very strong and fit and I suppose he has good balance too. It must be from riding Nero. Either way I was half-dead and all I carried was the radio and our toothbrushes and some knickers and things. The sun was so hot we didn't need too many clothes. Good thing too 'cause there's no way I could carry them. When the beach got quiet just after eight we snuggled up together and watched the water. That never gets old. You'd think it would but it doesn't and I can't explain why. We ate sandwiches from the shop down the road and drank a few cans of Harp. I still don't like beer but it does make me laugh, well, Matthew makes me laugh but things definitely sound funnier when I've had some beer. There was a man on the beach walking his dog. It was after ten and still bright. The dog was chasing its tail and the man was standing watching and waiting. Eventually the dog got tired of that and jumped up on the man. He gave the dog a hug like the same kind of hug you'd give a person. The dog panted and ran off and the man followed, his dog barking and yelping high on freedom. He was too far away to see his face but I bet it was a kind one. I bet he's a really nice person. He probably has a good job, maybe he's a doctor or a banker and he's probably married and he loves his wife and he's probably got kids who don't have to lock their doors at night. In fact they probably don't even have locks. To say nothing of a great big padlock like Matthew has put on my door for me – he's so handy.

So we watched the sea and Matthew was quiet and kind of far away. And I knew what he was thinking. Two weeks left. In two weeks he'll be back in boarding school. We try not to think about it but it's hard when every shop is full of back-to-school stuff. We keep agreeing to live in the moment but how can we live in the moment when we know that soon our life together as we know it will be over.

Am I being too dramatic like Joanie Flynn three doors down who cries at the drop of a hat and pretends to faint when she's in trouble? It doesn't feel too dramatic. Matthew pretends he's fine about going back but I know he's not. Last year he was bullied – he only told me that recently. He was embarrassed about it. The school told his dad and his dad had to get involved and he said his dad knowing was worse than the bullying. His dad called him names but the boys were suspended and the bullying stopped. Before a few people talked to him but no one now does because he's known as a rat. Stupid fools. They'd rather let bullies run riot than put a stop to them and be called names. I told him as much and he said it was easy for me. Everyone says that but I don't think it's easy. I just think I'd rather go down fighting! He laughs at me when I talk like that but I can tell he likes it.

Before this weekend we didn't go the whole way because we were scared about me getting pregnant and it's really hard to get protection. Sheila is using the natural method – she says it's all about the cycle. She talked about fertile days and non-fertile days and egg production and I just switched off. She got a library book and now she's an expert. She will definitely make a good nurse. Then the other night in our cosy fabric-conditioner-smelling sleeping bag it just happened and I'm scared about being pregnant but I'm glad we did it. It was right. Matthew did it before last year with a girl in Boston so I pretended it wasn't a big deal but it really was. I felt like, well, actually, I don't know what I felt like, a grown-up maybe. I don't know. I didn't think I could love him more this week than I did last week but I do. Looking into his eyes when he was moving inside me something clicked. I can't say what but in that moment I was inspired and everything made sense. It sounds so weird and maybe I'm a spaz but suddenly I found a place in the world. And I don't mean that I'm his and that's enough. I mean for the first time the future became clear and not some distant island. I'm going to be a writer. I'm going to put my heart, my soul, my experience, my lack of experience, my dreams, my hopes, and my love most of all my love, I'm going to put it all down on paper. Some day when I really have something to say I'm going to write because everyone loves a good story.

We've been talking more about going to America after the Leaving Cert next year and particularly Kentucky. There are universities in Kentucky and I could go to one. My school work is strong even if I do talk all the time. I could get in, at least that's what Matthew says. I could study English and Matthew could work in Keeneland. He asked his dad if he could organise it one night last week and his dad said he would and then he said he doesn't care if Matthew ever comes back but that's because Matthew's dad is a shit but his friend Ronnie runs Keeneland and he's a great man. Matthew says he will take us both in. He has a big family and his wife Marjorie and all the kids (eleven!!!) ride and they have hundreds of stables and stable hands and the workers are treated like family and they have big barbeques every weekend and a huge porch with a swing and everyone's welcome at the dinner table and it's like a real family, big and loving and fun. Matthew could break and train horses and I could study and we could have a life together. It's so real I can touch it. God, I hope I'm not pregnant. Maybe I'll read Sheila's book.

Mam won't talk to me because I let Dr B in the back door. He thinks there's something wrong in her head. He wants to do some tests but she won't go with him. HE came home and she was shouting at Dr B and then of course he started shouting because he just loves to shout. Dr B left but he asked me to keep an eye on her. I don't know how that's going to help but I said I would.

Dr B is getting really good at riding. We've been riding together a lot lately. I'm still a bit nervous but I pretend I'm not and Dr B and Matthew don't seem to notice. Dr B has nicknamed me Trouble. It makes Matthew laugh so I don't mind, in fact I like it. Hi, it's nice to meet you! I'm Trouble!!!!

HE hasn't had any work for a few days and he's itching for a fight. She's so quiet and withdrawn all the time, it's even hard for him to pick a fight with her. He's looking my way again but I'm not scared any more. In my head and my heart I'm free. In three weeks Matthew is going back to boarding school. He's going to do everything possible to come home at least once a month no matter what his dad says or does. Then all we have to do is get through eleven months and we can start our new lives. eleven months isn't long. Eleven months is nothing. Roll on next July!!!!!

Chapter eighteen

I knew I knew you

Aidan always cleaned when he did something his internal moral barometer deemed to be wrong. He cleaned when he told his mother to fuck off after a particularly nasty row about personal insurance. He cleaned when he lied to his friends about being sick just because he wanted a day off. Then again that's the problem with working with friends: lies are problematic and guilt-ridden. He cleaned when he used George's credit card to buy tickets to Macy Gray after a fight about cheese. He cleaned when he stole a T-shirt from GAP for a dare by a guy whose name he couldn't remember and he cleaned when his sister called and asked him to mind her three kids and he pretended to have flu. Aidan was cleaning his apartment when the phone rang. He took off one Marigold before answering.

"Aidan."

"Andrew?"

"I know this is coming from nowhere but could we meet sometime this week?"

"Look, if it's about Sue and the builder –"

"It's not."

"Oh. Right."

"I'd really appreciate it."

"Okay." *What the hell does he want? Make up an excuse. Oh fuck, come on, think of something. He's waiting. Think, you fucking moron.* "I'm free tomorrow evening."

"Good, great, Okay, tomorrow then. Brilliant. Thanks. See you then."

"Andrew?"

"Yeah."

"When and where?"

"Oh." Andrew laughed a little. "Sorry. Anywhere in town suits me."

"How about The Westbury." *No one knows me in The Westbury.*

"Perfect."

"See you then."

"See you then. And Aidan . . ."

"Yeah."

"Thank you again."

Aidan put down the phone and seeing as Sue and Harri weren't picking up their phones he called Melissa. She had finished crying fifteen minutes beforehand and was on her second whiskey. She could have told Aidan what happened but she was too ashamed. She was even considering hiding the fact that she'd almost lost her son from his father. She answered the phone brightly.

"What?"

"You're never going to believe who called me?"

"George Michael?"

"No."

"Damn it, what's the point in hanging around with homos if it doesn't get me closer to George Michael?"

"Are you finished being Dublin's answer to Joan Rivers?"

"Okay," she sighed. "Go on."

"Andrew."

"Andrew Shannon?"

"The one and only."

"What the hell did he want?"

"To meet me."

"You're not going to meet him, are you?"

"Yeah."

"Aidan."

"What?"

"He's a prick."

"Melissa, life is not that simple."

She sighed because she knew he was right. "I wonder what he wants."

"No idea."

"Maybe he's gay." She was being sarcastic and yet judging from Sue's version of their non-existent sex life it was a one in a million possibility.

Aidan laughed. "And I'm Tipper Gore's wet dream."

She laughed. *What the hell made him think of Tipper Gore?* "Yeah, I suppose the notion is pretty outlandish. Speaking of which, what the hell was Sue thinking arriving with that Keith person?"

"She wasn't. She's just a little lost, that's all."

"That makes all of us. Did you hear where Harri's gone?"

"No."

"To Wicklow."

"Jesus. That was quick."

"I hope not too quick." She hadn't necessarily embraced the idea when Harri had called her the day before, especially as she couldn't go with her. Then again she had been the googler and so in a way she blamed herself. *It's too soon. Take some time. Google a bit more. Read your dad's file. Have a holiday. Read a book. Get back with James. Fuck it, get back to your life. I wish I could get back to mine.*

"Melissa."

"Yeah."

"Can you keep a secret?"

"No."

"I'm serious."

"So am I."

"I want to tell you something."

"So tell me but I cannot guarantee that I won't tell the next person I see."

"You sound like Harri and it's pissing me off."

Melissa laughed. "Just tell me."

"No, forget it."

"You're being a baby."

"You love Gerry, don't you?" he asked out of nowhere. "I mean you bitch and moan but that's what women do. Am I right?"

"Be careful. You may be on the phone but I will find a way to hurt you."

"Seriously."

"Of course I love him." Melissa smiled to herself, remembering earlier that morning her husband's familiar kiss and the warmth when she spooned him. Quite suddenly she felt like crying again. *I nearly lost our son. Jesus Christ, I nearly lost him. Get a grip, Melissa, calm down, he's home, he's in bed, he's safe. You're fine. Drink up. Pretend it's all okay.* "What's this about?" she asked after drinking deeply.

"Nothing," he said. The moment for truth had been lost. "Well, anyway, I'll give you a buzz after I meet Andrew."

"What the hell does he want?" she repeated.

"I don't know. And tell Harri to call me when she gets back. I can't believe she didn't tell me what she was up to – having said that I was in one of my moods last night."

"I noticed and will do."

Aidan hung up the phone and sighed to himself. *How the fuck am I supposed to meet Andrew when I've at least a week's worth of cleaning to do.*

* * *

By the time Sue had finished looking at furniture in Bray and by the time they had driven to Wicklow town and stopped for something to eat it was a little after four. The town was narrow to drive through, bustling with people and a maze to find parking in. There was nothing by the pier or on the street behind it and the main street was far too busy. Eventually they found a space by the old jail.

"Oh look, they do night tours!" Sue said, drinking from her takeaway coffee cup as they headed back to the car.

"Great," Harri sighed.

"It's not going like you planned, is it?" Sue asked.

"Not really, no."

"Sorry. I'm getting in the way."

Harri felt sorry for her friend. She'd been bedraggled since she'd walked out the door of her own home and God love her she couldn't seem to find her way back to normal. If Harri was lost, Sue was more lost and the builder was a symptom of that.

"It's okay. I don't know what I was expecting. Maybe we should take the night tour of Wicklow jail and go home." She deactivated the car alarm with an annoying beep beep. The two women sat in.

Sue turned to her friend. "Look, why don't I check out all that Wicklow town has to offer while you head to the graveyard? You don't want me there."

Harri smiled. "You don't mind?"

"No. It looks like there are some half-decent shops around here." Sue grabbed her bag and before exiting the car she pulled her friend towards her and kissed her on the forehead. "Good luck, Harri. I hope you find what you're looking for."

"Knowing what I'm looking for would be enough," Harri admitted with a slight smile.

Sue got out and waved Harri off down the street in search of the graveyard.

* * *

Brendan completed his afternoon sitting at four on the dot. Despite a rampant vomiting epidemic, all was well with the Wicklow folk and he intended on making good use of the rest of his day. First he would grab a takeaway coffee in Donnali's, then he'd head on over to the graveyard before he'd take in eighteen holes of golf. The coffee shop was busy with tourists and locals alike.

"There you are, Dr McCabe. I was saying to Sarah we haven't seen you in an age."

"Keeping the head down, Martina."

"That vomiting bug is desperate."

"Yeah. it's knocking people for six."

"My Malachy is in bits with it, at least that's what he pretends."

"Bed rest, Martina, bed rest and liquids."

"Unfortunately, doctor, you've just described his entire life."

He was on his way out the door coffee in hand when he nearly walked into Sheila Doyle.

"Dr McCabe."

"Sheila."

"Are you well?"

"Fine, just heading up to visit with Liv."

Sheila's face fell. *The 11th!* "I forgot," she admitted, embarrassed.

"It's been a long time," Brendan said smiling at her.

"I was her best friend. I should have remembered."

"Don't be silly, Sheila, you've a house full of kids, a business to run and an insulin-dependant husband with a stubborn streak a mile long."

"*You* remembered," she said quietly.

"The benefit of living alone. How's Patrick anyway?"

"Good. He's driving me mad but good."

Brendan squeezed Sheila's shoulder. "I hope I didn't upset you," he said.

"No and thanks for reminding me," she smiled and waved him down the road. *I can't believe I forgot you. Jesus, Liv, I'm sorry.*

* * *

Sue made herself busy in the local boutiques, finding a particularly tasteful silk top within three minutes flat. *I believe my visa will take some battering today.*

She and Harri had not discussed her attending George's opening with Keith – in fact the conversation had been carefully avoided by both parties. Sue didn't really know what she was doing. The consequences of her actions had only dawned on her when Aidan had explained that her husband and daughter could arrive at any moment. She had all but collapsed and even after they had left the premises and were heading into The Front Lounge, a bar her husband would never have frequented, she couldn't rid herself of the bitter taste of fear or failure or something else she couldn't quite put her finger on. She looked over at Keith who was uncomfortable in a gay bar. *What the hell am I doing?* He was uncomfortable with the whole evening if truth be told. He had never signed up to be a boyfriend and going to a wine-tasting was the remit of a boyfriend as opposed to a casual lover. Sue had pretty much tricked him into it and he wasn't happy. Neither was she. And it was impossible without serious therapy to even attempt to contemplate why she had done such a thing. Keith left after one drink. Aidan was having a laugh with some of his friends from the scene. Sue knew one or two of them but they were on a buzz and didn't have too much time to spend talking to a middle-aged woman with a sad face. Aidan tried to cheer her up with a sambuca and it was at that point she had hailed a taxi back to Harri's.

Alone on the pull-out bed in Harri's sitting room Sue had tried to make sense of her new life.

Beth wouldn't take her calls. Her husband might as well have relocated to the moon and the married man she was having casual sex with had no interest in leaving his wife or being her boyfriend. She was free but Keith was still married. And even if he wasn't, would she really want him in her life anyway? *He's holding me back*. It was at that moment that Susan Shannon made a pledge to herself that she would not see her married builder friend again. And not because of guilt about the woman whose husband she was shagging and not because her friends were silently judging her even if they pretended they weren't and not because she was afraid that her daughter would find out. And just because she wasn't considering a stranger's marriage didn't make her a bad person – a little selfish maybe but not bad. Susan decided that she was a good person who had just walked out of a dead marriage because she had wanted more and the married builder Keith was never going to be more. She lay awake for a long time that night reliving her marriage, the good as well as the bad, and remembering her daughter and family's milestones. She cried and she even laughed a little and she said goodbye to her old life and in her mind she let go.

So today was a new day, a new beginning for both Sue and for her partner Harri and to celebrate Sue would shop until there was nothing left in Wicklow to buy. *Jesus, I'd love to get my hands on a decent spiral mixer or a hand-painted wooden spoon.*

* * *

Harri made her way through the graveyard slowly as she had no idea where to start and so it was only natural to begin at the beginning. *I'm never going to be that lucky.*

She was on her knees trying to make out a name and cursing herself for not bringing her glasses when a man passed and she thought about asking him but then reconsidered on the basis that it would have been rude to assume that every one in Wicklow knew everyone else dead or alive and so she allowed him to pass without a word while coveting his takeaway coffee. *I'm gasping.* She managed to cut herself on a bramble and bruised her knee when she tripped over a stray pot. *This is stupid. I'm never going to find her.* There was an office at the entrance but it was closed and there was no such thing as a map of plots and Harri was tired and emotional and sick of hurting herself. *If I bang into one more bloody gravestone!* But still she walked on, reading each gravestone she passed.

* * *

Brendan made himself comfortable on the grass. "Hi there, Trouble!" he said, looking at Liv's name printed in black. "Thirty years and I swear it seems like yesterday. I wish you'd written that book. I would love to have read that. I bet you it would have been a bestseller. It's all about time – you were just out of time, Trouble, and none of us saw it coming. I promise I would have saved you if I could have. But you know that. I had a fling in San Francisco, you'll be delighted to hear. He was forty so I suppose you could say I'm a cradle-snatcher. He works in design. We didn't do much talking about design though," he laughed to himself. "You would like him. He's the kind of gay man you always wanted me to be. Self-assured, proud and happy. And I am. I'm a different man to the one you knew back then another lifetime ago. I think you'd be happy with the way I turned out, at least I hope so. I do miss you, Trouble."

He was silent and sipping on his coffee when he saw a woman slowly making her way from gravestone to gravestone. As she got closer she became more familiar. Her hair, her bone structure, her mouth and particularly the look that crossed her face when her ankle gave way on gravel. Brendan stood up.

"You're looking for Liv," he said.

Harri stopped dead in front of the man with the takeaway coffee cup. She nodded.

"She's here," he said.

And Harri made her way over to where he was standing slowly and carefully and with her heart and soul having taken up residence in her mouth. She looked at the name on the gravestone and the date and from there she looked to the man who was ashen-faced and staring.

"Happy birthday, Harri," he said.

"Thank you," she replied in nothing more than a whisper.

"My name is Brendan McCabe." His eyes were boring into her.

"The doctor," she managed

"Yes."

"I'm not ready for this," she said and it was then that her legs went from under her.

September 2nd 1975 - Tuesday

Today I said goodbye to Matthew. I cried until I felt so sick that all I could do was lie in my bed. He cried too. Henry took us to the train station because his stupid dad has gone to France. Matthew had enough cases to suggest he'd be gone forever. I can't stand it. The summer is over and he is gone and I can't stand it. Everything in me is aching from my head to my toes and inside I'm screaming. Henry waited for a while and then he said his goodbyes and ruffled Matthew's hair and told him he'd miss him and he promised to take good care of Nero and I was already crying because Henry was saying all the things that Matthew's dad should have been there to say and then Henry was gone and we were alone and I was still crying and he was trying to be strong.

On Saturday night Matthew and his dad had the biggest fight. I was there. It started because Matthew asked him if he could come home every weekend. Loads of the other boys in his school get to go home every weekend but he said no. Matthew argued with him and said it wasn't as if his dad would notice whether or not he was home. His dad lost it and the things he said were so hurtful and they weren't true either.

Matthew could be anything he wanted to be. He isn't a fool or a waste of time. He could never be a disappointment. The hurt in Matthew's eyes when he said those things will stay with me forever and later when he cried it was like being knifed. I mean it. It felt like a knife slicing through my insides. That has never happened before and I really really hope it doesn't happen again because it is highly unpleasant. When his dad said he was glad Matthew's mother was dead so she didn't have to see what a loser her son was, Matthew was going to punch him. He raised his arm and made a run at his dad and I pulled him back by holding on to the back of his jumper. I don't know why. It was instinct. Mathew shouted at me afterwards. He said I shouldn't have interfered. He was right. I should have let him punch his dad. I feel really bad about that. I need to learn to mind my own business. Matthew was angry with me for a while and it hurt almost as much as seeing him cry. Matthew's dad is so mean, really mean. You can see it in his eyes. He's cold through and through. He always seems angry and he likes to hurt people. He was enjoying himself. I think he's a very sad man and I wonder how Matthew and I got so unlucky. If his mam had lived and if my dad had lived our lives could have been so much better.

The train pulled in and nearly took my legs from under me. People were boarding and it seemed like forever we were standing there looking at each other, desperate. He's off to a cold boarding school where he doesn't talk to anyone from the start of one week to the next and I'm back in my room with the door locked and eleven long months ahead. Sometimes life is too hard. Today I cried so loud that I actually heard myself as though I was standing outside my own body and witness to its breakdown. I'm worried for him. I'm worried he won't make it another year now he knows what it's like to be loved and to have friends.

Last night on our last night Sheila, Dave, Matthew and I went to Keoghs' farm. It was Dave's idea. He wanted to send Matthew off in style. As usual Sheila and Dave started the night off with an argument. She maintained that her granny always warned her never to cross the glen after dark. As Keoghs' farm was past the glen and Dave thought Sheila's granny was full of shit he stormed off leaving Matthew, Sheila and me standing there. Eventually he came back and talked Sheila around especially as he'd gone to a good deal of trouble to leave a picnic basket with snacks and beer at the farm. I'd never been to Keoghs' farm before and I have to admit I wasn't that keen on spending my last night with Matthew by a haunted farmhouse after crossing the glen after dark. I mean, what if Sheila's granny was right? Anyway we went up there and it really did feel weird. The fact that the old farmhouse is big, imposing and derelict doesn't help and there is an eerie vibe to the place, but the weirdest thing is the dead orchard. Every tree in the whole orchard is standing there stone dead. It's like something from a film. Dave and Matthew went inside but there was no way I was going in there and Sheila was white in the face and so nervous she kept running behind a dead tree to pee. She says nervous bladders run in the family on her mother's side. We had the picnic in the dead orchard. Dave had gone to a lot of trouble with snacks and beer and cheese sandwiches that he made himself. He even had candles and a flash light and one of his dad's golf clubs in case of a spiritual encounter. I don't know what he thought a golf club would do in the face of a restless spirit but to be fair he admitted that he wasn't sure himself. Matthew said he'd read somewhere that you just tell a ghost that you'll pray for it and it would vanish. I really hoped he was right because my skin was standing on end and poor Sheila spent most of her time squatting behind a tree. Nothing happened. There was not a ghost to be seen and it was nice. We told ghost stories, drank beers and talked about the good times we'd had at the carnival, by the castle and on the strand. Dave apologised to Matthew for thinking he was a stuck-up posh git when he met him first and Matthew took that well. When we had left them Matthew said it was the first time in his life he felt like he had friends.

Poor Matthew, he breaks my heart. He's in that place now and he's alone. I wonder if I close my eyes and concentrate really hard can I communicate with him?

No.

Shit.

HE's home. I can hear him shouting. He's drunk and Mam is crying. I wish I had Dave's golf club now.

He's gone now. When I got into the kitchen she was cowering down by the sink and he was standing over her getting ready to pounce. He's lucky his stupid gap-toothed friend called because if he hadn't he would have got a dinner plate over his head. I'm so tired of this. I miss Matthew. Matthew, please come home.

Chapter nineteen

One day a time

Aidan was early. Aidan was always early. He brought a newspaper and was reading an article on conservation in the Appalachians while munching on a plain chicken sandwich. He was on his second cup of tea when Andrew made an appearance. He sat in the comfortable chair opposite and began by shaking Aidan's hand and thanking him for turning up. The waitress was standing beside them within seconds. She took Andrew's order for coffee and a croissant.

"So," Aidan said.

"So," Andrew repeated.

"Why am I here?" Aidan asked. After all he was Susan's friend not Andrew's. They were polite to one another and had spent some time together at various events but they didn't know one another, not really anyway.

"I have a problem," Andrew heard himself say.

The waitress returned with coffee and a croissant and both men fell silent, allowing her time to lay down the tray.

When she was gone Andrew continued. "You're probably

wondering why I'm talking to you." He laughed a little. "It's because I don't know who else to talk to."

Aidan was getting nervous. *What the hell . . .*

"Three years ago I started having problems. I ignored them. They didn't go away. Two years ago the problem got worse. I kept ignoring it and while I was busy pretending nothing was wrong my wife had an affair."

"What are you trying to tell me?" Aidan asked.

"I can't have sex," Andrew admitted with his head hung low. "There, it only took three years to admit it," he laughed but his laughter was hollow.

"Why are you telling me?"

"I don't know. Because I couldn't tell anyone else and you're so open and free and –"

"And gay."

"And gay."

"Being gay doesn't make me an expert on dicks, you know."

"I know. I just thought maybe you've come across it or heard something about the problem," Andrew said, rubbing his face. "Oh, I don't know, I thought maybe gay men talk about things."

"You've tried Viagra?"

"Makes me dizzy and those other brands too. Nothing works."

"There's a clinic in James's St. I'll come with you."

"I'd really appreciate that."

"Andrew?"

"What?"

"How could you not tell her?"

Andrew shook his head from side to side. "I suppose I'll have the rest of my life to work that one out," he said sadly.

"She thought you didn't want her."

"I know."

"It nearly destroyed her."

"I'm sorry."

"Jesus, Andrew, people like you belong to another time."

Andrew and Aidan separated on Grafton Street. Andrew promised he'd call Aidan with the details of his appointment. Aidan had tried to talk him into speaking to his wife but Andrew was adamant that he didn't want her involved.

"Why?"

"Because."

"Because what?"

"Because she's gone, Aidan."

"Only because you let her go."

"I don't want her pity."

"Oh balls, Andrew. She's your wife."

"Yeah. Tell that to the builder."

He was in Jurassic Park having a drink when he spotted Lorcan the twenty-four-year-old he'd slept with two nights before. *Balls*. The whole point of going into Jurassic Park was that all those under the age of thirty stayed on the other side of The George, the youthful fun side where every day is Mardi Gras and age is just a number and not indelibly marked on your face.

"I hoped I'd find you here," Lorcan said, sitting beside him at the bar.

"There should be an over-thirties age limit in here," Aidan said keeping his eyes fixed forward.

"I thought you were going to stop playing hard to get after the other night."

"I was drunk when I said those things. You're twenty-four and I'm in a relationship."

"So?"

"So don't start."

"You like me."

"I really don't."

"You do, that's why you can't look at me. It's too painful."

Aidan laughed.

"I really like you," Lorcan said with his head tilted so Aidan found it difficult to avoid looking at him without becoming awkward.

"I'm in a relationship."

"You are not happy."

"That is none of your business."

"Aidan, every time you break up with him, you come to me. Every time you fight with him, you come to me. Every time he does something you don't agree with, you come to me. We like the same things, we laugh together, and we're attracted to one another. I'm patient but not infinitely so."

"I shouldn't have knocked on your door the other night," Aidan said. "It's not fair on you."

"He's never going to get you the way I do," Lorcan said.

Aidan laughed. "You don't really know me."

"I know you better than he does." Lorcan left Aidan on that note.

Why is it so easy to have the answers for everyone else's relationship and yet be completely and utterly useless about your own?

⋆ ⋆ ⋆

Melissa was already on the computer when Gerry answered the door to Aidan.

"Jesus, it's coming down out there," he pointed out to a sodden Aidan.

"Really? I hadn't noticed," Aidan replied dryly while dripping on Gerry's mat.

"Yeah, yeah. Get in." Gerry grabbed a towel from the bathroom under the stairs and handed it to Aidan who wiped his face and patted his hair dry. Gerry took his coat and draped it on the heater.

"Coffee?"

"I'd love one. Where are the kids?"

"Blissfully in bed."

Aidan checked his watch. It was just after eight. "So where is she?"

"Upstairs on the computer. She's been printing stuff off since you called. What's going on anyway?"

"Oh nothing."

"Right." Gerry knew better than to interfere – besides there was a match starting. He handed Aidan the coffee. "You know where to go."

Melissa was staring at the screen when he went into her makeshift boxroom office.

"Well?"

"Well, it could be anything. Listen to this. 52% of males between the ages of forty and seventy have reported some degree of impotence. Can you believe that?"

"I'd rather not."

"Age is one factor in ED, that's short for erectile dysfunction. The majority of men with ED do not seek or receive adequate advice or treatment." She was nodding. "Remind you of anyone we know? Still can't believe it. What a moron. If my Gerry hid something like that from me I'm murder him."

"There are days that if your Gerry buttered his bread with the wrong knife you'd murder him. He's still here by the grace of God, the poor bastard."

"Ha, ha, you should think about going on the road with that kind of material," she said without looking away from the screen.

Aidan smiled at her. She was in her element, glasses at the tip of her nose and clicking away, accessing the fountain of all information before regurgitating facts and figures. Although Aidan had promised Andrew he would not say a word about his problem to Susan, he had not made such a promise about mentioning it to anyone else and so in the wake of his encounter with Lorcan he had called her from Jurassic Park. Andrew had asked him for his help so he would give it and to do that he'd have to know a little bit about what he was dealing with and as his laptop had died on him three months previously it was only natural that he call upon his friend the googaholic.

"Psychological reasons account for one third of cases. Do you think it's psychological?"

"I'm not a doctor."

"Okay, physical causes of ED. Erection occurs in response to signals to the brain, erectile tissue, cylinders, sponge-like, blah, blah, blah. Fibres contract, the sponge is wrung out."

"Jesus, Melissa."

"I'm only reading what's there. Okay, where was I? Oh, draining veins open up."

"Okay, that's it, read it your head."

They sat there in silence, Aidan with his cup of coffee reading a poster about a stressed housewife on the wall in front of him and Melissa reading the ins and outs of a flaccid versus hard penis.

"Here we go. Possible physical causes of ED. Diabetes. He doesn't have that. High blood pressure. He could have that."

"Jesus, I have that," Aidan said. "I mean it's not outrageously high but at my last check-up my doctor said it was a little high." He was slightly pale.

"It has to do with hardening of the arteries."

"Oh God."

"Calm down. You're fine. Oh and smoking."

"He doesn't smoke."

"Not now but he did for about twenty years."

"Oh God, I smoked." Aidan was beginning to feel very sorry he'd sought Melissa's googling expertise. *Sometimes ignorance is bliss.*

"Multiple Sclerosis. No. Parkinson's disease. No. Prostrate surgery. No. Spinal injury?"

"I think we'd have noticed."

"Yeah. Okay, how about some cures?" she said while click-clicking.

"Yes, please." Aidan was still suffering slight shock. *A little high. What does a little high mean? How high does it have to be before your dick stops working*?

"Drugs. He's tried them. They don't work. Okay. A mechanical vacuum device causes an erection by creating a partial vaccum which draws blood into the penis," she looked from the screen to Aidan. "Not ideal, is it?"

"Not really, no."

"Oh look, here's a diagram. Jesus!"

"I don't want to see it, I don't want to see it!" Aidan called out, putting his hands over his eyes. It was at that point that Gerry walked in.

"What the hell is that?"

"A penis pump."

"Sorry I asked!" He backed out, closing the door behind him.

"It's not for me!" Aidan shouted after him.

"Oh!" Melissa said while making a face.

"What?" Aidan really wasn't sure he wanted to know.

"Many men achieve stronger erections by injecting drugs into the penis."

"Oh no. No. No."

"Okay, moving on. Surgery which can implant a device, reconstruct arteries or block off veins that allow blood to leak from the penis."

"Poor Andrew!" Aidan said, shaking his head. "Poor, poor Andrew."

Aidan left Melissa's with a heavy heart.

* * *

George answered the door in an apron.

"I didn't expect dinner," Harri said.

"I was cooking anyway."

"Do you always eat after nine?"

"No, if I did I wouldn't be the perfect male specimen you see before you," he said with smile.

"Where's Aidan?"

"Off radar."

"Oh."

She sat down at his kitchen table and it was only when she smelt the food that she remembered she hadn't eaten all day. He dished up chilli and opened a bottle of wine – something he said would compliment it but Harri was more interested in water as her brother was known for his fire-alarm chilli.

"Well?"

"I met the doctor," she said. "He was there at her grave."

"The doctor who found you," he clarified.

"Yeah."

"Odd."

"Bloody odd. He knew me."

"What?"

"He knew me. He knew I was looking for her and he called me by my name."

"Well, maybe Dad told him what he was calling you."

"But why would he remember and what was he doing there and why was he involved in the whole thing in the first place?"

"I don't know why. Didn't you ask him?"

"I couldn't. I froze. Actually I thought I was going to have another stupid panic attack but he made me breathe with my head between my legs." She shook her head and sighed. "My head was between my legs."

"I think that's the least of your worries. What did he say?"

"Not much. As soon as I could breathe I ran. He called after me but I just wasn't ready. You know. I thought, I'll go to Wicklow. I'll look at a gravestone. How hard is that? I didn't expect to have to deal with the living. The living have no business in graveyards." George nodded in agreement.

"He called out that his name was McCabe and he was in the book and he'd love to see me again."

"You want me to come with you?"

"I didn't say I was going."

"You will."

"You have a new business to run."

"So we'll go next Sunday."

"Are you sure?"

"Positive."

"Okay but don't tell Mom or Dad."

"I promise."

After that they ate the chilli and George talked about his business and the write-up the shop received in the *Independent*. He spoke about Aidan and his inability to reach him. "He just needs a few days to cool off. It'll be fine." He spoke about their parents. "I just can't seem to get past it. I don't know why."

Harri talked about her concerns for Susan. She had hoped that getting away from Andrew would strengthen her friend but she seemed to be falling apart. "She cried herself to sleep last night."

"It's early days."

"I know."

"What about you?"

"Oh, I often cry myself to sleep." She grinned but she was telling the truth. *I wonder what James would make of Brendan McCabe.*

* * *

Susan worked late. Her day had begun badly and was getting worse by the second. Delay after delay had occurred leaving her in the middle of a room without silk wallpaper on one side, an unfinished kitchen because the carpenter had walked out in a huff when the delivery men brought the wrong kitchen and four extra chairs that nobody would take responsibility for. She had called Aidan hoping he'd help out with the wallpaper crisis but he was odd on the phone saying he had important business to attend to, business which he couldn't discuss. This was very unusual for Aidan because Aidan would talk about anything. He had hung up before she could push him. *If you want something done, Sue, do it yourself.* She finished papering at ten and spent another hour removing the boxing around the kitchen cabinets so that they would be ready to install. She left a message with the shop saying that if their delivery man wasn't there to collect the chairs by 10 a.m. she'd put a hold on her client's credit card and burn them. She made it back to Harri's for midnight.

Harri was drinking cocoa and watching another effing *CSI*.

"Oh, Harri!"

"Sorry. Couldn't sleep."

"I know the feeling," Sue said, slumping on the sofa.

"Cocoa?"

"No, thanks," she sighed.

"Why didn't you call me?"

"Ah, it was fine. I got the job done. How did you know?"

"Aidan rang. He said you needed help but when I rang you'd turned your phone off."

"He was acting weird."

"He's avoiding George."

"How did your job in Swords go?" Susan asked.

"Good. He's a nice guy. He knows what he wants. He has good taste and a big budget."

"That's what I like to hear." Sue smiled. "A few more clients like him and I'll be out of your hair."

"I like having you here," Harri admitted.

"Thank you," Sue said and her eyes welled up.

"Have you heard from Beth?"

"No." She shook her head.

"She'll come around."

"I hope so," Sue replied, wiping a tear away. "I really hope so."

Harri went to bed soon afterwards leaving Sue to her pull-out bed.

Harri made a promise to herself to take her mom out to lunch. She couldn't imagine causing her own mother the same pain she saw in her friend's eyes.

September 26th 1975 - Friday

Matthew's not coming home. Henry said he got in a fight with some other boy and had all his privileges taken away. Henry said I shouldn't cry, that he is fine but I know he's not. Matthew's not a fighter, he didn't start it. It's not fair. His stupid dad could have told them he wanted his son home but he didn't. I hate him. Henry said Nero is missing him too. Dr B has been taking him out. Sometimes I ride with him on Betsy but Betsy seems tired lately. I know how she feels. I tried to call him on the phone down town but they wouldn't let me talk to him. It's like he's in jail. School isn't supposed to be jail. Everything is wrong. I can't sleep. I have a headache for the past three days.

I forgot to lock my door last week. I never forget but somehow I did. I woke up and HE was on top of me with his hand over my face. I tried to scream but nothing would come out. It was like I was rendered dumb. I could hear myself screaming in my head but there was no sound. He was grabbing at me and trying to part my legs but I managed to cross them and I held them together, vice-like. He'd have to break them. His hand slipped and I bit him as hard as I could and when he yelped my mother called out from her room asking who was there. I could hear her shuffling. So he slapped me and got off me and I heard the door close behind him. He'd taken the padlock that Matthew had installed so I asked Dr B for a loan because I was short of money being back at school, paying for lunches and having to buy that stupid book that I lost and I need to make the money I got working last and besides that I wanted him to ask me what the money was for. I wanted to tell him. And he did ask and I did tell and he wouldn't let me go home. He told me I was to stay with him in the gate lodge that night and that he would sort something out. He called Father Ryan and he came down just as Dr B was making us some tea. They went into the other room and I couldn't hear what they were saying. Afterwards Father Ryan said my allegation was very serious and asked me if I was aware that God was always watching. I told him if he was and, seeing as Father Ryan had a direct line, he could just ask Him what happened. I was being cheeky but he didn't respond, instead he just nodded and said he would deal with it. He agreed it was best for me to stay in Dr B's spare room that night but only if Minnie Jones his housekeeper stayed too. Minnie arrived after eight with a face on her. She had an early night and Dr B and I stayed up talking. He said I wouldn't have to go back if I didn't want to. I told him I had to go back, my mam needs to be taken care of. He said that Father Ryan would talk sense into HIM and I laughed. Dr B and poor Father Ryan, they really think you can talk sense into someone like him! There is no talking to someone like him. Dr B should just have given me the money for the new lock in the first place.

Father Ryan did talk to him and he denied it and Father Ryan got a punch in the face for his trouble. He said I was a lying little whore when I eventually did go home. Mam didn't even seem to know what was going on, she was acting like it was just another stupid argument. Dr B called and he threatened him but Dr B didn't back down. He said he'd be watching and if he even suspected anything he'd call the guards and if the guards did nothing he'd call some friends who didn't care about Church or law and would smash his face in as soon as look at him. He was frightened. I could see it. He looked at me as though I was making everything up and he spat on me after Dr B had left. Mam was in bed sleeping but really I think she was just pretending to be asleep. She can't handle any of this stuff. She's not able for it. Dr B has bought me a new padlock and I'll never forget to lock my door again.

I've been writing to Matthew and he's been writing to me. I keep the letters folded in my diary and read and re-read them and when I close my eyes I can hear his voice. In his last letter he was so excited about coming home. And now he can't come. He must be devastated. I wish I could see him. Ten months to go. Only ten months to go.

September 19th

Liv,

Only one week to go. I can't wait. I've been counting down the hours and the days and the minutes and the seconds and well you get the point. I miss you. I miss you. I miss you so much it's worse than a kick to the balls. When I get home let's go riding through the woods and we can have a picnic by the waterfall while the weather's still good. Next month will be too cold. How's school? How's Sheila and Dave? Tell them I said hi. I'm studying and keeping to myself and living for the weekend. I've no news, never do but I love you.

Love, Matt

P.S. Liv, I used to be lonely but I'm not any more.

Chapter twenty

Men will be men

Dinner started off well. The lamb was delicious and fell off the bone. Matt had brought a decent wine, one of his old friend's favourites. Brendan didn't broach the subject of his chance encounter until the dinner was long over and they were playing poker.

"Dealer shuffles," Brendan said handing the cards to Matt. "How was Clara?"

"Good," he said, shuffling. "She's thinking of relocating to the UK." Before dealing five cards each.

Brendan picked up his five cards and viewed them before resting them on the table. "That's come from nowhere."

"Not really," Matt said, resting his own cards face down. "She's been talking about it for a while."

"You didn't say anything."

"Nothing to say. What's your bet?"

"One euro."

"Feeling rich!" Matt laughed, tossing in his own euro. "How many cards?"

"Two."

"Dealer takes three."

"Will you miss her?"

"I don't know. I'll tell you when she's gone." He took back Brendan's discarded cards.

"I visited Liv yesterday."

"Good. Are you betting?"

"Another euro."

"I'll see you."

"I saw Harri there."

Matthew stopped as though something inside him had powered down. He became very still.

Brendan put his cards down. The game was over. He got up and lifted a bottle of brandy from the shelf and wiped down two glasses before putting them in front of his paralysed friend and pouring. Brendan drank but Matthew didn't move.

"She looked so like her," Brendan said. "Not as tall but her face was so familiar." Matthew remained silent.

"She got a fright, she didn't expect to meet anyone but she knew who I was, Matt. She asked me if I was the doctor."

Tears leaked from Matthew's eyes.

Brendan bowed his head.

"Did she talk to you?"

"No. Not really. She needed help controlling her breathing and once she recovered she ran but I called after her. I told her I was in the book. I told her to call. I hope she heard me."

"She was due to get married last month."

"What?"

"She didn't make it to the altar. It was the second attempt. Poor guy, James something."

"How do you know all this?"

"I've been keeping tabs her on since I returned from the States fifteen years ago."

"You never said."

"Since that night by The Eliana when I held her, a part of me never let go." He shrugged. "How could I? She was all I had left of Liv. I used to wait every year. I'd think she'll come and find me. I was beginning to think it wouldn't happen. Do you think it will happen?"

"I don't know," Brendan said sadly. "When she saw me she said she wasn't ready."

"I've waited thirty years. I suppose I can wait a while longer."

He left his brandy untouched. He went home soon after.

Brendan nursed a second brandy on his sofa. *All this time he never said a word.*

* * *

The appointment had been for half one. Aidan finished working around twelve, got home in time for a shave, a wash and change. There were three messages on his machine from George and four missed calls. *I can't deal with you right now.* He met Andrew in the hospital car park. He had decided against making any comment regarding Melissa's research. As his mother always said, if you've nothing positive to say, say nothing at all. Andrew was shaking visibly.

"Are you all right?"

"Grand."

"You're shaking."

"I know."

Aidan wanted to say it wouldn't be that bad but judging by what he'd read it could well be and maybe Andrew had carried out some research of his own.

"You'll be fine," he said when they were sitting in chairs, ironically the same chairs Harri and Andrew's daughter Beth had been sitting on one month earlier.

"What do I say?" Andrew asked slightly breathless.

"Say 'I can't get it up'," Aidan whispered.

"Right. I feel sick."

"Hospitals have that effect on people – it's perfectly normal," Aidan said, patting his arm.

"I don't think I can do it," Andrew said standing up.

Aidan pulled him back into his seat. "Don't be stupid. You can and you will."

Andrew sat quietly. They didn't speak after that. Instead they waited to hear a nurse call out his name. If someone asked Andrew what had eventually driven him to seek help he wouldn't have been able to answer, at least not immediately, but if he thought about it long and hard he probably would have said he had nothing left to lose. When his name was called and after a little push from Aidan he was up and on his feet and in the doctor's office listening to the door close behind him.

Aidan waited five minutes, ten minutes, fifteen minutes, twenty minutes, half an hour. *Jesus, how long does this take?* After an hour Andrew appeared but he was on a gurney, his shirt was open and there were patches on his chest.

"Andrew?" Aidan shouted while running up the hospital staff racing with the gurney.

"Please give us room, sir," one nurse said.

"What's going on?"

"Your friend is having a heart attack."

Oh sweet Jesus!

* * *

George was in the cellar doing a stock take when his phone rang.

"I thought you'd left the country!" he said.

"Andrew is having a heart attack."

"Excuse me?"

"Andrew Shannon is having a heart attack as we speak."

"How do you know?"

"I'm in the hospital with him. He's been having a problem with his dick. I said I'd go with him, hold his hand or whatever. He went into the office and he was fine. He came out of the office on his back having a heart attack."

"Christ! Why did he ask you?"

"I don't know, George. I hardly think that's what we should be focussing on."

"Calm down, Aidan."

"You'll have to tell Sue."

"Why me?"

"Because I can't do everything. I have to go. We're in James's St." He hung up, leaving George dumbfounded.

* * *

"Hey, George!" Sue said from her mobile phone while perched precariously on the second highest step of a ladder.

"Hey, Sue!" George said a little too airily to sound like himself.

"Are you okay?"

"Are you near a chair?"

"I'm on a ladder. What's up?"

"Get off the ladder."

"What's going on?"

"Are you off the ladder?"

"George?"

"Just get off the ladder."

She got off the ladder. "I'm off the ladder. Are you happy?

"Andrew's had a heart attack."

Silence.

"Sue?"

"Yes."

"He's in James St. Aidan's with him."

"Is he all right?"

"I don't know the details."

"Did you say Aidan's with him?"

"Yes."

"What's Aidan doing with him?"

"Long story. I think you should go to the hospital and maybe call Beth."

"She won't answer me. I'll get Harri to pick her up from work."

"Okay. Good. Let me know if you need anything."

"Yeah, okay." Sue hung up in a daze. *I should go to James's St. How do I get to James's St. from here? I should just go. I'll remember the way in the car.*

★ ★ ★

Andrew had many a nightmare in his day but this one was particularly nasty. He dreamt that he was having his dick examined when an almighty pain took hold of him and it felt like nothing on this earth. He grabbed his left arm and chest and slumped and the doctor whose hand was wrapped around his dick said something and called for someone and suddenly he was on a gurney with Aidan racing behind it.

Waking up to realise it wasn't a dream was a kick he could have done without. *He was alone. Where's Aidan? Oh God, somebody find Aidan. He can't tell anyone I'm here.*

★ ★ ★

Aidan was outside getting some air, drinking coffee which was surprisingly good from a real coffee shop in the hospital concourse which seemed more like shopping mall than a hospital. *Shops, restaurants, a feckin' juice bar. Since when have you been able to eat and drink healthily in a hospital?* He held his phone close to his ear and spoke loudly to combat the level of noise and bustle around him.

Harri was in the car and on the way to pick up Beth from the boutique she was working in. She had him on speaker. "I'm going through the park so if we get cut off I'll call you back."

"Okay," he said. "So what are you going to say to Beth?"

"I'm going to tell her the truth."

"You can't tell her the truth."

"Why not?"

"Because you can't tell her that her dad had a heart attack while having his dick inspected."

"She's not a child and I've no intention of saying that. I'll just say he was in the hospital having a check-up when he had a heart attack which is exactly what happened without the graphics."

"Fine. I wonder when it would be appropriate for me to leave?"

"Is Sue there yet?"

"No."

"When Sue gets there."

Aidan sighed. "Right. I better go back."

"Okay. I'll see you if you're still there."

Aidan hung up and walked back to where Andrew was lying awake, alert and deeply embarrassed. Aidan steadied himself outside his friend's husband's cubicle. He pulled back the curtain with a smile plastered on his face.

"Well, Andrew Shannon, you certainly know how to give a man a scare."

"You called Sue, didn't you?" Andrew was clammy, weak, nauseous, tired with all kinds of liquids flowing through his veins and the memory of torturous pain still fresh in his psyche.

"No," Aidan said.

"Thank you," Andrew said with hands clasped in simulated prayer.

This exposed the two cannulas, one sticking out of each hand allowing for the administration of the required intravenous fluids, making Aidan feel a little light-headed. He turned away, fixing his gaze on a white locker with a missing handle.

"I called George," he admitted to the locker. "George called Sue."

Andrew sighed.

Aidan was on a roll. "I also called Harri who is collecting Beth from work and bringing her here."

Andrew was silent for approximately seventy-five seconds while absorbing the information that Aidan had just vomited. If he wasn't knocking on heaven's door he could have got up and out of the bed, marched Aidan to the nearest window and thrown him out of it. *When I get out of here you better run.*

After seventy-five seconds had passed Aidan explained to Andrew that although it was highly likely that his reason for being in the hospital in the first place would come to light, relatively speaking and considering Andrew's current circumstance, his dick was the least of his problems. Aidan had not come to this conclusion lightly. He had spent the previous night awake and worried for the health and safety of his own dick. *I wonder if I asked, would someone here check my blood pressure?* But Aidan was sure, having genuinely feared he was watching his friend's husband breathe his last, that when it came to a dick and a heart, the heart wins. And while contemplating life and death on a hard hospital chair while imbibing a non-fat latte, he had surmised that the heart beating dick theory was in fact an analogy appropriate to the state of Andrew's marriage. This epiphany was one he could not but share with his weary new friend and whether it was Aidan's utter belief in his own reasoning or the fact that Andrew's heart had momentarily failed or maybe it was just the drugs, but it made sense to Andrew.

Aidan sat back in his chair content. *My work here is done. Sue, hurry the fuck up.*

* * *

Sue drove at forty kilometres the entire way to the hospital. She couldn't manage to push her foot on the pedal – instead it rested, almost hovered. She didn't actively drive into the James's St car park, instead the car seemed to take her there. So many questions clouded her mind. She parked the car and when she took her hands off the steering wheel she realised that she was shaking. She had a little cry before she got out and was grateful for the rain that came from nowhere and soaked her through. Others ran with newspapers, or handbags over their heads, but she couldn't break into a jog never mind a run. She had come off a ladder and her world had switched a gear into slow motion.

She stuttered at the desk when she asked the woman with the jam on her face for directions to the accident and emergency room. At the accident and emergency she asked a nurse, stumbling over the word 'wife' as opposed to stuttering the word 'Andrew' but the effect was the same in that it made her want to bawl.

Like Aidan before her she spent a short time collecting herself outside the cubicle which held the heart patient who used to be her husband.

When Andrew saw her it occurred to him that she looked worse than he did. *She still cares after everything, she still cares.* He noticed the shake in her hand despite her attempt at concealing it behind an oversized handbag. *What is it with women and large bags?*

She was attempting to smile but that annoying dry-mouth syndrome had returned, ensuring her lip stuck to her gum.

Sweet Jesus, Aidan thought, standing up. *What's wrong with Sue's face?* He guided her into the chair he'd been sitting on. She sat without a word. He leaned in. "Would you like some coffee?" he asked, speaking slowly and annunciating each word like a random passer-by would do to a begging deaf mute. "I can get you some coffee. There is a lovely coffee shop. Seriously, it tastes great."

"I'm fine," she said and even through the haze she could sense her friend had lost it a little.

Fuck it, Aidan thought. *Maybe I'll say I want coffee or no, maybe a juice. I'm sure coffee has an adverse affect on high blood pressure. I'll have a juice and then I'll leave.* "I'm going to get a juice. Do you want a juice?"

"No."

"Right." He was just about to exit when the question came.

"Aidan?" she asked.

"Yeah."

"What are you doing here?"

Aidan looked at Andrew who shook his head and sighed. Aidan left the cubicle and instead of getting juice, he went outside and hailed a taxi.

* * *

Harri entered the shop and looked around. She couldn't see Beth anywhere. She walked up to the counter and was annoyed when the woman fixing the till receipt pretended not to notice her.

"I'm looking for Beth Shannon."

"She's on a break," the woman said without removing her gaze from the till.

"Do you know where she's taking her break?" Harri asked in a tone that suggested she was ready to kung-foo fight.

"No," the woman responded in an equally frosty tone.

"You must have some idea."

"Well, I don't possess the girl and I left my divining stick at home so you're out of luck."

Harri nodded. "Her dad's just had a heart attack."

The woman's eyes rose to meet Harri's and it was instantly apparent that she was sorry she'd been such a bitch. "She's in Burger King."

"Thank you," Harri said and left.

Burger King was jammed and Beth was still queuing when Harri found her.

On the trip to the car Harri explained her father's circumstance. The information stopped Beth in her tracks but there wasn't time so Harri gently guided her into the car.

"Buckle up." Beth buckled up. Harri started the car. "Everything will be fine," she said, quite pleased that she wasn't freaking out, driving into walls and forgetting her own name. *I don't know what people are talking about. I'm great in a crisis.*

She accelerated and the car felt spongy.

"Harri."

"Yeah."

"It might work better if you take off the handbrake."

"Right. Will do."

Beth went from shock to anger in record speed. She decided that her father's heart attack was her mother's fault and she was venomous.

"I hate her. I hope she burns."

"Beth!" Harri warned.

"She could have killed him!" Beth pouted.

"Oh Beth, seriously, no, don't do that."

"Do what?"

"Don't make this about blame."

"Why not?"

"Because you don't know what you're talking about."

"I know she had an affair and broke his heart, today being the physical manifestation of same."

Today being the physical manifestation of same! Who talks like that?

"Beth, you do not know the full story of your parents' break-up."

"So tell me."

"Do you really want to know everything?"

"I have a right to know."

"Really."

"It's my family too."

"Okay. Fine. Do me a favour. Close your eyes."

Beth sighed long and loudly before doing as she was told.

"Now picture your parents having sex. Better still picture your mother on her knees."

Beth's eyes and mouth shot open at the same time. "Harri, what is wrong with you?" she almost shouted.

"So do you want to know everything now?" Harri asked.

"Noooo!" Beth shouted while elongating the O for the purpose of clarification.

"I believe I've made my point." Harri said in a manner which suggested a certain amount of self-satisfaction.

Beth was silent.

"Your parents are people. People are fallible. Your parents have their problems and you wading in with only half of the information will not help anyone. You judged your dad and gave him a hard time but you didn't know the whole story. So now I'm asking you to learn from that, to realise that you don't know the full story and you shouldn't judge. Stop judging and forgive her. Forgive them both."

"Have you stopped judging your parents? Have you forgiven them?" Beth asked.

Harri bit her lip while recalling the stilted lunch she shared with her mother and the last monosyllabic conversation with her dad.

"No," she sighed.

"Well, then!" Beth said with her hands in the air.

"Look, Beth, adults are really good at giving other people advice. Unfortunately we are not so good at taking either our own or anybody else's which begs the question as to why after millennia we bother giving advice at all. The thing is we all make mistakes and we know we're making mistakes because we're looking at the people around making the same mistakes. The human race has an extraordinary propensity towards stupidity. But bearing that in mind, I'm asking you to listen to my advice and to take it. Break the cycle, Beth."

Beth sat back in her chair. *An extraordinary propensity towards stupidity! Who talks like that?* "You're really weird, you know that?"

"I wasn't aware of that, no, but I'm listening and I'm taking what you've said on board." Harri said turning into the hospital grounds.

Beth grinned. "Okay. I'll take your advice but only on one condition."

"What's that?" Harri asked.

"You take your advice too."

Harri smiled and nodded. "I'll try."

October 9th 1975 - Thursday

Matthew's dad is dead! Oh my God. Oh my God. Oh my God.

October 10th 1975 - Friday

I was waiting with Henry when Matthew arrived. He looked weird. His face was grey and strange to me. He hugged me and held on for ages. I was grateful. I can't explain how grateful I was. Henry took him home and the housekeeper made him something to eat and she was crying and Henry was saying the nicest things and Matthew was being really strong. Even though he hated his dad it was very sad. Even though I hated him it really was very sad. His grandparents arrived and his granddad said that we should all go and that he wanted some time alone with his grandson. So I left. It was after ten so Henry drove me home. He said that Matthew's dad was driving in Monaco when he had an accident. He was with a woman. She was dead too. I asked him about what will happen to Matthew. It was only when I saw his grandparents I started to worry. What if they take him away? They live in Meath. They can't. Please God, don't let them take him.

October 11th 1975 - Saturday

Matthew said his grandparents haven't discussed anything with him other than arrangements. The body isn't coming home until next week! Matthew can stay at home until after the funeral and then he has to go back to school. His grandparents asked Matthew what his dad was doing in Monaco but he didn't even know he was there. He's holding up well seeing as he's worried about what's going to happen too. He cried because he remembered that the last time he saw his dad they fought and said horrible things. I told him that I thought that his dad was just really sad that his wife died and for some reason he just couldn't let her go and over the years it just kind of made him bitter and that maybe looking at Matthew was too sad for him. Matthew thought about that and said that it kind of made sense. Now he thinks I'm really wise. I'm not wise. I told Dr B about the fight and he said those things. I would never have thought of that. But I can't say anything about Dr B to Matthew because he'd go mad if he knew I'd told anyone. Anyway it seems to have helped and that's what counts. I still can't believe Matthew's dad is dead.

October 18th 1975 - Saturday

Matthew's dad came home on Thursday morning. The removal was Thursday night and the funeral was yesterday. Matthew's been doing really well all week and he hasn't cried since last Saturday. It seemed like the whole town was at the funeral. I didn't know

Matthew's dad knew so many people. Sheila and Dave came and they bought a wreath between them which was really nice and made me feel a bit sick I didn't think of buying one but I don't really have the money and I don't think Matthew noticed. Still I feel bad about that. Dr B told Matthew he would always be there for him which was really nice. Father Ryan said the Mass and it was nice. He talked about all Matthew's dad's achievements. I knew he was rich but I didn't realise he was so good at what he did. He's done a lot. I suppose that's stupid of me but I just never really thought about it. Matthew's gran cried a lot. His granddad didn't. He just sat there with her hand in his. Henry helped Matthew carry the coffin. Aside from his grandfather I didn't know the others. Sheila said one of them was an Abbey actor. I've never been to the Abbey so I wouldn't know. Matthew's quiet. He just lies in his bed and listens to sad music mostly Carole King's 'So Far Away' and T-Rex's 'Cosmic Dancer'. He listened to those two songs for hours. It started off being really sad and then it just got so boring. I switched off. He doesn't want to talk but that's okay. He doesn't want to touch and I understand that. He doesn't really want to do anything. He reminds me of my mam a bit. I hope he's okay. I hope he'll be okay. I hope nothing has to change but then everything changes. He's going back to school tomorrow night and his grandparents still haven't said anything to him about his future. That family are really strange.

October 19th 1975 - Sunday

Matthew's gone back to school. I can't believe it. I missed him. His grandparents wanted to take him out for a meal and then drive him to Dublin. Henry said it was all very last minute and he couldn't call me because I don't have a stupid phone. He's gone. I don't know when he'll be back. I don't even know if he's coming back. I don't know anything. I never got to say goodbye. I just can't believe it.

October 21st

Liv,

I'm so sorry I missed you but my granddad wouldn't let me call in to say goodbye. I don't want you to worry. He talked to me and he agreed that I'm old enough to stay in my own home on breaks from school. He was running a business at fourteen so I have no business acting like a child. He's spoken to Henry who's happy to supervise and this is the best bit – I can come home every weekend if I want. Henry said he'd have me home anytime and granddad thinks it's a good idea for me to be around the horses more and learn the business. Can you believe it? I'm coming home on Friday night. Today is Tuesday (sorry I couldn't write yesterday, I had to go on a school trip to a stupid cave) so by the time you get this letter I might be on my way home.

Love Matt

P.S. Everything is going to be fine.

Chapter twenty-one

I know what I said before but this time it's true

Harri stood up from her seat and looked at her parents.

"What are you doing, my darling?" Gloria asked.

"I forgive you," she said.

Gloria looked at Duncan who looked back at Gloria before resting his eyes on Harri.

"I know that you thought you were doing the right thing. I know that if you hadn't taken me in I would probably have gone into care or something and I've had a very good life as a Ryan. I'm glad I'm a Ryan."

Duncan smiled. "Well," he said. "Well," he repeated. "What?" he asked someone unseen.

Gloria smiled and her eyes welled up. "We're so happy you feel that way, Harri. We love you so much."

"I know," she said. "I know you do and I love you and so does George even though he's intent on holding it against you for at least another month or two."

"Oh, darling, that's just George," Gloria said with a laugh and a wave of her hand.

Harri sat. "I'm going to be having dinner with Matthew Delamere tomorrow," she said and her parents' faces fell.

"I phoned Dr McCabe. I met him at Liv's gravestone and he told me I could call him and I did and he asked me to dinner and he said that Matthew would like to meet me," she gulped. "At first I hung up on him but then I called him back and agreed."

She waited for a response. Both parents remained quiet.

"I just want to meet him," she said.

"Of course you do," Duncan nodded. "It's only natural."

Gloria remained quiet.

"Mum?"

She nodded and smiled and then she stood up. "Can you hand me your plate, darling? These dishes won't wash themselves!" She laughed and picked up her plate signalling that the conversation was over.

* * *

When she had first received the shock that her husband's blood pressure was off the charts and that this was responsible for both his Erectile Dysfunction and heart attack, Sue had been stunned.

"Erectile Dysfunction?"

"Yes," the doctor had said.

"Erectile Dysfunction," she repeated.

"Mrs Shannon, I take it you are aware that you husband has suffered with ED for going on . . ." he looked at his chart, "three years now but we're taking steps to control his BP and obviously we'll have to discuss diet, exercise etc. We'll get the heart healthy and then we'll deal with the ED."

"Erectile Dysfunction," she said, nodding her head. "Right. Thank you."

She walked away from the doctor who hadn't finished his medical update. *It takes all sorts.*

It would be unusual for a wife to want to punch her husband while he was attached to a heart monitor but if Sue was honest she'd have admitted that's exactly what she wanted to do. Because the instant the doctor had told her that her husband was suffering from Erectile Dysfunction the problems they'd encountered, beginning three years before, all fell into place. *How could I have been so stupid? Wait a minute! How could he have been so stupid? And so cruel. I thought he didn't want me any more.*

She calmed herself down with a celery, apple and carrot juice that the girl behind the counter in the juice bar swore had a calming quality. The girl didn't lie because by the time she was sitting by her husband's side the desire to punch him had disappeared, leaving only a terrible sadness in its wake.

"I'm sorry," he said. "I'm so sorry."

"You killed our marriage because you were embarrassed," she said in a voice drenched in tears.

"I know," he said. "I know what I've done."

"I thought it was me," she said. "I thought you didn't want me."

"I was a very stupid man," he admitted.

"A stupid, vein, arrogant and ridiculous man," she said.

He nodded his agreement and smiled a little because if she was calling him names maybe they had hope.

"Sue."

"You had your chance, a million of them. I said goodbye to you."

"But you're still here," he pointed out.

"For Beth."

"Beth is at home in bed."

"And Keith?" she said, looking at him close enough to see him shudder.

"I'll forgive you if you forgive me."

"That's big of you," she said angrily. *This is your entire fault. The whole ruddy lot of it. None of it had to happen this way. Fuck you, Andrew!*

"I know you're angry."

"Quick alert MENSA, there's a genius in the room"

Andrew laughed a little. He loved it when his wife was sarcastic and he hadn't given her the opportunity to be in such a long time.

"Don't laugh."

"Sorry."

And suddenly it dawned on her, despite the anger and recriminations, for the first time in a long time Susan and her husband Andrew were on a level playing field. They were both at fault and they were both victims. *Interesting.* What was also interesting was that their daughter was behaving in a manner approaching kind, considerate, benevolent almost.

"Are you hungry, Mum?" "I got you a sandwich just in case." "You look tired, do you want me to take over?" "Are you okay for a coffee?" "Dad need anything, anything at all?" "Mum, you look like you could do with a hug." Beth's turnaround was not merely unexpected, it was miraculous and had an effect on both her parents.

On the third day of Andrew's internment in James's St hospital he reached for his wife's open hand, reminding her of the painting on the couple counsellor's wall. *It will take time and work but we might just be okay.*

★ ★ ★

When Harri got home she found Sue packing.

"Well?"

"I'm going home."

"Good."

"Baby steps," Sue said. "Baby steps." But she was smiling and seemed happier than she had been in a while.

Harri was delighted in her friend's new-found hope.

"It might not work."

"I know."

"We still have a huge amount of stuff to work through."

"I know."

"There is a lot of pain there."

"I know."

"Will you stop saying 'I know'?"

"Okay." *What is everyone's problem with me saying I know when I do know?*

Harri helped with moving her stuff to the car.

"Thank you for everything," Susan said gratefully.

"It was really good to have you." Harri meant it. Susan's presence had helped ease her loneliness and it may have even finally broken her *CSI* habit.

"I will not watch one more second of that bloody show."

"Ah please!"

"No."

"It's my apartment."

"No."

"That is so unfair."

"Live with it."

Harri waved her friend off and took a bath. *Tomorrow is a very big day. Do not mess it up. Do not have a panic attack. Do not end up in hospital.*

* * *

They took Harri's car but George drove. He would never in a million years concede to be driven by Harri.

"Why?"

"Because you're crap."

He seemed to be obsessed with that fact that she didn't keep a map in her car.

"We don't need a map. It's a straight run on the motorway."

"That is not the point."

This is going to be a long drive.

George was airing grievances so that he could talk and he wanted to talk because he was nervous. George always talked when he was nervous. "Look at that. I mean what is the government thinking? How many more fucking flats are they going to build? You know, in ten years Irish people won't know what a piece of grass looks like." "I am sick to death of people overtaking without indicating. What is so hard about indicating? Indicate, you pissing moron!" "You know what kills me about NASA. They kept going back to the moon. There's nothing there, move on!"

Harri was happy to listen and smile and nod her head when appropriate because it was helping to keep her mind off the impending appointment and her heart rate steady. The gate lodge was surprisingly easy to find, being that it was stuck out in front of a property that seemed to go on for several miles.

"So this is what a peasant feels like," George said turning into the driveway.

Harri was silent.

"It's fine Harri. Everything is fine."

She nodded.

"Breathe."

She nodded.

"Keep breathing."

Brendan opened the door and waved to them both. George got out of the car and shook his hand.

"George Ryan."

"Brendan McCabe."

"Nice to meet you."

"Nice to meet you." Brendan turned to Harri. "It's good to see you again, Harri."

She nodded.

"She's a little overwhelmed," George said, guiding his sister around the car.

"Of course – come in," Brendan said smiling.

Harri's legs felt like lead and she was all but dragged in by George.

"Glass of wine?" Brendan asked. "Dinner will be ready in half an hour."

Both Ryans decided against wine. Harri was busy wondering where Matthew Delamere was.

"Matthew shouldn't be too long."

She nodded.

They were sitting around the table and George and Brendan were laughing about Harri's fear of foreigners when Matthew opened Brendan's front door to let himself in.

"It's not exactly a fear, it's more a sense of discomfort."

"You've cried over it."

"He's exaggerating and besides he has a fear of tiled floors."

"It's not a fear, it's a sense of discomfort," George said and Brendan laughed.

Matthew listened at the door, afraid to go in.

"George speaks four languages," Harri said proudly.

"Harri works with tiles," George said, emulating his sister's pride.

Brendan laughed. "What do you do?"

"I'm an interior designer," Harri said.

"Impressive."

"Not really but I like it."

The door opened and Brendan smiled. "Matt."

Harri sighed deep and audibly. George squeezed her hand before jumping up to shake Matt's.

"George."

"Matt."

"Nice to meet you."

"Nice to meet you too."

Harri stood and faced Matt. "Hi."

Matt nodded and smiled. "Hi."

The room was silent and tense.

"Who's hungry?" Brendan asked in an attempt to break the stare-off.

Dinner was an extraordinary affair in that it wasn't extraordinary at all. Brendan and George behaved as if they'd known each other a lifetime and Matt and Harri while quieter still found things to say.

"The last time I broke my leg. Which leg was it?" George turned to Harri.

"The right."

George nodded. "The last time I broke my right leg I swore I would never snowboard again. People think skiing is harder but I don't find that to be the case."

"How many times have you broken your right leg?" Brendan asked amused.

George thought for a second or two before looking toward Harri.

"Once. You broke your left twice."

"I thought I broke it three times."

"No, two breaks and a torn ligament."

"Jesus, that was sore!" He involuntarily rubbed the back of his leg. "So, Matt, you must have fallen off a horse once or twice."

Matt nodded. "Once or twice."

I just said that.

Brendan, sensing a lull in the conversation, decided to ask George to help him with dessert.

They got up, leaving Matt and Harri alone.

"You're smaller than she was," Matt said.

Harri wasn't sure how to respond so she didn't.

"You have the same hair – you even wear it the same way."

"I was thinking of getting it cut," she said. *Change the subject, you're freaking me out.*

"Do you ride?"

"No. George does."

"Would you like to ride?"

"No but thanks."

He was staring.

"You're being weird," she pointed out and he laughed.

"I'm sorry." He was staring again. "I expected you to be more athletic."

"Do you say everything that comes into your head?" she asked in wonder.

"A lot of it," he admitted.

"It's very annoying," she concluded.

"You're exactly like her." He shook his head. "That's the kind of thing she would have said."

Happily it wasn't long before Brendan and George returned from the kitchen with home-made cheesecake. Afterwards Brendan insisted that Matt take Harri up to the stables.

"It's a ten-minute walk and besides Henry is dying to meet you," Brendan said.

"He's like my second father," Matt said. "I promise you'll be back in half an hour." *Stop staring at her, Matt, and for God's sake don't make any more comments.*

The walk was nice and quiet.

"It's beautiful here," Harri said, taken by the hundred plus shades of green, the old trees, the dirt path, the sounds, the fresh-smelling air and the general weight of passing time in the air.

Matt just nodded and walked on, remembering the past when he was younger and the girl walking beside him was the girl he loved.

"You're thinking of her, aren't you?" she asked.

"If I'd had a choice I wouldn't have let you go," he said.

"Oh."

"I'm sorry," he said shaking his head. "Usually I'm good with women."

"Lovely," she said.

"I shouldn't have said that I'm sorry. I don't know how to be around you."

"Be yourself."

"You don't seem to like me being myself."

"True," she laughed.

Henry was cleaning out Derby Girl's stall.

"Henry!" Matt called out.

Henry walked into the courtyard and stood still a second before putting his hand up to his forehead and shaking his head. "There you are," he said with his old eyes watering. "There she is, Matty," he said, sniffing. "You're smaller," he said with a single tear flowing, "but that's al lright."

Harri felt like crying with this old stranger.

Matt was steadfastly stoic. "She's a smasher, Henry," he said to the old man.

"Ah well, she comes from good stock."

After they had walked Henry back to his lodge.

Afterwards Matt told Harri about how Henry had taken care of him after his own father died. "He's a good man," he said.

"Did he know that she was pregnant?"

"Oh no. Nobody knew."

"Can I ask you something?"

"Of course."

"How did you think you could keep it a secret?"

He shrugged. "We were kids."

December 25th 1975 - Thursday

My last period was 30th October. I think I'm in trouble. I've been feeling sick. I've been throwing up and my chest is so sore that last night it woke me. I haven't said anything to Matthew because he's still trying to get over his dad and anyway there might be nothing wrong. I'll wait another few days. No, I'll wait till the New Year. If I haven't got it by the New Year I'll say it to Matthew. The first week of the New Year, that's when I'll tell him. Matthew is spending Christmas with his grandparents in Meath leaving poor Henry all alone. I'd never thought about Henry being alone before, not until he was asked to watch over Matthew. Now every weekend they're like two peas in a pod. It's nice, we all muck in together with the horses and we ride and Dr B comes up and he helps too and it's like we've got our own family which is good because I might as well have no family here.

HE took a job in Galway for the month, at least that what he told my mam. I don't think she cares much about anything any more. Today we had chicken for Christmas dinner. I cooked it. Mostly we just watched TV. She gave me a pendant though it was my granny's. It's nice. I bought her a bottle of perfume and a book but she didn't even look at them. Not really anyway. We just sat on the sofa, time passed, and now I'm up here writing it all down, not that there's much to write. Matthew will be home the day after tomorrow so everything will be back to normal. Well, at least I hope so. Maybe I'll talk to Dr B or maybe not. No. I'll just wait and see. It's probably fine. Sheila and Dave have been having sex for ages and she hasn't got pregnant. Everything will be fine. Happy Christmas to me.

Chapter twenty-two

If I could change . . .

Harri and George had a lot to talk about on the way home from Wicklow.

"Brendan's nice," George said.

"He seems nice," she replied.

"Do you know what he told me when you and Matt were at the stables? He said that the first person he came out to was Liv."

"No!"

"I swear."

"That's so strange," she said.

"Funny old world."

They talked about Matt a lot.

"I like him!" George laughed.

"But didn't it freak you out the way he kept talking about the way I looked?"

"Natural."

"What about the way he says everything that comes into his head?"

"You do that."

"But I have to be asked."

"True," he agreed.

"He thinks I don't like him."

"Do you?"

"Yes. No. I don't know."

"I'd say lots of women like him." George was smiling.

"Oh seriously, George, don't do that."

He laughed a little. "He's a looker."

"George, please, I get car sick at the best of times."

"Henry sounds like a nice man."

"He made me want to cry."

"You know what I think?"

"What?"

"I think the girl that died in the woods in 1976 was really loved."

"Me too," she smiled. "Me too."

⋆ ⋆ ⋆

Deirdre was sitting in her chair by the heater under the large window which looked out onto the grounds. Matt rested his hand on her shoulder.

"Hi, Deirdre."

"Hi, Matt."

"Sorry it's been so long." He sat in the spare chair next to her.

She shrugged her shoulders. "Has it?"

"Deirdre."

She blinked at him.

"Remember I told you a secret a few years ago."

She nodded. "About the girl who looks like my Liv."

"That's right."

She smiled and blinked at him.

"I met her today. It was awkward," he laughed. "I think I made a bit of a tit out of myself." He waited for a reaction but there was none. "You'd really like her, Deirdre. She has that look, the one that puts you in your place the moment you say something she doesn't like."

"It'd frighten the devil," Deirdre said with a little giggle that seemed to come from a faraway place.

"That's the one," he laughed. "Maybe some day I could bring her to meet you. I mean not today or tomorrow and maybe not for a while. I mean I don't know when I'll see her again and things are very up in the air but maybe some day I could bring her here. Would you like that?"

She blinked at him.

"Deirdre?"

But Deirdre's mind had moved on to somewhere else.

"Well," he said, getting up. "Maybe one day."

Doctors would often discuss and debate Deirdre's depression and associated altered behaviour which had been diagnosed soon after her daughter's death. For thirty years Deirdre had been in and out of mental institutions where she received any number of treatments. Unfortunately it was only following an EEG test in the mid nineties that it became clear that the cause of Deirdre's mental condition was a brain injury, no doubt a result of the domestic abuse she suffered throughout the nineteen-seventies. The diagnosis came too late in her case and so they would be forced to continue her treatment with medication although it had long ago become clear that Deirdre would not find her way back.

Deirdre had returned to her little home in Castle St many times over the years but never for long, and during her times of internment the tiny mortgage payments had mounted. When it became obvious to all those around that she was unable to take care of herself, Matthew had moved her to a care home and paid all her bills because it's what Liv would have wanted.

Seeing Deirdre always made him sad because in that last week Liv had been so sure that her mam was going to be all right – but then that was Liv, determined to look on the bright side no matter what. *We were only kids.*

* * *

George only realised how tired he was when he opened his front door. It had been a hectic week at work and driving to and from Wicklow in one day was no joke, especially when there was a bloody two-hour traffic jam on the way home because of not one but two broken-down trucks.

"How the hell does that happen? Look at them side by side taking up the whole fucking road!"

Aidan was waiting on the sofa. He was quiet. The TV was off. George knew it was time and so he sat down.

"We don't work," Aidan said.

George nodded.

"We keep trying. I'll give us that." Aidan smiled. "And I don't want to hate you and if we keep going . . ."

"Me neither," George said.

"I will really miss you," said Aidan with a slight smile.

"You will really be missed," George replied sadly.

"You are selfish and have issues that you may never resolve but you are fascinating and worldly and fun and passionate and you are kind and I wouldn't take back one minute of our four years together," Aidan said with tears threatening.

"Maybe the minute we had a gun stuck in our faces after you mooned out a bus window in Egypt," George grinned.

"Yeah, okay, I'd take back that minute," Aidan laughed.

"You're camper than Christmas and sometimes I know you're just doing it to annoy me."

Aidan nodded.

"You're loud, you're bitchy, you're patient – you have been very patient. You're funnier than most people I know and when I said I loved you I meant it."

Aidan sighed and stood up. "Goodbye, George."

"Goodbye, Aidan."

They hugged while fighting tears. Aidan left quietly and George sat alone and heartsick in his apartment in the centre of Dublin's bustling city. *If I could change I would have changed for you.*

* * *

It had been a long week and, between George and Aidan and Harri and her new dad and Sue and Andrew and the whole bloody lot of them, Melissa was ready for a quiet uneventful night with her husband.

She took Jacob up to bed.

"One more *Scooby Doo*," he begged.

"No."

"A half a one."

"No."

"One more, Maha-maha-mahamy!" he wailed.

"Jacob, you can maha-maha-mahamy me all you want, love. You can scream, you can shout, you can roar, you can do that kicking thing you do on the floor but you are not watching another *Scooby Doo*."

Jacob thought about this for a second or two before screaming and shouting and roaring and doing the kicking thing on the floor until, exhausted, he passed out.

Gerry was downstairs rocking Carrie who was suffering from a cold.

"Is she all right?"

"She's still stuffy, poor little mite," he said, looking down into her little face.

"It's the crèche," she said. "She picks up everything in that crèche."

"It's not the crèche," he sighed.

"It is the crèche," she argued.

"She's a person and people get sick."

"Not that often!"

Gerry sighed dramatically. "Okay, okay, let's get that Mrs Rafferty to come and mind her at home until she gets better."

"Fine," she said. "Look, I've been doing some figures and if we get rid of the two cars and maybe buy one a few years old and if we cut out a family holiday for a few years and tighten our belts I could leave work."

"No."

"Gerry!"

"Melissa, we can't afford it."

"But we'd save on crèche fees."

"Oh the bloody crèche again!" he said, wiping Carrie's nose.

"You know what? Fine. Fine. Fine. I'll just die standing, will I?"

"I have no idea what that's supposed to mean," he said. *Jesus, here we go again.* The door slammed. *Looks like it's just you and me, kid.*

* * *

Harri opened the door in her dressing gown, with a big smile on her face.

Melissa held up a bottle of wine. "Can I stay?"

"Why not, I've just got rid of Sue."

Melissa flopped on the sofa while Harri opened the wine.

"I still can't believe you met your dad."

"I know."

"I still can't believe Sue and Andrew are giving it another go."

"I know."

"I still can't believe George and Aidan have split up."

"I know."

"Everybody else is moving forward and I seem to be stuck in the same old rut." She clinked Harri's glass.

"He's still not budging then?"

"He won't even discuss it."

"Still, you've worked so hard to get where you are."

"I know."

"You might hate being at home all the time."

"I know."

"But then something's got to give."

"I know." Melissa smiled.

"If only you could go part-time."

"It's just not an option – the firm is too small and my job is too big."

"What are you going do?"

Melissa picked up her glass and thought for a moment. "Have you taken Matt up on his offer yet?"

"No."

"If you do, how would you feel about company?"

"But it's mid-week."

"Exactly. I think it's time Gerry got a taste of my life."

"Oh, you wouldn't!"

"Oh, I bloody would!"

"I'll make the call."

Melissa clapped her hands together. "Road trip, road trip!"

★ ★ ★

It had been a week since Matt had met his daughter for the first time in Brendan's kitchen. He'd waited until Wednesday before he'd made the call inviting her to attend a horse show in Seville. He sold it on the basis that she'd get to see what he did and it would be a nice midweek break and maybe it would be easier to get to know one another on neutral ground. He'd sounded nervous on the phone and he'd sounded like he wasn't used to sounding nervous.

"I don't know," she'd said.

"Think about it."

"Okay. I will."

"Good."

There was a slight uncomfortable silence and then the phone call ended. When she rang him on the Saturday morning to confirm she would go, along with her friend Melissa, he was delighted.

"Fantastic! I'll show you a great time."

Later she went home to her parents' house. Her dad was sunning himself on Nana's bench. She kissed his furry cheek and sat beside him.

"A good day," he said looking up at the bright day.

"It is," she agreed.

"Last Sunday was nice too."

"It was," she laughed.

"How was he?"

"Fine. Nice. Weird."

"I suppose that's to be expected."

"Dad."

"Yes, love."

"No matter what, he's not you."

Duncan smiled and he rubbed his beard on her face the way he did when she was a child. She pushed him off laughing.

"Your brother is inside with your mother," he said conspiratorially. "He's been here most nights this week."

"Still missing Aidan."

"It's early days," he nodded. "And what about you?"

"Me, well, I'm going to get James back."

He turned his head to look at his daughter. "Well, good for you!" he slapped his thigh. "That's the best news I've had in a long time."

* * *

She listened to the ring tones and thought about hanging up but it was too late.

"Hello?"

"James."

"Harri."

"Is it okay that I'm calling you?"

"I was just thinking about you."

"Ha. How funny."

"Are you okay?"

"I'm good," she said. "I'm really pretty good."

"Good."

"James, the last time we were together you said I needed to find myself or something – well, I'm doing that. I've visited with my mother which, granted, is just standing in front of a stone but I've had dinner with Matt, my father, and his doctor friend and I met old Henry who you would just love and I'm going away to some horse show in Seville with them next week and it's weird but it's not weird either and I miss you. Every day. And I know it's not much and I've a ways to go but can I ask you to hold on?"

"Yes."

She laughed. "Okay. And James?"

"Yes."

"I was thinking of a Christmas wedding."

"Don't push it."

"Understood."

"Call me when you get back from Seville."

"I will." *I love you, you knock-knock-joke-telling weirdo.*

January 30th 1976 - Friday

Okay, slightly panicked. My period has still not come and I decided to wait before upsetting Matthew because it might have been a false alarm and he had a hard Christmas with his grandparents and school is difficult and I only get to see him on weekends. I'm making excuses. I'm a coward. I'm a pregnant coward. I'm so sick all the time and tired. I fell asleep in biology class today. The teacher was doing the reproductive organs which was ironic. I keep puking and puking and puking. If puking was an art form I'd be Leonardo Da Vinci. I think I've lost weight too, my school shirt is swimming on me. It's weird. I wonder how long that will last.

I was riding with Dr B on Monday evening and it was freezing. Betsy was not one bit happy and I don't blame her. I wasn't too happy myself but I promised. I was thinking about talking to him and maybe I would have but then I thought I don't know if he has a duty to report it, like he had a duty to report HIM coming into my room, not that the police did anything about it, but what if he has a duty to report me and they do something about me? Pamela Whelan's older sister Pauline (there are four girls in that family and they all begin with P!) got pregnant two years ago and she was sent to a convent in the midlands and when she came back she had no baby and she's been a bit weird ever since. And Dave told Sheila about his cousin Loretta. She got pregnant and was sent to England and that was four years ago and the family never speak of her. He doesn't know what happened to her. I'm in big trouble. Anyway I was thinking of telling Dr B and then I thought I wouldn't and then he told me that he had met someone. I nearly died. Dr B has found someone. I'm happy for him. They met at some dance in Dublin and he's only seen him three times but they get on great, they both like cards and chess. He has a car and a full time job as a factory manager. It's brilliant. I told him I was so happy for him and I wasn't lying. I even forgot that I was pregnant for a while. I have to tell Matthew this weekend and I'm dreading it. He keeps talking about Kentucky being only six months away. I thought after his dad died that our plans would have to change but Matthew won't inherit until he's twenty-one and Matthew's dad's friend still wants him to come and Henry thinks it's a great idea and now I've gone and ruined everything. He's going to hate me.

Please Forgive Me I Should
have read Sheila's book

February 1st 1976 - Sunday

Matthew and I had a huge fight. He said I had lied to him and that I should have told him and that all this time he's been making plans and now they are all messed up. He was so angry. I said I thought it would go away. He said I was like my mother. That hurt but he was right. I stuck my head in the sand just like she does and now I don't know what to do. He wouldn't talk to me. He said he couldn't look at me and I'm desperate because I know I was wrong and I know I've hurt him but I just want him to hug me and tell me it will be okay. I don't want to go to a convent and come out with no baby and a bit mental. I don't want to go to England and disappear. And what if HE finds out? I'm in big trouble. Matthew, where are you?

February 2nd

Liv,

All I could think of on the train was you. I shouldn't have said those things. I sounded like my dad and I didn't mean to make you cry. I know you weren't lying. I know you were trying to make the best of things the way you always do. I want you to know that we'll be okay. Maybe we can still go to America and even if we can't I'll marry you. I'd marry you tomorrow. Maybe Henry could talk to my granddad and we could get married as soon as the exams are over, we'll see. I just don't want you to worry. I think you were right not to tell Dr B. I think it's better if we keep it to ourselves for a while. My grandparents are very old-fashioned and your mother isn't very well so we'll say nothing at least for a while. Please don't worry and please don't cry any more. I'm so sorry. I love you. I'll see you at the weekend.

Love Matt

Chapter twenty-three

No, no, no, no, and no

Sue and Harri met Aidan in Paddy Cullen's bar. The place was jammed as usual but they found a seat at the very back. Aidan looked well having just returned from a week-long getaway to Playa del Ingles. He was tanned, relaxed, fresh-faced and happier than the girls had seen him in a long time.

"I always thought Playa del Ingles was a horrible kip," Susan said.

"Oh it is, but it's a gaytastic horrible kip – besides if you spend a few quid it's not so bad."

"I'm not going to ask what you got up to." Harri grinned.

"Better not to," he said, nodding and curling his lip the way he always did when he was thinking something filthy. "And George?" he asked as it was better to get it out of the way.

"He's good."

"Still hanging out with his mother?" Aidan asked smiling.

Harri gave Sue a dirty look before returning Aidan's gaze. "Yes, he is but he's fine."

"I'm glad. And you, Miss Harri. I hear you're heading to Seville."

"Next week."

"And Melissa . . ."

"Is still planning on walking out on her husband and two kids for four days mid-week. We're calling it Operation Fuck You Gerry."

Aidan laughed. "A bold move."

"Desperate times and all that." Harri smiled.

Susan was quiet.

"Sue?" Aidan said and she smiled at him. "How are things with Andrew?"

"Difficult," she said honestly. "Sometimes it feels like we're strangers." She bowed her head and sighed. "But we're working on it and at least Beth is back to being a moody cow so we're back to some normality!" She laughed a little.

"And how's his dick?" Aidan said attempting a whisper.

"Surgery soon, maybe before Christmas."

"Say no more!" Aidan said with his hand up. "I'm sorry I asked."

They spent a very pleasant night catching up so Aidan waited until the end of the night to reveal to his two friends that he was leaving.

"Leaving where?" Sue asked.

"Ireland," he said.

"Bollocks!" Harri laughed.

"Remember my friend from California?"

"The one with the electric car?" Sue guessed.

"No, *he* lives in California but he's from Berlin. I'm talking about the guy from California living in London."

"Oh the one who cries when he sings that song from *The Lion King*?" Harri said with her finger in the air.

"Yes."

"Well?" Sue pushed.

"Well, he's been contracted to do a massive refurbishment job in Kent. It's an old stately home, a listed building. I'd get back into conservation plastering, pargetting work, lime washing, lime plastering and all the good stuff. The stuff I'm good at. I'm sick of painting and decorating brand-new builds. I worked hard to get good at what I do and in the past two years I've got lazy. I took the work because it was there and it was easy but I want more."

Sue raised her glass. "I think it's great."

"Don't go!" Harri said with moist eyes.

"It's not forever," he said smiling.

"You don't know that," she said and he nodded his acquiescence.

"I'll miss you, ladies." He raised his glass to meet Sue's.

"Ah, there's plenty more fag-hags where we came from!" Sue said, laughing.

Harri leaned over and kissed his cheek. "I love you," she said and he knew she meant it.

"I love you too," he answered.

Melissa didn't get to say goodbye. Carrie was still sick, Gerry had a conference and Aidan was leaving the next day.

* * *

George wasn't used to working all day or indeed most evenings, in fact George wasn't used to working much at all. He'd managed to avoid any real work until this his thirtieth year and, although a long-held dream was realised, he was beginning to recognise the value of hard-earned money. He was tired most evenings and yet he found his apartment to be nothing more than an empty space without Aidan. As Aidan never formally lived there and had a place of his own, George didn't realise how much time they'd actually spent together in the apartment. He wasn't used to being alone. He didn't like it. He tried to make the best of it but when that failed he drove to his mother's house where she would fuss and cook and pour him wine and they'd laugh about things that not very many other people would find funny including his father. As soon as Aidan left George, Gloria and Duncan were forgiven. George's forgiveness, although born of necessity, was gratefully received in the Ryan household.

"Oh, darling," said Gloria, 'I haven't told you Mona's jumping out of a plane for charity."

"Moaning is jumping out of a plane?"

"For the paraplegics."

"Does she know a paraplegic?"

"No, darling, but as I said to her she's only a jump away."

George and his mother cracked up laughing while Duncan mumbled about them not being as funny as they'd like to think. *Being a paraplegic is no bleedin' joke.*

When at last George returned to his own abode Harri was on the phone before he managed to put his coat down.

"How did you know I was home?"

"I had a feeling. Do you know about Aidan?"

"What about him?"

"He's moving to London."

"Oh."

"Are you all right?"

"I'm fine."

"Are you sure?"

"Positive."

"OK. I just wanted you to know."

"Thanks," he said in a tone that suggested that he was light, happy even.

"What?" she asked suspiciously.

"Nothing."

"Do not lie to me."

"Okay. Okay. Calm down, put away the axe."

"So."

"Brendan called me."

"Brendan who?"

"Brendan McCabe."

"And?"

"And we're going for a drink."

Silence.

"Harri?"

"No way."

"He's nice. He's attractive. I like him."

"He's fifty-odd years of age."

"So?"

"So it's mad, it's madder than mad. It's mental."

"I like him."

"No. No. No. No. No. No. And no!" She hung up.

George put the phone down. *I like him.*

March 27th 1976 - Saturday

If my last period was on October 30th we think I'm about four and a half months. If we leave Ireland straight after the exams nobody will know until we get to Kentucky. It's a risk but I'm still small, probably because I puke the minute I smell food. I can't remember the last time I ate anything other than a carrot stick. I really love carrot sticks and I hated them before. My tummy is rock-hard. Matthew said it's like a boxer's. You can't see anything when I'm dressed but the last night when Matthew came home and we were in his room I took off my clothes and my belly was huge. He kept laughing and touching it and making me do poses in front of the mirror. It's not so big this morning. It sounds mad but it gets way bigger at night. I hope it stays that way. I don't mind if it's big at night as long as it's small during the day.

Sheila's suspicious - it must be the nurse in her. She keeps asking me about what I've had to eat. I need to be careful of her. I love Sheila but she has a really big mouth. My mam hasn't a clue. She just does her own thing which is nothing really. HE's back a few weeks but he's busy unloading paper at the docks. Mam has really let herself go. She used to dye her hair but it's really grey now. Long grey hair looks weird. I can see why people think she's scary. Dr B is still trying to get her to do some tests but you might as well be talking to the wall.

I'm also trying to steer well clear of Father Ryan but for some reason every time I turn around he's there. Always asking questions, always trying to talk about patience and love and God and I don't know what else. I switch off. I think he still feels bad about talking Mam into letting HIM back in, only for Dr B to tell him that he tried to have sex with me. Poor Father Ryan, he's trying his best. He was visiting the school the other day and we sat together at lunch. Sheila ran off, she didn't want to be seen with a priest, but I don't care. He's nice really and sometimes he's even funny. He doesn't like cars and he gives out about them a lot and he doesn't like the heat. Who doesn't like the heat? He said it makes him itch. He likes it cool. I said he should move to Poland. He said he'd think about that. He ruffled my hair just before he left in the same way Henry ruffles Matthew's hair. It's nice to have someone look out for you even if it is a priest who would shove you in a convent as soon as look at you if he knew you were pregnant. I hope I stay small. I hope they don't know. Sometimes I get hungry and I'm not sick but I try not to eat because if they find out it could all be over, everything we've worked for. Matthew said no matter what we'll get to Kentucky. He'll make sure of it. I know we'll get there. I can't wait. four months to go!!!

Chapter twenty-four

Reality bites

Harri's phone rang in tandem with her alarm clock. The clock screamed beep-beep, shortly followed by her phone singing the Pussycat Dolls' 'Loosen Up My Buttons'. She shot up in her bed. *George, will you stop messing with my ring tone!* She turned off the alarm and picked up the phone.

"Up."

"Good. Synchronise your watch because Operation Fuck You Gerry is a go," Melissa said in a whisper from downstairs in her kitchen while Gerry and Carrie slept soundly above her head. Jacob was ensconced in front of *Scooby Doo* with a bowl of cereal.

She'd made Jacob's lunch and packed in his schoolbag by the front door. The day before she had ensured that the kitchen was well stocked with food and that Mrs Rafferty would be turning up at eight thirty as usual to take care of Carrie (who had recovered from her cold but still "had a few sniffles" – or so Melissa had told Gerry). But after that and for three days Melissa's family were officially on their own.

She retrieved the suitcase she'd hidden under the stairs and was waiting outside for the taxi when he pulled up. *Seville, here we come!*

* * *

Harri was queuing by the check-in desk. She wasn't talking, instead she just handed her ticket and passport to Melissa and walked off. Melissa took no notice of this as Harri was clinically unable to communicate before the hour of 8 a.m. As it was two hours before eight Melissa was not only prepared for silence but only too happy to bask in it. She was nearly at the top of the queue when Harri returned with two coffees. She handed one to Melissa in silence, Melissa received it in silence and together they stood sipping until called to cross the yellow line.

The plane wasn't full. Melissa liked to sit by the window. Harri liked the aisle seat. The middle one was free and so became a place to house newspapers, magazines, a make-up bag and bag of bon-bons which Melissa insisted on sucking on both ascending and descending. The plane took off fifteen minutes after eight and so talking was allowed. "My dad's sister Noreen's ear started to bleed on one of these flights," Melissa said, tipping her head to the side and scrunching her mouth into an O shape. "Can you imagine? Blood pouring from her ear. My father always said it would never have happened if she was sucking."

Harri thought of a dirty joke but it was too early to bother delivering it.

"So are you nervous?" asked Melissa.

"A lot of Spanish people speak excellent English."

"Not about that."

"Oh. Yeah, it will be weird but we have our own room and it's not like we'll be joined to him at the hip, plus he's working, you know, horse trading or whatever so . . ." She shrugged.

"Are you excited?" Melissa asked with a grin.

"Is nervous the same as excited?"

Melissa thought about that for a minute. "Not sure – it might be.

I'm excited. I can't wait to meet him."

"Don't flirt. If you flirt I'll die."

"Of course I'm not going to flirt! I'm a married woman and besides he's your father."

"He's only five years older than Gerry."

"It's mad, isn't it?"

"Yeah, it's mad."

Melissa sniffed. "Do you feel a change in pressure?"

"No."

Melissa popped a bon-bon just to be sure. "I wonder how the kids are?" she said before looking out at the white fluffy clouds beneath her.

* * *

Gerry turned off his alarm at 7 a.m. and reached across the bed to find an empty space. This wasn't unusual. Melissa was probably walking the floor with Carrie but if that was the case why was Carrie crying? When the crying hadn't stopped and instead become louder and more intense he got up.

"Melissa?" he called.

"She made my breakfast and left," Jacob said from the bottom of the stairs.

Gerry looked down the stairs. "What are you doing, son?"

"Watching *Scooby Doo*."

"Okay." He walked into Carrie's bedroom where he found a very distressed little girl. "Oh, don't cry, Daddy's here. Don't cry!" She wasn't complying. So he walked with her. "Shush . . ." She bawled. He introduced a bounce into his step. "Shush . . ." She bawled louder. He bounced his little girl in his arms while attempting to reach his wife on her mobile phone. Her phone was off. *Blast it, she said nothing about having an early meeting.* It was only when he went to the kitchen that he noticed the note on the fridge door.

Dear Gerry,

You say we can't manage without two wages. You say that we both work hard. You say that most of the time I make a fuss about nothing – after all, Jacob goes to crèche and Mrs Rafferty minds Carrie. You say it's not so hard and maybe you are right but to be sure I think we should test this theory. I'm in Seville and won't be back until Friday morning. Mrs Rafferty will be here at 8:30 and Jacob will have to be in crèche by 9.00.

Good luck,
Your loving wife,
Melissa
xxx

He laughed a little. *This is a joke. She's joking.* "Melissa! Ha ha, very funny!" Silence. "Melissa!" She*'s not joking. Oh my God, she's not joking.*

"Dad, I'm hungry."

"I thought your mother fed you."

"She did but I'm still hungry."

"Okay."

"Dad, get Carrie to stop crying."

"Okay."

"Dad!"

"What?"

"I'm cold."

It was at this point that Gerry realised his son was naked. *Jesus.* Okay. "Where are your pyjamas?"

"I took them off."

"Why?"

"I wanted to."

"Right, let's go upstairs."

They trudged upstairs.

"I want Spiderman."

Gerry put the batman boxers back in the drawer. "Here we go, Spiderman!" His son stepped into the boxers and he pulled them up. "Right – jeans."

"I want cargo pants."

"Can't see them."

"Okay. I want . . ."

"Jacob, see these jeans in my hand? You're wearing them."

Jacob shrugged as he wasn't too pushed either way.

Getting the child's top on was hardest, especially with a weeping Carrie in his arms. When the child was fully dressed Gerry sighed, happy to have achieved a remarkable feat.

"Dad!"

"What?"

"My Spiderman boxers feel tight."

"What?"

"I think they're too small."

Oh God, kill me.

With Jacob back in Batman jocks and redressed, they trooped to the kitchen. Maybe she's hungry. He put Carrie in her chair. She roared. He picked her up and smelled her. *Oh, dirty nappy alert!* He walked back up the stairs to his daughter's room and changing table.

"Dad, where's my breakfast?" Jacob called from downstairs.

"In a minute!" he shouted down.

"But, Dad!"

"Jacob, give me a minute." *Where's the nappies? Where the hell are the nappies.? Oh, okay, here they are. Right, nappy wipes. Where are the wipes?*

"Oh sorry, Carrie, Daddy didn't mean to lie you down on the cold wipes." *Okay, clothes, she needs clothes. Anything will do.* "Carrie, if you just stop crying Daddy will finish dressing you and then you can have a lovely bottle."

"She eats food in the morning like me. I eat food in the morning," Jacob said, suddenly standing by his father's side.

"Okay, okay," Gerry said leaving his daughter in a fresh nappy and a T-shirt. "Let's go."

"Dad, you can't leave her with no pants."

"Jacob are you hungry or not?"

"I told you I was."

In the kitchen Carrie threw her food around but she had stopped crying. Gerry was happy if one spoon of food in four made it into her mouth. Jacob was eating his breakfast in front of *Scooby Doo.*

Just as Gerry was about to take a bite out of a slice of toast he heard Jacob crying. "What's wrong?" He ran into the sitting room to find Jacob's upturned bowl on the floor and his breakfast all over him.

"Back upstairs." *Melissa, this is not funny.*

Mrs Rafferty arrived at eight thirty on the dot.

"Mrs Rafferty," Gerry smiled. "Welcome."

"Thanks," she said, looking at him strangely. "Where's Melissa?"

"Seville."

"She never told me."

"That makes two of us."

"Oh," Mrs Rafferty said, nodding, before giving a little wink. *Oh yeah, I've seen this before. She's blown a gasket, he'll be lucky if she doesn't bankrupt him.*

Gerry handed her Carrie who was covered in orange gunk. "I'm sorry, I know she's supposed to be dressed but if I don't leave now Jacob will be late for crèche and I am never going to make it into work."

Mrs Rafferty nodded. "No problem."

"Right, Jacob, get your schoolbag – come on, let's go."

"Gerry."

"Yes."

"Maybe you should get dressed first."

Gerry looked down at himself. *I'm standing in front of Mrs Rafferty in a pair of jocks. Sweet loving Jesus!*

* * *

There was a car waiting for them at the airport. A man with a sign reading *Harri Ryan* was standing by the gate. Melissa went ahead and conversed with him until they reached the car. It was a limo.

"Fancy!" Melissa said grinning.

The driver opened the door and the ladies stepped inside. He closed the door and within seconds they were on their way.

"He speaks English," she said. "Nice man, he used to be in the army."

"You were only talking to him for two minutes."

"I have a gift," she said while playing around with the remote control. "Some TV?"

The Hotel Hacienda Benazuza's white walls climbed from deep green grounds into an azure blue sky.

"Wow!" Melissa was looking out of the limo window with her guidebook in her hand. "It says here it's a tenth century farmhouse. Stunning, isn't it?"

Harri smiled and agreed. "It's beautiful."

The car stopped at the hotel entrance. The driver got out and opened the door.

"You're a gentlemen, Enzo," Melissa said.

Harri smiled at him. "Thank you."

He nodded. "You're welcome."

"You see, Enzo doesn't bite," Melissa said grinning.

"Well, you did make me promise," Enzo said to Melissa and they both laughed.

Jesus, they were only talking for two minutes.

* * *

Matt spent a lot of his morning in his hotel room walking around in circles. Alfio sat contentedly on the patio reading a Spanish newspaper.

"Just sit," he said.

Matt appeared and leaned on the balcony.

"Do you think it's too soon for this trip?"

Alfio smiled. "This isn't a new girlfriend."

"Aware."

Alfio laughed. "I think it will be great."

"We've only had a few hours together and now I'm dragging her to Seville."

"She wanted to come."

"I just want her to like me."

"She'll like you."

He sighed. Alfio smiled to himself. He wasn't used to his boss being out of control, especially with women. It was interesting to him.

Matt disappeared into his room and returned having changed his jacket.

"Is this a better jacket?"

"She won't care about your jacket."

"Alfio!"

"It's a better jacket. Can I get back to reading now?"

"If you don't want to be disturbed, read in your own room."

There was a knock on the door.

"She's here," Matt said before clapping his hands together and exhaling in a manner reminiscent of a fighter before entering a ring. He made for the door.

Alfio got up and came into the room.

Matt opened the door, revealing Harri and Melissa.

"You must be Melissa," he said, shaking her hand. "Welcome to Seville!"

"Thank you, Matt," she grinned.

Do not flirt with him.

"Harri."

"Hi," she smiled.

He turned to Alfio and back to the girls. "This is my sidekick Alfio."

Alfio smiled and approached to shake the ladies' hands. "Don't be scared," he said to Harri, "I speak English." He grinned at her.

Harri was confused and this confusion was written clearly on her face. *How does he know?*

"Brendan mentioned something," Matt said laughing.

Melissa was busy staring out the window. "Would you look at that view!" She walked out onto the balcony. "Can anyone else smell orange?"

Alfio followed her and they had a discussion about the local orange blossoms.

Matt sighed. "Is this okay?"

"What do you mean?"

"Being here. Is it okay?"

"It's nice," she said. "As long as you don't point out how short I am, that I have an evil look or that it's really weird that I'm not athletic."

He laughed. "I am so sorry."

"Apology accepted."

The hotel had won some food awards and, as it was early evening and the bar had a beautiful outside area, they ate there.

"I could live on tapas," Melissa declared before looking at her watch. "What time is it in Ireland?"

* * *

Gerry's secretary knocked on his door and entered. He pointed to the phone to show he was on a call. She knew he was on a call. He'd been on the same call for forty-five minutes and his nanny had been on the phone three times during the course of his call. She held up a sign.

YOUR BABYSITTER IS LEAVING YOUR HOUSE IN 15 MINUTES.

"What?" Gerry shouted into the phone. "No, sorry. No. Ah Ernest, could I get back to you with those figures? Something has just come up here and, ah, it needs my immediate attention. Okay. Great. Great. Great. Okay. Great." He hung up and looked at his watch. "No. No. She should stay until five."

"Not on a Wednesday," Lorraine said. She pointed to the phone. "She's on hold."

"Oh God, it's Wednesday. Shit!" He grabbed the phone. "Mrs Rafferty, I am so sorry! I forgot it was Wednesday. No, I understand your time is precious. Yoga is very important." He sighed. "The best I can do is forty-five minutes. Well, maybe there's a later class. Okay,

I'm leaving, I'm leaving now."

"So I'll cancel your meeting with Noel?" Lorraine queried.

"Fuck!" Gerry cried out. "Yes, fuck it! Cancel."

He was met at the door by a very pissed-off Mrs Rafferty.

"I'm sorry! I hit prime time traffic."

"I've missed my class. I might as well have stayed on."

Well, why didn't you then, you old witch?

She left after he'd apologised some more.

Carrie had a tooth coming down which Mrs Rafferty pointed out accounted for her bad humour. Jacob was bored with *Scooby Doo,* it was raining and he wanted to go swimming. Having become stressed out past the point of return sitting in traffic, Gerry needed a drink. He poured himself a gin and tonic and sat on the sofa, opening his tie. Carrie started to cry when Jacob hugged her too tight.

"Jacob!" he shouted, frightening the shit out of Jacob who was only being nice.

Jacob started to cry. Gerry considered joining his children. One day not even down and Melissa had made her point.

* * *

George was led to his table by the maitre d'. He shook Brendan's hand and sat.

"I ordered a glass of house red while I was waiting. I hope you don't mind," Brendan said.

"Not at all." George smiled. *But we're not drinking house with our meal.* It was odd that neither man felt awkward and idle chat was unnecessary. It was odd that although they had only met once they felt like old friends. *I know you.*

Brendan laughed when George talked about his youth growing up with Harri as his twin and the way they were the way they still were now.

"When we were five I jumped out of a tree."

"One of your broken legs."

"An arm and Harri ran into the kitchen and instead of telling

Mum that I was in a heap in the garden she punched her in the knee."

Brendan laughed. "Punched her?"

"She thought if she punched her and ran out that Mum would follow her and that's exactly what happened. Mum chased her screaming about her knee until she stopped at my feet with Harri pointing. She's never been good in a crisis but somehow she always muddles through."

"Seeing her brings Liv back and it's hard," Brendan said sadly.

"I'm sorry."

"Oh, don't be!" He shook his head with a big smile plastered on. "The best things in life are hard won."

"I don't get it."

"Seeing Liv in Harri hurts but it also brings great joy."

"She must have been a good friend."

"I know she I was only seventeen but I think she was the best friend I ever had."

"I don't know what I'd do if I lost Harri."

"You'd mourn her and then you'd move on."

"I wouldn't want to."

"No, you wouldn't."

"And Matt, has he moved on?"

Brendan grinned. "You know Matt's dad lost his wife when Matt was a kid. He never got over it. He became bitter and twisted. Matt swore he'd never be his dad and he's not. He's a good man, kind and he loves life. He loves women!" He laughed. "Maybe a bit too much and, yeah, he still loves her but he'll find his way."

Brendan got into a taxi outside the restaurant and rolled down the window. "We should do this again."

"Absolutely."

"Good night."

"Good night."

George watched the car disappear down the road. *Oh crap, I really like you, and Harri's going to kill me.*

April 25th 1976 - Sunday

At the start of the month my tummy was sticking out and staying out and it was getting way too hard to cover up so now that I've stopped being sick I decided the best thing to do was to eat all around me so that I'd look fat. Skinny arms and legs and a big belly is too obvious but fat arms and legs and a fat tummy and a big jumper just might get me through. I've been eating and eating and eating. Mam even made a joke about it the other day. I couldn't believe it, we were in the kitchen and she said that if I ate any more I'd burst and she thought it was funny because she laughed a little and that was really good to see. HE was there too but he was hung over and listening to something on the radio.

Dave called in the other night. He said that he had something to tell me and he was very serious. He asked me to go on a walk and so we took a walk around the town. He said that he'd seen HIM and he was with another woman and they were kissing outside The Pole. I told him I didn't care and I hoped that he'd go off with whoever she was and leave us. I pity her though, she hasn't a clue what she's getting herself into. He thought it was a bit weird that I didn't care but then he doesn't know the half of it. He said he liked me with a bit of weight on. I nearly died. Anyway he said that Sheila thought I should know and that he was glad he'd told me. Sheila's so funny - she's in school with me every day, she's my best friend and she gets Dave to tell me. People are odd. I mean she knows I hate him. In fact that news really has cheered me up. I feel like celebrating. I think I'll have a bun.

I was over in Dr B's the other evening playing chess. He thinks if we keep playing I'll discover I really do like it. WRONG. Anyway we were playing and I was giving out about some stupid annoying rule involving a basic pawn strategy or some other shit and out of nowhere he was crying!!!!! The man he'd been seeing didn't want to see him any more. He said he was messed up and told him he should get help. Dr B is not messed up. I told him I'd love to find that man and give him a good talking to. That made Dr B laugh a little. I asked him why his friend said all those mean things. He said he'd talked to him about his concern about going to hell. Father Ryan has been adamant that if he acts on his desires he'll end up in hell. I told him not to worry, that Father Ryan says that to everyone, even married people if they use contraception. So if he is in hell he'll be there with the rest of us. He laughed again but you could see he was worried. I get worried too sometimes. Maybe I will end up in hell and if it's half as painful as Double Science on a Friday afternoon I hope not. Anyway I told him that if he wants to debate good and evil and whether or not he's either, he should stick to doing it with Father Ryan and not to do it when he's in bed with another man. He went red and said he never mentioned where the conversation took place but I could tell. He told me that life would be very dull without me which was a really nice thing to hear. Seeing as he was so open with me I was desperate to tell him that I was pregnant but I promised Matthew so I didn't. I hope he forgives me.

Chapter twenty-five

It's my trip to Seville and I'll cry if I want to

The Palace Of Exhibitions and Conferences with its gold-coloured dome roof looked like something you see in *Star Wars*. A little man-made lake rested outside, reflecting its grandeur and beauty. The place was packed with people, horses and livestock. Harri felt a bustling energy that came from the floor and filled her from her feet up. Every inch of the place was draped in colour. The arenas were spectacular, lined in red earth, and on display were Spain's purebred horses. Some of them were pure white and stood out against the colourful background. They had viewed the show-jumping, driving and dressage, moving from arena to arena, part of an ever-increasing throng.

Matt was busy explaining to Melissa the difference between Pintabians and Arabians so they walked off together, leaving Harri and Alfio by the ringside where judges viewed studs from a particularly successful stud farm in Northern Spain.

Alfio leaned in to stare at one particular horse. "You see his natural ease of disposition."

"I see him standing there."

He laughed.

"I think they're beautiful though. I was always so afraid of actually having to get up on one that I never really took the time to look," she admitted.

"Is that how you feel about foreigners too?"

"Ah!" she squealed and he laughed. She joined in. "Maybe."

She asked him about himself and he told her about his background growing up on a stud farm in Argentina. He told her about his champion polo days and about the accident that had ended his career. He told her about his love of training and how he'd met Matt in Uruguay and that when he called him a year later heartbroken and in need of work Matt had flown him to Ireland straight away.

"He's a good friend," he said.

Harri was more interested in his story of heartbreak and after a few protestations he told her about Maria, the love of his life, who left Santa Cruz for a physiotherapy job in Buenos Aires. Harri asked him why he didn't go with her but he replied that his whole life was in Santa Cruz.

"So why are you living in Wicklow?"

"Because after she left, I couldn't stay there."

"So why didn't you follow her to Buenos Aires?"

"I did," he admitted, "but it was too late. She had found someone else."

Harri established that Maria had been really annoyed with Alfio for not supporting her in her dream after she had invested many years in supporting him and his polo playing. She also confirmed that he had waited eight months before following her, so realistically a girl who looked half as good as he had described would be dating by then. What she didn't understand was, if Maria was the love of his life, he didn't just go for it

"Go for it?" he repeated.

"Call her, tell her you still love her, you were stupid and you'd move to the end of the world for her."

"It's been two years."

"So what have you got to lose?"

She allowed him to think about what she'd said. *That's what I'm doing. James, batten down the hatches, I'm coming to get you.*

* * *

Melissa and Matt were seated at the bar in the hotel.

She was charmed by him and yet she had started to fret a little about the family she'd abandoned at home.

"Call them," he counselled.

"If I call, Gerry will tell me something terrible, I'll freak out, get on a plane and that will defeat the purpose."

"But you can't relax," he pointed out.

"Matt, this isn't about relaxing – this is about proving a point."

"Right."

They remained seated in the bar in silence.

It had not gone unnoticed by either party that Harri had done everything in her power to avoid Matt.

"She's just freaked out," Melissa said after a while.

"Me too," he replied. "She didn't want to come, did she?"

"No. Not really. I suppose I made her."

"I shouldn't have asked. I made such an arse of myself when we met I just wanted to make it up to her."

Melissa laughed. "She doesn't think you're an arse."

"What does she think?"

"She's confused."

"Well, I know what that's like," he admitted. "I shouldn't have rushed things."

When it became apparent that Harri would not be rejoining her new-found father, he and Melissa made their way to the hotel restaurant and ordered some food.

Over dinner Melissa talked about her problem. "You see, Gerry thinks it's just a phase. He thinks sooner or later I'll be back to myself, but I'll never be back to myself because that was the old me and this is the new me –" she waved her hands, spilling a little wine, "the stay-at-home-with-the-kids me." There were tears in her eyes. "I mean I don't like that notion either. I didn't get a degree and work my arse off for the past twenty years for nothing. But Matt, I am a mother first. That's it. That is the reality. I am a mother."

Matthew did a lot of nodding that night. Melissa wasn't really looking for his opinion or even advice, she just needed someone to listen.

"You are such a good listener," she sighed, a little teary having drunk three glasses of wine too many. "Harri is lucky to have you."

Matthew smiled at his new drunk friend. *It's a pity she doesn't think so.*

* * *

Alfio spotted Harri in the garden. "I thought you were dining with Matt?"

"Don't feel like it," she said before sitting on the bench.

He joined her. "It's all a little much?"

"I shouldn't have come. I'm not ready for this. It's too much."

"Matt never does things by halves."

"I came for Melissa really. I thought it would be easy but every time I look at him I feel weird."

"Weird how?"

"I can't explain. I have so many questions but I'm not sure if I want the answers. He's a stranger and yet when he looks at me it's with such great expectation. I can't handle that. He keeps talking about the way I look and I know he thinks I resemble her and it's creepy. He seems like a nice man but I'm not sure that he's the kind of man I want to know. I don't like horses, I don't care how pretty they are. I don't like country estates, welly boots and fleece jackets. I don't like the way he looks at me so intensely when I talk. I don't like that he knows so much about me, that he's been watching me from afar. I don't like that he can't seem to let go of a girl who died thirty years ago. I don't like that he keeps texting me. I hate texting."

Alfio laughed. "Are you finished?" he asked with a grin.

She smiled a little. "I don't like that he's flirting with my best friend. There, I'm finished."

"He's been waiting for this for thirty years."

"I know."

"He's missed you for thirty years."

"I know."

"He just wants to get to know you."

"I know."

"He's not just some stranger who wants something from you and he's not just about riding horses, welly boots and fleece jackets. He's smart and funny and kind and, yes, he's a womaniser and flirt but he's also a gentlemen and like you he's just a little lost."

"I'm scared," she admitted. "He's been waiting for this for so long. What if I'm a disappointment?"

"You're not," Alfio smiled.

* * *

Matthew escorted Melissa to her room. "I had a lovely night," he said.

"Liar," she laughed.

Harri opened the bedroom door and Melissa passed her silently, leaving her standing face to face with Matthew.

"Sorry I disappeared."

"It's okay. Sorry I pushed you to come here."

"You didn't. Melissa did."

"I shouldn't have asked."

"I shouldn't have accepted."

He laughed a little and she smiled. "We sound pathetic."

Matt nodded. "I have an idea. Why don't we just have breakfast tomorrow? All I ask is one hour."

"Okay," she agreed, "one hour."

* * *

Breakfast was stilted and, despite both of them making an effort, for a large portion of their hour together they sat in an uncomfortable silence.

"Do you ski?"

"No. George does."

"Oh. I love to ski."

"Yeah, so does he."

Silence.

"Ever lived abroad?"

"No. You?"

"America. Kentucky."

"Nice?"

"Beautiful."

"Oh."

Silence.

"The eggs are really good," he tried again.

"Yes, they're lovely."

"I love eggs."

"Me too." *This feels like a really bad date, oh my God I'm feeling panicked.*

Silence. Breathe. It's all fine. Breathe in and out. In and out. Not too quickly. In. Wait. Out. Wait.

"Are you okay?"

"Fine." *In. Out. In. Out. I have no idea what to say to this man.*

Harri managed to regain composure but lost it once more following an embarrassing misunderstanding with the waiter which seemed to confound both of them.

Matthew valiantly attempted to recover.

"How about we ask each other a question?" he suggested hopefully.

"Okay, you go first."

"Is your dad a good man?"

"Yes," she smiled, "he's better than good."

Matthew smiled. "I sensed that. I'm glad I was right."

"Did you want to keep me?"

"I was seventeen."

"That's not what I asked."

"No. I had just lost Liv. I was turned inside out. I was a mess."

"I understand."

"It still hurt to let you go."

She smiled. "This has been nice." She got up and left, having given him fifty-five minutes of her time.

Back in the room Melissa was attempting to sleep off a hangover. She woke to her friend crying at the end of the bed.

"What's wrong?"

"It's never going to be like it used to be," she sobbed.

"I know," Melissa soothed. She got up and joined Harri at the end of the bed. "But that doesn't mean it's the end of the world."

"It fucking feels like it!" Harri said making Melissa smile. "The waiter thought we were a couple."

Melissa laughed so heartily Harri was forced to join in.

⋆ ⋆ ⋆

Gerry was on red alert. "Okay, Melissa, you want to play games. Fine." He decided that the previous day had been a nightmare only because he wasn't prepared. *That will not happen today.* The alarm when off at five and approximately two minutes before his daughter awoke crying. He walked around in circles before attempting to take her into the shower. She didn't like the shower so he got out quickly and without washing. He tried to get dressed but she really did not like it when he stopped moving and after nearly tripping on his own trousers he wrapped himself in a towel and gave up.

He laid Jacob's clothes out on his bed so that when he awoke they were ready.

"That's what you're wearing," he said, pointing to the clothes. Jacob started crying. "I'm not listening. I am not listening." *Oh God, I sound like Melissa.*

He put Carrie in her chair with a jar of food she could throw around and while she did that he made Jacob some toast.

"I don't want toast."

"You're having toast."

"But."

"It's one day – just eat the toast."

And while Jacob ate toast Gerry dressed. He ate the end of Jacob's toast and took Carrie upstairs to clean and dress her.

"Don't forget my lunch."

He made Jacob's lunch.

"I can't find my bag."

"Where did you put it?"

Jacob shrugged.

Gerry spent fifteen minutes looking for the bag which he eventually found in the hot press.

At eight thirty on the dot Mrs Rafferty arrived. He handed her the baby.

"Jacob, let's go."

Jacob arrived into the hallway "Hi, Mrs Rafferty."

"Hi, sweet man." She looked him up and down. "That top looks huge on you."

"Dad said he doesn't care."

"Right."

"Bye, Mrs Rafferty," Gerry said, pushing his son out the door.

He had to take Jacob inside the crèche personally as it was a rule. Then Cara the teacher wanted a word with him.

"I don't have time."

"Excuse me?"

"Seriously, I'm not a bad parent, I just don't have time!"

He ran out the door and got into the car before she could follow him.

Traffic was back to back. He called Lorraine.

"I'm going to be fifteen minutes late."

"They're already here."

"Christ."

"I could entertain them if you want – maybe a medley from *Grease*?"

"Lorraine."

"What?"

"This is not the time for funny."

Gerry was twenty-five minutes late for his meeting and his fellow attendees were not too impressed.

As Mrs Rafferty was working until five he filled his briefcase with work he could take home and left the office at 4.15 p.m. making it home for 4.59 p.m. Mrs Rafferty had her coat on. From five o'clock to eight he ran around the house after Jacob playing cowboys and Indians, cooked, fed his two kids and cleaned the kitchen as Mrs Rafferty had made it clear that she was not a cleaner. He then dressed his kids for bed, changed his daughter's nappy three times, read his son three stories and attempted to drink two coffees, neither endeavour successful. At 8.05 he opened his briefcase at his kitchen table and by 8.25 he was face down on the table and fast asleep. He woke at 10.00 p.m.

"Sue?"

"Hi, Gerry."

"I need you."

Sue laughed.

"She told you what she was doing to me, didn't she?" he said.

Sue admitted that she had.

He sighed. "I give up."

"What can I do?"

"I have to be in work for a conference call at eight."

"I'll be in your place by six forty-five."

"Oh, thank you! Thank you, Sue. Thank you. Thank you so much."

Sue arrived at six forty-five just as she had promised. She took over handling the kids while Gerry got dressed, reviewed key figures for his conference call and ate an actual breakfast. He was gone by seven fifteen. At eight thirty Mrs Rafferty arrived and Sue took Jacob to school. After spending the afternoon picking up fabrics for a client she returned in time for Mrs Rafferty to leave at five. Gerry got home just before six. Both kids were fed and sitting in front of *Sponge*

Bob Square Pants. Sue served Gerry his dinner and sat drinking a coffee while he ate.

"I had no idea," he said. "I mean I lived here and it's not like I don't pitch in but I had no fucking idea."

Sue laughed. "When I had Beth, women didn't really work."

"Well, now I can see why."

"It will be tight," Sue said.

"You've no idea," he admitted.

"But it will work out," she smiled.

"I just worry that she'll leave her job and realise that she hates being home. I tell you, Sue, I think I'd rather die painfully."

"You're exaggerating."

"No. I'm really not."

"I think she will miss it. She's loves her job but she just can't do it all and as it turns out she just wants to be there for her kids. Who'd have guessed?" Sue smiled.

"She can always go back," he said, rubbing his forehead.

"Or she might want to do something else."

"When the kids go to bed I'll play around with some figures."

"Tell you what? I'll put the kids to bed and you start right now."

"Thanks, Sue," he said, kissing her on the cheek. "You are a star. Andrew is a lucky man."

"Yes, he ruddy is," she said with a grin.

July 9th 1976 - Friday

HE was drunk and he bumped into me and I lost my balance a little and then he grabbed me and his hand must have felt my hard stomach because he knew. The minute he touched me he knew it was more than fat. He'd been calling me names and I didn't care. I said to Matthew he could call me anything he wanted, I don't even hear him anymore, but when he touched me and he looked at me I knew it was going to be bad. He hit me in the face with a closed fist. I thought my eye was going to come out of the back of my head. It knocked me down. It was so loud even Mam heard it and she came running and then he screamed that I was a slut and he was pulling at my clothes and she jumped on his back and wrapped her hands around his neck and she looked like a woman possessed and she screamed that she would never let him touch me and he was choking she was holding his neck so tight and I swear no matter how hard he tried he couldn't shake her. He fell to his knees before she let go and then she kicked him and told him to get out and he did. He just left. And afterwards she put ice on my eye and when it wouldn't go down she took me to Dr B. We walked together through Devil's Glen and if she realised I was pregnant she didn't say anything, instead she just breathed in the fresh air as though she'd forgotten what fresh air smelt like. She didn't really talk but when I said thanks for helping me she stopped and she kissed me on my forehead and told me she loved me with all her heart and then we walked on in silence and all I wanted to do was cry but it hurt too much. Dr B took away the scrunched-up knickers filled with ice that I was holding up to my eye and he said it was nasty but I'd be fine. Mam waited in his sitting room and watched '*Coronation Street*'. He asked me what had happened and I told him nothing but he knew I was lying and then he asked me out straight if I was pregnant and I said yes and asked him how he knew and he said he guessed and instead of being annoyed he apologised for not noticing sooner. I told him not to worry, that I'd gone to a great deal of trouble so that people wouldn't notice. He checked me out and he said that he was worried that I might go sooner than we thought. I told him that I couldn't because Matthew and I were going to Kentucky next week. He asked how and I told him Matthew was doing everything. That's when he rang Matthew's house and told him to come down and that's when everything went a bit weird and basically he said that our plan was rubbish, not in those terms but that's what he meant. By the end I was crying, Matthew was crying and Dr B was pacing and Mam was still watching the TV even though '*Coronation Street*' was long over. And then some time after that it was agreed that Matthew would go to his grandfather and seek his permission to marry me. It has something to do with money and the estate or something, I don't know, I switched off.

Anyway Matthew said he would and then we were engaged and we hugged and Dr B made tea and we clicked our mugs and Mam was still watching TV. Dr B said if she won't listen to reason he might have to put her into hospital forcefully. I asked if he could really do that and he said he could. I told him about how she'd saved me and that I really thought she was improving and I do, I really do. He said he'd keep an eye on her but our priority was Matthew going to his grandparents. He's leaving the day after tomorrow. I can't wait.

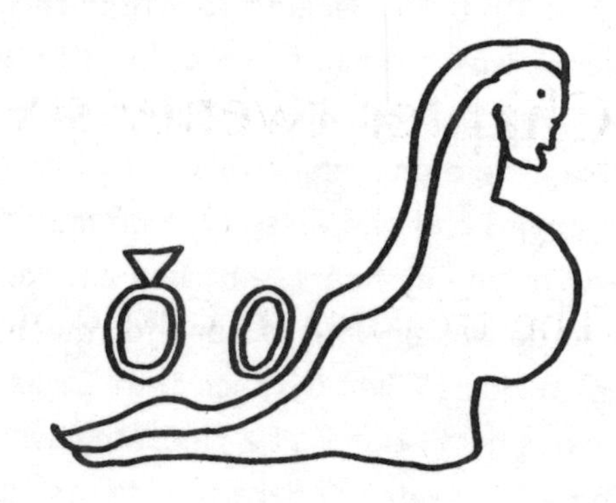

Chapter twenty-six

The treasure in Castle St

"Okay. I have a question," Harri said holding the phone up to her ear and sighing into the receiver.

"Go on," Matt prompted.

"When did you fall for Liv?"

"Oh, that's easy. One day in the stables my father came out of nowhere screaming about one of the horses being lame. I exercised the horse so of course it was my fault. He called me every name under the sun and all the while she was standing in the stable behind me. I knew she was there and I liked her so I was really embarrassed."

"So what happened?"

"After he stormed off she walked up to me and nudged me. I was so red I didn't want to look at her but she smiled and told me not to worry, that all dads were dicks." He laughed at the memory. "I fell in love then and there."

Harriet laughed. "All dads are dicks! What a beautiful story." They both laughed. She was making her way around the market with Melissa who was tired and hungry. "I should go."

"Okay."

"Enjoy the horse show."

"I will."

She hung up.

Melissa turned to her. "So let me get this straight: he brought you to Seville so that you could communicate on the phone?"

"It works better like this."

"To each his own, my friend. To each his own. Now let's eat. I'm starving."

Alfio knocked on Harri's door a little after six. "I called my ex-girlfriend."

Harri opened the door and allowed him in. "Well?"

"She's married."

"Oh. Shite. Sorry."

"No. It's good. I've been holding on to what was for too long."

"You look like you might cry."

"That is because I might."

Oh Jesus. "Well, what does Matt say?"

"He says what he always says. Get laid."

Charming.

"But, you know, this time I think he's right."

"Good for you."

"Thank you, Harri. You've opened my eyes. It's been painful but necessary."

"You're very welcome."

He left before Melissa made it back from the pool. "Are we meeting Matt for dinner or what?"

"No, drinks afterwards."

"Great."

"With Alfio."

"Nice guy."

"Looking to get laid."

"Not that bloody nice. I've a husband and two kids to get back to."

Harriet smiled. *And I've got James whether he likes it or not.*

* * *

Gerry was waiting in the airport for Melissa with flowers and a large apology. She was just grateful to be home and hugged him tightly and asked after their kids who Sue was kindly minding. All the way home they talked about how they could manage and what they would do and even after they made it home they sat in their driveway talking.

"You're sure?" Gerry said.

"I'm just so tired," Melissa said.

"I know," he admitted.

"It won't be forever."

Gerry kissed his wife. "Rather you than me," he smiled and they hugged.

"It won't be forever," she repeated.

Melissa would be sad to leave her job and her friends and she knew she'd miss the gossip and the jokes and the work and money and the benefits but her job was demanding and so were her kids and she knew she just couldn't do it all any more. She handed in her notice two weeks later and that night she had the first good night's sleep she'd had in over a year. *Hello, world, I'm back.*

* * *

Matt insisted on walking Harri to her car in the long-term car park.

"So is it okay if I call you?" he said.

Harri smiled. "It's fine."

"Good," he said. "I suppose you know Alfio is going home."

"Well, he couldn't hide out in Wicklow forever."

"He was the best trainer I had."

She laughed. "That's tough shit."

He laughed. She got into her car and he waved her off as it was too early in their relationship to hug.

She drove out of the airport and straight to Malcolm's where

James was still staying. He opened the door.

"Hi," she said grinning.

"Hi," he replied.

"So I've come back from Seville and while I was there I told an Argentinean guy to take a chance on the woman he loved and to be honest it didn't really work out, but fuck it because now I'm here asking you to take a chance on me. I love you. I want to marry you and you know what they say, third time lucky."

"How romantic of you," he laughed.

"Yeah, well, I'm a big romantic."

"No, you're not."

"No, I'm not," she admitted, "but I could change."

"No, you couldn't."

"No, I couldn't. So are you in or out?"

Malcolm arrived home with two bags of chips, a kebab and a battered burger only to find his flatmate's tongue down his ex-fiancé's throat. *Ah well, all the more for me.*

⋆ ⋆ ⋆

In the month following Harri's trip to Seville she spoke with Matthew Delamere often. The phone was so much easier than face to face. She felt calmer and she felt he did too.

"You know what I don't get?" Harri said into the phone while propping up her pillow to make herself comfortable.

"What?" Matthew asked whist sipping a glass of wine in his conservatory.

"Brendan found her. But what the hell was he doing out in the wood in the middle of the night?"

"He said he was going for a run."

"And you believe him?"

"At the time he was a celibate gay man so I suppose anything is possible."

"Poor Brendan."

"You know once, years ago and when he was very drunk, he told me he heard her calling him."

"Telepathically?"

"That's what he said."

"That's impossible."

"That's what I thought but then I remembered something."

"What?"

"Liv used to try to contact me telepathically when I was in boarding school. She always got so pissed off when it didn't work."

"Bloody hell."

Matthew laughed. "I'm sure he was just running off some frustration."

"Yeah."

Harriet said goodnight and thought about what Matthew had said and she wondered about whether or not she'd mention it to James who was in the other room halfway through a box-set of CSI. *I'll just sleep on that one.*

* * *

One morning not long after that conversation Brendan was sitting at his kitchen table reading the newspaper, indulging in his second cup of coffee.

"Brendan?"

"Harri?"

"Yes."

"Well, hello."

"I hope you don't mind me calling this early in the morning."

"Of course not."

"Do you mind if I ask you a question?" she asked with the phone held to her ear by a raised shoulder so as to facilitate making toast.

"Go ahead."

"On the night Liv died, why did you call Uncle Thomas?"

"Who the hell is Uncle Thomas?"

"Oh, I'm sorry. Father Ryan. Why him?"

"Because Liv's mother wasn't a well woman. Her stepfather was an animal who had just been escorted out of town and poor Matty, well, he was just a boy. I promised Liv I'd take care of her and I failed. After all the business with her stepfather Father Ryan felt that he'd failed her too. I knew he'd help and he did."

"Brendan?"

"Yes."

"That night in the wood did she really call out to you telepathically?"

Brendan was slightly shocked by the question. He was silent for a moment. "Call me crazy but I really think she did."

"Wow," Harri said.

After that they chit-chatted for a little while and long enough for Harri to burn four slices of toast but for Harri it was the end of the call that was the most intriguing.

"Harri?"

"Yes?"

"How's George?"

* * *

It was one month before her wedding. The Shelbourne was jammed but Harri could spot Matt a mile away. She waved and he smiled at her. She rose and he kissed her cheek. They sat.

"How's Clara?"

"Good."

"I'm glad."

"James?"

"Great."

He grinned. "I broke up with Clara."

She laughed. "So when you say she's good it means that she's better off without you."

"Thanks a lot." He grinned. "I'm going to remain single for a while."

"Single or celibate?"

"I haven't decided."

It had been six months since they had first met and, although it was still new and sometimes strange, Matt and Harri had formed a nice little friendship. It turned out that although they had not many common interests they were quite alike in that they both valued honesty over propriety.

"Nervous?" he asked, surveying the menu.

"Not a jot."

"So you've no plans on stuffing up a third wedding then?"

"Nope."

"Good for you."

"Thanks."

The waitress was a blonde in her late twenties.

"What can I get you?" she asked.

"Well, my dear, that depends on what you're offering," he said, flashing her a grin.

"Don't you dare!" Harri warned.

It was never going to be a traditional father and daughter relationship but Harri already had that kind of dad in Duncan Ryan and she found that she quite enjoyed her time with Matthew on a completely different level which was new and interesting.

Before they left he mentioned her mother's old house on Castle St. He told her that he'd bought it a few years beforehand and that it was hers if she wanted it.

"A wedding present," he said.

"It's too much."

"No. It's not. It's rightfully yours and besides there's a huge amount of work to be done. I was thinking it could make a nice little holiday home."

"We have a place in Wexford."

"George says it's a dive."

She laughed. "It is a complete dive."

"Well, the house on Castle St is probably not much better but I think in its time that place saw a little happiness. Go and see it. Think about it." He handed her the keys. "You don't have to take it if you don't want to."

"Thanks," she said, taking the keys. "I don't know what to say."

"Don't say anything. Just go there. I think you'll like it."

"I will," she smiled.

"One more thing. Liv's mom, Deirdre, left her room exactly as it was on the night she died. It's untouched," he smiled, "like going back in time."

"Thank you," she said and suddenly she was welling up. "Thanks."

He nodded and they said their goodbyes.

* * *

George was seeing Brendan for four months before he had the courage to tell Harri.

"I really like him."

"La la la!"

"Harri, I really like him."

"La la la!"

"Are you going to stop that?"

Harri took her hands away from her ears. "He's twenty-five years older than you."

"I know."

"He was my dead mother's friend."

"I know."

"He's my brand new father's best friend."

"I know."

"Stop saying 'I know'." For the first time Harri realised truly how annoying it was. "Do you really think you have a future with this man?"

"I do. I really, really do." He was speaking in earnest and she knew it.

Bloody hell. "Fine then."

"Really?"

She nodded and laughed. "It's not like you're not going to do anything but what you want to do anyway."

"That's true, after all I am known for being selfish," he smiled. "Thank you, Harri."

"You're welcome, George."

* * *

Six months together and it seemed like Brendan and George had never been apart. They shared the same interests, dressed similarly, both enjoyed the finer things in life and most noticeably they were comfortable together as though they really and truly fit. The gap in each of them had closed.

Harri enjoyed spending time with her brother and his new boyfriend but to Brendan the presence of George and his old best friend's daughter in his life meant the world.

"I'm really happy," he admitted to George one night lying in bed, warm and relaxed. "I can't remember being this content."

"Me too," George said.

"I was so lonely," Brendan said with a slight smile, "for so long."

"And the romantic in you likes to believe that your friend Liv had a hand in us meeting."

Brendan's smile widened. 'You know me so well."

George laughed. "Well, whether it was Liv or fate or just bloody good luck, I'm grateful."

* * *

It was two weeks before the wedding. Harri rang Sue from the car. Beth picked up.

"Well?" Harri asked.

"He's still in surgery. Do you know what they are actually doing to him?"

"I don't want know."

"They are reconstructing –"

"Beth, I do not want to know."

"Mum keeps making dick jokes. Like why did the dick cross the road? Because it could."

"That's not funny."

"I didn't say they were funny. Dad's laughing though so that's good. Oh, she's back from the loo – I'll put you on to her – seeya, Harri."

"Seeya, Beth."

"Hi," Sue said.

"Well?" Harri asked.

"He should be out shortly. I'm starving."

"Me too."

"I'd love a chicken tandoori."

"Exactly what I was thinking." Harri looked at James who was driving. "We'll have to stop for a chicken tandoori."

"Are you in the car?" Sue asked.

"On the way to Wicklow."

"You're going into that house, aren't you?"

"Yeah," she said.

"Best of luck."

"Thanks."

"Right, I'd better go," said Sue.

"Tell Andrew I said hi."

"Will do. Love to James."

She hung up and Harri looked at James and sighed.

"What?"

"Nothing."

They stood outside the house for less than a minute. Harri put the key in the door and opened it. They walked around the downstairs, the tiny hall with the steep staircase, the back kitchen that led to a long overgrown garden. The front sitting room was small but full of light. They made their way upstairs with Harri leading. The first stop was the bathroom which was a surprisingly large room.

"Are you thinking what I'm thinking?" James asked.

"This room is perfectly proportioned to house a Raindance Rainmaker Shower," she sighed.

"Bingo!" he smiled.

Liv's bedroom had her name on the door. Harri stood outside

looking at it for a moment or two. The name Olivia was faded, almost gone. She opened the door to reveal a small room with a small bed, a locker stuffed with girls magazines, nail varnish and creams. The wardrobe housed her clothes: jeans, tops and a smock or two.

"Jesus, people are wearing them again now," James pointed out.

Her school uniform hung there but was pushed to the side and on its own. The desk by the window was tiny and there was engraving in its soft wood.

Liv loves Matthew

One day at a time

Kentucky

James found a big padlock in her top drawer.

"What the hell is this for?" he said, raising it in the high.

Harri shrugged before sitting down on the bed, a little overwhelmed.

"Are you okay? You look pale?"

"I'm fine."

"Sure?"

"Can you feel her presence here?" she asked.

"No," he admitted. *And if I could I'd run out of here like my arse was on fire.*

"Me neither and I'm glad. I'm glad she left this place."

It was James who noticed the slight bump in the mattress.

"Well, it's old."

He lifted it. "I told you – see, I've found something," He held up a thick book.

"It's a diary," she said, eyes glistening.

A few letters fell out. Harri picked them up. "They're from Matt."

She opened the first page of the diary and read aloud.

"January 1st 1975. And so starts another year. God, I hope it's better than last year. Sheila said it has to be because everyone knows that every year ending in five is a good one. Sheila really is a SPAZ!!,"

She laughed and hugged the diary tight. "It's her," she said with tears falling.

"Who knew we'd find treasure," he said, holding her close to him.

July 11th 1976 - Sunday

I woke up feeling sore and all day I'm getting cramps. I was making Mam some breakfast and had to bend over with the pain but then it went. She seems brighter since HE left. He collected his clothes yesterday and it was Father Ryan who drove him to the station. I don't know where he's going and I don't care but Sheila said that her dad said that one of the lads that normally drink in The Pole was in his bar last night and he said he's going to London. It's so great that he's gone. I swear even when I've got cramps I'm smiling. I really think a few months away from him and Mam will be back to her old self in no time. My eye is healing up well which is good if I'm going to be getting married soon. Matthew left to go see his granddad this morning and before he left he slipped a letter through my door only because I said since he'd finished school I really missed his letters. He is so romantic.

It's late and the pain is much worse. Mam's in bed asleep. It's raining. If I go now and take the short cut through Devil's Glen I'll get to Dr B's in half an hour. It's probably nothing but better to be safe than sorry. I am so sick of not having a phone!! Maybe If I close my eyes and concentrate really hard I can communicate with him so that he can meet me halfway.

No.

Shit.

Before I go. Today I took a walk in the afternoon because I thought it might help with the pains. I haven't really spent much time by The Eliana since HE grabbed at me there but today I stayed for a whole hour just looking out to sea. I know I'm always saying I can't wait to leave Wicklow but I love it here too. Wicklow's in my bones so no matter where I go I'll never leave it and that's okay by me. I better go before the rain gets any worse.

One last thing! I'M GETTING MARRIED!!!!!!!! Hello, I'm Liv Delamere!!!!

July 10th

Liv,

Tomorrow morning I'll be on a train to visit my granddad to get him to agree to me making you my wife. Dr B Is right, it's the right thing to do but more than that it's the only thing I want to do. I want to call you my wife. I love you more than I knew it was possible to love. My heart is full and it's full of you. Henry says angels exist and I think he's right because I'm going to marry one. (Don't puke, I'm serious!) I can't wait to come home to you. I can't wait to make you my wife. See you soon, Liv Delamere.

Love
Matt

Chapter twenty-seven

The Wedding - Take Three

The date was December 27th 2007, and it was the third time Harri was set to marry.

She'd slept like a log the night before, with her fiancé beside her.

"I'm not doing it unless we go to the church together," he had said.

"But it's unlucky."

"Could it possibly be any more unlucky then being left at the altar twice?"

"Good point."

James was in George's room with Malcolm and Brendan helping him with his tie, his vows and her nerves.

"What did you say? Honour, protect and what?" Malcolm said with a mouth full of toast.

"He said honour, protect and cherish," Brendan said. "That's lovely."

"I'd speak up though if I was you – I thought you said honour, protect and banish."

"Big day," Harri's dad had greeted her with a wink on the landing.

"Big day, Dad," she agreed grinning.

"Three times a charm," he said.

"Fingers crossed," she said, kissing him on his hairy cheek as he passed with his paper heading toward his en-suite bathroom for a well-earned shite.

Her mother was calling her from her own bedroom.

"Darling, there you are. The aquamarine outfit or the pale pink?"

"Those are from my last weddings. It's not like you to recycle."

"Well, I've promised your father I'll reduce my carbon imprint and my visa bill and seeing as I didn't actually get to wear them to anywhere other than an A&E department . . ."

Harri laughed. "The aquamarine."

"Good choice. Now get going. Mona will be here in a half an hour and ever since Desmond dropped out of school she has a face on her like a donkey's hole." Gloria winked and Harri burst out laughing.

"I love you, Mum."

"I love you too, my darling."

Back in her room and after a long shower she made her way over to and sat on the chair that accompanied the table that looked down on the pretty stone patio and across to the ancient oak tree. The rain poured down from a heavy grey sky.

"I couldn't give a stuff," she said, hugging herself in the comfortable towelling dressing gown her mother had given her six years before when she'd first left home to move twenty minutes down the road to the UCD college campus. She sat there and thought about Liv for a while. *You would have been a lovely bride, Liv.*

There was a knock on the door and George was in and lying on the bed before Harri managed to say the words "Come in".

"Moaning is here. Mum's making her a coffee so you have five minutes before the all-important hair and make-up."

"Thanks."

"You look incredibly relaxed. Have we met before?" he asked in jest.

"Ha ha."

"Are you all right?" he said seriously.

"Never better."

"It's pissing rain out."

"Let it rain."

"Dad and Matt have cracked open a vintage bottle of brandy and they're halfway through it."

"I hope they drink it all."

"James is planning on singing 'Unchained Melody' at the reception."

She laughed. "He bloody will not!"

"My God, I think that we may actually be going to a wedding today."

"You can count on it," she said.

Duncan and Harri stood under an umbrella by the church door. She stepped inside and he closed the umbrella, shook it and laid it down on the floor. Inside she could see all the people she loved: Melissa and Gerry and Jacob and Carrie, Sue and Andrew and Beth holding hands with the boy who gave her crabs. George and Brendan, Matt and her mother, Aidan who had travelled from London with his boyfriend Quan, and all the other people kind enough to turn up a third time.

And on the altar was her Uncle Thomas, known to everyone else as Father Ryan, bursting with pride, happy that at last little Harri knew the truth. And when her dad walked her down the aisle, in her heart she carried with her a teenage girl called Liv.

May 1st 1976 - Saturday

I woke up this morning dreaming of Kentucky. I saw horses and hay and trucks and land that went on for miles. I saw a big old farmhouse with a veranda and a swing chair big enough for six. I saw me in a meadow and Matthew riding a horse so fast he was blur. It was really nice. I felt warm and whole and free and happy and safe. I felt safe. And when I looked down I saw a baby, a really cute one just lying beside me, bald and thin and wrinkly, and although it doesn't sound like it the baby was really cute with a squishy face. She was holding my hand and smiling. And then I saw another one! This one had hair and was a little bit tubbier and was yelling and didn't look one bit happy. So I picked it up and I think she was a girl but I'm not sure and I held her and told her not to cry and I stroked her and she listened to my heartbeat and she stopped. And I knew it was a dream and soon it would be over so I held her as tightly as I could and whispered into her ear but I couldn't hear what I said which makes me think I didn't say anything because surely I'd know. And then she was gone. Dreams are weird. And then I woke up. And all day I've been feeling a little nostalgic so I sat in my room and read my diary and I didn't realise how much I say 'anyway', and 'weird' and 'shit'. I say 'shit' a lot. And I switch off a lot too and I don't know if that's a good thing. Plus I really, really can't draw. I think I'm nostalgic because soon I'll be leaving here and endings even the happy ones are sad but then again every ending is a new beginning so that's okay.

The End